I, JEHOVAH

I, JEHOVAH

Caleb Levi

To order additional copies of this book, contact:
Xlibris Corporation
1-888-795-4274
www.Xlibris.com
Orders@Xlibris.com

PRELIMINARY NOTE

Caleb Levi is a scholar outstanding in the field of Ancient Languages and Culture. His work with the Sumerian language and relics is well known. Not so publicized but equally distinguished has been his research in the biblical and religious area along with his study of certain rare and controversial documents. This latter work is often the subject of hot debate among other scholars in the field.

Though the authenticity of his sources is constantly challenged, Professor Levi stands by them and so, in spite of opposition, we have seen fit to publish this book.

We are, however, publishing it as a novel, a work of fiction. That means that all characters including Jehovah, as well as all incidents in the narrative, are to be considered as imaginary . . . products of the literary creativity of the author.

This goes along with Professor Levi's own wishes. But if scientific investigation should ever prove beyond a shadow of a doubt the total authenticity of his two basic documents, we promise to issue a subsequent edition as a nonfiction volume.

STATEMENT BY CALEB LEVI

I have had to date almost exclusive access to certain ancient documents in transcribing and reconstructing events in this narrative history.

Chief among these has been what I believe to be nothing less than the personal narrative . . . almost what we moderns would call a diary . . . of the entity who eventually came to be called Jehovah. I have added little to it, mainly a couple of transitions where there seem to be gaps. On the contrary, I have cut out considerable portions in the interest of maintaining a simple, direct story line.

Also, I have rendered the narrative in modern colloquial English where ancient and exotic metaphors and modes of expression might be incomprehensible to the modern reader. Included in that editing process are the conversion of measurement into modern English units as well as a number of other changes. Again, these modifications have been made only to increase the document's readability without altering the sense of what is described therein.

I wanted the story to speak as plainly as possible for itself without its impact at all being blurred or diminished by unnecessary language barriers. Its ending is necessarily based partly on speculation, partly on information supplied in the second of the two aforementioned ancient documents.

And so, all the academics . . . the research information and the footnotes . . . I leave for a future volume, which may well occupy the rest of my life to complete.

Meanwhile, my publishers and I have decided to present this work as fiction. As a novel . . .

That way the main story . . . important as it is . . . can be divulged to the public . . . without them having to wait twenty years for the detailed authentication that academic protocol demands.

—Caleb Levi

My name is Yahweh.

I am Anunnaki to the core . . . if I am not that, not a member of that ancient race, then I am nothing. And that is the nucleus of my story.

For us, Earth was the Golden Planet.

We had to come here because without the gold our own planet, Nibiru . . . could not much longer survive.

It was that simple. Extraordinary circumstances dictated that Gold was to be the elixir of our life.

Without it we would all die.

Not that Earth looked golden at all from Space. It did not. On the contrary it looked cool and inviting.

In the deserts of Space, it was an Oasis hanging there against the black, black heavens.

I myself loved it from the first as I watched it approach from just behind the pilot's compartment of our Mother Ship.

It drew you into it. The swirl of white clouds above deep blue of oceans. There was a mystic, clean, pure quality about it that I loved from the beginning.

Maybe, of course, I was heavily influenced by our probe reports.

I knew in advance the air was pure, better than on Nibiru . . . the vegetation lush and green . . . the water supply enormous and unpolluted. But above all, the most necessary element in the picture, the gold . . . the probes had told us . . . ton after ton of it buried underground.

Nothing less than our salvation, and ours for the taking.

Which made me, as I saw the planet looming ahead of us so globularly inviting . . . breathe a sigh of relief.

****

We had two enormous problems on Nibiru, both of which promised to be resolved with a plentiful supply of gold distributed in the right manner.

The first problem was that our atmosphere was beginning to tend to drift off into space. That, if not remedied, of course could be fatal to our continued existence.

The second problem was loss of heat. If that wasn't fixed in some way, we could all eventually freeze to death.

Our scientists had come up with this solution. Extremely fine gold particles to be distributed in the upper atmosphere all around our planet. It did two necessary things. One was to keep the atmosphere from drifting, the other to help retain the planet's heat.

Together those two things spelled survival for the Anunnaki.

We did not have an orbit like those of Earth and the other obvious members of the Solar System. Rather we shared our fate more with the comets than with any other planet . . . and that had to do with the ancient and complex origin of what is the present Solar System . . .

For one thing . . .

We on Nibiru were much more far ranging than any other planet . . . going so deeply into space that the sun at the far end of our orbit began to look more like a distant star than our personal sun.

In fact, our orbit is so vast it takes 3600 Earth years to complete . . . which makes our year equivalent to that length of Earth time.

Other than that vast difference between us, Earth and Nibiru have much in common . . . which may tend to explain some similarities between the Anunnaki and the Earthlings.

To begin with, deep back in time before either of our races existed, there was a brushing by, or glancing collision in space between Nibiru and another solar body. That solar body was separated, with one portion eventually to become the new planet Earth . . . and the other to form what is now known as the asteroid belt.

That at least is what our own astronomers tell us.

In the chaos of the great collision and its aftermath, there was sharing and mixing of soils and bacteria, all of which contributed to some extent to a tendency to a common evolutionary process . . . though in that the Anunnaki had at least a million year head start . . .

****

But as I said, our planet now was in a state of crisis, and to resolve that crisis we had to have the substance of which Earth had such a plentiful supply.

Gold.

And so, our First Mission had been a holy one from the beginning. Anything we might do on Earth had but a single purpose . . . to preserve Anunnaki life and civilization. And of the sanctity of Anunnaki life, there is no question. As a loyal Anunnaki myself, I feel only the deepest pride in saying I would do anything to preserve that life.

****

But I am not writing of the First Mission, except in retrospect.

As I find time to write this, we are in orbit above Earth. I am with the Second Expeditionary Force. Oh, yes, I was also with the First . . . the First that ended so disastrously, of which I will try to tell something, however briefly.

But now . . .

Now we are back again, for a reason which has once again to do with our own threatened existence on our Home Planet Nibiru.

There are no inhabitants on Earth now.

Let me repeat that.

No inhabitants.

Or so we believe, officially, at least. I personally believe it too . . . for how could there be? A flood with water levels rising three hundred feet. I saw it as we left . . . no, there could be no survivors. It was impossible.

I am writing this because I want to keep some kind of record.

Why?

Because the Official Record of events in my experience is never the real one. Politics always enters in, which includes very prominently the elements of rank and privilege, which in Anunnaki social order are everything.

And justly so.

But not in my account.

In mine . . . in mine, pure honesty and straightforward narrative will prevail . . . let all chips fall as they may and where they may.

The story to be told is a great one, of enormous scope and importance. Of that I am aware, as I am equally aware of my own key part in it . . .

And so . . .

Once we are landed and set up in our new headquarters, I will continue this, and will do so into the foreseeable future.

To help my own clarity of comprehension, I will start off with a greatly condensed version of our common history.

Earth and our Home Planet of Nibiru have astronomically always been intertwined. Our astronomers have told us that, and I have no reason to doubt it.

But now we are ready to leave orbit and I have my duties to perform. Besides . . . I don't want to miss a single moment of this second great adventure . . .

****

We have been here on Planet Earth five days now . . . at last have our temporary quarters established . . . and so I can write again.

So far we have seen no human survivors of the Great Flood, which is exactly what everyone expected. But there has been no time to explore . . . all our energy has gone to set up a basic headquarters around our former Space Station on what we named the Sinai Peninsula. Which may exist still beneath the many layers of mud and silt . . . and which we will try to excavate in the coming months.

Meanwhile, in these free evening hours I will try to condense the basic facts of our First Expedition . . . before I make any attempt to start keeping the record of our Second.

****

Here are those events of the First Expedition. I will just jot them down here in the very briefest manner . . .

Enlil was in charge of the First Expedition, its Commander. His assistant was his half-brother Enki, and both were sons of the exalted leader and mighty ruler of Nibiru, the great patriarch King Anu.

We established our space station in the region that we came to call Mesopotamia, territory watered by two rivers that we christened Tigris and Euphrates. I should mention that I myself with only two assistants made the first rudimentary map of the entire Earth on a two month scouting excursion early in our occupation of the planet. So it was as a consequence that many of the geographical areas I personally named . . . and of all the Expeditionary Force I accumulated the most comprehensive knowledge of Earth's topography.

But at first that was considered of little importance or consequence. What was important was the yellow metal that only Earth could supply us.

And very soon after our first arrival . . .

Mining for gold began.

First from the Persian Gulf waters . . . not successful.

After many Earth years of effort, we gave it up . . .

Next was the continent I had named Africa . . . lots of gold as our probes had shown us previously . . . but deep in the ground. We went about it as best we could. It was hazardous, hard . . . physically strenuous work . . . and despair was never far away.

We persevered because the fate of Nibiru hung in the balance . . . but at last it was too much for everyone. I, as a high administrative aide to Enlil, was one of the few excused from the work schedule.

At last it came. An out and out crisis.

After a cave-in in which 15 Anunnaki were killed . . .

After that, there was a kind of unspoken mutiny. No one would go into the underground mines anymore.

Enki, Enlil's half-brother and second in command, volunteered a solution.

It was a radical one . . . but then everything about Enki was always radical and unexpected.

What he proposed was to my conservative ears both horrifying and . . . potentially very useful.

He wanted to create a new race of Earthlings.

That opened my ears.

Not, he explained, to be our equals. Not to be anything close to that . . . which idea I found to be at least a little reassuring.

No, this race was to be created just to fill a need of the Anunnaki. Nothing more . . . but nothing less, either. Basically they were to be a race of slaves. Slaves to carry out our bidding, and just intelligent and capable enough to do so, but no more. They would not, he emphasized, be in any way a threat to us.

I was not so sure. But I listened carefully, and considered all factors, not least of all my own political future . . . which in turn depended upon Enlil and his decisions.

****

In private, after long consideration, as Enlil's unofficial chief counselor, I advised Enlil to accept Enki's plan . . . and were it to become a success to take credit for it . . . as was his due as Commander of the Expeditionary Force.

Were it to fail . . . well, he could disown it as a crackpot idea pushed by the flighty Enki . . . an idea he had been unable to forestall in view of the crisis that faced him.

Which would give him considerable political advantage with his father King Anu back on Nibiru.

As his advisor, I wanted him in a no lose position, and thought I had come up with one.

Meanwhile I did other things to enhance my own status in the Anunnaki hierarchy.

I scouted around vigorously and found with my metal detectors a rich mine running through a hillside in Africa.

This was potentially very important.

Thanks to that discovery, our production could continue for the

next few Earth years at least without our men and women being sub-
jected to the prior dangers of deep underground mining.

Meanwhile Enki proceeded with his plans to produce a work-slave.

Enki had already for some time been conducting experiments
with the animal life on Earth, some of which I had observed. His
hybrid monstrosities held a lot of interest for me, but so far I had seen
nothing useful in them. His lion-ape instead of being fierce and agile
was instead an easy prey itself due to poor mobility and a kind of
sickly weakness.

Still, he kept trying.

He tried several combinations with the ape, trying to fabricate
now a kind of work beast for the Anunnaki gold mines. But there
were too many deficiences in every prototype produced . . . most
notably the lack of intelligence and language ability sufficient to carry
out even the simplest of instructions.

At last he saw what he had to do to have any possibiliity of success.

He took the sperm of some of our most robust younger men of
the Anunnaki Expeditionary Force and injected it into the eggs of
females of the primitive ape-man species. These were watched over
carefully in vitro until they reached a certain viable point, and then
were placed inside the wombs of five of our female crew members
who volunteered for the experiment.

Four of the five rendered what looked to be workable offspring.

I immediately advised Enlil to start to lend support to the project
on a tentative basis, pending further results as the first and subsequent crops attained their adolescence, making them able to work.

There were a hundred stories at least in the checkered history of
the development of our work-slaves. I only want to recall and put
down here a few of the more important ones in the most elemental
fashion, to help in my own perception. Any increased accuracy of
perception on my part should help me to advise Enlil.

Any successes by Enlil in turn would augment my own success,
which was what interested me most.

****

Early on in Enki's experiments arose the life span question.

From the first I told Enlil to prohibit Enki from ever giving any Earthly entity any but the earthling animals' exceedingly short life span.

I pointed out to him the obvious dangers of having any such inferior race to be given anything more.

Slaves with long range goals were dangerous by definition to our objectives.

We wanted these creatures to be vigorous and strong and able to work long hours under arduous conditions in the mines, true . . .

But . . .

But we did not want them to question their masters nor try to emulate them nor aspire to be as we were. They were to spend their short lives in strenuous work following all our explicit instructions . . . then die quickly and quietly, to be replaced by a new generation of equally submissive and contented work-slaves.

If any were ever fabricated that had our own life expectancy of a million and a half Earth years, we would have an enormous problem on our hands.

Enki followed those instructions, though I thought he might have felt differently about them than Enlil and I did.

There were several incidents that proved me right on that.

Everyone saw one enormous problem when the first four specimens reached early adolescence.

These humans, as we had come to call them, were simply far too intelligent.

Furthermore . . .

Their intelligence was of a unique variety. Simple, direct . . . but of unbelievable clarity and brilliance. They seemed perhaps even as intelligent as we . . . and therefore were very dangerous.

I myself took charge of the important task of disposing of them. Which turned out to be really simple to carry out, they were so altogether trusting and unsuspicious by nature. That part of their personality was good for us because it led to what we had to have . . .

total control. But the intelligence . . . that had to be greatly diminished and I so informed Enlil.

Enlil made it a written order to Enki, who had no choice but to obey. His solution was genetic, modifying certain specific genes so as to produce what he thought would solve the problem. I had him explain it to me before I recommended approval to Enlil, because in my mind Enki was altogether too friendly with the human specimens he was producing . . . perhaps overawed by the power of his own invention in their production.

The gene alterations, he said, would produce a kind of impervious membrane which would separate the right and left hemispheres of the brain. The logical and the intuitive would no longer have a direct interrelationship as of course they did in us . . . rather he thought that the personality thus produced would be at constant war with itself, forever trying to resolve the conflict between instinct and logic, between intuition and orderly thought. It seemed a good idea.

Pehaps even a master stroke of strategy. Worthy of my support, and even, I admit it, producing a bit of envy in me for what had been so deftly accomplished. Turning applied physiology artistically on the lathe of our political goals.

And it worked.

The new crop proved successful in all respects, and production was immediately stepped up . . . so that very soon we had a force of some 200 laborers, which we quickly put to work in the deep mines. When workers were hurt or killed in accidents, these humans were saddened sometimes to the point of becoming temporarily incapacitated . . . but the salient and most important element was this . . . they always eventually went back to the work and continued with their assigned tasks, whatever they were.

****

Gold production went up, and it seemed our major problem had been solved.

But not completely.

Here was where Enki's liberal tendencies and misplaced sympathy for the humans came to the fore . . . to cause us untold problems still once again.

****

True, this was after almost a hundred thousand Earth years had gone by . . . during which time the stocks of gold reserves on Nibiru were raised to what looked like a level sufficient to last a very long time . . . with King Anu being very happy with our efforts, apparently insuring a considerable bump upwards in my own career. During that same time, of course, countless generations of human work-slaves had come and gone . . . their short, work-filled lives flitting by us like butterflies flitted by them on sunlit mornings . . . but not like that either, since their own mornings were spent far from sunlight in the damp darkness of the twisting mine shafts under Africa . . . where the presence of butterflies was unknown.

****

But, to my way of thinking, at least . . . if not to King Anu's fatherly way of regarding his son . . . Enki was always rash and unpredictable.

This quality of his came out at last and led to a big change in our entire policy towards the humans and the working of the mines.

For a long time now the pregnancies and births had been carried out exclusively in the laboratory . . . in vitro, with no further need for birth mothers to participate in the production process. This was good in that it prevented what could have become another mutiny, this time on the part of our female crew members. The bad part was it gave Enki all that time in the laboratory to experiment further genetically with the developing embryos . . .

Apparently he fell prey to temptation or weakness, and made a big, big mistake.

I believe he finally made a genetic change that would permit the hybrid Earthlings to reproduce themselves. Then it follows that he must have given some kind of instruction to the Earthlings concerning sex and procreation.

I am just guessing here, because none of us knew.

Accused of that on my advice to Enlil, after the first natural human birth from a human female occurred, Enki denied it, claiming there must have been some kind of natural environmental or evolutionary change which had taken place. That line of defense in the end saved Enki from official censure. But I did not believe it, especially when the births did not stop at one, but soon became epidemic.

****

Censure or not, Enlil was apoplectic about the situation. His edict soon followed.

Which was this . . .

Humans would no longer be cared for by us. Our African settlement of Edin was thereafter to be closed to all Earthlings and they would have to make their own way in the world. Plant and gather their own food, construct their own shelter. But that did not relieve them from their responsibility concerning the work in the mines. Oh, no. That work must continue as always, and for anyone who might dare to try to escape it, the penalty was death.

That had been my recommendation, and I was glad to see Enlil follow it, over all the pusilanimous objections of Enki.

This was a setback to our administration, for several good and cogent reasons . . . which I had made sure to point out to Enlil to help him towards the right decision to remedy the ill. Humans who could have families would tend to be more far-sighted than they had been . . . plus they could now form into units tied together by blood and thus potentially cause all kinds of trouble.

I didn't like it at all, and was quick to tell Enlil so.

Fortunately the work went forward on a more or less even keel. There was more grumbling on the part of the workers, and they were not so docile as before. However, I soon found a way to put an end to that by a simple strategem.

I merely let it be known that any damage to the work process by anyone would quickly be compensated for by some kind of immediate and inexorable damage to their own family. And by and large this quelled almost all problems before they ever eventuated. I got this policy instituted over the objections of the ever vacillating Enki, who would have simply appealed to the "better nature" of the humans in negotiating any difficulties.

****

In using my best and smoothest arguments in private to convince Enlil of his brother Enki's underhanded tactics in helping the Earthlings, I had at last perhaps gone too far . . . that is, I succeeded far better than I knew.

That plus the fact that Enlil had long before become utterly bored with our Mission on Earth and his role in it. He longed for the Home Planet, wanted to be close to his father Anu.

Close to the throne, you mean was what I thought.

Then, too, Enlil had started to drink heavily of the crude alcohol we brewed from a species of the local grain. When he drank, he became impatient and impulsive . . . two dangerous qualities for a Mission Commander, or any heir apparent to the Anunnaki throne.

I tried to caution him and to short-circuit many impractical ideas he wanted to put into action. I was in general quite successful in this, but not always.

And then circumstances combined to bring everything into a state of crisis. A crisis bigger than any of us had ever had to face before . . .

****

It happened even as our own great planet, Nibiru, was approaching Earth near the perigee of its 3600 Earth year orbit.

Customarily, this brought us a visit from King Anu or his

representative, since the proximity of the two planets made such a trip both short and easy.

This time, however, was different . . .

The first I learned of it was the cancellation of the usual visit. Only later did I learn why. And this learning came at the expense of my almost having to confront Enlil, a risky maneuver at the best . . . but fortunately I was able to pull it off. I felt my loyalty to him demanded that I do it . . . and I was right.

His state was far gone in a surprising direction. The obstacles to carrying out the Mission . . . his impatience at being so long away from Nibiru . . . his resentment at not being openly named as successor to the Throne which implied he was being held in a kind of suspensory comparison with his brother Enki . . . all this seemed to be channelled into what had now become a hatred of the human race he had been instrumental in creating.

Those were not the only things bothering him. He didn't like how our crewmen were having sexual liasons of their own with the Earthwomen . . . or so he said. I happened to know he had had his own romantic flings with various of them over the years . . . and had been greatly offended when one of them actually chose an Earthman over him in some kind of final confrontation. That at least was the rumor.

But what he talked of to me was discipline and its lack. He thought it very bad for his crewmen to fraternize with an inferior race. Bad for morale, bad for the essential element of Anunnaki life, which was always and at all costs to maintain the sacred hierarchy, the hierarchy that gave order and continuity to our lives and culture.

His many edicts had done nothing in stopping the fraternization and left him facing a dilemma, he said. Either to punish his own men, which meant punishing the majority, an impossible command position . . . or making himself seem lax by allowing the situation to continue unabated.

"But it will continue no longer!" He suddenly shouted the words and pounded his pudgy fists hard against the top of his wood-hewn desk.

He knocked back a large slug of alcohol, narrowed his heavily lidded eyes at me and . . . suddenly he was telling me the whole secret story.

His staff scientist had told him the facts about the situation months before. I was, he said, the only top official besides him to know the whole truth up to this point.

A staggering truth, indeed . . .

Earth had only months to live.

Earth at least as we knew it.

****

It all had to do with the South Pole, which the staff scientist had been observing over a period of years.

Rapid changes were taking place now.

The global warming we had all experienced was causing a frightening scenario to eventuate.

The ice at the base of the pole was becoming increasingly softer, leaving the millions of tons above it in danger of toppling into the ocean.

Unbalance would then become the immediate problem. There might be some wavering of the geographical axis, causing widespread destruction on every surface area of the world. Whether or not that occurred, something else just as nefarious would. Water levels would rise precipitously . . . perhaps as much as 300 feet. The most likely result would be that all life that lived on land would be annihilated, leaving only some of the sea creatures to survive the catastrophe.

Enlil, in his drunken state, in what was to me a bizarre twist, seemed exuberant about this prospect. He chuckled more than once in his narrative of the situation, and I saw he was way out of control.

"But . . . but . . . Your Excellence, what can we do about this terrible situation?"

"Do . . . do?" His laughter was hearty, triumphant. "Why . . . enjoy it . . . to the uttermost . . . the uttermost. That and . . . get out of here . . . this nowhere . . . this forsaken outpost. The Home Planet . . . THAT is where we will prosper, you and I, Yahweh."

****

Under my questioning the withdrawal plan came out.

Secrecy, Enlil said, was the watchword. Under no circumstances were the Earthlings to be told of their plight. The Anunnaki would simply depart under cover of night. Silently and without saying goodbye and with no hint to anyone of what was to come.

As to what would come and exactly when it would come . . . that was a problem already solved. Susceptible to such a solution principally because of the approaching Nibiru. Our big planet swooping on its orbit between Mars and Jupiter would inevitably introduce a strong gravitational force affecting Earth. That gravitational force would be the trigger that would cause the toppling of the South Polar ice cap into the sea.

The scientist had no doubt about it. I believed that, for should he prove to be wrong his own life might be forfeit if I knew Enlil's character.

****

"We will watch the whole debacle from orbit before we catch our ride home on the passing Nibiru." Enlil chuckled softly as if telling me some private joke.

I really didn't know what my own reaction, other than surprise and shock, was at first . . .

Not until later that night.

****

I woke around midnight, listening to the crickets chirping outside. Then it came to me.

It was really all political.

As such it would depend more on subsequent, almost unpredictable events than it would on the act itself.

To abandon Earth and the Mission. That was something serious, something which could be career ending. For Enlil, for me.

Not that I had any love for Earthlings. I did not. They were exactly what they had been conceived to be in the first place. Beasts of burden. Work-slaves, whose function was to mine the gold Nibiru needed to survive. My feelings for them did not go beyond that, nor would it have been right for them to do so . . . we were dealing after all with inferior beings whose welfare was not our concern. To help them at any point that did not directly concern our Mission was to go outside the parameters of that Mission . . . and in that process perhaps put the Mission and ultimately the Anunnaki as a race in jeopardy. As a loyal Anunnaki, I could not subject our sacred race to that unauthorized risk.

And if . . . as we had been told . . . the gold stocks on Nibiru were now such that it seemed they would be sufficient for at least six thousand Earth years without further mining . . . then there was no immediate crisis to be combatted.

At any rate, I had a different card to play in this very political drama as the situation eventuated.

The environmental crisis on Nibiru might yield to another approach. I knew of one which I was holding in reserve to use for Enlil at the right time for it . . . that was simply to look for another home for the Anunnaki race. Surely there must be one available out there somewhere. If not in this galaxy, then in another.

Then Enlil would be a hero, and my own future would seem assured.

And if we could manage to bring charges against Enki for his reckless attitude towards the human race, to the point of putting the Anunnaki objectives in imminent danger . . . then . . . then I could almost see the crown upon Enlil's head, and myself seated on his right hand as his most trusted advisor.

At last my thoughts blended into the chirping of the crickets. I fell into a deep sleep and dreamed of myself polishing a golden crown . . .

****

I personally woke a large number of our personnel the night of our departure.

I saw the surprise and disbelief in their at first uncomprehending eyes, of course. And then the gladness . . . the happiness to be going home.

In Enki's eyes I noted a different reaction. It looked to me something like shock and an unanswered question. Which just gave me more satisfaction.

Certain technicians of course had been preparing us for launch for days . . . but without knowing it were anything more than another drill.

****

Most of the personnel were still half asleep when we obtained orbit in our great Mother Ship, our scout ships hangared inside. I waited until some time had passed and they were more alert before reading to them Enlil's pronouncement . . . the pronouncement I myself had written.

I put it in terms of triumph for the Anunnaki. Of our Mission, of our race . . . and the triumph of our science over unavoidable catastrophe, both on Earth and on Nibiru. The reaction was good in general, though I caught the anguished expression passing across the face of Enki.

Above all, though, and most important to me and my future . . . Enlil himself looked pleased.

****

We continued in orbit for two whole Earth days . . . we had plenty of time to see the image of our approaching Home Planet grow successively larger on each of those days, which caused plenty of excited talk.

And then . . . then it happened.

****

It was at first like an advancing blur across the face of the planet . . . the wrinkled wall of water that started in the south and slowly . . . we knew it was actually very fast . . . swept north.

Over time the continents, or most of their land area, were erased by blue water. What we could see of the face of Earth under the turbulent dark clouds told us that.

****

We were glad we were not down there, happy to have escaped that terrible fate. Some may have thought of the Earthlings during those hours in orbit as we observed the catastrophe below. Enki's now perplexed expression told me he did, and others grew strangely quiet.

But then, that somber mood lifted soon after we fired our own rockets and were racing for home that loomed ever larger before us.

Home . . .

****

So it was over, the whole Earth adventure.

Over . . .

****

I tried to think of it as just a cycle, an episode in my own steady rise towards power. That was my perspective and I wanted to keep it that way.

As part of the cycle, we had given birth to a new species, the Earthlings, or humans. All right. It was a necessary step towards our own survival. Nothing more, nothing less.

Yes, there was a certain emotional impact involved to see it all swept away in one powerful surge of natural force.

But there was more than that involved. Much more. The future of our planet. Of the Anunnaki as a race. In my mind, to insure both of those Enlil must come to the fore and dominate over the frighteningly liberal Enki . . . who if ever in power could bring ruin and decay into our great and noble history.

My own role was of key importance. To keep Enlil on course, not letting his excesses result in his negating himself and our future. So it goes without saying that I had to prosper if our planet, our race and our great cultural and technological heritage were to continue to prosper. Thus it was I cast personal doubts aside and seized upon each moment of opportunity as I knew I must.

Humankind destroyed? That was of minor importance if in the process the Anunnaki heritage was preserved. They were our creation. We were not theirs.

****

Back home, back on Nibiru, at first everything seemed to go our way.

Enlil was feted and universally praised for his decisiveness . . . for his courage and farsightedness . . . because who knew what future trouble the Earthlings might have caused . . .

He was seen as a true son of his father Anu, the obvious successor to the throne.

That was wine to both our thirsty egos.

But . . . time passed and things changed.

The problem again was environmental.

The atmospheric loss on Nibiru began to escalate exponentially. Our gold supplies so hardly wrenched from Earth and that had seemed sufficient for thousands of Earth years . . . suddenly were not.

That unexpected and unforeseen situation made all the politicians see things in a different light.

The unfortunate thing was this . . .

That new light drained the blood from Enlil's countenance and transfused it into the face of his brother Enki. Enki became now positively roseate with what looked like victory, his judgment in trying to preserve the human race after all vindicated in the light of the latest hindsight.

We, on the contrary . . . Enlil and I as his advisor . . . began to be seen as the villains of the entire Earth episode, our judgment flawed.

To say this was a painful experience for me, is to say the very least about it. I was hurt, Enlil was furious with me, our mutual future looking very dark.

Enlil's fury naturally turned towards Enki. He wanted to challenge him to combat to the death to save his honor and prestige.

I cautioned him not to. No matter what happened he could only lose. His life, at worst. And even if he triumphed it would only be defeat in disguise.

Anu and the Anunnaki in general would remember always it was Enki who had advocated the conservation of the Earthlings. Just as he now advocated his return to Earth, to once again re-establish the human race as a work force to save Nibiru.

A position that, in the face of the crisis, quickly gained political support.

Enlil was devastated, cowed.

"Let it go," I counselled him. "Turn their eyes in a different direction."

An idea had occurred to me, the one I mentioned earlier.

An inspiration.

A life-changing, destiny-changing inspiration.

"Why not . . . why not now ask for another Mission that will take everyone's attention off Earth. Make you, Enlil, once again the cynosure you deserve to be . . ."

"What . . . what are you talking about?"

"Just this. The only Mission that will matter in the long run. This planet is dying. Nibiru will not survive. All of Earth's gold can not keep that from happening eventually. We have to recognize that before anyone else does. That will make our future for us. To know that what we need is not to repair this broken home of ours any longer . . . but to seek a new and better home."

I let the impact of what I had said sink in. With Enlil, that always took time. I waited . . .

"Earth? Are you talking about Earth? We can have it anytime. It is ours."

"Ours, yes. But too small for our race. No, I had a different idea in mind."

"Speak, Anunnaki mine, speak!"

"We don't have to stay in this part of the Universe."

His eyes lit up and I saw he was getting the idea. Finally.

It is hard to be an underling, a mere lieutenant, when you know your own capacities are to your Commander's as the stars are to our moons.

But what can one do? Time and circumstance eventually make fools of us all.

But I had my clinching argument ready. The one that would cement me into the graces of Enlil, and I spoke it strongly now.

"Then . . . THEN . . . you can take your vengeance on Enki."

"How?" His questing expression told me all too plainly the fool still did not comprehend.

I gave words to the obvious.

"After you find a new home for the Anunnaki . . . even as you let it be known what and where it is, this great prize and that you have done it . . . you secretly yourself return to Earth and prepare your revenge against Enki, your nefarious brother who loves the brutish Earthlings so much."

He liked that word "brutish". I could see it by the sparkle and movement in his green eyes. I made a mental note to repeat it often, however much of a misstatement of fact it were.

"Go on, go on. How could I do that?"

I drew it out for him, poor fool.

Exactly how he could surreptitiously re-establish himself on Earth . . . in a place far from Enki's to be newly established headquarters so as not to be detected. As an adjunct, I gave him only a hint of how I might ingratiate myself with Enki, become an important member of his staff, get myself appointed in charge of reconnaissance on Earth.

He still could not see it.

I gave him more conjecture, with details.

He himself this time, I said, could create a new Earthling. A quite different version than the anterior one.

But his sights had to be set higher.

I labored at my task of explication, drew it out for him.

Not an Earthling like Enki's final version, a common laborer to work the mines.

But instead a race of warriors!

A race of warriors such as had not been seen since the distant days of my own grandfather, who had genetically engineered the Dinosaurs . . .

He was listening to me intently.

I could tell the idea enchanted him. He quickly became drunk with it, comcomitantly with the wine, raising the glass to his lips and pacing, weaving a bit from side to side, his eyes alight.

Suddenly he stopped, a pensive look on his face.

"But Enki . . . how will I know what he is doing? How can I prepare my attack against a foe of whose activities I am ignorant?"

"Simple." I smiled at him and clapped him on his ample and muscular shoulder.

"Simple, because . . . you will have a trusted spy right in the middle of the enemy camp. I will do everything to get the assignment."

His look in response was gold to my soul.

I went on to tell him how, to gain our ends, he and I must stage a bit of theater for the consumption of King Anu and his power group of officials and politicians . . .

There would be a disagreement, an argument . . . whose upshot would be that I would be dismissed from his staff. He would afterwards make remarks here and there in the right circles to the effect that I, Yahweh, was, for his taste, too much an admirer of the personality and politics of his brother, Enki.

****

Enlil was given his requested Mission to scout out possible new planets for the Anunnaki.

Concomitantly, King Anu gave Enki the Mission of returning to Earth and continuing the quest for gold so that Nibiru could continue to survive meanwhile.

And I . . . I was appointed Communications and Reconnaissance Officer on Enki's staff . . . exactly as I had hoped and secretly intrigued for.

Everything was in place. But as I knew well from bitter experience, that did not at all mean that things would eventuate the way I hoped they would . . .

****

Still, here we were now in Earth orbit, preparing to land and begin our Second Mission . . .

****

The Second Mission would be very like the first as far as its objectives . . . those were the same as before, to mine enough gold to keep life on Nibiru possible.

But the nature of that mission, I knew, had to be very much different. How could it not? . . . with Enki in Command.

Enki and Enlil might be brothers, but inside they were as different as any two entities could ever be. Still, as Enki's Chief Aide, I would practically be almost as powerful as he as his second in command, due to the strong influence I hoped to exert over him . . . just as I had done and was doing with his brother Enlil.

Since I controlled the information Enki got, since appointments were made through me, since I was his Chief Aide . . . I saw unlimited opportunities ahead of me, and pledged to avail myself of every one of them to carry out my own objectives . . .

We would make my dream of Invincible Warriors come true, Enlil and I, right here again on Planet Earth where my grandfather had wrought his own greatest triumph. We would accomplish this, Enlil and I, behind Enki's back, of course, and without his knowledge.

That was my plan.

If things went the way I thought, the trusting Enki would never suspect a thing, never know his brother was even on the planet . . . much less imagine the grand scheme I would have in place. And when that grand scheme had been carried out, it would take Enki so totally by surprise he would be unable to stop us from realizing my great dream.

Enlil and I would rule Earth and everything in it. All its people would be the work-slaves and warriors we would create. There would be no dissension, no disagreements, no rebellions and no discussions. Enlil and I would be Earth's gods. Its only gods . . . to whom total obeisance and allegiance would always be demanded, always be slavishly given.

That to me was the very best, the essence of the Anunnaki Way . . .

And now . . . on station in orbit for our Second Mission to Earth . . .

The planet looked not so different from the first time I had seen it a third of an Earth millenium ago. The ubiquitous waters that had rushed over its entire surface at our hasty departure were no longer evident. The continents looked in just about the same general outlines and proportions as before . . . from that altitude, at least, almost as if the Great Flood had never happened.

I reminded myself that from the very first I must keep my eyes peeled for Enlil's arrival . . . well, not my literal eyes, of course . . . my ears, perhaps. On his secret arrival, he was to transmit a pulsed code signal only on the special communicator shared exclusively between him and me.

I had joked with Enlil before even he left Nibiru on his Star

Quest that he might well beat me to Earth. It was a joke, yes, of course . . . but with a germ of truth to it, too. Though his quest for a habitable planet for the Anunnaki might take many years as measured in Earth time, one factor could make my joke a near reality.

That factor was his potential use of the recently discovered Time Corridors . . . which could cut travelling time enormously for interstellar voyages such as his.

Not that I minded a few Earth years going by. That would give me time to establish myself the way I wanted to be established with Enki. To win his faith and confidence and set him up just right for the Big Surprise.

I had no way of knowing at that time the first big surprise was destined to be mine . . .

****

That surprise was not evident until we Anunnaki on our Second Mission had passed several months on Earth.

For one thing, there was so much to do.

The first was to re-establish our Space Center. The entire area looked different now, because everything was buried under a layer of calcified mud, making it look to us as if our great base had never existed.

At first we thought to rebuild. But then the technicians came up with an idea. They would try cutting through the mud with laser technology, to see first how much of our buildings and equipment had survived.

It was heavy, tedious work, but we then found that more had survived than we would have expected.

It was decided to strip away the mud, or rather set the lasers to vaporize it, and it only, without damaging our buildings or their contents. Working in that way, a lot was salvaged and in six Earth months the base was operative again on a primitive level.

It was shortly after that feat was an accomplished fact that I took my first Reconnaissance flight.

It was a flight that was cut short because . . .

Because I could not believe my eyes.

When I had checked it out further, I quickly turned back to base. I had to report this to Enki, and fast.

****

I entered Enki's headquarters office, closed the door carefully behind me, took a deep breath and started to open my mouth and blurt it out.

"The Earthlings are here! They're . . . somehow . . . back!"

Even as I said it I noticed something odd about Enki's own mouth . . . a strange, tight little smile. And a kind of twinkle in his eyes.

Hardly the reaction I expected. Unless . . . a staggering thought hit me. Almost knocked me over. But of course, it had to be. "You . . . you knew . . ." was all I could get out.

"Sit down, Yahweh. As my Top Aide you need to know a few things. It's time."

I took the chair he indicated.

I couldn't seem to stop talking. "But the Earthlings . . . they were supposed to have been destroyed. The waters . . . we saw them . . . how? Why? . . ."

Now I knew I had to get a grip on myself. Which meant to shut up and listen. Otherwise, who knew what kind of dangerous political waters I myself might be flooded by? So with an effort I listened carefully to everything that Enki told me.

"I had good reason for saving some of the Earthlings, even if I had to do it secretly and against my brother's order. I hope, as his ex-advisor, you can believe that and understand. I'm sure you will as all the details come out. Even Enlil finally must understand and approve . . ."

He rose and began to pace the room, his arms gesturing expressively.

"Just to give you some of the reasons. For one thing, they had done us yeoman service in our Mission to save Nibiru. As such, they deserved saving. Second, they were our creation. We had a certain responsibility for them. Third, they were an interesting scientific experiment, one which deserved to be followed through on. But the most important reason of all . . ."

He paused in his pacing and looked straight at me, which was my chance to say something.

But I knew better than to fall into that trap. What HE was going to say next might change everything and I above all didn't want to come down on the wrong side of all this Big Surprise.

So . . .

I pressed my lips together firmly, felt my jaw muscles tighten and tried to look eager and on his side, even though I wasn't sure yet exactly what that side was.

"Well, Yahweh, you know it. You see it. We NEED them . . . the Earthlings. Just as long as our own planetary crisis exists . . . and I for one was never convinced it was over, as Enlil was. That was his mistake . . . but I wasn't going to endorse it, either."

Now I felt it safe to speak. Carefully, though. "But . . . but how . . ."

I let the question just hang there, served it up to him as if I were his admirer, which I pretended arduously to be now, every time a good opportunity like this one came along.

He responded in a good way, lowering his tone to one of confidentiality. One loyal Anunnaki to another.

Good . . .

"Still, Enlil was my Commander. I could not disobey him. It was a quandary for me. What could I do?"

I leaned forward to show my intense interest, but let him take his time in framing his response to his own question.

"I was prohibited from revealing the facts about the coming disaster to any Earthling. I could not go against that prohibition. But . . . there was no prohibition about talking to a wall . . ."

His smirk here I found despicable . . . while at the same time I flashed a tentative smile at him inviting his revelation.

"So one evening in the darkness I talked to the WALL on one edge of our compound. I told the WALL about the disaster, gave the WALL detailed plans of how to build a craft . . . an Ark . . . against the coming deluge, and how to stock it with a certain number of people and animals. If the human patriarch known as Noah happened to be on the other side of the wall at that time in response to my notice to him, well . . . that was no concern of mine one way or another."

I saw a look of ultimate satisfaction on his face.

"And so, we now have our workforce for the mines. Ready to go when we want them. No delays, all of them eager and loyal to me, their benefactor and savior. And . . . what do you think of all this, Yahweh?"

He looked at me curiously, his eyes narrowing.

Watch out.

I knew what to say. I expressed my admiration for his perspicacity and foresight without saying anything negative about Enlil, which would have been too bold and obvious.

I thought under the circumstances I handled myself well.

That night in my quarters I made copious notes of our conversation and its ramifications.

They might, I thought, come in handy later. Very handy in the case of one possible eventuation of all this at sometime in the distant future which I saw as entirely possible and even likely . . .

I speak of Enki's trial back on Nibiru, when Enlil could bring against him what his brother so richly, in my opinion, deserved . . . charges of treason against his Planet and his Race.

****

The short Earth years kept flying by . . .

I will say this for Enki. He very promptly got the gold operations in production again. But it was on the basis of what I perceived at the time to be deliberate deception. He had to pretend that what was being done was for the mutual benefit of the Earthlings and the Anunnaki. I would have made no such pretense. We were their gods and their creators . . . our word was law, they were fortunate to have been given their existence by us, and they had no other choice.

As simple as that.

Too simple for Enki, I guess. He continued with his childish games with the Earthlings, and in the process did us in my estimation much harm.

My feeling was . . .

You have a choice . . . you can be friendly with an inferior people or you can demand their respect and obedience at all times . . . but you can not do both. It was Enki's great error to think that you could.

I saw it as my eventual duty to relieve him of that misconception and save the dignity of the Anunnaki. But everything in the ripeness of Time . . .

Meanwhile I was busy with my other, more mundane duties.

We needed a power base and a communications center.

So my energies were focused for quite a while on the Great Pyramid we had constructed in the land I had earlier decided to call Egypt during our First Mission.

We had to reconstruct it now on this Second Mission, and it was not easy.

But I had a crew of technicians as well as a human work force at my disposal and I made good use of both.

The layers of mud and debris had to be lasered off first.

The outer layer of gold had been washed away in the deluge and had to be reapplied. The one inch layer of limestone and the inner layer of gold were still there.

So then I needed only to have my technicians supervise the re-installation of the giant thermocouples in the desert sands around the base of the pyramid to once again have our basic electric capacitator in place. The great crystal and the set of minor crystals that formed part of the charging system were basically intact and only needed to be cleaned up and polished and reset.

Then there was the interior insulation to be taken care of. As to the control systems they were basically intact. The great sweep of the enormous flood had largely been excluded by the design of the pyramid. So the technicians did the minor repairs and rewiring and some modifications concomitant with the Anunnaki advances in technology since the time of the original installation . . . and we were back in business.

I personally supervised the sending of the first message to King Anu to that effect.

There were general commendations all around in the messages from the Home Planet, of which I of course received my deserved share. It was tempting to let things slide and to merely bask in the reflected glory of Enki, but I could not rest while there was what I considered a deadly cancer growing on the Anunnaki government . . . in the form of Enki's misplaced liberalism with an inferior people. I saw it, it was thrust into my face every day.

I began to travel further and further afield in my scout ship in my duty as Reconnaissance Officer. In carrying out such duties I became conscious of another disquieting fact.

Earth people had settled in many different places around the globe. Not only that . . . they seemed to be doing much better than I would ever have expected from such backward peoples.

Their lives were primitive, yes . . . nevertheless they seemed to have adapted themselves to a variety of enivironmental conditions, and I asked myself how that could be.

At last I dared to ask Enki himself about it.

He smiled that infuriatingly superior smile of his . . . the cat that had eaten the canary . . . and then explained it all . . .

Back at some point in time on the First Mission he had added something to their genetic mix . . . a designed element of his own . . . he referred to it now as the adaptability gene. Which allowed them to overcome limitations and modify not only their biology but their mental and pyschological outlooks . . . as necessary, to cope with whatever conditions might come up.

Well, that computed with what I had observed. In the Eastern regions, a yellow race with upslanted, heavily lidded eyes. In Africa people observably darkening and otherwise protecting themselves against a searing and intense sun.

And I thought within myself . . . to do that . . . to give them such a power . . . was that not a potential threat to us, the Anunnaki, their creators? Who knew to what extremes it might someday lead . . .

what rebel fires might be lit by that very adaptability gene at work within them . . . and . . .

My mind balked at carrying out all the possible consequences.

But I made mental and some written notes later of all of that . . . more grist for my mill in Enki's eventual trial for treason.

****

Over the years we saw generations of our Earth-slaves come into maturity and work and die . . . but I here admit Enki got a lot of use out of their ridiculously short and inefficient lives.

The undeniable result was . . .

We sent vast stores of gold back to Nibiru aboard our shuttle craft.

But he was much too liberal with them. How could they consider us as imperial and imperious gods if we looked too closely after their own welfare? And yet, Enki, in his limited way, continued to do so.

His policy in the mines literally made me sick. He shortened their work hours, instituted costly and unnecessary worker protection devices and . . . this was incredible . . . liberated them from further work after twenty years, bringing in fresh crews to take their place . . .

Yes, he had sufficient reserve worker pools to be able to do this. But . . .

It was added trouble and work for us and not part of the Mission parameters.

So where did he get the authority to do that?

Above all his policies brought into jeopardy our godhood, the essential thing that gave us our inherent dominance over the race. To inferior minds such as theirs, one never knew what the reaction might suddenly escalate into.

So in my estimation failed Enki in what should have been his leadership role.

At last we heard news from King Anu as to the status of Enlil and the results of his search for a possible new planetary home for the Anunnaki.

In a very distant constellation, to which we had given the name of Zeta Reticuli 2, Enlil had found a possible successor to Nibiru . . . should the necessity for such ever be confirmed.

That shot a thrill through my heart. Success to the enterprise meant a lot in Enlil's standing as Anu's eventual successor over Enki. I knew that, of course.

But Anu's reaction to the find . . . that was just as important to my future . . . to the Anunnaki future . . . which I also knew.

That came out slowly over a period of time in the form of many different messages from the Home Planet.

Anu and his advisors were studying the problem and what would be the best course for the Anunnaki as a Race.

For the time being, he announced at last, there would be no change . . .

As long as Nibiru could be kept habitable by the supplies of gold from Earth, he inclined towards keeping things as they were. It was possible the causes of the atmospheric crisis would lessen. Or even, failing that, that new solutions might be found. But for the present, he said, the best thing was to continue the Earth Mission with its successful results in preserving Nibiru.

It was made clear, too, that Enlil continued his explorations to try to turn up some even better alternative to Nibiru for a new home.

Only I knew better. It was part of our plan to maintain that illusion.

Maintain it while Enlil made for Earth, the intention to land far away from Enki's headquarters, and to institute our own program for Conquest of Earth and the elimination of Enki.

Which in its turn would inevitably have to lead to the Succession of Anu by his son Enlil as exalted ruler of the Anunnaki.

****

I had some time previously found what I had thought might be an ideal location for Enlil to begin building our base of operations on Earth.

It was far out in the Western Sea . . . halfway around the world from the Anunnaki base in Mesopotamia. That was one advantage. Another was that no Anunnaki was liable to stumble upon it accidentally since it was so far out from any large land mass, isolated and alone on the broad and seamless ocean.

There were four large verdant islands, which gave us enough space I thought, to carry out our plans to create the Invincible Army . . . with no interference or oversight from any nosy Earthling neighbors.

Of course everything was subject to Enlil's approval. Knowing his sometimes capricious ideas and illogical whims, I was afraid he might come up with some idea of his own . . . such as . . . perish the thought . . . locating as near as possible to his brother Enki to get the confrontation over with as soon as possible. I knew he was capable of thinking just that way, hoped that this time at least he would be more sensible. But you never knew.

I had sent him Earth coordinates of the islands via our special communicator long since, and waited somewhat anxiously now only to hear from him . . .

****

One evening the slight buzzing like a bee from the little communicator in my pocket came while I was alone in my quarters. That was no accident. I had asked Enlil to buzz me only during evening hours my local time and fortunately I saw . . . or heard . . . that he had complied.

So far, so good.

On the tiny screen of the communicator appeared the visual equivalent of our pulse code along with coordinates that I quickly recognized. The islands. So he was there!

I breathed a sigh of relief.

****

Early the next morning I was off on a Reconnaissance Mission of my own design, quite different from the one I communicated to my men . . . and yes I would be going alone as I liked and was accustomed to doing . . . and pointed out to them I would be absent three or four days and not to worry about me.

As I set off in the scout and gained appropriate altitude to where I could see the curvature of Earth, at that one particular moment it seemed like nothing so much as my own great round recreational ball to do with as I liked.

That was exactly what I hoped it would eventually turn out to be . . .

****

As I neared the area where the four verdant islands lay in the great Western Ocean, high up as I was, I saw it from afar . . .

The great interstellar space ship that had carried Enlil vast distances across the Universe to the constellation Zeta Reticuli 2, which would be Option B for the Anunnaki . . . our New Home if the environmental situation on Nibiru ever necessitated it.

It was nice to know we had that option in reserve . . . nicer yet to know I had influenced Enlil to undertake the Mission that now, with its success, could only help to carry him to ultimate power when his father Anu at last came to the end of his long life.

I actually felt my hands tremble as I set my Scout down beside the vast Mother space ship on the largest of the four islands, so eager was I now to put our plans in motion . . . and to attach myself to the rising wave of greatness I felt sure we were about to immerse ourselves in.

****

My thoughts, yes, quite naturally, had gone to greatness, to achievement, to the very stars of accomplishment . . .

Separation had made me forget how petty and impatient Enlil could be.

He seemed more concerned with his immediate comforts than any transcendental goals.

I had to adjust instantly to fight off the negative influence of his thinking and his presence, and to put things back on track.

Oh, there had been this problem and that . . . disappointment A and disappointment B, delay and discomfort thus and so and everything too long and uncomfortable . . .

Well, yes. I did not try directly to point out to his royal self that for most of us life was never just a picnic in the park . . . no, I was too smart to risk his displeasure that way . . .

Instead I praised his appearance and above all his great accomplishment. Put it in perspective for him so he could perhaps for the first time, I realized, understand what it was he had done. Even so, all that might have fallen short were it not for element B . . .

Element B was something I served with a great flourish to Enlil at the very beginning of our talk . . . a generous sample of the latest Earth alcohol our technicians had succeeded in brewing . . . and it was something of an accomplishment in itself, light in body and tasty but at the same time very powerful.

It had its wanted effects on Enlil, and the conversion of his attitude with a little time was startling. He was slapping me on the back and telling me how he had missed my companionship and my counsels.

At last he wanted me to draw out the dream for him again so he could . . . he said . . . relish it for a while.

I thought it more likely he had forgotten it completely.

But . . .

I was only too eager to oblige.

Once again with broad strokes I painted it for him in the air . . .

How we could raise and train our Invincible Army here on the islands. Using genetics to produce warriors such as had never been seen in the Universe . . . except perhaps for my grandfather's dinosaurs.

These could be fabricated from the DNA of our human work-slaves who were available to us to kidnap from any part of the globe, so omnipresent had they proved. I did not miss my opportunity here to describe Enki's clear treachery in going against Enlil's own edict prior to the Flood. I recreated it now in fact in such personal terms that I saw the reaction in him.

He pounded his fist into his palm. "Enki . . . Enki . . ." Words failed him here and he had recourse to his glass again. Then just shook his head with an expression of hate I had seldom seen on him.

I pounced on my opportunity to elaborate further. About Enki's present liberal administration of the work in the mines. Of his obvious attempts to pose as a friend to the Earthlings, and how he lowered himself almost to their standards . . . rather than striking fear into their hearts as befitted his status as an Anunnaki, a god to these lowly work-slaves who would not have even existed without us.

I told him of my worst fear.

That Enki even some day might incorporate into the Earthlings the DNA for our long lifespans rather than their own pitifully short ones.

From their point of view it would make them practically immortal. Then the threat from them, already great, would become almost unlimited. They could even think to aspire to be like us.

"Monkey see, monkey do." Enlil pronounced the words without humor and I saw his hand tighten on his glass.

Now I could go ahead with the outline again of our plan and have it mean something emotionally to him in this moment.

"We can bring Enki to trial. For treason. I have been gathering evidence. His own words to me will convict him. On several charges which we will have drawn up.

"But first we must have force to back us. What he has failed to do, we must do. Establish above all the Anunnaki Way of Life. We must reign supreme, and the work-slaves must keep their appointed station."

Enlil nodded, once again pounded his right fist into his left palm. He looked at me. "Tell me once more, how must this best be accomplished?"

"We must make a strike on his base. Take over the administration of the Earth Mission."

"Well, that . . . we could do it now. Tomorrow . . . I have nuclear bombs." Enlil's great rolling eyes expressed his eagerness.

"No. We have to have your father Anu's opinion on our side. Otherwise we stand to lose everything. What we must do is capture the base without any great harm to the personnel. That we can do with a surprise ground attack. Then hold the trial, the court-martial on the charge of High Treason. And for that we need . . . our Invincible Army. Which you are going to develop here. We need them not only to make the strike. We need them subsequently to hold at bay and conquer any Earthlings that dare to challenge our authority. They are many in number and have an unreasonable loyalty to Enki, so enchanted they are by his smooth lies and his oily, treasonous ways . . . do you understand me?"

His expression told me he not only understood me, but was now my eager ally, ready to do anything to accomplish our goals.

****

Time . . . the days, the months, the years . . . so fleeting on Earth as compared to Nibiru . . . hundreds of Earth years seem the blink of an eye to us Anunnaki, though generations of Earthlings are born and die within the narrow boundaries of such an inconsequential stretch of Time.

We Anunnaki are not constantly hemmed in by crises, as I have observed the Earthlings are. Of course their very survival is constantly under threat, being as backward and ignorant as they are, making hundreds of unnecessary mistakes each day, exposing themselves to dangers we have learned to routinely avoid millions of years in the past. Then they feel as they mature they must immediately mate . . . if not they possibly miss their only chance to reproduce, since the traitorous Enki gave them the power . . . next they must look for a way to somehow try to raise their children against all survival odds, and then . . . and then they are entering old age and must prepare themselves for death, a subject they understand nothing about . . .

For me, for all Anunnaki, it is nothing like that. We dominate the environment rather than it dominating us. There is always time for everything, and time itself is a commodity we will never be short of. Mating? If we do not mate today or next week or next year or next century it is no great matter. After all we can reasonably expect to mate in our lifespan many thousands of times, and probably with many hundreds of different women, which is part of our Anunnaki heritage.

It is the women who control the birthrate, which if it ever got out of hand, could be disastrous for us.

They conceive only when they wish to, and there is a limit for each female, strictly imposed and regulated, at least on the Home Planet. There everything is hierarchal, of course, as good order demands. A Queen or Princess can have as many children as she might desire. The noble ladies must limit themselves to a dozen children. Our management and technician class women may have only 3 offspring during their long lifetimes . . . while the common class women are prohibited from having any children at all except by special request, and then if permission is granted it is for a single child only.

It galls me to see Earth women reproducing themselves right and left with no restrictions at all, when they are obviously far inferior even to our lowest class females who must obey strict rules. This, however, is only what must be expected when someone in authority of liberal persuasion such as Enki is given free rein to do what he wishes in defiance of all normal law and order.

Of course Earth is only a crude outpost, and it might be argued that it does not matter if anarchy prevails here. But it does matter, to me at any rate. If nothing else, my own self-concept and the self-repect and prestige of our entire race is at risk under such conditions.

But time, as I said, is on our side . . . our best ally and the Earthlings' worst enemy. It is the saving grace in our precarious relationship and must never in any way come to be altered or challenged. And so people like Enki, who think otherwise, must not be permitted to continue to exercise power here.

It was now almost a hundred Earth years since my first rendezvous

with Enlil on the Western islands . . . and if at first it seemed that
nothing much had changed, in fact a lot had.

Our plans were well under way. Of the genetic experiments to
produce the ideal soldier for our Invincible Army there was much to
be reported. On my frequent scouting trips I had had countless opportunities to observe that great work in progress . . . to observe and
to contribute my own suggestions, some key ones of which I was
proud to see incorporated towards the final result.

I was proudest of all, perhaps, of my radical suggestion that was
at first opposed by everyone. Enlil and the chief geneticist and Enlil's
military chief. None of them could see it, what I saw . . . not then, but
they were each eager later to rewrite history and claim they always
had been in favor of it from the beginning. I do not waste my time
contesting these outlandish claims from Anunnaki who should know
better . . . rather I try to use their own momentum generated in their
political lying to try to attain still other goals of importance to me.

And so I did in this case, gradually shaping the upcoming agenda
to fit my purposes not theirs.

But the main thing here was that the project was proving to be a
success. That such a success generated many fathers was not exactly a
surprise to me. For had my idea been a failure it would have remained
an unclaimed orphan and its parentage immediately attributed exclusively to me . . . and it would have been I who would have suffered
all the negative consequences, not them. None of this is new to any
talented underling who must serve the interests of those in power . . .
who often, after all, have not a tenth of the necessary comprehension
and intelligence to really have a perspective on what is going on.

Yes, my idea was bold.

Yes, it was revolutionary.

Yes, at first glance it may have seemed unworkable.

But that is the point. With me, it was not at first glance. I had
spent weeks running it through my mind and turning it around and
looking at it from all directions before I made so bold as to bring it
up.

Nothing there was to support my position, and certainly no

administrator was going to put himself in jeopardy by coming out in
my favor. The only thing that did support me was the result . . . and
that . . . that was enough . . . that was fantastic.

I do not have any deep knowledge of genetic science, and of the
actual technical aspects of it I am admittedly ignorant. But, as some
of our Anunnaki say about art, I know what I like . . .

In this case I wanted the most malevolent, violent, crudely savage
warrior it was possible to achieve. And yet I wanted that same warrior
totally malleable and subject to command with no initiative of his
own . . . and with a monolithic loyalty to his Commander that would
never know there even was a possibility of questioning that authority
in any way.

Yes, that is what I wanted.

And what I finally saw I was getting.

A warrior so fierce and cruel, and at the same time so subordinate and responsive to command that it fulfilled every dream I had
ever had. I saw my grandfather's dinosaur created again before my
eyes, except this time in human form.

Well, almost human form . . .

We had to take the human DNA as one of the bases, of course . . .
we needed his intelligence, which while not nearly on the plane of the
Anunnaki, still, was far above that of any other Earthly beast. Our soldier must be smart enough, after all, to carry out orders and understand
something about the nature of his assigned mission.

Of course we wanted him bigger and stronger than normal Earthlings. Sufficiently huge so as to strike terror into the hearts of any
humans unfortunate enough to stand in the way of what he wanted.
And so he came to be, this warrior . . . some seven feet in height, his
great primitive face glowering down in fury upon any perceived obstacle in his path.

That had to do with part of my idea. Which was to graft gorilla
DNA into the final mix . . . the physical characteristics of the gorilla.
The primitive deepset eyes and salient bone structure almost biologi-
cal armor in itself, not to mention a terror-inducing appearance. The

weight, the bulk, the massive muscular structure . . . all that helped to produce the effect I sought.

Many genetic animal mixes had been tried previously, but few of them had been successful. The sea surrounding the four islands was the recipient of a hundred failures in the ongoing genetic experiments. Monstrosities, each of which for one reason or another became a behavioral failure. Some with four arms or eight legs, or a cluster of eyes or any other physiological anomaly you might imagine . . . the only thing in common being they were dysfunctional . . . failures.

But early on due to my suggestion we had the intelligence of the human and the power and bulk of the gorilla successfully blended together. But I knew . . . or intuited . . . there was a missing element. I wanted something so fierce as almost to defy imagination. And I dared to go after it, to suggest it.

The crocodile, I said. I would like to see some DNA of the crocodile added to what we already had. To top off our already successful cocktail of creation.

They laughed. Scoffed. Treated it as a joke. Changed the subject.

I persisted. To the point that at last Enlil ordered the geneticist to do it. Give it a try.

Of course I told him I didn't expect to SEE actual crocodile physical characteristics. What I was after was deeper than that. What I wanted was some muted version of the essential savage NATURE of the crocodile . . . those instincts incorporated into our warrior.

They all now admit what we have is indeed the perfect warrior, though each wants to take the credit for adding the final vicious element, the crocodile influence.

What mattered was what I told Enlil. That this was it. What we had been searching for. We would produce it in sufficient numbers for our task. Which was to attack the space station and take it over, along with capturing Enki . . . we could then declare Enki as a traitor and set up his immediate courtmartial. His trial would be followed by our taking over the Mission and the Administration of Earth.

Things were looking very, very good. The rest was just a question of time and sagacious administration. That latter was in short supply, but with my frequent visits I would be there to furnish its lack.

Soon, I thought, we would become Earth's rulers. Which was a halfway station to later becoming the choice of Anu as his successor, which meant the rule of the entire solar system.

And I, as Enlil's trusted advisor, would be the real power behind the throne.

****

Meanwhile the Earth Mission under Enki went on.

We mined and packed and sent back to Nibiru millions of tons of gold, that served to keep our planet habitable, which otherwise it would not have been.

Behind that golden curtain, King Anu had not wavered in his decision to keep the Anunnaki on Nibiru for as long as the planet remained a viable home . . . he obviously was not eager to mandate any change that might prove dangerous or traumatic . . . he did not, as we say proverbially, wish to go from the frying pan into the fire.

Our gold then, was, and continued to be the lifeblood of our mother Planet.

But as fast as Enki supplied that lifeblood, he simultaneously was involved in draining it away.

That at least was my opinion. Based on what I saw and heard and continued to see and hear with each passing year of the execution of the Mission.

His concessions to the Earthlings were nauseating.

He came dangerously close to treating them as equals.

I noted it all down in my secret notebooks for use in the courtmartial.

I saw him in the act of treason many times.

Joking with Earthlings. Fraternizing with them. Taking their complaints and suggestions seriously.

He put everything into jeopardy. Our standing, the success of the Mission . . . things neither he nor I might conceive of in the moment, but which might later prove to have been fatal mistakes impossible to erase.

The Earthlings, yes, thought of us as gods. Which to them we were and should always be. But as to how long that concept would endure was anybody's guess. Enki's conduct left the question always dangerously open . . .

Yes, we all of us had fleeting love affairs and sexual liasons of one type and another with the human women. They had proved to be quite attractive in a rather vulgar way that to us perhaps seemed enticingly exotic. But this had nothing to do with the correct and proper administration of our Mission.

We knew that, but apparently Enki did not. He gave them privileges and a respect totally out of proportion for a class of work-slaves whose only official function was to extract gold from the mines.

Many times he invited one or more of them to his headquarters. This in itself was a violation of proper procedure. For one thing, he had the Anunnaki Master Protocols there. What if an Earth woman would have stolen one or more of them? They had all the information and procedures it had taken us millions of years to amass and distill and accumulate. With them in their possession the Earthlings could eventually aspire to become our equals in everything except duration of lifespan. But no, not even that was sacrosanct, because the protocols contained knowledge and techniques as to how to alter DNA to produce our own almost eternal lifespans.

High Treason, then, in my opinion was the only term that could be correctly applied to Enki's actions.

I noted down, too, that his headquarters was exaggeratedly elaborate, that he had used Earth laborers in its construction, which was itself a violation of security.

Then, too, in my opinion his headquarters was too far away from the Space Station . . . not a good strategical decision on his part which, while not treasonous in itself, at the very least showed an incompetent lack of judgment.

He had his personal headquarters/residence built in the mountainous region that the Earthlings had come to call Mount Olympus
and whose name I adopted on my official maps. Of course with the
establishment of the Headquarters there it soon came to be known
among the Earthlings of the region as the abode of the gods.

On the one hand, I was glad to have all this evidence accumulate
against the dangerous Enki.

On the other, it angered me down to the depths of my being. An
inferior race should never be given the temptation to think of themselves
as anything higher. That way lay danger and anarchy which could lead
step by step eventually to the destruction of everything we held dear.

Well, I knew the antidote to that.

The correct use of Enlil and the forces on Atlantis . . . the Invincible Army that would yet lead us to triumph over the forces of Evil.

****

I like to KNOW with total assurance beforehand that things will go
the way they should, the way I plan them.

Not just guess.

One way to do that is through experiment.

And so I stated it strongly to Enlil on one of my visits to Atlantis,
which was the name Enlil had given our island Kingdom.

I talk here of a visit hundreds of years later than our first
rendezvous.

The situation had changed. All to our advantage.

That is, now we had thousands of our ideal warrior.

Now, it seemed, we could move on Enki with every assurance of
success.

Well, not every assurance, either.

That was the point I made to Enlil.

I needed a test.

A test of the real capacities in a real situation of the Invincible
Army . . . before we put it into action against the traitor Enki.

****

Atlantis over the centuries had become a thriving city. I pride myself on being involved in the principal planning and architecture. I obviously was not the architect, nor the planner . . . yet my input was respected and I saw some of my most important ideas carried out.

The central largest island was the hub of everything. There it was that the city proper was developed. The main streets had central canals and overhead transportation cables carrying our Anunnaki to any destination quickly and esthetically. There were only some 200 of us, which were, besides Enlil and myself, the crew of the great Mother spaceship plus his technicians and staff and special personnel such as the geneticists. And our reason for being there was not to create a beautiful city. Not at all. The city was an almost accidental by-product of the objective I had strived so hard to implant firmly in the minds of Enlil and all his subordinate crew . . . which was the creation of the perfect warrior.

There were now thousands of them on the main island. Of course they had to be housed, and a thousand logistical details had to be attended to. The city, beautiful as it came out, was designed to develop this central concept. There were many open fields . . . there had to be . . . where warlike drills could be carried out and mock battles fought. Endless rehearsals were staged for the eventual assault on Enki and his forces, as well as domination exercises to insure the Earthling population could be first terrified and then conquered . . . beyond any possibility of their ever dreaming of any future resurgence or rebellion.

That was the basic philosophy behind much of the design of the city, and that was where my imprint was clearly visible . . . though of course the architects and engineers carried out all the mundane details of design and construction. If Enlil believed it was all his doing . . . well, that in the end was all to the good. I had spent a great deal of time and effort to make him think exactly that. The road to power, contrary to what one might think, has strange detours and demands a peculiarly unselfish person to effect the eventual ends desired.

My imprint however did not end there.

The architects had wanted to put all the important administrative buildings on the main island.

My feeling was they could put most there, but not all.

Not all our eggs in a single basket.

And so I prevailed to have put on the smallest, most insignificant of the four islands, two things that were very important. The great hospital and the Military Planning Center . . .

My choice of this island was not arbitrary. Far from it.

It was the only one of the four with a mountainous area on it.

I nestled our hospital and Military Planning Center in the irregular creases and valleys between those mountains. Again this was not capricious on my part. In so doing I made them at once almost invisible and also invulnerable to all but the most pinponted and exact military attack.

True, we were isolated in a remote region of the Atlantic that in the normally foreseeable chain of events no one probably would ever see until after we took over the administration of the planet.

But . . . I liked to have things always prepared on the basis of the worst eventuality possible.

For that same reason I insisted the buildings on the small, mountainous island should be camouflaged.

And prevailed in this at last after much argument.

So that from high overhead the island looked like nothing more than that. An island, yes, but an unpopulated mountainous island mostly overgrown with greenery and dominated by rocky outcroppings in its highest part.

This was part of my philosophy not learned in any book or protocol of the Anunnaki. Offense and initiative and surprise were the paramount factors in that philosophy . . . but not by any means did that negate the need for conservative, defensive strategy. I saw no valid reason for not incorporating both into my Master Plan . . . and was proud that I did so.

****

The ripening of the time was something I could feel in the deepest part of my anatomy. My bones, my blood, the beat of my heart told me in no uncertain terms that the crest of opportunity was right before me.

But not yet exactly here.

No. That crest could only come after our Invincible Army had been put to some kind of test . . . that I believed, and that I insisted on to the impatient, ever impulsive Enlil, who was ready as always to risk everything tomorrow on what amounted to a roll of the dice.

Well, not me.

What I looked for was guaranteed results, not rosy probabilities.

You could style it as a difference in philosophical outlook. But for me. . . .

That was to give too much honor to the processes of Enlil's alleged mind. The closer I had come to those mental processes, the more I had been frightened by the yawning chasm of emptiness that loomed before my astonished perception. I saw very clearly that everything . . . the future of the Anunnaki . . . of Earth . . . all depended on me. It was a heavy burden to bear, and while it caused me many sleepless nights, I saw that to refuse to face up to my responsibility could only result in the most dire results for my Race, including its chances for eventual survival.

I had figured out the parameters for the test. It must be against superior numbers . . . which was the primary situation we must face in our initial assault on Enki, and on any later defensive strategy against the rebelling Earthlings taken in by Enki's deceit in posing as their friend and ally.

In my scouting flights I had discovered a primitive tribe near the eastern coast of the southernmost Western continent. I had observed them to be warlike, had seen them agress against the tribes north of their own territory with success.

They seemed perfect for the purposes of the test. They were of course Earthlings, assuredly with no recent genetic mix with the Anunnaki mission members. They were . . . to give them their best due . . . primitive . . . savage . . . aggressive . . . simple and straightforward in their barbarous and cruel outlook on life . . . and totally selfish. Almost a reflection of our own Perfect Warrior . . . except physically and psychologically, I thought, on a much lower scale as far as motivation and instinct and pure ferocity were concerned. At least the ultimate development of those qualities was what we had striven for, and in my opinion achieved.

But it still remained to be seen.

The test would tell.

I arranged it all with Enlil and he in turn put everything at my disposal.

The day came . . .

****

I personally piloted the great Mother spaceship that had brought Enlil across half a universe to Earth. In the great central hold behind me there were a thousand warriors impatiently gnashing their teeth for the opportunity to kill and conquer.

I set us down in a clearing just beyond which . . . behind a narrow neck of jungle . . . was the principal concentration of the primitive tribe of conquerors that would so soon become our foes.

It was just before dawn, but with our nightvision windows in operation, of course I saw everything clear as day. Saw their sleeping village which would soon awake to the most horrendous assault they had ever known . . . that perhaps anyone had ever known.

I set our warriors loose with no preliminary . . . sicked them like hungry dogs . . . dogs, no, like hungry wolves . . . upon the enemy.

What a vision that must have been to that enemy . . .

Something they had never seen before except perhaps in their worst nightmares.

A surprise mass attack by seven foot tall enemies whose like on Earth had never been seen before . . .

Their recessed eyes glowing intensely like coals in the dark.

Their guttural shouts the very aural equivalent of an announcement of imminent death.

And their behavior . . . what I, hanging low above them was able to observe at first hand . . . would have struck terror into the souls of anyone, Anunnaki not excluded.

With them it was not enough to strike and stun. No, they had to kill. But neither was that enough.

They wanted to annihilate.

Yes, every man, woman and child was killed, in the most vicious, unthinking, systematic way possible.

But in addition, their bodies were disintegrated with direct supernumerary force going far beyond any rudimentary essential requirements of killing. The Ideal Warriors I had helped design, I saw wanted to strip away any possible concept on the part of the enemy that they were beings with any right to live. As if only in that manner would they be completely neutralized.

It came to me then what the slaughtered primitive tribe must feel, would have to feel in their last instants of life on Earth . . .

That they were vermin. Nothing more. Just vermin to be exterminated from further plaguing Earth. Inferior entities with no right to exist.

And that . . . that was what I wanted. Not just conquest. Not just death. Not even just the extermination of noxious vermin. But to establish the feeling in them even as they died that they were worthless.

That would be the key . . . the ultimate key . . . to the proper domination of the Earthlings. Something that Enki could never see, but which would help form very soon the shape of the proper punishment for such incompetent blindness of someone in command . . .

****

In the months that followed the successful test, Enlil and his other advisors and I talked often of exactly what should be our stategy and our plan of attack against the arrogant and incompetent Enki . . .

What eventuated out of all these discussions finally were two basic plans . . .

The first was this. We could make a direct attack on the Anunnaki

Space Station on the Sinai Peninsula. Take it by surprise, unleash our warriors and quickly occupy it.

But . . .

That left the headquarters of Enki on Mount Olympus. Any sane plan would have to include a simultaneous attack on that.

While we could do it, the logistics became more complicated, and I for one did not like complications. My key to success had always been to keep things simple inasmuch as such was possible.

And so I proposed the second plan.

I might entice Enki aboard my reconnaissance craft. Mouth whatever excuses or lies might be necessary . . . but somehow get him landed on Atlantis.

I with a certain amount of felicity could anticipate his surprise, his distress . . . his liberal mind unable to comprehend how a trusted subordinate and apparent friend could be guilty of not telling him always the strict truth of any situation . . . it was exactly that puny and puerile mind that had caused all this necessity for correction in the first place, something that was, too, I was sure also beyond his limited comprehension.

In fact, the only ones who appreciated the true parameters of his dereliction of duty and his treachery were myself and Enlil . . . and Enlil only because of my long and careful education augmented by the sharp direction of his own ambition.

But after our peremptory Courtmartial . . . after my presentation of the evidence I had accumulated . . . ah, then things would change.

Then we would feel the very levers and fulcrums of physical reality react to what we would prove . . .

And we, the true Anunnaki, the patriots and preservers of order in the Universe would prevail.

Enki would be shorn of his disguise and shown for what he truly was. The essential shameless traitor, the sell-out to the interests of an inferior race that had no intrinsic virtue outside of what we ourselves in our generosity had given them . . .

I was fairly sure that my presention of the second alternative would triumph . . .

I was relaxing on the veranda and looking out with satisfaction over the ocean vastness as seen from the fourth island where our Military Planning Center was situated . . .

When . . .

Something so ridiculous happened I immediately attributed it to an electronic failure . . .

Our defense alarm sounded . . .

A chill ran through me. Because if I was wrong . . . if the alarm were not the result of an electronic failure . . .

It could mean only one thing . . . some aerial craft had penetrated our air space!

****

My mind was ablaze.

Like a forest fire it raged within my head . . . seeking one thing. An answer.

How could it happen?

I had been so careful.

Perhaps it was nothing. An illusion. Vagrant electronics.

But no, it was not.

There WAS a craft in the sky. The radar showed it . . . my eyes from the veranda confirmed it.

The ship could only be from the Anunnaki base.

But how?

It came to me, with an accompanying shudder. For some reason, Enki must have become suspicious. Perhaps about my frequent reconnaissance missions into the Western ocean regions. And one day . . . this day . . . perhaps he had tracked me . . . had me followed.

Was that unlikely scenario possible?

There was no time to think any deeper than that.

Atlantis had been discovered by Enki's forces. That was a fact, even though the scout ship itself had turned away and quickly disappeared back in the direction from which it came.

The overwhelming question now was . . . what was to be done?

How could the situation be salvaged?

****

After a lot of heated discussion at the emergency meeting with Enlil's military staff in the Military Planning Center, what I already knew before it started became crystal clear to everyone.

There was no salvaging the situation. Our position was a desperate one, no doubt about that. All our previous golden plans were now out the window. Blown to smithereens by this new and totally unexpected development.

The only question was what to do.

I knew the answer and saw I must leap into the breach left by the lack of decisiveness and leadership on the part of Enlil, whose eminence kept the three members of the military staff in check.

"Only the most drastic action can save us now," I said, looking at the four who sat there still half stunned by the unexpected development.

They were silent.

"You know what I mean," I said quietly. "Everything has changed. Everything is now just a pure and simple question of survival. Unless we act fast we lose everything."

The ranking military officer looked at me now square in the eye. "You're talking nuclear?"

I nodded.

The military looked even more stunned, but Enlil leaned forward and his eyes brightened. I seized the opportunity to make my point.

"Enki has thirty tactical nuclear bombs. They're stored at his headquarters on Mount Olympus. I've seen them."

One of the military raised his hands and turned them outwards in a kind of plea. "Why? Why so many?"

"For construction. Mining. Anything that might come up. He's used a couple already in Africa for deep mining. They're small but . . . large enough. The big question is . . . how many do we have?"

Enlil looked blank and turned to his chief of staff.

"Two. Just the two we carry aboard the Mother Ship."

"Just one is enough," I said, "if we do it right."

I quickly outlined my plan to them . . .

We had to demolish Enki and his headquarters on Mount Olympus. That would leave them without their leader and without any more nuclear bombs. The Space Station with all its resources would be intact and by moving fast we should be able to take it over, taking advantage of the Anunnaki force's shock at what we had done to them.

We could justify everything later with King Anu by saying that Enki moved first on us, with his nuclear weapons . . . that what we did was self defense and, in view of Enki's documented treason, for the good of the Race.

Of course we would quickly move our Invincible Army into the area of the Space Base for its intimidation power in our fight to establish order. No one would dare to challenge us or our story.

Enlil's smile now was a mile wide. With his usual grasp on reality, he looked like a man who thought it would all be just a picnic in the park. I knew better, but under the incredible circumstances what else could I do?

At least I could see my plan had carried the day. But then I received a slap in the face.

I wanted to be the one to deliver the bomb. It was logical. I knew the area. We only had one chance at this and it had to work. No margin for error, no second chance. Failure might mean our own deaths, one way or another . . . though I personally doubted that Enki would ever use nuclear weapons against fellow Anunnaki because of his puerile, pusilanimous nature and his dangerously liberal ideas about relationships in society.

But Enlil would not hear of it. For whatever reason he wanted me there on Atlantis and insisted on sending his cousin, one of our pilots, to do the job. What his motives were in that I did not know . . . nepotism, perhaps, endemic among Anunnaki royalty much to our detriment . . . or because he liked his cousin overmuch or didn't like his cousin . . . it was all obscure to me.

The crisis gave us no luxury for delay. Everything was arranged in a matter of minutes. Our two bombs were quickly downloaded from the Mother Ship and into the Military scout, but I cautioned the pilot to use one and only one, and gave him every direction possible to lead him to his target. Besides that I told him to look for Enki's gold colored Flagship which was always parked in the open hard by his headquarters personal mansion. That way he could not go wrong.

And, I cautioned him, if he found himself being followed on his return, he was to take a diversionary action by heading south towards the pole until any pursuers were lost. Under no circumstances was he to risk bringing them back to Atlantis.

****

The next few hours . . . how can I describe them?

Strangely they were calm. There was nothing to be done. We were ready to move . . . the Invincible Army was passive as lambs to our commands and the Mother Ship was ready to receive them in an instant.

All we needed . . . and all we waited for . . . was our Military scout to return, and to receive the report of the successful completion of the mission.

I remember I spent most of the time in reorganizing my own thinking, so set over the centuries towards other ways of achieving our ends. But maybe, since our hand was forced, this was best. Enki would be out of the way forever and at last this Planet Earth would be ours.

Nibiru would be next . . . for when the aged King Anu at last passed away there would be no doubt as to who would be his successor. And I, Yahweh, as his Chief Aide would hold in my hands the power I had always wielded over the wishy-washy if at times whimsically insistent Enlil. In other words I would be the power behind the throne, which was just exactly the way I wanted it.

So no one waited the return of our Military scout more anxiously than I.

And then, at last, growing quickly from a mere dot in the distance against the clouds, there it was!

****

He was to set down right outside our building, the Military Planning Center on our camouflaged headquarters on the smallest island, so there would be no delay in our mobilization plans.

And so he did. Then taxied his ship into the camouflaged underground hangar. But as he went by me he gave me the thumbs up signal.

My dreams coalesced before me into some kind of beautiful but extremely fleeting vision, and I felt an exhilaration and exaltation like I had never known.

Enki was destroyed, his treason vaporized and made null now forever, and soon we would be in charge of the planet . . .

****

The sky?

While the pilot now parked the Military scout in the camouflaged underground hangar beside the Hospital ship and I waited to talk to him, to congratulate him . . .

My vision wandered upwards towards it.. the sky. Why not? What more natural? It is the direction of victory, the psychological celebration the soul seeks in moments of triumph.

I saw a dark speck there in the far distance, which troubled me immediately. But wait. Maybe it was just an illusion . . . nothing more than a tiny opening in the clouds themselves. And then the pilot was there before me . . . I clapped him enthusiastically on the back.

"Any problems in finding the target?" I asked him, just to make conversation, really.

"Clouds," he said. "There were lots of clouds. But I dropped my bomb."

"Did you . . . did you see the results of the explosion?"

He averted his eyes, and I suddenly became aware his face was pale. Very pale.

"I couldn't. They had a craft in the sky. I had to get out of there."

"Were you followed?" I found myself shouting the words, then shaking him violently by the shoulders. "Were you followed?"

That was the thing. I had given him explicit instructions that if anyone were to follow him after the mission, if there were any pursuit, he was to head towards the South Pole . . . until he lost them.

I looked at the sky again. What had been a speck now was the size of a coin.

It suddenly occurred to me. How to check. My secret communicator with Enlil. I had left it in my rooms at the headquarters of Enki. If I tried it now and it still worked then the mission had been a failure.

I turned to Enlil. "Your communicator with me . . . do you have it on you?" He handed it to me, a puzzled expression on his broad features. And I quickly saw the truth. Yes, there was a rebound response. That showed clearly the communicator on Mount Olympus was intact.

Which showed equally clearly the headquarters was intact. There was only one conclusion. The raid had somehow gone astray, the nuclear bomb undoubtedly dropped on one of the many uninhabited mountain peaks surrounding Mount Olympus. The pilot's pale face and averted eyes now made perfect sense.

I swung somewhere from my knees, I guess. Anyway, the blow was strong enough to knock Enlil's idiot cousin sprawling.

Enlil just stood there looking at me aghast.

I was aghast, too. Why would I not be?

Enki was alive, his forces undamaged! And now our roles would be reversed. The hunted would become the hunter . . . and we were the prey.

Even as I thought the horrifying thought, my eyes confirmed it. The image of the coin in the sky now had metamorphosed clearly into the shape of a great and terrifying Anunnaki Mother Ship.

****

And then the world ended.

The shock of the blast knocked everybody down. Some were never to get up.

The flash of light of the explosion had left me blinded at first.

But gradually my seared eyes revealed what I rather would not have seen.

The Main Island of Atlantis was no more.

Great orange clouds roiled and boiled over it and were now shooting up into the high atmosphere.

I remember wondering how Enki could have done such a thing to his brother, to his fellow Anunnaki. But then the answer came, one that I had not considered before. If he were the friend of humanity, did that not automatically make him the enemy of his fellow Anunnaki? And here we had the proof . . . it was the last thing I remember before passing out.

****

I never expected to recover consciousness again.

But I did.

And almost wished I hadn't.

To see the ruin of all my dreams displayed before me was something that someone of my particular ambition found almost worse than death.

But the survival instinct is a strong one. It drove me, because there was nothing else to give me any motive force.

The Main Island was a blackened, twisted mass, seething with smoke and . . . I despair of remembering the rest. The Invincible Army vaporized in an instant.

What had saved us . . . the ones who still lived . . . was our camouflage and our position on the smallest island. That was something I could take credit for . . . but to take credit for anything amid that destruction was an absurd concept and my mind immediately swept it aside.

Those of us who lived . . . we were very probably, I knew, but walking dead men . . . had received who knew how much radiation from the blast, probably lethal amounts. I knew that and at the same time refused to know it . . . because my mind could not accommodate that unwanted fact.

But somehow I got us together. Enlil was there, with the blankest most uncomprehending of all expressions on his face. I had no time to answer his babblings.

There were . . . I counted . . . 13 of us still alive.

The fortunate thing . . . not fortunate at all, really, but the result of my conservative concerns in my planning . . . was that the two ships parked in their underground hangar were intact and even free from radiation damage. I speak of the Military craft, our scout ship, sent on the mission to destroy Enki, and a Hospital ship . . . both parked safely in the underground hangar. They were to be our salvation, if indeed there were to be any hope of salvation.

I did my duty. I shut up the babble of Enlil . . . led the way into the underground hangar . . . helped the most weakened into one or the other of the craft. I would pilot one and the other I found a live pilot for. I told him to follow me. There was obviously nothing left for us on Atlantis. Even as we taxied out of the hangar we felt the earth shaking violently beneath us.

Once in the air, I circled what had only an hour before been the proud city of Atlantis. Not once but two or three times. Why? I don't know. I still was not functioning with anything like intellect. Everything was reflex or instinct.

What I saw happening below was something I could not absorb at the time. But it was enough. Enough to make my only possible decision clear in my own dimly functioning mind.

Maybe I just wanted to be sure that there was no coming back. So I could be correctly oriented towards our future. If we were to have any . . .

I knew the direction of that very conjectural future. My bones, perhaps, intuited it. West.

The big Western Continents were the only conceivable place for us now. As far away as possible from Enki and his Olympian and Mesopotamian bases.

Almost blindly . . . my vision impaired and functioning at only half capacity . . . I headed that way.

****

There was a black, bitter taste in my throat.

I knew well enough where it came from.

Betrayals. So many betrayals . . .

How could Enki, the great friend of humanity, the naive liberal who wanted to be a brother to the inferior races . . . who thought everyone could get along and co-exist . . . how could such a person go against his own apparent principles and attack us with nuclear weapons?

I tried as I headed us towards the setting sun, to answer my own question.

Yes, his military staff would have . . . and should have . . . advised him to do it, of course. I would have. But he had always been resistant to anyone's thinking except his own . . . except in this case, apparently.

What a time for an exception, I thought, feeling the bitterness in my throat coagulate even more.

I could have been with him, with Enki, at the summit of power now with Enlil eliminated from any realistic hopes of the succession to the Anunnaki throne.

But no. I had given all up for Enlil, to help him in his rise to ultimate power . . . though because of his own incompetence I had had to draw pictures for him every step of the way and carefully steer him . . . because if not he would have carelessly thrown everything away long before.

Well . . . it was all water under the bridge now. That made me laugh. Because it was the other way around. It was the bridge, or bridges . . . Atlantis had three of them to connect the smaller islands to the main one . . . which were underwater now. Not only the bridges but the four islands themselves. The nuclear blast had started the

Earthquakes that we had felt before escaping in our two ships . . . the
Earthquakes that at last had finished the work of Enki's bombing.

Now for the first time my mind permitted me to review and
understand what my damaged eyes had seen as we circled above the
disaster.

They had seen the last of Great Atlantis . . . our materialized
dream of dominating a better, more productive Earth . . . with a kind
of final convulsion, break up and then sink beneath the waves . . . just
before I had instinctively decided we must, for our salvation, for our
lives . . . head towards the setting sun.

The bitterness kept coming at me in the wake of things.

There were other betrayals besides Enki's . . .

Enlil's idiot cousin, our bombing pilot. Had he followed my instructions, we would be securely ensconced in the position of power
over this planet right now . . . Enki vaporized, his warped dreams
dead, the full surge of Anunnaki tradition securely in place under our
administration.

All the pilot had to do was what he was told. What I myself had
done my best to imprint upon his consciousness. But it was too much
for his flighty, feeble mind, true cousin that he was of Enlil's . . . he
simply could not hold true to the course of what was necessary for
success, thus revealing the same character fault of his Royal cousin.

It was that same deficiency of character, perhaps genetically induced, that for whatever whimsical reason had made Enlil deny me
the opportunity I had so earnestly sought. To be the pilot of the plane
that would have made a success instead of an abject failure of the
assigned mission . . . that would have changed the destiny of the
world for the better, that would have made us the only true gods of
Earth.

At this moment we would have been drinking alcoholic toasts at
the base in Mesopotamia to the new reign over Earth, to the final
victory of good over evil.

Instead . . .

Instead we were perhaps 13 dead men who had not yet realized
they were dead. Who were flying towards their graves in the Western

Continents, all their energies unknowingly directed towards becoming food for worms in some as yet unknown location.

What a comedown for Earth's gods!

Irony could not get more bitter than that, for the most outstanding members of an ancient race . . . a race that prided itself above all on dominance and control and the most orderly paradigms of progress . . .

And I was not ignorant of the deeper ironies. All this had come about due to Enki's failure to grasp the realities and necessities of his own situation. How gods had to be gods, not friends to a vastly inferior race, to humanity. They could be one. They could be the other. They could not be both. Not ever. The two goals were mutually exclusive. It was a proven truth Enki could never appreciate, that no one could make him see.

In that sense, the deepest betrayal of all was still Enki's. His ignorance was so deep that he would yet turn nuclear weapons upon us, the true champions of what was best for Earth and the ancient race of the Anunnaki . . .

I swallowed hard at the thought, and nausea almost overcame me.

As we approached the Western Continents, the northern one, the sun was setting.

It was a gorgeous sight, which on a happier occasion, I would have much appreciated.

Now . . .

Now, nothing seemed right.

The setting orb of the sun was enormous, but the rays of light emanating from it were reddish, which to my imagination made it seem tinged with blood . . . and for that reason, beyond all logic, ominous.

So extreme was my anxiety, that in my confused state I questioned everything. Was the sun really just setting or was it dying?

Maybe it was, for us.

Was this the last light we were ever to see?

Because even though the sun might rise again tomorrow, the question was . . . would we?

Or had we already tasted our own doom . . . just that we were too wounded and disabled to be able to rightly perceive it . . .

With an effort, I thrust those negative thoughts aside.

We were over land now, the nightmare we had experienced in the middle of the sea far behind us.

The Western Continents, which even I had not yet thoroughly explored . . . perhaps they held some key for us, some as yet unknown remedy even for deadly doses of radiation.

Yes, some part of my mind said.

Yes.

Here. Here we might nurse ourselves back to health. Maybe even someday put our dreams of Earthly conquest back together.

We had been gods. . . . we would be gods again . . . even if only to the most primitive of races.

I swore it to myself even as I felt the swelling of my face intensify.

I ignored some part of my being that was making subversive statements. That whispered to me that even the Earthlings who had once been our abject slaves were now superior to us. Might live longer and in better health. Might very soon come across our radiation ravaged dead bodies and in their savage way have us for dinner . . . or worse, hang our corpses from trees as positive demonstrations of their own superiority . . . or nail us up to crosses so their barbaric children could shoot arrows into our ravaged bodies . . . while laughing and insulting in their abject ignorance the very gods who had created them.

I thrust all this aside from my fermenting mind at last, but it was not at all an easy thing to do.

We were pretty far inland now and on the other side of a range of mountains.

Darkness had fallen and I let down below the overcast to try to seek out a landing spot. I turned on the night vision and as I did so suddenly felt a wave of fatigue sweep through me such as I had never known before.

I knew of course it was not just fatigue, but the result of injury.

Of the deep injury caused by the intense wave of radiation from the nuclear blast we had all received back on Atlantis.

I fought it off. Momentarily.

Somehow I got us down and saw the other ship behind us also settle down not far away.

I knew we had landed on a flattened area of a hillside on the edge of a plains region and that was about all.

And no sooner done than I, still at the controls, lapsed into a deep sleep. But a sleep, no . . . at least not like any I had ever experienced . . . more like a swoon, a little death . . . an excursion into a dark place from which hope had been excluded.

****

How long we slept I have no idea. My guess is not one night but two, with of course the day in between also.

And even then I would not normally have awakened for some time longer I am sure.

Instead of experiencing again our living nightmare I was deep into one of those pleasant dreams where responsibility and sense of duty have no purchase. Where any beautiful woman who offered herself was quickly taken up on her offer, where there were no confrontations or tragedies and where life flowed like one of the many pleasant rivers on Nibiru. Nibiru . . . our lost home . . . it was pleasant to dream about it, but maybe what put me there was the repetition of the word into my sleeping ear.

"Nibiru. We must go back. Immediately."

Enlil's insistent voice was what brought me back to consciousness.

With consciousness, the truth of our situation rushed in and I almost vomited right there, all over my revered Commander.

Somehow I managed to sit up and run my fingers through my hair. That was a mistake.

Through swollen eyes I saw strands and thatches of hair sticking to my palms. Now I WAS going to be sick. I staggered into the nearest bathroom and got rid of all the contents of my stomach.

Got a glance at myself in the mirror. Which was mistake number two.

I looked as if someone had fricasseed me like some fowl for dinner. My face was seared, my eyes a pair of slits in the middle of swellings. I was in fine shape.

When I forced myself to come out, I saw Enlil was hardly any better. What I didn't know was where he was getting the frantic energy necessary to bombard my ears now with things I didn't want to hear and was unprepared to deal with.

But there he was coming at me again. "My revered father, the Great Anu . . . we should go to him . . . appeal to him . . . to execute that traitor Enki and put me in sole command here."

As far as I could see we were the only ones awake of the seven in the Military scout ship. Good. I didn't want the others to overhear this. It might be infectious. If any of us lived long enough for it to make any difference, that is.

I tried to muster up a smile and could only imagine how ghastly that must have looked. "Your Excellence . . . this is a matter of the utmost delicacy. Perhaps you and I in private . . ."

I gestured towards one of the many empty compartments. We went in and closed the hatches and were alone, out of possible hearing range of anyone.

"Your Magificence, " I began. "Your heart is right, as always. But there are problems."

I had to outline it to him as to a child. Hardly a new experience. "We are on weak ground here. We are in the right, of course. Enki is the great traitor. We know that. But your revered father Anu does not. He looks on Enki as a beloved son, just as he does you. All my notes describing Enki's traitorous conduct sank with Great Atlantis. We have no evidence. While Enki will claim we attacked first. That you kept your presence here secret. Against what we know to be justice, he might win, your father being very aged and in his dotage, not the clear-thinking beacon he once was. And just as a practical matter, we have no way of getting to Nibiru now. This ship and the Hospital ship . . . neither are spaceworthy . . . they were brought here aboard the Mother Ship, but they are not designed to navigate in the great vacuum of space."

"So we are marooned here?"

"Yes. For now."

His swollen features reflected his dismay and bewilderment. He had never thought of any of the things I had so briefly mentioned. None of them. That thought almost made me sick again.

What I did not tell him but what I knew was this . . .

Could we get to Nibiru, which we could not, we would not stand the ghost of a chance of winning our case. The law on Nibiru was one thing . . . its application quite another. The real law was that the status quo rules. The victors there write history, the survivors rule and the dead and the past keep their secrets. King Anu himself was living testimony to that. I knew he had usurped the throne in a power move by a few Anunnaki . . . but it was something not talked about, a fact glossed over in our histories.

I tried to leave him with the idea that what we must do first was try to regain our health, then think about revenge on Enki.

Well, that was how my morning began. Combatting Enlil's delusions.

And it didn't get any better.

Not at all.

****

There were thirteen of us who landed on the northernmost of the Western Continents the previous night, but only twelve of us who woke up.

By sheer coincidence, the dead man happened to be the errant pilot, Enlil's idiot cousin . . . the one who had cost us the opportunity to rule this planet and whose incompetence had relegated us to our present pitiful state. *Poetic justice* was my first secret thought.

Later I was to learn it was not coincidence at all, but a second product of a second class mind trying to cope with circumstances he was unable to comprehend in a timely manner. While the rest of us hit by the atomic blast all at least had the good sense not to unnecessarily expose ourselves more, he had climbed one of the hills to stand there shaking his fist and screaming at our aggressors, even though they were by that time long gone. Ineffectual theatrics, I thought, were part of the DNA pattern of Enlil and all his relatives. Well, now at least there would be one less to worry about . . .

I conducted a brief ceremony on the grounds between our two ships. Then with the laser aboard the Military ship his lifeless body was vaporized as we all looked on. It was my decision. I would not risk leaving him to be the possible prey of animals or savage humans.

I thought I had caught a glimpse across the grassy plains below us of movement . . . and not of wild animals either. But when I tried to focus my afflicted eyes I saw nothing more than just wind making the four foot high grass move back and forth.

I took the opportunity of the memorial to make a little speech. I knew, if I knew anything, that Anunnaki have to be given a program and a purpose, a way of looking at the future and coping with it. Otherwise they are lost. And that's understandable. So I stepped into the void left my Enlil's sullen silence. I saw he was lost in some universe of his own where he was undoubtedly exacting immediate revenge on his brother Enki.

I talked about what had happened. About how it came about only through unforeseen eventualities and was the culmination of Enki's treachery. But that what we had to think about now was our own pathway back to health.

That was because I saw the unspoken question in their swollen, bleary eyes. Who's next? Will it be me? And when . . . tomorrow? Are we all going to die in the same way as the Anunnaki whose body we had just incinerated?

At that point I deliberately put their question to Doctor Atra, right there in front of them all.

I could not have been more blunt.

"Doctor, are we all going to die?"

His eyes were almost as swollen as mine, but I could still see the surprise in them.

He tried to sidestep. He raised both hands, palms upwards, mutely shook his head.

But I was not about to let him escape so easily.

"We must know."

"But . . ."

"No buts, Doctor. We are all going to rest now and hope for more strength. But I want a full report tomorrow. Here, at this same spot, between the two ships. Eight o'clock."

He nodded. What could he do? I had focused everyone's attention on him. To keep it away from me. Maybe . . . maybe he could come up with something.

Of course he came to me afterwards as I knew he would and we talked.

"What do you want me to tell them? I don't know what's going to happen. Radiation poisoning . . . we know so little about it."

"Don't you have Medical Protocols on the Hospital ship?"

"Just the standard ones. But this is special, something never expected . . ."

"Search them. The protocols. Come up with something. A program for us. I want to hear it tomorrow with the rest."

"Yes, sir."

****

It was amazing. I never expected any result other than the shifting of blame from my shoulders to his.

But obviously Doctor Atra had found something. His bearing told me that, and his words bore it out.

"There is a remedy to what we have suffered. And it works. But there are two negative things. One is that the prognosis . . . well, it takes a long time. The second is that we may have to do things that we have never done before . . . that we may not like to do."

I stepped forward at that point, more to show I was in command rather than anything else. Such things are important.

"What things, Doctor? Everyone wants to know. What things?"

I thought his eyes were less swollen, and I gained a little optimism from that, though mine in the mirror that morning were still slits looking out through a seared face.

"Well, first, let me say this. Yes, we will all die soon if we do not apply this remedy. There is little doubt about that."

Diplomacy, I thought, was not the Doctor's long suit. But then it never had been. His medical brilliance, however, and his willingness to accept anything authority told him to do or say . . . those were his strong points that counterbalanced any weaknesses.

Our ten walking dead reacted with a stir and a murmur to the shocking statement, nothing more. Why not? It was hardly unexpected news and if they felt like I did, then they hardly had enough energy to care. Then, too, they were Anunnaki, military people, and ready to walk into Hell if ordered to do so.

Doctor Atra went on.

"What the protocol tells me that we have to do is this. Our internal organs need help. They need to be renewed. That is our road back to life. We are anemic. But much worse than that. Our blood due to the radiation has probably stopped producing hemoglobin and the many hormones that we need to survive."

I intervened again, once more showing my authority to any who might doubt it.

"Tell us, Doctor Atra. Tell us now without any more medical explanations. What is it we need to do?"

"Well, the protocol describes it, the procedure. It worked in a couple of isolated cases. Each of us needs to take in the blood supply and the essence of the internal organs of healthy beings . . . but in concentrated quantities and continuously over a long period of time."

I continued to ask the key questions, prodding him onwards to I knew not what conclusion. Whatever it was, it would take the onus off me and leave it with him. Of course, if it proved to be a success, I hoped to be around to take the credit for it.

"How long does this take? To get us back to perfect health?" I asked the question that I knew all were thinking.

"According to the computer studies . . . included in the protocol . . . well, it is quite a long time."

"How long, Doctor Atra?"

"Ten thousand Earth years."

****

My life is a testimony to order.

I like to take things in an organized manner always. To keep my objectives clear and the main purposes always in mind. And if you have this attitude and work to implement it, then . . . then you keep your agenda simple. What you have to do, you do . . . but that way you never have to try to cope with things piling up on you, with everything changing all at once.

But that was the unique situation I was into here, and I had to find a way to deal with it.

Alone in my own compartment I tried to assess our situation.

We had two ships and twelve men.

We might all die tomorrow as far as anyone knew, but hopefully not. Doctor Atra had given us a way out of that . . . maybe . . . if we wanted to follow his strange prescription for ten thousand Earth years. Of course, as I later learned in private conversation with him, there was no guarantee of success even then . . . since the protocol was based on rare, anecdotal results, not any kind of fundamental proof.

My choices, however, as to what we had to do, what decisions had to be made . . . were quickly narrowed down to one. We had to get food and soon or we would die of starvation without having to wait for the effects of radiation to do us in.

I had to think fast. We were in such weakened condition, all of us, barely able to walk and move around, sleeping most of the time . . . not in prime condition to go hunting animals for food . . .

Of course if animals wandered by we might be able to pick them off with lasers, then tractor them aboard. But according to Doctor Atra, it was not just food we had to have, but blood . . . preferably human blood with the generating power of ground up human organs thrown in.

And a sudden inspiration came to mind.

I went to the Proteus index and came up with what I thought might inspire the action we needed.

I had seen more distant movements on the Savannah, once or twice caught glimpses of Earthlings scantily clad, with long hair and bands around their heads.

Now I studied the landscape more using augmentation and our electronic scope . . .

I saw a small band of savages, looking our way . . . looking our way and talking together, gesturing and pointing at our two ships where we were parked on a slight rise with a view over the grassy plain.

I use the term savages advisedly, because these beings were obviously inferior to the Earthlings I had dealt with under Enki in the gold mining operations of Africa. Their skins were like nothing so much as burnished copper, considerably darker than even our own damaged skins, still seared from the flash of the bursting nuclear bomb that destroyed Atlantis and our dreams.

I concluded that their skin color was likely the effect of the adaptability gene the great traitor Enki had given to the Earthlings before the Great Deluge.

I was aware of other things immediately, too.

Several thousand years of this tribe's isolation here on the Western Continents doubtless had brought deterioration in everything pertaining to knowledge or culture . . . language . . . everything.

We would be dealing with real primitives here, I could see.

Well, with primitives there were two major things we could use. Religious awe and force. I could count on those to get me what I wanted . . . at least I hoped so, and it was that concept that motivated my plan now.

I activated the Military craft's Proteus.

It projected the holographic image of a sort of generic saintly figure with arms outstretched and a great halo of shining light all around him. I positioned it just in front of our two ships. I had arranged the focus towards the Savannah, towards the band of natives I had been studying through the electronic scope.

At the very least, the image should protect us. But I hoped for much more than that.

Then I fell into my bunk like the rest and sought whatever solace might be found in sleep.

****

When next I awoke, a little less nauseated, a little less groggy, but sharply more hungry, I gradually remembered what I had done, then got up to come to check the results of my maneuver, if any.

And I saw my intuition on what would work with these savages had not gone astray.

Not if my eyes were telling me the truth . . . which because of their still swollen condition, maybe they weren't.

What I seemed to see was this.

Sometime . . . I assumed during the night . . . the savages had arranged a kind of circular tribute for us just outside the range of the radius of the image I had put on display.

That is what I interpreted it as, at least. There were stones spaced all around the radius of the circle. They must have had some kind of ceremonial meaning for the savages. But more importantly was what appeared on top some of the flatter stones. Food.

The sight gave me strength and since I was the only one awake I went outside to check . . .

Yes . . .

Meat. Cooked meat. With a nice aroma . . . well, nice, no, not exactly . . . a delicious aroma to a starving Anunnaki. And some kind of grain that looked as if it had been perhaps boiled into a textured consistency. Both contained in crude stone dishes.

I looked warily around to see if I were not about to be the victim of a surprise attack, this being but the bait perhaps for some savage ambush.

Then . . .

My famished body went to work with a motivation and mind of its own.

I sampled both kinds of offerings with my hands. Not bad.

Not bad? In my famished condition it was a feast. Probably the most delicious I had ever tasted . . . though I knew that in a normal condition I might well have brushed both aside as too inferior even to contemplate. . . . so do circumstances make liars and hypocrites of us all.

I made sure to satisfy my own hunger.

Then went to wake our crews.

This obtaining of the native food offerings, I knew, would not hurt at all to establish still once again with Enlil and with the rest, my claim to be their natural leader.

****

The food and the obvious domination obtained over the savage tribe's mentality by my maneuver did much to raise the general morale . . . and my own status in the eyes of the men.

We were all still sick and suffering, but now, though in varying degrees, not quite so weak, not quite so much the prisoners of circumstance we had been before.

I felt like giving my personal thanks to the inventor of Proteus. Its technical prowess had perhaps saved our lives, at least for a little while longer. I knew the other things it could do, and would keep them always in mind. Proteus could camouflage our two ships perfectly. Make them blend with whatever background the ship was passing through. Pass under an overcast sky and your ship became a cloud. A starry night and your ship became a selection of stars with a pure black background. If you were silhouetted against the sun the silhouette would disappear and you would become the sun as far as anyone looking at you could discern.

And then there was Proteus on the personal level. I had an activator on my belt as did Enlil and we were the only ones. We could become fire, or water, a god or a devil, a lion or a giant bird . . . there were a thousand choices in the index as to just what we could appear to be. I knew in our situation it had the potential to become very useful.

Look what it had done for us already here.

As I said I felt the impulse now to thank its inventor and creator.

But I restrained myself.

For a very good reason.

The inventor had been none other than the traitor Enki . . .

****

I don't know why everything has to be my idea. You would think in the normal course of events someone else would occasionally come up with something that would help.

And yet, I do know why that is, too, if I put myself to really think about it.

First, Enlil is not someone who will ever understand the real situation, much less come forth with the solutions to problems. As a Royal he has not been raised to be exposed to vexing practical dilemmas, but rather to run away from them and let other people bear the burden of their ultimate solution.

Second, the others . . . typical Anunnaki . . . are so in awe of Enlil and his Royal, almost holy status in the Anunnaki hierarchy . . . that their minds freeze at the very idea of thinking around him. They believe that all right thinking emanates from him as does light from the sun!

Well . . .

Maybe I shouldn't blame them.

I used to think that, too, I admit. But hard experience has taught me otherwise. Though it is a lesson I must always strive to conceal from other Anunnaki . . . or run the risk of losing my own preferential post as Enlil's chief advisor.

After all had eaten, we were notably better, physically and in our general outlook.

But as always happens, one problem solved leads to another, sometimes even more difficult.

I knew what it was, but was not at all eager to face up to it. I refer
to Doctor Atra's challenge, which I myself had inspired him to make.

The question was, how was I to accomplish it?

The answer came to me that night in a dream.

****

I said it was a dream, though some might call it a nightmare.

I was learning fast that the line between dream and nightmare
was something judgmental and a luxury of interpretation that in our
present situation I no longer could afford.

Not if I wanted to save our lives.

If I procrastinated, or became too delicate in my moral decisions
here, the only sure result was that we would all die. And Enki would
win. Enki would be the uncontested ruler of Earth, and eventually
the sole ruler of the Anunnaki. And I . . . I would be food for worms
along with all the rest of us, Enlil and the crews.

No, I couldn't accept that Fate. Not without at least putting up a
fight against it.

So I outlined it to them. What we had to do.

And then I did it.

****

The next time the savages brought us offerings of food, I was awake
and watching, this time from the Hospital ship.

As they put the offerings over their ceremonial stones I projected
a second sacred image beyond the first. Outward beyond them, so it
would form a visual shield between the savages leaving the offerings
and their village, or others in their group waiting outside the to them
sacred ring.

As it happened, there were twelve of them remaining inside the
sacred inner circle when I did this.

Too bad for them.

It was not my fault we needed blood and the essence to be extracted from ground up internal organs. That blame could only be laid at the feet of the supposedly great Enki, who in reality was great only in the degree of his treason to the Anunnaki cause and the Anunnaki way of life.

I took them all, all twelve of the savages, very quickly with the Hospital ship's laser apparatus. Simple. Set on stun, aim, and shoot. Twelve times.

Then I tractored them aboard into the great central emergency room of the Hospital ship.

After that, it was all up to Doctor Atra, who I would afterwards hold strictly in account.

On my prior command, he was waiting . . .

And I knew from his briefing to me what he would do . . . what he had to do if our lives and our possible road back to health were to be preserved . . .

First, the blood would all be drained from each of the savages.

Step one.

Then . . .

The internal organs would have to removed. Crushed and ground and finally liquified and added to the mix of blood. That was Doctor Atra's own Rx, which I was trying to accommodate now as best I could.

****

The next day I called us all together. Under Enlil's name, of course. My illness had not made me lose my mind.

The place of meeting was in the Hospital ship. In the central emergency room.

I looked around at us. A sorry crew at best.

I was not the only one suffering loss of hair. Almost everyone had white patches showing through whatever they had previously been blessed with as a crowning glory.

Our faces all were seared and burned to various degrees.

The irony was not lost on me that the savage peoples we were dealing with now, at least as long as they did not see us close up, looked upon us as gods. And yet they in all their crude existence, in their primitive and uncultured, uneducated state, were better off than we. More attractive, healthier . . . I could not stand to hold any longer the thought.

The thin metal containers that Doctor Atra handed around now to us . . . smoke rose from their sides reflecting the refrigerating process they had undergone.

I knew of course what they contained. We all did.

Some portion of the blood of 12 savages plus their vital organs, or at least the essence of these last.

That was what Doctor Atra had told us would give us back our future. Even though that process might take ten thousand Earth years.

I stepped forward into the leadership gap left by Enlil, whose full, loose lips seemed to hang helpless over some personal abyss that left him impotent to say or do anything.

"Fellow Anunnaki. Honored and exalted Enlil. I propose a toast."

I had thought about saying something complicated and elaborate. But in the moment I settled for simplicity.

"To our health."

I paused for effect, then tilted the light metal container back slightly and gingerly tested its contents.

Hmmm.

Not bad. I had expected to be revolted by it. The surprise perhaps showed on my swollen face.

Then I raised the container high before with a flourish drinking deeply, watching to be sure the other eleven drank with me.

I looked at Doctor Atra. I did not want to say too much. To do so would only detract from the moment, from its potential triumph.

"This . . . this is mixed with something."

Doctor Atra looked at me. "Yes. I found a wild apple tree just over the ridge behind us."

Doctor Atra then took a large metal container from the refrigeration bank and poured each of us a refill.

A thousand thoughts ran through my head. The primordial one was a question. Had I slaughtered these 12 savages unnecessarily?

But no . . .

No, that was a thought that had only the life expectancy of an icycle in the tropical regions as I summarily cancelled it out in my mind. In the first place for an Anunnaki to be concerned about the lives of ignorant savages was absurd and of no moment. And second, if there were any blame to be attached to what I did, which there was not . . . well, such blame could only fall on the shoulders of the malevolent Enki, the author of our present lamentable condition.

The others were looking at me, including Enlil, awaiting my signal.

"To our health," I said again, this time with an anticipatory smile. And drank deeply, this time with something almost approaching enjoyment.

****

We went into phase two of our recuperation.

We all felt a little stronger with a little more energy during the eight days the blood supply lasted.

Then it was over and we had a new problem ahead of us.

We had killed the goose that laid the golden egg. I saw that. Understandably the little tribe of savages no longer wished to return and worship at the shrine we had so obligingly offered them.

I was weighing various possible solutions in my mind when something happened. We heard a thundering sound and looked outside.

The sight that met my eyes was fantastic.

There was a whole herd of great shaggy beasts like none on Nibiru that was moving its ponderous way across the grassy plain not too far from where we were. I felt the terrain's vibration even inside the ship.

Doctor Atra and I discussed the pros and cons of killing one of them, eating its meat and drinking its blood. He approved the first and vetoed the second, saying it might well do us more harm than

good. He insisted the blood must be human, according to the protocols.

Following his Rx, I managed to get the Hospital ship off the
ground and go after the herd. I swooped low over them, feeling the
immense momentum and power encapsulated in the great beasts'
peculiar rocking, plunging movements. The thought crossed my mind
they were like nothing so much as Prairie ships navigating their way
through the deep waves of Savannah grass swaying in the wind. I
killed one with a laser blast, watched it stagger and fall back and
finally plow headlong into the tall grass, then quiver and lie still, its
great bulk now useless in its self defense.

Useless to it, but not to us.

I landed the ship nearby and watched while our two medical
technicians managed to find enough energy to use their small and
specialized medical lasers in stripping the animal of some of its best
parts.

These I ordered properly prepared and packed into the largest of
our onboard refrigerator-freezers under Doctor Atra's supervision once
we were back at home base.

That was a problem, refrigeration space, if we wanted to keep
any but a week's supply of blood for our crew. Doctor Atra had already complained about it to me, and I had come right back at him
with an order. Search the protocols again or use his own brains, but
come up with a solution. Soon.

Meanwhile, back at our camp, we learned to roast the meat of
the shaggy beast over an open pit I ordered dug with much travail on
the part of the diggers . . . protected all the while from the sight of the
savages by the circular icon around us.

Had they seen us, it would have been quite a shock. Our faces
pocked and streaked and seared, our bodies emaciated, we would
have seemed more like demons than the gods they had so unwisely
chosen to worship . . .

****

The meat of the shaggy beast was tasty and plentiful. But we needed in addition to it human blood and the essence of human organs to effectuate our own eventual regeneration.

It was some days later when I witnessed an interesting event.

I was checking visually on the village of savages, mulling over in my mind if we should perhaps attack them and carry away another twelve to once again supply us with at least eight days of the blood and organ essence so necessary to our recovery.

But, to my surprise . . .

Someone else beat me to the idea.

As I watched through the augmentation lens an immense horde of other savages swooped down out of nowhere on the little village. The marauders each carried some kind of hatchet with a big knob on its opposite end . . . obviously a weapon that could be used either to club or chop. I watched them do both in a merciless and methodical fashion, their war whoops wounding the air around them in bone-chilling fashion. They quickly reduced the village to zero as far as living beings were concerned. They then rode away in triumph.

I followed them through the electronic scope, watched them for some time, saw where they entered the far foothills near the horizon and carefully plotted its position on a sketch of the area.

That was for future use.

But for now, one present problem was solved.

I alerted the medical team again and personally piloted the Hospital ship to a landing close by the scene of the slaughter.

In spite of their weakness, the Doctor and the two medical technicians, aided by four of the remaining crew, by the end of the day had harvested over a hundred bodies . . .

****

We had a supply of blood and essence for something like three months, and enough meat of the shaggy beast to last half that long.

But our refrigeration units were jammed to the gills and I again prodded Doctor Atra to find a solution to the blood storage problem . . . to which he said he had an idea, but it needed more investigation and some experiment. I let him know he had to work it out soon or our prospects of survival were not good.

I had an idea of my own, one that perhaps was obvious in the unrolling of events, but that nevertheless no one except myself seemed to see.

I called the crews together and explained it to them, but only in the broadest of outlines. It had to be that way, because when it got down to details I had no idea if it would work or not. But if it did it was a mechanism that might mean nothing less than continued life to us.

****

It was night when we took off.

I piloted the lead craft, the Military scout, and with the electronic night vision activated saw all I needed to see.

Nestled in a clearing right in the middle of the low, wooded foothills was the extensive encampment of the tribe I was looking for . . . the same tribe who had so efficiently slaughtered our former worshippers.

I picked out a grassy plateau a short distance above their camp. I calculated it would be perfect for us in all respects. The height in itself tended to inspire a kind of physiological awe in those who had to climb to see us, and their passage would be up through rocky and rugged country.

As we approached and landed, both our ships were displaying the religious archetype I had earlier selected for our former worshippers, and I was going to leave it on constant display. Considering the warlike nature of this tribe I also ordered force fields as an added protection for both ships just in case the religious icon did not take with these very relentless killers.

And so we were in position. Time would tell if my plan would work . . .

****

The nature of my plan was simplicity itself.

Obviously this savage tribe of marauders had won domination by a single trait. Their warlike ability to exterminate any other smaller tribe.

That in itself stirred the old ambition in me. Lost Atlantis dreams . . . to have an Invincible Army that would help us to dominate and rule Earth.

But that was something dwelling strictly in the outermost regions of my mind . . . what was motivating me was that this tribe apparently presented us with at least the possibility of overcoming part of our basic problem for survival . . . which was the availability of human blood, not in quarts or gallons or flagons or even tubs . . . we needed rivers of blood, and not only that, the rivers could never run dry for long or we would die.

While Death was something I personally felt I could face if there was no way out, what galled me most in my dying . . . in our dying . . . would be that Enki, the structureless and slimy Enki, he of no principles, would win . . .

That . . . that I could not take. Enlil might mouth similar words but ironically it was I all along who felt that much more than he . . . down to the very limits of passion.

****

So this was the solution.

If everything worked out.

We would make ourselves the religious idols for this warrior tribe. That was first.

And . . .

As they conquered all the other smaller tribes in the region . . . after each conquest we would make our harvest. Of internal organs, of blood . . . and so, over the many centuries, if Doctor Atra's prescription were to prove efficacious, nurse ourselves back to eventual health.

****

As the years went by my plan worked to something very near perfection.

It was a symbiosis made in heaven.

Our new tribe killed and conquered and carried out their savage instincts to the uttermost . . . we, in our turn, harvested their kill and grew once again by slow and infinitesimally perceptible steps back towards health and life.

Sometimes, too, we blessed their kill and helped its progress by making our appearance in one or the other of our ships over the battle site on the side of our savages . . . always striking terror into the hearts of the opposition.

Doctor Atra at last . . . somewhat outside the time limit I had given him . . . came up with the solution to the storage problem.

Using the centrifuge and a complicated procedure found in one of the footnotes of the least likely protocol, he had fabricated it . . . a way to convert the great quantities of blood into a storageable form.

And so at some point in time we went upon a new regimen.

One glass of fresh blood for each of us per day. The other ten quarts or so the Doctor had calculated we needed daily if we ever hoped to recover, were now available in a new form. A kind of spongy wafer, different from the wafers on which the protocols were recorded, of course . . . this one had no slick surface, but was perforated and, as I said, spongy and whitish in appearance. And in flavor, bland but not bad. Not bad at all . . .

I still didn't dare look into a mirror, but . . .

I felt a subtle change.

I for the first time since the Atlantis disaster began to look more towards life than death.

****

The life we led in our symbiotic relationship with our new group of conquering savages was in many ways an ideal one, given the inherent limits of our basic situation.

That was, even after hundreds of Earth years had gone by, we still lacked strength and were far from regaining anything like our former appearance.

We Anunnaki are by nature strong, handsome physical specimens. While the human race we created had a superficial resemblance to us, yes . . . still that was more like the resemblance of the moon to the sun rather than the resemblance of two stars to each other.

The stuff of human beings was genetically inferior because of the short span of their lives for one thing . . . because of their ascendance from the ape for another.

Any flash of beauty they might attain was subject to an almost instantaneous process of deterioration due simply and exclusively to the inexorable passage of time.

That was it. They were never more than the puppets of Time, and at its far from tender mercies in every aspect of their lives.

As for us, their makers . . .

We kept our beauty for hundreds of thousands of years, as measured by Earth time, once we attained adulthood . . . and with hardly the slightest physical change. So naturally we appeared as gods to any Earthling . . . and in comparison were gods.

But . . .

The exposure to Enki's treacherous nuclear attack had changed all that for us.

We were certainly no longer suns, nor even moons . . . asteroids perhaps . . . ugly, burned out asteroids scarred and pitted and disfigured by meteor collisions over millions of years.

But even though we were pale, scarred, gaunt spectres of our former selves, we began once again to feel surge through our loins certain desires that had been sadly notable by their absence.

This signalled to me that Doctor Atra's strange regimen was at last beginning to produce results, even though those results as yet at least had not produced much in the way of visible exterior improvement.

That was the way it worked, he told us every time anyone asked . . . the internal organs had to rejuvenate themselves first, an extremely slow and lengthy process . . . only once they were back to something like their

original shape and function would we begin to see improvement reflected in our exterior appearance.

With the wafers we had made a great leap forward, however. We
all agreed on that . . . the desires we began to feel confirmed it.

As to what to do about it . . . the solution was not far to seek.

We were gods to a cruel, savage tribe . . . a tribe whose leaders
easily understood the basic desires of males, even if those males were
gods, once those desires were effectively communicated.

I took upon myself the job of doing so one day.

The tribe's language . . . they called themselves the Su . . . was not
too distant from our own . . . badly deteriorated, of course, from even
the very basic cultural content coming from our African miners . . .
deteriorated, shortened and always, always oversimplified, everything
brought down to the crudest essentials.

Well, sex fit into that last category, and so I found it not difficult
at all to get my meaning across to the tribe's leaders. I did not appear
before them personally, no, of course not . . . that would have been
very detrimental to our image, something as gods we could hardly
afford.

I rather projected our desires through the medium of voices in
the night. Voices which appeared as if by magic in the heads of both
the warrior chief and the high priest.

It wasn't magic but technology. I had tractored them both aboard
and had Doctor Atra and his two technicians put little receivers in
their ear lobes. They were pacified first and administered a drug afterwards so if they remembered the incident at all, it seemed to them
like a great spiritual adventure.

And ever after I could give them any instructions I wanted and
they would be carried out quickly and to the letter. Day or night.

But the first ones were in the night. That I be brought two
women . . . not any women, but two young virgins, two of the
most beautiful of all the tribe. It was understood these two would
not be returned. They were meant to play a mysterious role in the
welfare of the gods, their future not to be questioned.

I then took my leisurely pleasure with the two in a private

compartment of the Military ship. I did whatever I wanted with them . . . they were after all electronically pacified out of their minds. They did not know if they were dreaming life or living a dream . . . and with the pacifier's effects they did not care. All their inhibitions, if such primitives ever had any, were put to sleep . . . and so they reacted on a purely physical level . . . like animals. They were literally open and receptive to each and every one of my advances.

And so I drank my fill that night of grunts and groans, of stomachs contracting in great sexual ecstasy, of rolling eyes and sighs and a deluge of lickings and little bites, the sliding of wet lips, deep kisses and uncontrolled and uncontrollable body contractions . . . always a driving towards a mutually desired destination.

I awoke much later from all that feeling better than I had in at least a thousand Earth years. Back before Enki's treacherous attack, when I had truly been a god . . . at least as far as Earthlings were concerned.

But awaking now meant facing the reality that day imposed. As a leader I knew what that meant. The ability not to shirk important decisions. And I did not.

The thing was this. These two maidens, even though in a pacified half-dream state, had nevertheless done something strictly prohibited.

They had seen me the way I really was . . .

That, obviously, was dangerous . . . dangerous and unacceptable.

They could not be allowed to go back to the tribe and report that what the tribe conceived of as their gods were in reality monsters. Horrible, inferior monsters.

Yes, I would have used Proteus if it had been possible to project a more godlike image. But even Proteus has its limitations, and at such close and intimate range it can not be effectively used.

So, I did what I had to do as a loyal Anunnaki. I turned the two sleeping girls over to Doctor Atra.

They became grist for his mill, or rather for his centrifuge. And so their lives fulfilled a second usefulness, one of which all of us could partake.

****

As we began feeling better I began to feel the need for a certain amount of cultural uplift myself.

Reading material to fill some of the idle time. Books.

We had them, imprinted on electronic wafers which we projected onto the walls of our compartments when we wanted to read. The problem was on the Hospital ship the books were mostly medical.

As on the Military scout they were mostly on military subjects.

It was true that in each case there was also a sprinkling of general interest books, too. But only a sprinkling.

The information wafers that we had were only an infinitesimal part of the Great Library of Anunnaki information.

So we were operating at a great disadvantage when compared with Enki. He had available to him all the distilled knowledge of the Anunnaki race in its entire history. While he had a full dinner, a feast . . . we had only crumbs.

It wasn't fair.

You see, everything on Nibiru is organized. No one has to reinvent the wheel.

Even a spaceship is just organized technology which is basically information. Applied information.

The complete set of wafers . . . the set that contains absolutely everything, the Master Protocols . . . were held by only a few people.

Enki was one of those.

So was Enlil. The only problem with Enlil was that his set of the complete information wafers had gone down to the bottom of the sea in the attack on Atlantis.

Those wafers are enablers. They enable anyone to be a technician, a strategist, a great leader . . . anything. Anything that has come from the millions of years of experience of the Anunnaki race.

You could say that the entire Anunnaki society was distilled into a box of 2 inch diameter wafers. Technology, philosophy, government . . . how to do it . . . it is all there. A system with the essence of genius . . . given in such a form that it can be applied by idiots.

Even by Enlil . . .

What it amounts to is this. We stand on the shoulders of giants

of our past, and with the wafers we make sure never to lose an inch of
that gigantic stature so hardly won. It is what has made us great as a
race and will always preserve us so.

I began to think about that. How we might possibly get in our
possession a complete set of the information wafers, the Master
Protocols. Somewhere along the line we had to do it, if we ever hoped
to dominate the planet.

****

Another episode soon highlighted in my mind the need for the Master
Protocols, the complete set of information wafers.

The idea of cloning ourselves had come to me.

The reason for that, as the centuries went by, was this . . .

We twelve surviving Anunnaki continued to enjoy the life style
furnished us apparently in perpetuity by our symbiotic relationship
with the Su here on the Western Continents.

All our food necessities were furnished us by the Su.

We had to do nothing in its procuring, in its preparation and in
its being offered up to us every day by the members of the tribe.
Fierce and cruel as they might be, and were, on the battlefield, that
did not apply in their relationship with us, their gods and saviors.

And anytime I wished fine adjustments to the policy I could obtain it by merely voicing it electronically into the earlobes of the Chief
Warrior or the High Priest.

And the supply of young nubile women for every one of our
twelve man crew never stopped. Sometimes we kept our favorites for
more than a single night. Even for as long as a month before they
were passed along to Doctor Atra's not so tender mercies.

And the supply of blood and the vital essence of internal organs was just as unceasing. The Su never stopped attacking other
smaller neighboring tribes . . . though I succeeded in instituting a
new policy . . . the one of not slaughtering all life in the conquered camps and villages . . . I wished to preserve the women, at

least the young ones . . . for either our pleasure or for the Su and future procreation.

It is true that none of the women of these primitive tribes were like our Anunnaki women. Still, even with their bronzed skin and straight black hair . . . products of Enki's adaptability gene I am sure . . . they effused a certain savage attraction with none of the concomitant demands of Anunnaki women. Total sexual domination was achievable on our part.

Of course with the Pacifier, we attained that. The Pacifier is unmatched as an electronic instrument that quickly could put them or anyone into a kind of hypnotic trance . . . receptive to anything or anyone. It works to translate anyone instantly under your power, and is a device we have used effectively in case of necessity ever since our first arrival on Planet Earth.

For me, taking a beautiful Earth woman was like enjoying a sunset. A nice, impressive, but quickly passing experience. Not something to try to fashion a life around. Sunsets, after all, are possibly so beautiful only because by nature they are and should be ephemeral.

And may I say I have enjoyed many, many beautiful . . . sunsets. Before and after Enki's shameful nuclear attack.

But none of us . . . none . . . with all our activity over hundreds of Earth years had been able to impregnate a single woman of the savage tribes.

Doctor Atra's tests of those favorites we kept in the ships for a month or more proved that.

Impotent we were not. Not any more. But what we were was medically certifiable sterile.

It was a shame. Because Enlil and I equally had never forgotten our eventual objective of revenge. I had already begun to think along the lines of conquering all of Earth's tribes one by one. Instilling their loyalty to us one way or another. So when it came time to make our move against Enki we would not lack for allies. And on achieving our objective, we might count on a multitude of loyal tribes.

And then one day the related idea entered my head.

To help us carry out our objective we might very well begin to use clones.

We were sterile, and would be for the foreseeable future.

We could not produce children, which would have been an enormous plus in implementing our program of world conquest. Our children, even though they would be half savage, still would also be half Anunnaki. We could influence them more easily in any direction we wished to go. The genetic attraction, almost like gravity, would be our link with them, and make them ideal to carry out our plans. As natural leaders, with more endowments than normal humans, we could easily begin to build tribes around them . . . tribes whose loyalty to us would then be almost genetically ordained and therefore something we could count on to help us in our dream of world conquest.

But . . .

We could not do that . . . not yet.

In the interim, while we waited for that power to return to us, there was something we could do.

Produce clones.

The clones could serve us. Do a lot of work which we ourselves would not wish to do. Either because it lowered our status as gods, or simply was too repetitious, tedious, laborious and mundane.

I broached the idea to Doctor Atra and set him to work upon it.

He did a number of experiments, none of which proved successful.

What he needed, he said, was the full medical protocols contained only in the complete set of information wafers, the Master Protocols.

It was another reason for carrying out a plan, one which had already occurred to me . . . but the risks were too great to allow me to undertake it. Because in the process of trying to gain a little improvement . . . we might lose everything.

That was a chance I did not want to take.

****

The thought occurred to me that the Su were very close to being the kind of warriors we needed to help us eventually dominate Earth.

What more could we ask, really? They were fierce, cruel, totally merciless . . . and above all, unthinkingly loyal to us their gods. They would do anything we asked, die for any cause we might propose, or just as easily die for us for no cause at all.

Of course, even with all those desirable qualities, they were nothing like our Invincible Army of Atlantis.

How beautiful that would have been to unleash upon an unsuspecting world!

Just to think of what we had, and had lost . . . was terrible still for me to contemplate.

But I had to face hard cold facts.

The truth was we had no way of working towards such an army again, at least not in our present circumstances.

On Atlantis we had had a dozen genetic specialists with no other duties than to produce our ideal warrior for our Invincible Army . . . the army that would have, were it not for Enki's perfidy, long since conquered this world. Not only that but vast laboratories and loads of special equipment, as well as a set of the complete Anunnaki Master Protocols. We had none of that here. Doctor Atra tried, but as yet he could not even produce a single clone.

We would have liked to raise the general quality of this tribe of Su with our own DNA. That was an easy program to carry out . . . simply impregnate a considerable number of the Su women, and then let nature take its course. The most desirable hybrids produced by such an ongoing process, due to Enki's treacherous and unauthorized genetic manipulations, would be already fertile and ready to produce their own offspring.

An easy program to carry out, yes, ordinarily . . .

But in our present condition . . .

Our radiation ravaged DNA would undoubtedly lower rather than raise the general quality of the Su tribe. They at least were vigorous and healthy, while we . . .

I still would not look at myself in a mirror, and if by accident I caught a glimpse now and then it was always just as strong a shock as it had been the first time after the nuclear blast at Atlantis. I was a

monster, a freak . . . and I knew it. It should have been no shock . . .
after all, what I saw every day in my eleven companions was no different. We were all monsters.

And yet, too, undeniably increasingly healthy monsters, although
to date the improvement was all internal, nothing that showed on the
outside. It was difficult to have faith that someday we would be restored to our former godly grace, yes . . . but the Anunnaki protocols
do not lie, and Doctor Atra had assured us that at some far point in
the slow dance of the centuries, at last we would have our vindication
and our return to physical beauty and grace.

But the Su . . .

It occurred to me that if I could just succeed in lowering my
sights and forget for the time being of ever again creating an Invincible Army . . . if I could do that . . . and attune myself to lesser,
secondary but achievable goals . . .

Then . . .

The Su could be our nucleus, our model for what we eventually
wanted to do all over the world. In each region . . . if we could have a
dominant tribe, in effect an army . . . blindly devoted to whatever
ends we might prescribe . . . then the total effect might hopefully be
almost the same as having a single Invincible Army.

The idea began to intrigue me beyond measure . . .

It raised my hopes and my spirits to a level neither had seen for a
long, long time. Beyond the horizon, which admittedly might still be
very distant, I could in a very tentative way now visualize the sweeping away of Enki into the dustbins of history and the ascension of
Enlil . . . his path always guided of course by his Chief Advisor . . .
into his proper place in the grand scheme of things. On Earth . . . and
eventually, too, on Nibiru.

Nibiru . . .

What happened there could change everything here. Make dust
of my dreams of power . . . or contrarily, imprint them across the
stars. I have always believed that Destiny is something to be shaped

by those who know how to do it and have the courage to do it . . . my whole life to date is a testament to that.

Yes, but . . . I also knew only too well that I at present had no control over events on our Home Planet.

Of course the crux of any drama enacted there at this time was the atmospheric crisis.

And as to that we remained in ignorance, necessarily, having no access to the communication facilities that Enki had at his headquarters on Mount Olympus, or at the Space Station on the Sinai Peninsula, or at the Great Pyramid in the land we called Egypt.

We were exiles from all the centers of power. All right. But what Enki and his cohorts did not know, what they did not know on Nibiru . . . what no one knew but us . . . was that we were alive. Not alive and well, no, not yet.

But at least not in that ultimate exile called death.

I had to know certain things. The prime one was this. Was Nibiru still the Home Planet of the Anunnaki?

Or had the atmosphere at last failed? All the supplies of gold mined by the humans and transported back to Nibiru to be injected into its stratosphere . . . was it at last all for naught? In such a case the Anunnaki would have moved already to their New Home. The one discovered and explored by Enlil in his far journey to the constellation of Zeta Reticuli 2.

If the second possibility were true, then our own position would change. Change drastically.

That would mean Earth would be abandoned to us. At least I assumed it would be. After all, what was the Anunnaki mission on Earth? Simply to mine gold to save Nibiru's atmosphere and its planetary heat from being dissipated into space. As for Enki, the hated Enki, our malefactor who would always sell out the best of Anunnaki ideals to benefit the base humans . . . he would inevitably be ordered back to the new Home Planet in Zeta Reticuli 2. Light years away from us, he could no longer interfere.

Then, what would we do on Earth?

The answer to that was clear as night stars in my mind.

We would . . .

Establish what should have been established in the first place, were it not for Enki's perfidy. A planet dominated by Anunnaki hierarchy, by the best of Anunnaki ideals. Earth would have one god, and one god only, as was appropriate for any planet inhabited by an inferior race. Blind loyalty and obedience to that god would produce the ideal society. Everything would flow like water, though structured by the unique procedures embodied in the Master Protocols, products of the distilled wisdom of many generations of the Anunnaki.

I write all this because . . .

Because the time was fast approaching. The time when the great planet Nibiru would once again, after 3600 years of navigating the blackest, furthrest regions from the sun and the other planets, return once more to its closest approach to Earth.

As always, it would pass between the orbits of Mars and Jupiter. And we would have it visible in the night sky during that time for a period of about a month.

We had only a pair of rudimentary astronomical telescopes aboard our two ships, which after all were only equipped for planetary duties.

Still, I hoped intelligent use of them would be enough to answer the overwhelming question . . .

Was Nibiru still the Home Planet of the Anunnaki?

****

Nibiru could have been a dead world by now.

Yes, that was a possibility, I told myself, as I peered each day to try to ascertain something from what I saw through the telescope.

Or Nibiru could have been just the same, basically, as when we left it. There was no way we could learn that through our telescopes.

What I hoped to see was a secondary sign that would tell us everything.

With Nibiru's near approach to Earth, there should be a visit.

It was logical. An opportunity in space and time not to be cavalierly wasted.

To send a space ship down to Earth when so near was no great feat.

So the expectation was that it would be done.

It might or might not be important. That is, the ship could carry the Great Anu himself . . . or his representative, which I thought more likely . . . I knew that King Anu at his great age no longer had the lust for travel he had exhibited in his youth.

Or . . . it might carry some kind of supplies and nothing else.

But in any case there should be a ship.

If . . .

If Nibiru were still inhabited.

If there was no ship, that would tell me one thing, and one thing only, with a ninety per cent probability.

That yes, the move had been made. To the new Home Planet.

That Nibiru was now a dead Planet.

And that we were already the de facto rulers of Earth.

And so it was I gave my utmost attention to my personal telescopic observations of the region between Mars and Jupiter.

Of course I had help. Round the clock someone was constantly in vigilance . . . to see if any spaceship were seen to leave Nibiru.

Three weeks went by and there was nothing. . . . nothing to report.

And then . . .

There was.

There was . . .

****

My hopes again lay trodden in the dust.

I had been almost sure that the Anunnaki had made the Great Migration by now to a new home on the planet in Zeta Reticuli 2.

And of course, if that were true, it logically followed . . .

That Enki would have been there, too, by now, leaving Enlil and I and our men alone on Earth.

And so . . .

Unobstructed, following my plans, we could build an Ideal Kingdom on Earth in a relatively short time . . . an outpost of what we could make the beginning of a New Anunnaki Empire. A Proud and True Empire . . . not of workers but fierce soldiers . . . which would leave us proof for all time against whatever outside force might come to threaten our ancient culture.

That accomplished, Enlil could then return in triumph to the new Home Planet in Zeta Reticuli 2, there to claim the crown from his father Anu. On two grounds. As both the discoverer of the New Home and the righteous restorer of true order all around Earth. And as a third ground, the cleansing Prosecutor, primed to expose the depth of Enki's treachery and put our own accomplishments into glowing perspective and the position of honor they deserve.

That would leave me to rule over the outpost Earth.

So I visualized the flow of events . . .

It would be Alpha and Omega to me to attain what amounted to the status of sole god of a planet . . .

It would fulfill me in ways I could not even yet verbalize. To achieve such status was a visceral, vital burning urge inside me, one that I could do nothing to resist.

Such a picture haunted my dreams and measured the extreme azimuth of my ambition. I, Yahweh, to be the Supreme One, controlling the fate of every living creature on this green and blue and white globe afloat like a round island in the desert seas of space . . .

Ah, Paradise!

But it was not to be. Not yet, at least. My dream, if not dead, was at least delayed.

We were not to be the rulers of this planet, because the nefarious Enki was still here, as evidenced by the visual sighting of the craft leaving Nibiru with destination Earth.

Nibiru was still the Home Planet of the Anunnaki and perhaps always would be. As long as that was true, it meant that Enki would continue to impose his traitorous stamp on Earth, no doubt trying to elevate

an inferior race almost to the status of the ancient Anunnaki . . . who had
earned their status over a period of millions of years of struggle.

I could only assume that the crisis on Nibiru was now under
complete control.

I speak really of a dual problem.

First, the atmospheric one and second the problem of the loss of
heat during the far reaches of the planet's enormous orbit . . . reaches
where the sun is too distant to give anything but a fraction of its
radiated energy, and almost all heat has to come from the planet's
seething underground rivers of lava.

Those, I knew, historically had been both a problem and a blessing. The problem was that there was always a danger that the subterranean pressures would build too high which, if not checked, could
conceivably someday destroy the planet . . . the blessing was that the
more active the rivers of lava, the more lifesaving heat was delivered
to the planet's surface on our long journey away from the sun.

Enki's gold mining then must be the principal reason Nibiru had
been saved from what looked like eventual catastrophe. The curtain
of fine gold particles, almost like a second sphere, serving equally to
retain the atmosphere and the surface heat, both lifesaving functions
for the Anunnaki . . .

Following that same path of my reasoning, it was logical to guess
that as a result Enki was probably considered now, in the light of
everything that had transpired, a great hero on the Home Planet.
After all, the original idea of mining the gold for the project here on
Earth had been his.

While we . . . Enlil and I and our fellow survivors of the atrocity
that was the destruction of Atlantis, that great city in the sea . . . we
had no status at all with Anu or anyone on Nibiru anymore. How
could we? . . . since surely according to Enki's lying reports we were
considered dead, and the villains of the whole Atlantis episode.

And bitterly it came to my mind, we still were. Dead, as far as
being anything like our former selves. So far at least we were still
hardly better than ghosts . . . pale, deformed, unhealthy spectres of
our former splendor.

Still . . . and it was the only thing that saved my state of mind . . . I hoped to use my considerable leadership talents to someday enable us to round a corner . . . where all the negative factors would one day turn around and fly flags strictly in our favor rather than Enki's.

That is what I lived for now, what I fought for . . . even though for too many long centuries our fight had been nothing much more than just a limited struggle for survival.

When that day of change would come I did not know . . . but I held on to it in my mind, yearned for it.

And then . . .

Then change did come.

But when it did, it was nothing like what I wanted. Not at all . . .

****

As I write this, several more centuries have already passed since the disappointment of the last passing of Nibiru.

They have been tranquil enough for us, those passing centuries. Our domination and direction of the Su has been complete. We needed to do nothing new to maintain ourselves and continue our fight to regain our health.

The only thing was it all became so intensely boring.

Yes, there were battles . . . yes, I got to pilot the Military craft, our reliable scout, during those battles, which temporarily again got my adrenalin flowing . . . to see the terror struck into the ranks of our opponents by our presence, especially when I projected the generic icon against the sky . . .

And . . .

If the battle ever started to go against us, of course I had other resources. Our lasers, our tractor beam . . .

But I tended to be conservative in all this, except when boredom got the better of me. Our Su were so strong and fierce, so experienced, so full of super confidence knowing the supernatural help that was always at hand, that they really needed nothing extra not only to win the battles but to methodically slaughter every man, woman and child of their opposition. It was their way, a way which I saw at last was impossible to discourage. On the contrary . . .

But then . . .

Then came the day of the change.

It started with something as minor as a flashing light.

On the control panel of the Military scout.

Still, that flashing light was enough to strike fear even into my own sturdy and not easily frightened heart.

It came near the end of one of the Su's battles . . .

I was able to finish up, however, and even to tractor aboard afterwards over the succeeding days a multitude of freshly killed bodies as grist for Doctor Atra's always busy mill, the source of many blood cocktails and legions of the lifegiving wafers which we must have if we ever want to once again somewhere in the far future become our former selves.

But the light had spoken and I had to pay attention to it.

Otherwise everything for our little group might come to a sudden and undesirable end.

I went to talk to Enlil about it.

I presented the problem to him. The solution. And by the time I finished talking he thought everything was his idea. That was an experience I had been through many times before, and that was really the way I wanted it. While I resented his taking credit for everything, at the same time it was the only way I could get my ideas and policies through to completion. The price was high, yes . . . but in dealing with Anunnaki royalty, if you were not prepared to pay it, you would not long be in any position of authority yourself.

"The power supply of the Military scout . . ." I told Enlil after all the necessary preliminaries of being humble and expressing my admiration for his sagacity. "It will fail in six months if we don't recharge."

He looked blank. "Recharge? But how . . . ? We can't do that. We have no way . . . do we?"

I relieved his ignorance at the same time I made him feel his question was a masterpiece of incisive inquiry.

He was informed, thanks to me, that the only place we could recharge the craft was at the Great Pyramid in Egypt.

When he raised his eyebrows and rolled his eyes . . . which was, pathetically, his most eloquent expression as to the impossibility of such a task . . . I was ready with my plan.

Yes, it would be dangerous. Very dangerous. Except for one thing that made it feasible.

I kept him in suspense for a moment to capture his sometimes wandering interest, then filled him in.

What made it feasible, I explained . . . was Enki's character, his fundamental weakness. His liberal tendencies.

First of all, almost for sure, he thought we were dead. Perished in the cataclysmic destruction of Atlantis. It would be logical for him to think so. I took the opportunity to remind him that we were unde-tected and that we survived in the first place only due to my own preparations in locating our headquarters on the smallest island, and camouflaging it.

I saw this scored a point for me with him, almost as if he had forgotten the traumatic episode . . . which in my estimation his strange mind was entirely capable of.

I went on.

Enki, I said, trying always to be the popular fellow rather than the ruler he should be, would probably not put a night watch on duty in the Great Pyramid.

And thinking we were dead . . . here I purposely stimulated Enlil's almost dormant hatred of his brother . . . and having no threat from outside . . . you could almost understand such an attitude. Almost but not quite, for me. I would have had around the clock watches there and everywhere. Eternal vigilance is the price of a secure rule.

What an irony, I thought, that he, Enki, is in power, while I sit here having to convince his brother as to the correct plan to follow in this emergency. Someday, I swore silently to myself, I would restore justice to the Anunnaki rule . . . but that day was not yet.

I made my basic point. That if I worked things just right, my chances of success were good. To recharge the Military scout. Which would keep our chances alive.

But I had in mind also to try to do along the way something else, which would make mine a double mission.

I wanted to take the opportunity, if the recharge were successful . . . to reconnoiter a location for our future base somewhere on the geographical area I had designated while still Enki's Chief Advisor as the Middle Continent.

It was a location strategically necessary in many ways.

Not too close to Enki, because we had to keep our very existence a secret. But this time, once we had regained something near our health, not so far away either. Within easy striking distance, was the way I put it to Enlil . . . once again to stimulate his apparently dormant desire for revenge on his brother.

I had a third motive . . . a private, personal one . . . for the mission. But I did not want to reveal it to Enlil.

I got his approval, which was all I needed.

I spent the rest of our time in the interview getting information which I needed. About the prospective New Home Planet he had discovered in the far constellation of Zeta Reticuli 2.

I found out for the first time certain details. That the planet had two suns and three moons. That it was almost twice the size of Nibiru . . . and had a temperate climate . . . all that was positive information and made me wonder why the Great Migration had not been already decided on by Anu.

Yet I knew his great age made him reluctant for any unnecessary change.

And then came the negative information. The atmosphere on the new planet was far from perfect. The oxygen content was low . . . Enlil and his crew had had to wear breathing apparatus during the entire time of their exploration of the planet's surface. The planet's greenery and plant life was not impressive. Of course, with time and the proper approach, all that could be improved. But it was another reason, for me, that the Anunnaki were still on Nibiru.

I found out too why the Military craft's power was going out.

They had used it extensively in their explorations of the new planet. That and the fact that the service record showed it was a very old machine to start with. Because normally such a craft was minimally good for something like ten thousand Earth years without a recharge.

Later I checked our Hospital ship and its prospectus looked secure for at least another five thousand Earth years. Surely, by then I thought, we would be the rulers of Planet Earth . . . the Great Pyramid and everything else in our exclusive possession.

****

Our power supply in the Military scout being low, I had to be careful.

My crew was minimal, consisting of a single person besides myself. I had picked Bronti, as our only engineer, to come with me on this vital and dangerous mission, the spearhead of our future hopes.

Because without at least our two ships, where would we be?

I knew the answer to that. Ill and deformed as we were, without the technology represented by and within our ships we would be nothing. Less than nothing. Less even than the cruel savages we dominated, less even than the primitive Su.

They, coming upon us in our true state, would hesitate not even a nanosecond in doing to us what we had seen them do to so many enemies. Kill us, scalp us (could they find enough hair, which was not always the case), and spreadeagle us on the ground as they had been taught to do with their victims in preparation for the evisceration to be conducted by the gods.

Such a theoretical picture was not one I liked to dwell on. I knew I had to make this mission a success or we were through.

I kept our speed low across the great ocean so as not to unnecessarily drain further our failing power supply.

As we passed over where Great Atlantis had once reigned supreme, our dreams in the acme of their ascendancy, I tried again not to think about it too much. Tried, but without success. The luster of those dreams . . . how brightly they would have illuminated this planet.

Long ago Earth would have become our clockwork Kingdom, everything ticking along in a model of absolute order and control.

As we neared the Middle Continent on the other side of the waters, I had to further drain our power, my hand reaching to activate Proteus.

I had no choice in that.

Were we sighted by anyone, the word might get back to Enki. Then things would change again in a way I did not like to contemplate.

What chance would we have then against his control? Control of not only the great Mother Ship that had brought him here, but all the technology available to him at the Space Station on the peninsula named Sinai . . . plus his links now with the ultimate power of King Anu on the Home Planet Nibiru.

As of now, we were only a few outcasts, long considered dead . . . I did not want to substitute the actual event for what at present was only a false conception in the mind of Enki.

With Proteus working, and placed on Blend, we were to any observers whatever our background happened to be at the moment . . . and thus in effect invisible.

I had to chuckle to myself. Softly, so as not to waken Bronti who slumbered in the co-pilot's seat now beside me. Chuckle, yes, and why not . . . as a person who always had appreciated irony?

Because I was using Enki's invention, Proteus, to conceal myself from him in the hopes of eventually . . . and I vowed I would do it, though it take eternity . . . removing his treacherous person from the Earth he had so defiled.

****

The Great Pyramid and the Sphinx are imposing sights . . . anytime and from any perspective.

Under moonlight, from the air, they definitely have a magic about them.

I circled high above them at first, looking the situation over carefully.

Well, we Anunnaki are expert in the construction of pyramids. There must be over 200 of them on Nibiru . . . and I am sure that many have been planned for the Zeta Reticuli 2 planet, should it ever be decided on as the new Anunnaki home.

A pyramid does not take that long to construct, nor is it beyond a medium range of difficulty. At least not if you have lasers with which to cut the big stones, and tractor beams with which to neutralize their great weight and put them in their place.

Of course you have to have, too, every procedure, no matter how minor or miniscule, on record in a Protocol . . . as we have long had. And of course trained technicians.

I, Yahweh, as one of my former duties with Enki had been administrative supervisor of the construction of the Great Pyramid in Egypt, the one I circled now so high above.

So I knew something about what myself and my companion on this mission, Bronti, were looking at.

I emphasize I was an administrative supervisor of the pyramid project . . . and as such I was not concerned with technology so much as assuring that all was carried out in an orderly fashion with adequate records being kept.

I was never one to dirty my mind with the intricacies of technology, even though Enki himself defied Anunnaki royal tradition in doing so. My concept was much higher. I was Aide and Chief Advisor to Enki and, consequently and correctly, far above such mundane details, which were for subordinates to carry out.

When all knowledge is incorporated into Protocols classified and stored on wafers . . . it would be folly and below my class to mix into the work of the technicians, no matter how much the rebel Enki himself did it.

My technician was sitting beside me even as we circled now, ever lower over the Great Pyramid.

Bronti, as an engineer, knew just about everything in a technical way there was to know about the pyramid. He had worked on the installation of the electronic gear, including the crystals and the recharging system. Not only that, we both had been privy to the codes involved . . . so I figured all would be open to us.

Open to us, that is, if as I had calculated, there would be no sentry on duty.

If there was . . . or any kind of security guard we could see from the air . . . I was prepared to laser-stun him, then pacify him.

That way, hopefully he would have no subsequent memory of us, or what we had done . . . would merely think he had fallen asleep, especially since we would supply him with a very sexy dream to take the place of what really happened.

But we saw no one.

I swept low and slow into the shadows of the pyramid to make extra sure of that.

No. No one.

In the process I came head on into the face of Enlil!

In the moment it was quite a shock, my nerves already on edge as they were on this precarious mission.

Suddenly to see Enlil's giant image rushing at me like that, seemingly like some dream spun out of moonlight and my own fears . . .

Of course it should have been no surprise.

Because it was no news to me that Enlil as Commander of the First Expeditionary Force before the Great Deluge had chosen his own visage to represent the higher element visible in the Sphinx.

Recovering quickly from the shock, I swerved our Military scout craft deftly away to keep my distance from it.

No damage done.

So far, in fact, I thought, so good.

The next question to be answered was . . . was there a night watch inside the Pyramid?

I didn't think so, as I had been at pains to explain to Enlil.

As far as anyone knew, Enlil and I and all our forces were ashes scattered across the ocean floor beneath the former Atlantis . . . and had been now for something like 4,000 earth years. And there was no other threat to Enki's unchallenged rule over Earth.

Still . . . as I said, I would have myself set such a watch were I still
Enki's Aide as I once had been.

Why?

To keep my forces on the alert, which was also good for discipline. And if there were no crisis, I would have manufactured one,
just to keep them sharp and on their toes.

But Enki . . . it figured he would go in the opposite direction.
Not to keep anyone unnecessarily awake when they could be home
asleep. Oh, no . . . not him.

Sometimes he made me sick. Often, in fact . . . something I had
to be careful to conceal when I had been his Aide.

The question I had always wanted to ask him was this. Did he
not realize that to the inferior Earthlings, and even to some Anunnaki
he was a god? And so must comport himself and be always arrogant
and demanding . . . because otherwise he lost respect.

But . . .

It was a principle he never understood, or was contemptuous
of . . . for all his great genius in genetics and invention.

Well, if you have no aptitudes to be a god, then you should
not be one . . . deposition was your eventual and richly deserved
future . . . though not by Destiny but by character default.

But there were many rungs on the difficult ladder of ascension
into Heaven . . .

I stood now just at the bottom of the ladder, even though I might
in the moment be once again high above the Great Pyramid.

****

I set the ship down softly in the sands on the side of the Great Pyramid that lay deepest in shadow.

Bronti and I then got out and walked to the North side . . . there
we found the secret entrance we both knew about that would give us
ingress with the right laser taps on its surface.

The panel slid back and we stooped and stepped inside the dark and musty passageway just before the panel automatically closed again behind us.

Besides our laser guns, we each carried a small laser flash which Bronti now used to light our way forward.

Not forward solely, however. Our way was also up.

We were headed for the top area of the Great Pyramid where all the electronic equipment was distributed.

We kept eyes and ears open on our ascent past the familiar corbelled arches . . . any unexpected sight or sound and we were both ready to act with our weapons.

And one came.

A grating, abrasive, urgent sound . . . like a cry . . . out of the black interior ahead. I grabbed for my laser gun and held it at the ready . . .

****

The cry was repeated.

Then ceased.

"What was that?"

I felt Bronti breathing hard beside me . . . before after what seemed a long time he answered my anxious question.

"Pretty sure nothing. Scary, but . . . I think just the contraction of the great stones with the cool of the night."

Cautiously, we continued.

****

Now we were near the top of the interior space of the Great Pyramid.

Where in niches and particularly designed recessed rooms rested the nerve center of the whole electronic system.

As to details, as always, I, Yahweh, as an administrator, was lost.

The overall picture, and maintaining that always firmly in my mind, was my talent . . . not the picayune piling on of technicalities that only served to blur that vision. Bronti knew about that, was in charge of that. I could not burden my mind with it. To do so would have put us both in danger. So Bronti now had to be my guide as to what specifically we had to do next.

But one great thing was already established, something that followed from my astute analysis of the mind of Enki. An analysis that gave us entrance where another of less deep thought would never have dared advance.

There was no night watch. That was Enki's weakness, his too careful consideration of the convenience and comfort of others . . . turned to our advantage through my own astute reading of his deeply flawed mind.

Bronti stopped, hesitated, swore softly. Then set silently to work. After a little time, I saw him throw a switch.

Above us the Great Crystal suddenly came to vibrant life. It sparkled and scintillated and threw down a million spears of light.

But Bronti was not through.

After fifteen minutes of frantic activity . . . I could see him coordinating sine waves on the small control screen . . . he stopped and reported confidently. "Ready to charge in twenty minutes."

"All right. Good. Meanwhile, while we're here . . . other things."

I wanted to check communications with Anu if there were any. There were.

Bronti found the right wafer, flashed its contents against the interior wall of the pyramid.

I took a few minutes to scan the series of communications. Their essence showed us that the gold mining mission was still underway, that the planet Nibiru was apparently still in a state of stability due to the continued infusion of gold particles into the atmosphere. There was no mention of us. No mention of the dead . . .

All right. At least now I knew.

"The Protocols. The Master Protocols. I have to have them."

I saw now in the light of the scintillating Great Crystal the site where, unless Enki had removed them, they had to still be.

Nothing revealed the presence of a wall safe. You had to know its exact location. Which I did . . .

Then you had to know the code. Which I did . . .

Three brisk taps . . . a pause . . . two taps . . . and then another three.

If I had got the location just right, then the sound-activated mechanism should make the metal plate holding the glass enclosed precious set of wafers slide out . . .

But nothing happened.

By quick visual triangulation I calculated once again where the exact center of the little safe should be. Tried again.

Three . . . two . . . three and . . . a rectangular section of wall slowly slid out towards me.

And I saw them, gleaming in the light from the Great Crystal overhead . . .

Our entire civilization lay there within a ridiculously small perimeter. They were . . . they were literally the keys of the kingdom.

Who had them had the way to do anything, achieve anything. The fruit of millions of years of knowledge transmuted into practical instructions that anyone could follow. Even Enlil, I thought.

"If I take them, the alarm will sound," I said. I knew that as Enki's former top Aide, as did Bronti as one of the chief pyramid engineers.

"I can deactivate the alarm for ten minutes only. You'll have to move fast."

"Do it."

As soon as Bronti finished his keystrokes on the control panel, I acted, trying to restrain what I deeply felt . . . which was covetousness . . . greed at the potential of mastery that lay before me . . . and tried to concentrate solely on the physical actions I had to take.

I took the three little glass boxes in my trembling hands. I opened the first one.

My eyes devoured the electronic wafers inside like my mouth did the edible wafers that had kept us alive all these years. They were very similar except these were smooth . . . electronically smooth. "Not much time."

I slipped the contents of the first box into the capacious drawstring bag that dangled from my neck. Quickly I did the same with contents of the second and third box.

"They . . . at some time they're going to notice the boxes are empty," Bronti said hesistantly. I saw he was afraid of angering me, as indeed he should be. As all subordinates always should be.

"No. No they won't."

"Why is that, my master?"

"Because if you can give me another ten minutes . . . I'm going to make duplicates and put the originals back. They'll never know we were here."

As Enki's Aide and Chief Advisor and Communications Administrator I had once had an office right here. I went there now and found it as I had left it. It looked bare, with only a crude desk and chair, both fashioned from pyramidal stone. But looks could be deceiving.

I found the series of buttons behind a sliding panel in the wall and pressed in my code. Another panel opened up to show various pieces of electronic equipment. My only interest now was to see if the electronic duplicator was still functional.

It was. I began the process of duplicating every one of the Protocols.

The Protocols included a protective system that did not allow them to be duplicated. But that system could be overridden, though only by Enki and myself. And that was through means of a secret code . . . one which all these years I still remembered, and pressed in now.

"The time," Bronti said, a little desperately, with one eye on the alarm.

My duplication done, I quickly put the boxes back in their original position and closed everything up. The wall was seamless again and there was nothing to show I had made the theft that could change the history of Earth.

****

Bronti stayed inside the pyramid to orchestrate the charging process.

My job was to bring our Military scout ship into position and keep it there while lowering the charging cylinder.

This I did with, if I say so myself, deft expertise.

The charging process started.

I saw multi-colored lights dart up and down the charging cylinder.

There was a humming sound gradually growing in intensity.

This was not new to me. I had done it once before. I knew that in thirty minutes we would have a charge to last at least 10,000 Earth years.

To me it was more like opening a door. The door to our future . . . we the dispossessed, the true and rightful administrators of not only our own future, but also the fate of Earth and eventually of what I hoped to make the Anunnaki Empire.

****

On the way back, over the Middle Continent, I asked Bronti to explain to me more about the charging process . . .

More to pass the time than anything else.

I didn't want nuts and bolts like a technician wants. Just the overall process in an easily understandable microcosm of words and concept for my own knowledge and possible future use in the manipulation of the levers of power. Of course it was all there on the Protocols dangling from my neck . . . we both knew that.

But he seemed to understand what I was looking for.

"The Great Crystal does it all. It gathers the electrical charge and amplifies it exponentially, then shoots it up the charging cylinder of the ship."

"Yes, but what happens to make us have power for another 10,000 years?"

He was flattered, I saw, by my question. Assumed an almost professorial air. "Well, it's simple enough. You know of course, my Master, the ancient formula of $E=MC2$ . . ."

"Every schoolboy does. But . . . what does that mean here in the recharging process?"

"Just this. We are taking the Pyramid's enormous energy . . . amplifying it through the Great Crystal, making it reverberate upon itself until it has incredible force . . . focusing and concentrating it through the recharging cylinder and into the Motive Power Box inside our own ship."

"Yes, yes . . ." I moved my right hand impatiently in the air. "But . . . but what happens then, eh? Inside the box . . ."

"Good question, my master. Well . . . what happens is that all the enormous energy concentrated into the special matter inside the Motive Power Box charges it far beyond what might otherwise be expected of it. There is even spontaneous creation of some new matter, I believe, from the vast waves of energy unleashed."

All right. I had an idea at least of how it worked. But I probed for more. It might someday be useful. "But the Crystal, where does it get its energy?"

He threw me a doubtful look. "But, my Master . . . you were there when we did the work. When the outer coatings of the Great Pyramid were applied, the thermocouples laid . . ."

"No. No, as a matter of fact I was called away that week on other . . . urgent business."

That, as it happened, was the truth. Though I have forgotten now the name of the beauty who called me away from the Pyramid work.

"Oh, yes. Well, it's simple enough. The thick layer of gold paint on the outer surface of the pyramid, a layer of neutral limestone mortar and a final layer of the gold paint on the exterior of that. That is your basic condenser, and the giant thermocouples then just keep it charged . . . highly charged."

"But the enormous charge . . . how does that get to the giant ruby crystal?"

Bronti shrugged and gave me a ghastly smile. But then . . . what other kind of smile could he . . . or I . . . give, with our still emaciated, almost skeletal faces?

"Through the accumulator. It's a little complex . . . brushes attached to a rotating sphere constantly collect the charges and feed them into a unit we call an electronic dynamo. It can safely hold everything we put into it until when it's needed. Then the release can be gradual . . . as in our charging . . . or sudden. Then in effect it becomes a generator of lightning bolts which we can direct towards any enemy."

Now he was getting to what I really wanted to know.

"Could we . . . could we hit Enki from the Great Pyramid?" The ghost of a plan began forming itself in my mind.

The ghastly smile returned. "Not if Enki is at his headquarters on Mount Olympus or at the Space Station in the Sinai Desert."

"Why not?"

"It's line of sight, my Master. Line of sight only. He's much too far away."

The ghost of a plan dissolved into nothing.

That was all right. I always had plans. If one died another quickly rose to take its place.

In the east, the sun burst over the horizon.

I was beginning to feel a little elation now. At least we had power . . . in more than one sense . . . and I had seen that Enki's state of preparedness was just what I had calculated it would be . . . basically non-existent.

The sheep would be asleep because the Shepherd himself slept when Wolf decided to launch his attack from the depths of night.

Instead of the glorious dawn like this one engineer Bronti and I were witnessing, the last light Enki would see . . . would be the flash from the detonation of a nuclear bomb.

I, Yahweh, when the time came, would see to that.

On the trail of that thought I had Bronti bring us two flasks of blood and organ essence mixed with fruit juice, and ten wafers each. We drank an extended and exuberant toast to the success of our enterprise, and nibbled down the wafers.

****

I was eager to return home with the spoils of our raid on the Pyramid.

I had the precious Master Protocols and with those we had access to every bit of Anunnaki knowledge ever collected, with practical plans and instructions as to how to implement whatever it was you wanted or might ever want. The Protocols were the building blocks of our entire civilization. It was a treasure, much more valuable than all the gold ever wrested from the mines of Africa.

That plus the Military scout craft was now assured of full power for at least another ten thousand Earth years, no matter what strenuous endeavors we might put her through. Without the use of this ship, we would have been lost.

Of course I could not head straight home, much as I might desire to.

No, not quite yet.

There was still the third part of our mission, but I was in no mood to unnecessarily draw that out. I called on my previous knowledge as Enki's Aide, then, to abbreviate it as much as possible.

I headed us towards what I already thought might be the most likely place . . .

I speak of where we might eventually establish our base of operations in the Middle Continent. Not too close to any of Enki's enclaves, of course.

And in a location that offered us the advantages we had to have. Secrecy. Concealment. A place from which we could establish our dominance over the Earthling populations and safely bring them into our cause. When the time was ripe, that is . . . which it was not yet. But these things had to planned out well in advance if they were to be successful.

The sea I had originally designated on my first rudimentary map I made so long ago for Enki as the Mediterranean, or Middle Sea, sparkled below us from the rays of the rising sun behind us.

There was the large pensinsula that I had called Iberia extending into that sea . . . and as we flew over it I could see it now was fairly thickly populated. That is, there were to be seen settlements, some kind of rudimentary agriculture and even an occasional village. We swooped low over those with no fear of detection since I had Proteus going full force.

There just ahead was a large island off the coast of this peninsula which I had my eye on. Our inspection showed it was as yet unpopulated. I thought it might be a possibility for our base.

We then flew north for a look at another area I had in mind. This was the neck of the peninsula that was mostly mountainous. I wove us through that collection of difficult mountains and liked what I saw. No Earthlings. So that, too, was another possibility.

I had enough for my Reconnaissance report to Enlil. I pointed our craft if not exactly towards home, well, towards whatever you might choose to call the place where exiles stay while they wait one day to go truly home.

****

Enlil was happy, Enlil was not happy.

He was happy about having the Military scout once again in full power operation, but worried that Enki might somehow detect our nocturnal visit to the Great Pyramid. I assured him that last was not likely.

He was happy about our having the Master Protocols again, but didn't seem to understand their pivotal importance in our situation.

I had to draw it out for him.

The Big Picture, however, didn't completely satisfy him. He wanted something more immediate. So I gave it to him.

"Cloning," I said. "We are still sterile, though one day we have reason to believe we will not be. In the meantime, if we can clone ourselves . . . it can lead to more control over the native populations for one thing."

He didn't know what that meant, I had to elaborate.

Then I told him how I now looked at the Big Picture.

Enki was on Earth to stay. The gold mining was something that would apparently continue for the foreseeable future. I told him how I had examined the key recent communications between Nibiru and

Earth, between King Anu and Enki, and how that was their gist. Nibiru would be saved, but only at the cost of Enki assiduously continuing to pursue his mission of mining Earth's gold, using the Earthlings to do it.

But . . . I made it clear to him. We could carry out the same mission . . . and much better than Enki. We would not betray Anunnaki principles in the process . . . we would maintain the sacred hierarchy which was what had made us great and which would preserve us always as a great civilization. We would not be subject to the failure which was endemic to Enki's mistaken policies, his pathetic attempt to be a friend to Earthlings . . . an obvious impossibility and innately treacherous in its very conception.

I told him that of course we had to strike at Enki. And strike hard. We would have our sweet revenge against his treacherous attack on us.

That would be the final step in what must still be a slow and careful process.

What we could do . . . what we must do . . . first . . . would be to take control of the general Earth populations. We would start here in the Western Continents. We had total control already of the fiercest band of warriors ever seen since our fantastic group on Atlantis . . . the Su.

Now we must expand our dominion. We must in the same manner take control of every tribe on the Western Continents.

Having done that, then we must establish our base on the Middle Continent, and begin our campaign of making those populations loyal to us, and to us only. I told him of my reconnaissance, gave him my recommendations as to where that base should be established.

At the right time, then . . . then we should attack, using our single remaining nuclear bomb to destroy Enki. We would then be the sole rulers of Earth and would administer it in the right way, not the Enki way. That would impress Anu, and with Enki justly annihilated for his treachery, our Exalted Ruler Anu would have no choice but to select Enlil as his successor.

All this was somewhat repetitious, but then, with Anunnaki

royalty, that was what you needed most to get your point across . . . repetition.

And patience.

And a feigned humility beyond imagination.

****

I was eager to put the new plan into operation. But there were details to attend to first.

I delivered the complete Master Protocols to Doctor Atra, instructing him to scan them all in case he might glean any new information on how to bring us back to complete health from our massive dose of radiation poisoning.

Then I was ready to set off on the first stop of what I was now coming to call our Pacification Program. It was actually nothing more than conquest and domination, of course, but applied in what I thought were cunning ways. Those ways I had pretty well perfected in establishing our marvellous state of symbiosis with the savage Su tribe.

I saw no reason why we could not use the same system to bring both the Western Continents under our complete control and command.

And so . . .

My first trip was to be but a scouting venture . . . but having my complete plan already in mind it would be easy enough for me to make a rudimentary map of where the principal populations were located, and how far each individual kingdom would extend and all the other logistical questions that needed to be resolved . . . in only the broadest of strokes at this stage, of course.

I really needed no help on this venture and so I planned to go alone. I welcomed the solitude, actually. That way no one could put arbitrary limits to my dream . . . I would visualize it my way without the static of interference or someone else's lack of comprehension of what I had in mind.

And then on the morning of my leaving . . .

Enlil sent for me.

****

"I have changed my mind. I don't think it best that we should waste time and effort on dealing with these savages here in the Western Continents."

Changed his mind, eh??? Sometimes he acted very like a woman, I thought, this supposedly great Enlil. What he told me next confirmed that thought.

Something could go wrong with my plan, he said. Any group of savages at any time could revolt against us . . . kill us all in our sleep, he said.

I pointed out to him that would never happen. The Su lived in total awe of us. They, or any other tribe, would never revolt against their god.

He seemed unconvinced.

What he wanted was to maintain the status quo with the Su, nothing more. Continue to nurse ourselves back to health, using the blood and internal organs of the savages slaughtered on an ongoing basis by the Su.

I told him that was fine as far as it went. But some day, in the Grand Plan of Revenge, we had to go after Enki himself, wrest control of this planet from his treacherous hands.

That got a rise out of him, I saw it in his eyes, the glisten of hate . . . but it only lasted a second or two.

"Go on your mission. I give you permission after all. See what you can see. But I mislike your idea. Still, on your return we can talk. How long will it take?"

I told him I would be back in 3 months maximum time, no matter what. He seemed pensive, but finally nodded assent.

I sensed he had some other idea in his head, one of which he obviously at this moment did not want to talk.

It upset me deeply, because in the end his word was law. And I wondered what he might be thinking . . .

****

My reconnaissance trip . . .

I will tell only the highlights here. First I headed south . . .

I found an interesting tribe near the large gulf towards the lower end of the northern continent. They were different from the Su . . . again Enki's adaptability gene had allowed them changes to adjust to the environment, or so I conjectured.

They were physically smaller than average, but from what I was able to observe they were mentally more acute.

Their women were exquisite.

I tractored two of them aboard and leisurely took my pleasure with them. I pacified them first so their memory of the experience would most likely be that of a strange, exotic dream.

And it was strange and exotic . . . for me, too.

I might have been a monster in appearance to them, and yet I'm sure I quickly became some kind of saint . . . as far as the obvious pleasure they took in my very assiduous and extended attentions. A nightmare turned to sweet dreams, I am sure far beyond anything their rude and savage male counterparts could ever offer.

I continued my journey south . . .

****

In the lower continent the populations were sparse and widely separated. That, I thought, had two sides to it. Less Earthlings meant a smaller force . . . yet as far as control, it would be easier because potential opposition would be less.

Bitter memories and old dreams of glory were both stirred inside me as I passed over the site where our Invincible Army had annihilated an entire tribe in a single thrilling morning.

How glorious our future seemed then!

For a while I lost myself in reverie of Atlantis. I realized still once again what, thanks to the perfidy of Enki, we had lost.

Then I forced myself to snap out of my momentary depression. If I did everything just right, and given enough time, we could still regain it all.

****

At the tip of the southern continent, I had hoped to find a truly advanced tribe.

After all, they were the oldest. The ones who first had ventured across the northern land bridge from the old world to this, the new. They should have had more cultural development.

But they didn't.

On the contrary they were even more primitive than the Su. The Su at least had a single burning desire around which they built their lives. That desire was to dominate, to be the masters of any other populations in their territory.

But these people at the southern end of the continent . . . had no passion. Perhaps it was because they had no opposition. No opposing tribes to fight against.

Their women were so unappetizing that I did not beam any of them up . . . some of them were as hairy as the men, who in themselves seemed more ape than human . . .

****

Coming north up the west coast of the southern continent, I again found an interesting tribe.

They lived principally high up in the mountain range that paralleled the coast.

They had the desire to conquer and dominate, I saw, which was good.

And their women were exotic. Slanted almond eyes and turned down mouths. The contrast I found exhilarating.

I'm sure a pair of them found me exhilarating, too. Even if only in the memory of what they thought was a pleasant, stimulating dream . . . where they were entertained by a very exotic kind of monster . . .

****

There were many other tribes I examined in my exploratory travels, but none of them were exceptional.

My work finished, I returned to the Anunnaki station, well within the three month time limit I had pledged to Enlil.

But then, as I approached . . .

What I saw from the air was quite a shock . . .

****

I circled around the area several times.

Our own enclave looked normal, just as it should.

But where were the Su?

Had they abandoned us? Had the unthinkable, that I had told Enlil could never happen, happened?

I hoped not.

****

Doctor Atra met my landing, and told me the situation.

The Su had been struck by an epidemic. What it was he did not know . . . it was outside Anunnaki knowledge. From the time it first struck to a month later . . . that had been the last life span of the Su . . . they were all dead, not a single survivor.

I felt my heart contract with that news.

The only good news was that we Anunnaki seemed resistant to whatever viral infection that had swept the Su into oblivion.

I was not impervious to the irony of the situation. The Su . . . the conquerors . . . the obliterators of opposition . . . had in their turn been conquered, been obliterated. Not by any human opponent, but by some microscopic marauder who showed even less mercy than the savage Su themselves.

The irony did not end there. Doctor Atra told me the Anunnaki were not in good shape either. The supply of blood and wafers had run low and was on ration. They could not harvest the Su bodies for fear of being invaded by the virus . . .

****

But then the very next day the picture changed somewhat . . .

It is never good to depend too much on the reports of subordinates, however trusted.

There were some survivors of the epidemic after all. This I found myself by walking around and looking inside the conical huts made by tying together leaning tree branches.

I had my belt Proteus turned on to make me appear as the same saintly figure we always projected around our camp.

I did not want to touch these surviving Su myself for fear of contracting the mortal disease, but I ordered Doctor Atra to have them rounded up and checked. This he did using our two medical technicians who undertook the actual work, of course . . . and the results of their examination was something of a surprise . . .

There was no trace of any virus in their systems. Apparently these few . . . there were twelve of them . . . for some reason had some slight difference in their DNA that made them impervious to the onslaught of the virus.

Our situation, I realized, was ambiguous and somewhat perilous in this sense. Doctor Atra could not be sure whether we were immune or not . . . it may well have been just our separation from the Su that kept us from being sufficiently exposed to contract the disease. Therefore I made a suggestion to him which he thought about somewhat doubtfully at first, but then later heartily approved, even insisted on its being carried out. I got permission from Enlil, and the strategem was executed.

It consisted of this. Two of the survivors were beamed aboard the Hospital ship that night. They were pacified, and then painlessly made more grist for Doctor Atra's perennial mill. So when I say the strategem was executed, it was a well-chosen mode of expression, implying a double and apt application of the verb.

The next morning each of us drank a toast to the late twosome, and ate ten wafers concocted from their blood and vital organs. The wafers were as always practically tasteless, and the blood that formed our toast, refrigerated until it smoked and mixed with some local fruit juice that had a peculiar sharp spicy tang to it, once again was not at all bad. After all, after drinking it now for so many milleniums, it would have been strange indeed had we not developed a certain taste for it.

The rationale, which was the basis of my idea, was this . . .

since these Earthlings, these particular Su, survived, their blood and internal organs which were immune to the assaults of the virus, might well make us immune also.

In questions of survival, there is no profit to be had in taking into account anything like sentiment. The very term itself was something anyway that should never come into play when talking about a savage, vastly inferior race. Enki might stoop to that, but never Yahweh. I, Yahweh, would always have the best interests of our ancient race, its traditions, its history and its future, uppermost in my heart.

****

In the light of what had happened Enlil now had to take a different view of my plan of Pacification of the Western Continents.

Clearly we could not stay where we were. With no new blood and wafers to sustain us, we would die as the radiation poisoning would once again establish its supremacy over our internal organs.

We lifted off and I circled the area a few times as just, I suppose, a way of saying goodbye. I felt the Su had been fortunate enough to fulfill a vital role for us under the difficult circumstances in which we found ourselves. I was sorry to lose such a fierce tribe who would have been the model for my Invincible Army in this lonely, backward part of Earth. But what I had learned would not be forgotten and would now be applied universally across both continents.

As we made the last pass the remaining ten survivors, four men and six females, came out of their tents. Their behavior was interesting. They raised their arms upwards towards us as if to stop our going . . . to their primitive minds maybe such a procedure even appeared to have a chance of working, who knows?

Then they fell to their knees and clasped their hands together. I could see their upraised faces working spasmodically as they tried to comprehend what was going on. It was, of course, completely beyond their very limited powers.

I made a mental note. Someday I would return. Because it was just possible these ten survivors might be able to regenerate their savage race. And if they succeeded in that over a period of years, it would be foolish of me not to use again that fierce power to help in my goal of totally dominating these two Western Continents. As for the immediate moment . . .

I knew the closest, safest place for us to go, and was ready to lead the way there . . .

****

The Mah-Yahs they called themselves.

I followed basically the same procedures as with the Su, with a few new flourishes as the circumstances permitted.

Using Proteus I flashed the image of the generic saintly figure across the sky over them, this time putting it in the form of a slow dissolving hologram.

That way, they saw it in the sky for a couple of days, before we even landed.

And so they were preconditioned to accept whatever would be offered by these obviously supernatural beings.

We positioned ourselves not far back from the edge of a white limestone cliff which dropped off to a kind of cistern or well far below.

And waited.

For a very brief time, actually. Then before our locally projected same image of what they must have supposed to be a divine being, just as I hoped, various tributes were offered up to us by bowing savages.

The most important, of course, was food. That was cooked,

quantious, and delicious. We didn't know what it was, but ate of it ravenously.

There was drink, too, in big casks. A white, milky liquid which we quickly found had a kick.

No doubt but what it was alcoholic. Highly alcoholic.

It quickly lifted our spirits.

Mine in particular. I saw success ahead with my proposed plan over the long future. And as for the stimulating present moments, all we Anunnaki were entranced.

We knew we had fallen into something big . . .

Especially when I tractored aboard twenty of the youngest, prettiest women . . .

The milky liquid, the stimulus of the new, different, exotic females . . . it all combined into a wild celebration inside the Hospital ship, which lasted half the night.

****

We quickly with the Mah-Yah tribe got back on to something like our previous schedule with the Su.

It worked out along these lines . . .

The high priests came before our electronically projected icon, bowing and scraping.

I beamed them aboard for an audience before me exclusively.

I first activated my belt version of Proteus, of course, so I looked almost as saintly as the icon.

I told them we were divine, had come from Heaven. That we were prepared to be their gods . . . to lead them to dominate a vast region . . . if they could prove themselves worthy of us.

Tribute . . . the prepared food was good and similar tributes must continue every day.

But beyond that . . .

We would collect every opposing warrior slain in battle as a sacrifice. This must be done, because should they fail to slay other tribes, then we must take sacrifices from their own ranks . . . that choice was up to them. But the great forces that controlled the rising of the sun and the advent of the stars at night must be appeased.

Also . . .

Those same forces demanded the sacrifice every week of a certain number of their youngest, most attractive virgins. Twelve of those.

Only in that way could their continued existence and success as a tribe be assured.

****

The weekly sacrifice of the virgins, I must say, was always a highlight of our activity.

It went something like this. The high priests had their altars directly across from us. We were of course, due to my astute selection of our site, on the higher side above the waters of the cistern, so we could watch the entire ceremony.

Not only watch it but with our augmentation lenses, could minutely study the physiognomy and features of the faces of each and every girl brought to be sacrificed to us. This was always interesting . . . to watch the facial expressions of the victims. Strangely, most were resigned to their fate and apparently accepted it, some kind of tranquil almost transcendent expression on their faces. Only a few exhibited the facial contortions . . . the working mouths and fluttering eyes that denoted panic and terror.

The sacrifices were done one by one.

Typically, the first girl either jumped or was pushed by the priests over the sheer side of the natural limestone cistern. We watched her plummet the thirty feet into the dark waters below.

If she were exceptionally pretty, or if someone in our group expressed a desire for her, we tractored her up as soon as she bobbed terrified to the surface . . . to the Hospital ship for group or individual pleasure, before delivering her up to Doctor Atra.

Others we sometimes let sink as genuine sacrifices to us.

Of course if we were in any way short of blood or wafer supplies we might just tractor her, pacify her and make her immediate grist for Doctor Atra's always hungry mill with nothing sexual going on between.

Had we not been still sterile it might have been different. Had we been potent, then it was to our interest to produce a great number of hybrids. These would be intensely loyal to us, would raise the general quality of the savage tribe and would let us get on more expeditiously with my plans for conquest of the entire Planet.

Then I would have electronically tagged the women, returned them to the tribe, and if and when they became pregnant I would have monitored their offspring and worked them into our general plan.

This was a subject that Doctor Atra and I had many discussions about in the ensuing years . . .

****

It was my opinion that since we were sterile, it might be worthwhile to now at least experiment with cloning.

It might help us establish our Western Empire in various ways. The clones could be trusted. They would be like us. That at least was my first way of thinking.

Of course, in our damaged physical condition that was part of the basic unanswered question. How much like us would they really be? Would they be like us in our present monstrous state . . . or would they prove to be the beautiful gods we ourselves once had been and now scarcely remembered?

Doctor Atra didn't know the answers to those questions, and of course I did not either. But what I wanted him to do was try . . . keep trying.

He dedicated himself for years to deep study of the Protocols I had stolen from the Great Pyramid. We lacked equipment, the specialized equipment required to clone. Instruments, the special laboratory set-up . . . that was not part of the standard equipment for a Hospital ship.

But over time he improvised.

Came up with something.

And at last was ready to at least experiment.

He cloned me. Took a cell from inside my cheek and put it into one of the scraped off, hollowed out eggs of one of the virgins.

He let that combination progress for a certain time inside a glass bottle. Then it was time to nurture it with a mother.

I was present by request when he placed it inside the womb of a pacified virgin tractored up from the cistern into the Hospital ship.

He marked her electronically and I returned her to her tribe.

Eight months later we tractored her back up for her delivery.

Only Doctor Atra and I witnessed it.

Neither of us was favorably impressed.

The newborn was definitely not something to be impressed by. Pale, underweight, undefined . . . I suggested we terminate him.

But Doctor Atra said no. As the experiment it was, we needed to see how it would develop. From failure, however ghastly, perhaps we could somehow formulate a future success.

****

We raised our monstrosity aboard the Hospital ship. We did not dare to let his mother raise him with the tribe.

What would they have thought of us, their gods, as the fathers of such a pale, weak being? Our domination and our status as gods might have disintegrated right there.

The strange entity grew and passed finally to adulthood. An adulthood as none of us had ever known or seen.

It . . . I hesitate to say him, although technically it was male . . . was about two thirds my height, but only half my weight. It had no hair to speak of anywhere on its head or body. Its mouth was a slit, its nose and ears only suggestions of what they should be. Arms and legs thin, far too thin. No musculature. It frightened me. It was like some kind of ghost . . .

I concluded my DNA was still so damaged by the radiation of Enki's treacherous bomb blast that destroyed Atlantis that this terribly weak specimen was all that could be presently produced.

I was almost glad we were sterile. Because who would want to ever have children that looked like this?

A child that looked not like a god, nor like a devil, either . . . but something perhaps like the ghost of the latter.

****

But Doctor Atra stayed my hand, the hand that out of shame would have destroyed his pathetic attempt at a clone.

And it was well he did . . .

Because, against all expectations on my part, in a strange way, my clone was to prove over the long run to be useful.

Physically he was very weak.

As a god, or as the son of a god, he was a total failure.

But casting all that aside, as a servant . . .

He was superb.

His personality was totally bland. He was compliant, content, took little nurture and almost no nutrients . . . emotions were something he apparently was not blessed . . . or cursed . . . with. He followed any orders of ours specifically, explicitly, with no questioning. Was apparently tireless and needed very little sleep.

After long observation I at last forgot my ego, forgot he was a clone of myself, and accepted him for what he was.

Not a reproduction of me, not a god, nor even the equal of a savage Earthling.

No . . . but all the same . . .

Something we badly needed.

****

In consultation with Doctor Atra, we decided that for experi-
mental purposes, the best thing to do would be to clone each one
of us twelve. Maybe my cloning for unknown reasons had gone
asymmetrically astray. Maybe the others, or some of the others,
would come out right . . . with godlike beauty.

So he went ahead on that basis and the interesting thing was
this . . .

They all came out just about the same.

Twins of my clone.

Doctor Atra concluded, as I had long ago, it was all due to our
still damaged DNA.

My next questions to him were these . . .

When, if ever, would that change? Could we ever again expect to reproduce ourselves in our original images . . . as proud
Anunnaki . . . superior physical specimens, beautiful and . . .
gods as compared to the crude and savage Earthlings?

He did not have a definite answer to my questions.

But his study of the Master Protocols I had stolen from the Great
Pyramid was starting to produce other results.

The regimen he had put us on milleniums ago. It was further
reinforced by what he had found in unexpected, isolated spots in the
electronic wafers of the Protocols under sometimes inappropriate
headings.

He had put them now all together.

What made the program really work . . . compressing centuries
into decades . . . was something he had not had accessible to him
before through the very limited medical protocols of the Hospital
ship.

No. These protocols detailed the one nuclear disaster on Nibiru
milleniums in the past and how it had been dealt with. That plus
some isolated cases of radiation poisoning that had happened accidentally during laboratory experiments.

What we were already doing was basic and correct.

But to accelerate the process, if we wanted to do that, then we
needed to add something. A catalyst.

The problem was that such a catalyst only existed on Nibiru. At least according to the Protocols.

It was a vegetable compound extracted from certain cacti on the Home Planet.

Obviously we had no access to it here on Earth.

****

We quickly fell into a routine with this tribe of Mah-Yahs.

In many ways it was as symbiotic as was the relationship with the Su.

Certainly they were not as fierce nor cruel as the Su had been. That was a disadvantage in my plan to conquer and dominate every tribe in the Western Continents.

At least so it seemed at first.

But as time went by . . . and I am talking of several centuries now . . . I began to see them in a different light.

Physically they were small, yes, but it was on the mental side where gradually certain qualities made themselves more and more apparent to me.

For one, they were somewhat curious.

That in itself was an astonishing phenomenon.

The Su always accepted things as they were. Some of their tribe were killed, well, they immediately accepted that as fact and did not dwell on it. Even though the slain might have been in life a best friend, or brother even, it did not matter. Things were the way they were and that's how they were. Things happened and they never once inquired into the reason why they happened. As a matter of strict fact, I do not believe the word "why" was even in their vocabulary. And I am not making some abstract point, here. I mean the word itself simply did not exist, or at some point had dropped out of their usage. So they had no verbal handle to grasp at in a search for under-standing. And, to my observation at least, there was never any such search.

In this, the Mah-Yahs were somewhat different. Not vastly, understand me, but somewhat.

They actually had the word "why" in their vocabulary, and perhaps for that reason, sometimes . . . it was rare enough, but sometimes . . . actually wondered about things.

I knew this from personal conversations with their high priests. Of course I had my Proteus belt activated to make me appear something like the god I once was . . .

They actually wanted to know about the Great Heaven they saw above them in the tropical night sky.

How it worked, what it all meant . . .

They were so bold, a couple of them, to ask that.

Not that I was going to tell them anything like the truth. That might have shattered their very limited and delicate minds into a thousand bits. And anyway, according to the Protocols the revelation of such knowledge to backward tribes was strictly forbidden. And I, Yahweh, was not Enki, the devil rebel who dared defy these sacred orders . . . and I would never be.

No.

What I did, however, as the centuries progressed, was to give bit by bit selected knowledge about how to observe certain patterns of the celestial bodies in the night sky.

Gradually it entered into their consciousness, the idea of the recurring seasons as governed . . . so they thought . . . by these same recurrent patterns in the night sky. It became an important part of their religion, whose mainstay of course was . . . we ourselves.

I again encouraged the belief, as I had done so succesfully with the Su, that to maintain this great clockkeeping procession across the night skies, which in turn was what kept Earth from imminent destruction and what kept the sun rising each day . . . to maintain all this it was necessary to regularly sacrifice Earthlings. This was for the greater good of everyone, I let them know.

It was an important stimulus in encouraging them to constantly be at war with all the neighboring tribes within a reasonable radius of their own base.

War meant pleasing the gods, meant maintaining the life of the fragile Earth. Since blood and slaughter was the constant ingredient to keep their universe from self-destructing, it only made good sense that the necessary victims whenever possible should not come from their own tribe, but from the captured prisoners or slaughtered warriors from the tribes surrounding them.

Added to all that, they had the absolute assurance they were the chosen people . . . the only tribe which had contact with the gods.

These psychological and religious factors gave them immense confidence in combat . . . something which I noted down for future use . . . and served to make them almost invincible.

And I, Yahweh, if I ever noted any dimunition of their confidence, would make sure to make a personal appearance in their next battle. I would let show the Military scout ship hovering above our troops . . . which in itself would strike such awe and fear into the primitive hearts of the enemy tribe that it almost assured immediate victory.

On occasion I alternated that with the religious icon, the generic one, so that the opposition would know to whom they should in the future pledge all their loyalty . . . those who survived, that is, if any . . .

I even, as time went by, saw some rudimentary exhibit of original thought among these Mah-Yahs. Someone among them actually built a kind of crude calculator in stone in an attempt to plot the positions of the planet we call Venus against the time when they should plant their crops.

I gave my approval to this because it was roughly correct, and very necessary to our own survival.

A couple of milleniums went by this way . . .

****

The way of life we led with the Mah-Yahs was very seductive. In a way we had fallen into our own trap.

My policies had created a tribe that met all our needs without us having to do anything much.

It was an easy life. More so for the devastated beings we ourselves still were, our normal ambitions paralyzed because of our physical afflictions caused by the traitor Enki.

We might still be monsters, yes. But in the interim, we were, in our very special circumstances, still living like gods.

We had beautiful, delicate, petite, perfectly proportioned exotic women in never ending supply to satisfy every sexual need.

We had a continuous supply of a wide selection of exotic foods prepared for us in ever changing styles.

Our daily blood and organ essence quota was something that was always met. And we felt ourselves growing ever so gradually stronger, if not yet better looking.

In addition . . .

Now we had twelve clones who could take charge for us of every mundane duty. They would perform perfectly any assigned task. If the assignment were risky, or onerous, as in the harvesting of blood and body organs from the legions of victims slain in battle, I sent the clones to do it, while we watched from the safety of our ships.

They had a power of their own, working oddly in our favor I saw at last.

They drifted like ghosts across the lives of the Mah-Yahs doing whatever duty I assigned to them.

And we did not lose face with this. Perhaps that was because I put in periodic appearances myself, walking through the villages of the Mah-Yah and with my gestures extending blessings to right and left. Of course this was done with my belt Proteus activated so I appeared as the same celestial being they had seen for so many centuries in our projected icon.

And so the clones came quickly to be seen as lower beings than the gods, but still supernatural, and who carried out the gods' wishes . . . which is what they more and more came to be, for us as well as them.

I thought my plan for my Pacification Program was going forward and working very well.

Obviously it was time to extend it, now that I knew all its parameters. And I began to do so.

****

On one of my reconnaissance flights, preparatory to launching a campaign to consolidate both continents into the final unity, out of curiosity, I went by our old site where the Su once reigned with such fierce authority.

To my gratification, I saw a small village of their crude conical tents. Yes, it was only a hundredth part of what they had once been. But it was incontrovertible evidence that they had at least survived.

I swept low over the little village.

And saw a sight I shall not soon forget. As the word spread, they all prostated themselves beneath me. On their knees, alternating their arms first to the ground in abject surrender, then raising them towards me, their eyes amazed.

I knew it would be easy now to reinstitute my former success with them.

But I had to wait until later. There were a hundred tribes ahead of them in the Great General Plan for total domination of the two Western Continents.

And later in my flight I saw something of potential importance as I swooped low over a kind of unpopulated desert region.

My intuition told me to take action.

So I did.

And brought back to our Mah-Yah headquarters a large collection of spiny cacti . . .

****

Doctor Atra made tests on every one of my cacti.

None captured his attention until the last. His analysis told him it was almost a twin of the cactus described in the Protocols . . . the one that acted as a catalyst in the curing of radiation ills.

For our next day's creation of bloody cocktails and wafers he added generous proportions of the cactus into the mix.

The day after that he checked us all with a variety of medical tests.

And I saw a little smile cross his seared face as he correlated the results . . .

****

That smile I had seen on Doctor Atra's face soon became contagious.

Because within three months the results became visibly reflected in every Anunnaki countenance.

Not that we suddenly regained our former godly comeliness. We did not.

But still . . . change . . . change for the better . . . was apparent.

Doctor Atra himself was exuberant when I at last asked for an informal report.

"We will continue this regimen . . . it speeds up the healing, I calculate with a factor of ten . . . this . . . this is sensational!"

So at last . . . at long, long last we were moving ahead. I threw myself now with renewed vigor . . . partly psychological no doubt, but also partly physical . . . into the task of making both Western Continents forever and irrevocably ours. Two massive land continents stretching almost the complete distance between the poles with very diverse populations . . .

That diversity of the populations was another consequence of Enki's irresponsible insertion of the adaptability gene into the Earthling's DNA.

I had known that for a long time, of course.

But now I was able to do something about it.

In fact, I thought my policies had done much to counteract that dangerously entropic tendency. Not by any genetic technology, no . . . but by my mastery of the techniques of effective subjugation of inferior tribes.

Religion . . . my brand of religion . . . based on a single deity with its comcomitant abject worship and mortal fear. That was the mechanism I had set in motion and that I would see through to ultimate success.

Soon all that Enki-inspired diversity would be melded into one single overriding belief and one single overriding desire. Belief in one god with the deeply ingrained, almost instinctive compulsion to dedicate their lives to serve that god . . .

****

The Pacification Program continued to go well.

It required us to move around, of course, spending time with each new tribe until all our policies were perceived to be firmly in place.

I saved us a lot of time by dividing our procedures up into stages. After stage one we might move on to a new tribe which I had chosen to dominate the other tribes in their area. Returning years later we would institute stage two, or three, which was the final one.

Still, because of the distance and the diversity, it took us some 800 Earth years to complete the entire program.

I called for an official celebration to mark the event, and Enlil agreed.

It took place high in the mountains that paralleled the western coast of the southern continent. I had earlier noted this tribe as one of the more interesting ones. For one thing, their women had large almond eyes which was a particular fascination for me, and perhaps the main reason I wished to hold our victory celebration on their mountain premises.

But they had other qualifications, too, that made them rather a far cut above the Su and other savage tribes.

When I first contacted them they already had a perfunctory interest in gold. They did not understand it or its uses . . . just that they were attracted to it. With my Proteus belt giving me the image of the sacred icon, and accompanied by three of my clones, I showed the high priests something about how to mine the gold and how to work it. They had actually shown some initiative in continuing the practice after I left them, so that now a few golden artifacts were in existence. I took most of them in tribute, of course, as was to be expected. But there was the prospect that much more could be produced.

At the height of our celebration, drinking the local liquor which had a nutty, oily flavor and was of high quality, though very strong . . .

I decided to send our twelve clones down on an important

errand . . . to bring us back from the custody of the high priests twelve selected virgins.

We then seated the maidens in twelve golden chairs molded and curved to comfortably accommodate the human form, which I had ordered specially constructed for the occasion.

Their rolling wild almond eyes were not rolling with terror. That had abated with the application of electronic pacification, plus their generous libations of their native liquor. Now it was anticipation . . . desire . . . a mad lust, as naked and primitive as their gleaming bodies . . .

Why should they not desire us? We were the gods, the supreme beings who regulated their lives, who gave them knowledge and who kept the golden sun in the sky and the bright stars steady on their courses through the night.

I made a sudden decision in the midst of the wild ecstasy of that communion. When it was over I would not pass these women to Doctor Atra to process. No, for the first time ever I would not do that. I would go against my own procedures.

And no, I had not lost my senses or my judgment. The mirrors told me everything. The mirrors I had so studiously and assiduously avoided for so many milleniums . . .

And this was the mirrors' long anticipated message.

That suddenly . . .

Incredibly . . .

I was not so bad looking. Not at all. To the extent that I didn't blame these women for now wanting to climb all over me. Who knows? They may have wished to do the same even without pacification.

My body had by this time finally come into some kind of conjunction with its former self. I was muscular and integrated into a form very reminiscent of what I had once been, if not yet entire.

My face was interesting. Not yet my former face, no, which had sent many Anunnaki women into a chaotic state they did not fully understand . . . on many occasions, I had seen them abandon professed principles and goals in the presence of a beauty that made a powerful statement of its own, against all politics and social mores and normal caution.

My eyebrows were not quite back. They had been plush as black velvet once. They still lacked luminescence and softness but they were in a state of replenishing themselves. So my eyelids, so long absent of hair. Now they had at least half of their former dense growth of lush eyelash. The yellowed portion of the eyeballs was once again in the process of becoming almost white.

Most important of all, my former scraggly looking scalp, punctuated only here and there with sickly hairs, had been rejuvenated. Now I had again almost as generous an allowance of black and lustrous hair as previous to Enki's treacherous attack.

And so . . .

I did not blame the young virgins for their all out lust against me, their assault on the fortress of my now strong and well-shaped body. My muscles rolled and snapped with my every movement. I was something once again like an Anunnaki male . . . as I saw in the scenes of the passion that was all around me, were the eleven others . . . including Enlil who seemed totally lost in the events taking place before our astounded eyes.

My idea of the celebration was as only a prolog, really. A prolog of many marvelous things to come.

For now that the Western Continents were ours, I knew it was time to move on. We wanted the whole Earth, and we would never have that while Enki ruled the richest and most productive part of the planet.

But with the West under our exclusive and complete dominion, I thought next would be the Middle Continent. And with that taken, we would be ready at last to move against Enki, ready to smash him into oblivion . . . the oblivion he had so monstrously planned for us.

But then something went wrong . . .

****

Maybe it was the gold. If I had left that out of the celebration, perhaps everything would have been all right.

Because maybe that was what triggered something in Enlil's mind. Of Nibiru with its golden curtain, the whole reason for our Earthly mission in the first place.

Anyway, when I talked to him later . . . after I had ordered returned the twelve virgins to their people . . . when the celebration was over . . .

When I presented my plans now for the Pacification and Domination of the Middle Continent, I received a shock.

His obvious reticence and lack of enthusiasm for what I was proposing astounded me.

And then it came out.

Yes, it might have been the gold that triggered his sentimental memories of Nibiru in Enlil's mind.

Or maybe it was an idea he had entertained now ever since Nibiru's last passing near Earth.

Whatever it was, the effect of his idea was undeniable.

What he wanted to do shook me down to the very marrow of my being . . .

****

It was a radical plan, full of danger.

Of course I knew the time for Nibiru to swing once again close to Earth was approaching.

We all knew that.

But Enlil . . . words almost failed me to contest his idea, it was such a surprise to me. First, that he would have the mental ability and perspective even to have conceived it. Second, my instantaneous recognition that it would put everything we had worked for in jeopardy. Desperate jeopardy.

Anu. That was the centerpiece of his plan.

Enlil figured his father Anu would take advantage of the proximity of Nibiru to Earth to pay a ceremonial visit, as he had done sometimes in the past.

He wanted to talk to his father. Before his father had a chance to talk to Enki.

He wanted to . . .

Intercept the Anunnaki ship while in its orbit preliminary to landing.

The personal contact . . . he thought that could sway everything our way . . .

My heart sank at his words . . .

****

As I said, Enlil's unexpected diatribe seemed to throw everything I had planned for into chaotic confusion.

To such an extent I spent a sleepless night after listening to it.

What part of the night was left after our wild celebration.

But then, the next day, in some unguarded moment of the mind when it came at me from an unexpected angle . . .

I saw it in a different light.

Maybe . . . just maybe . . . there was a chance that it would work.

I considered that for the first time in a positive light.

King Anu was aged. The sight of his son who he had considered dead for all these years . . . that would have an emotional effect, a blow for us to the center of his psyche.

Agreed.

But what I had tried to tell Enlil the previous night was that Enki would already have presented a different story to Anu. Making us look like the villains of the terrible nuclear episode. Indeed I had seen an implication or two of that in the correspondence I had to so quickly scan inside the Great Pyramid during our night visit there on the recharging mission.

On the other hand as I thought about it now . . .

What if, yes, it all went the other way?

That Anu believed Enlil.

Then Enki would be removed from power on Earth. Enlil would be the ruler.

I thought about it even further. Anu would want Enlil close to him as he felt his time to go perhaps was not too distant.

Which meant, as Enlil's second in command, I would be appointed to rule Earth . . .

I thought about it.

And the more I thought, the more I thought it was maybe worth the tremendous risk.

At any rate, in the end, if Enlil said it must be that way, that was the way it would be . . .

****

The Protocols gave us the information we had to have to entertain even a hope of carrying out Enlil's idea.

Including the ideal time for the launching of Anu's ship to effectuate the easiest entry into Earth's atmosphere . . .

Of course the ship could be launched any time and still enter Earth's atmosphere, but there was no reason to believe it would come at any but the most efficient, easy time.

Since normally only one orbit was required previous to entering Earth's atmosphere, we made our own plans accordingly.

We would be when the time came, as close as we could calculate, already in that optimum orbit. And ready to come alongside the Anu ship, communicate, and later dock with it. So Enlil could go aboard and make his plea. Perhaps change history. His own, and that of the Anunnaki . . . and of course mine.

If Enlil failed to convince, on the other hand, the prospects were nothing short of horrifying . . . it could mean prison and ignominy for all of us.

But . . . Enlil was Enlil, the natural son of our Exalted Ruler, King Anu . . . and I was only his second in command.

I saw of course one advantage to his plan. If it succeeded, there would be no combat. There would be a bloodless transfer of power with no casualties, no risk.

Enki under Anu's edict would be retired from command of Earth under the shadow of disgrace at the very least. Enlil would be Supreme Ruler of all the Anunnaki, if not immediately at his father's wish, then certainly in the near future when the aged King Anu would die.

Such an eventuality, or something like it, was what I hoped for . . .

****

The next time I saw Enlil I told him his plan was brilliant. And strangely, this time I wasn't lying. There really was a certain simple ingenuity to it. After milleniums of waiting, everything would be settled in a matter of a few hours. Of course, that was a double-edged sword . . . and I hoped that neither edge would end up being aimed at our necks, which was a real possibility.

We watched the night skies impatiently for weeks, awaiting the arrival of Nibiru. Then, when it did arrive, we spent days studying it through our two rudimentary astronomical telescopes. Even those were not strong enough to show us any detail on the planet itself. But we thought we might just catch a glimpse of a big Mother Ship leaving orbit for its rendezvous with Earth.

That did not eventuate, however, and our time window for optimum entry was fast approaching.

I took a co-pilot with me since we would be doing detailed work in the rendezvous and docking. He sat beside me while Enlil sprawled on the special sofa he had insisted be installed for himself back in Atlantis, his royal body comfortably ensconced on something like six pillows, his complete attention during most of the flight apparently absorbed in manicuring his fingernails.

I found it almost irritating me that such a genuinely inspired idea could come out of such indolence and a highly exaggerated air of general boredom. Such posturing to me did not seem to be such as would inspire confidence and loyalty in his subordinates, and it was an attitude I told myself I would never assume once in supreme power . . . and yet, it had its grotesque opposite side of the coin, too.

That is, his air of total relaxation in a way did inspire some confidence after all in the outcome of the mission. In the sense that, if the Commander were so unperturbed, then a logical conclusion might also be that there was nothing to worry about.

Of course, such conclusion was based on the supposition that Enlil knew what he was doing and was conscious of all the risk factors involved . . . and that, to me who knew him, bordered on fantasy in itself.

Still, everyone can be right once in a while. Maybe this was Enlil's turn.

As we say on Nibiru, even a stopped clock gives the right time twice a day.

The Military scout, this particular one, is not designed for interplanetary space travel. Orbit is the closest it comes to that, and for orbit it is adequate. The metal alloys involved in its construction even without a heat shield are enough to withstand the heat of re-entry.

Of course it helps that our computer system, as I understand it, keeps constantly varying the re-entry angle microscopically so as to effect a more gradual clash with the atmosphere, which causes consequently less generation of frictional heat.

Nevertheless there is a heat shield which can be extruded, and I planned to use it. Why not? An additional safety precaution which would also result in less wear and tear on our valuable and absolutely indispensable Military scout was something I could hardly afford to ignore.

But then if our rendezvous conference should prove effective, the scout would no longer be indispensable . . . we might have all of Anunnaki technology and equipment again at our sole disposal.

I kept that thought in mind. Through all the long hours that followed . . .

****

Days had gone by. The window of opportunity had passed.

It was obvious to all three of us that, for whatever reason, Anu had decided not to send a ship to Earth this time.

And yet, that made no sense.

Nibiru had never yet failed to send such a ship when its orbit swung close to Earth . . . not since the mission to mine gold had first begun. Well, except for the time when Earth suffered the Great Flood, which all the high officials on Nibiru had been advised beforehand was coming.

So . . .

What was going on?

Enlil insisted we remain for a couple of orbits more, even though scientifically now, there was no hope. I indulged his royal nonsense without a murmur, because that ability is what has put me where I am today and I know it. My respect for him, or lack of it, neither rose nor fell with this decision of his. It was something I was long since accustomed to.

Anyway, the extra orbits gave me time to think. About what might be going on.

There were at least two possibilities.

Maybe King Anu simply decided not to send a ship this time. For whatever reason. Okay . . .

Or . . .

And this one hit me like the proverbial flurry of asteroids . . .

What if . . . what if the Great Migration had taken place?

!!

What if the Anunnaki race were now living comfortably on their New Home Planet? So far away in Zeta Reticuli 2?

If that were true then the planet we were looking at . . . our ancient home Nibiru . . . might now be a dead planet, as to its any longer harboring the sacred race of Anunnaki.

Other enticing thoughts came to mind that made my heart seem to rise in my chest as they processed themselves through my brain.

If that were true . . . that Nibiru was now an abandoned planet . . . then it brought with it a necessary corollary.

Enki must also by this time have abandoned Earth!

After all, there would be no further necessity for his mission.

In such case, he, too, must now be on the distant New Home Planet in the constellation Zeta Reticuli 2.

It had to be.

Which meant, in such case, we were at last the sole gods of Earth.

I really wanted nothing more in life than that. Enlil might be the ruler in name . . . but I knew well that in actuality the ruler would be I.

I, Yahweh.

****

In subsequent days I pondered my next task.

I had to communicate all this . . . the meaning of the non-appearance of an Anunnaki ship from Nibiru to Earth . . . to Enlil gradually, day by day over a considerable period of time . . . so that his delicate emotions could permit him to absorb it.

He had, I suppose, constructed all kinds of mental blocks against it, thinking exclusively in the great triumph of his plan.

He was never exactly what you would call adaptable.

I prided myself on being that, to the maximum grade. A necessary quality for survival.

The question was . . . what to do next?

We were living our comfortable symbiotic life again back in the mountains of the southernmost Western continent.

That life seemed to have a message of its own. That it was not necessary to do anything new or dangerous because . . . because this life offered us everything.

And it did, it truly did. Security. Worship. Adoration. An endless supply of exotically beautiful young women. An equally inexhaustible supply of food, well prepared and tasty. Our daily supplies of blood and the wafers compounded from Doctor Atra's centrifuge . . . which in combination, and now with the new cactus catalyst, were rapidly leading us back to our former beauty and health.

But I had to find out the truth, which at last I made Enlil understand. Was Earth our planet now to rule?

If so, we could openly continue with our Pacification Program now, not only in the Middle Continent but in Mesopotamia and Africa . . . the entire populated Earth.

And we could take over the Space Station on the Sinai Peninsula. The Anunnaki ships would be there no longer, true. But the basic installation with all its technology would. As long as we acted expeditiously enough to keep it from destruction by the barbarian human hordes.

Because when the master is away, the apes will play.

We could also have access to the Great Pyramid, which was our Power Station and also a place of refuge in case of calamity or natural disaster. Now it would be for us, not Enki.

Lastly, we would have Enki's private residence and personal headquarters on Mount Olympus! I had seen, when quartered there myself as Enki's Aide, the vast array of technical advances there integrated into the overall architectural and residential beauty. Enki had his own laboratory on Mount Olympus, extremely advanced. Cloning, restitution of DNA . . . if we needed any of that, the absolute best place to possibly find it would be there.

We had failed to destroy it previous to the disaster of the destruction of Atlantis. All right. Perhaps there was justice to be done after all, at last . . . we would have it now as our own private domain.

With all those keys to power there was no doubt. We would rule Earth . . . in the true Anunnaki way, not Enki's deviant way.

For how long? A million years. Most assuredly. And barring unforeseen negative consequences . . . probably a billion. As a beginning . . .

We would be the Emperors of Destiny, never to be forgotten.

****

Those were my dreams.

Not dreams, really . . . logical, hard-headed conclusions.

And I fully expected to find that was the true situation.

But then . . . with Enlil's permission at last, I made my

reconnaissance of the Anunnaki area on Earth. The area where the Great Mission had been carried out and . . .

And I was cautious . . . prudent . . . as a great military Commander should be.

I activated Proteus. On Blend. To reflect to any observer from any angle nothing more than the background behind me, but not the physical presence of my ship.

I went to the heart of the matter immediately. The Space Station on the Sinai Peninsula.

In my mind I had expected to find it deserted. To swoop down and land and exult and entertain myself walking around its premises just like a new owner properly should . . .

But I saw them from on high . . .

The great Mother Ship. And four other ships parked there.

What was this . . . ?

My mind reeled at the sight.

****

My next destination was something I needed to keep firmly in mind as I tried to recover from the shock of what I had already seen.

That destination was Mount Olympus. Enki's personal residence and headquarters. Though, to tell the truth, now it was a formality only. I no longer had any hope that he was far away in the constellation Zeta Reticuli 2.

But en route I made a wide swing to the east and I passed over areas of Mesopotamia. And there I received a second shock, perhaps even bigger than the first.

It could not be. Impossible . . .

****

After that, my reconnaissance of Mount Olympus was almost an anticlimax.

But, still dazed, I forced myself to methodically note down the presence of Enki's personal gold Flagship parked alongside his main headquarters building. It was no surprise after what I had already seen in Mesopotamia.

Who else could be the treasonous author of that atrocity?

I headed back to report the devastating news to Enlil . . .

****

If I felt dazed at all this, it was nothing to Enlil's reaction.

He had hardly yet resigned himself to the fact his own plan had resulted impossible to carry out when the expected visit from Nibiru did not materialize.

He was still petulant about that.

But it had begun at last to dawn on him that as a consolation prize we would inherit Earth . . . without combat or struggle.

Now, my news that that was not the case . . . that Enki and all his forces were still here . . . left him visibly upset. Beyond upset, puzzled.

Then I had to report the last incredible part. What I had seen as I ranged far to the east and then north from the Sinai on my round-about route which took me eventually west back towards Mount Olympus.

Beautiful, fully developed cities in Mesopotamia. In my overflight I counted seven of them.

Enlil's large eyes rolled, he spread his arms wide . . .

"What . . . what does it mean?" He seemed to be asking the heavens the question as much as me. But I, as always, was the one who had to answer.

I spelled it out for him in seven letters.

"Treason!" I shouted the word. "Treason still once again. That is what it means. Your brother has sold out now completely the heritage of the Anunnaki to the savage Earthlings!"

I saw the hate instantaneously start to well up in his eyes. But it was not yet sharply focused. That was a problem both temporary and easily resolved.

I went on.

"These were Anunnaki cities that I saw . . . not anything the ignorant Earthlings could ever develop for themselves . . . not without at least another million years of evolution. These were Level 3 cities, up even to a few of our lowest level on Nibiru!"

"But . . ."

Here I dared to interrupt him. "Yes, of course, Your Excellence. Immediately your sharp mind goes to the essence of things. And you are right. All this is not only against all Anunnaki policy and doctrine concerning the Earthlings . . . it goes against the very core of what we are as a race. It is an atrocity. To blatantly share this way the hard-won secrets that have cost us millions of years of work and hardship to develop . . . with an ignorant and dangerous people so inferior. Who ironically are our own creations."

"Who were . . . who were . . ." His voice lost its force, failed him.

"Yes, Your Excellence. Who were only created in the first place for Anunnaki needs. To carry out OUR objectives. Nothing more than work slaves."

"And . . . and now . . ." He looked at me imploringly to once again formulate the thoughts that must have been struggling to emerge from his stricken mind.

I obliged him. "And now . . . now he would let the slaves take over the master's house. Worse, he would help them construct houses and cities of their own, every bit as great as those of their masters!"

Enlil turned around once and sat down on a pillowed sofa.

He ran his hands over his now ample cheeks. "No . . ." he breathed.

"Your Eminence it is . . . a slap in the face of Anunnaki history. An expectoration of beings little more than animals into the faces of their creator gods."

He stirred. "How . . . how . . ."

"How could this occur? Astutely put, Excellence, astutely put. The answer is only with the tutelage and full approval of Enki. He is the instigator of all of this. What his motives might be, only the

Creator of the Universe may know. But it seems he has this destructive idea in his mind . . . as we know from bitter past experience . . . this idea that he must be the friend to humankind . . . it apparently flatters him to have their gratitude and their praises . . . beyond all reason . . . beyond all loyalty he owes to his father Anu and the Anunnaki way of life."

It was too much at one sitting for Enlil. He was suddenly waving me away, his drooping eyelids over his great eyes announcing more than any words he could not cope with this.

I had no choice at this royal command. I left him. Before the hatch to his compartment slid shut automatically on my exiting I saw him already prone upon his pillows, the back of his right hand flexed upon his great forehead . . .

****

As usual I had only encroached upon the edges of the extent of the problem that was facing us with this new development.

What it meant to me beyond the elementary discussion with Enlil was much more complex, much more fraught with possible negative consequences for us, our hopes, our dreams, our ambitions . . .

How could this situation come about? It implied one of several negative occurrences.

King Anu at last was in his dotage. Senile, perhaps . . . what else could make him blind to this blatant treachery of Enki which went against all Anunnaki tradition?

Or . . . there had been a revolution. Or a coup. Some kind of change of power. Perhaps Anu had died and some radical Anunnaki had seized the throne.

Or . . . perhaps it was more simple and neither so complicated nor so surprising.

Whatever it was, I had to know. I could fight against anything . . . but first I needed to at least be able to perceive the profile of the unknown enemy that was coming at me from the dark . . .

****

This second mission to the Great Pyramid was different.

Yet it was the same as the first in many ways, too. All I needed was information, for one. For another, Bronti, the engineer, was again at my side.

But this time he was not my only companion.

The other two were pale and ghostly looking. Fragile and very quiet, completely complaisant.

Yes, I had a pair of clones on board.

So useful they had proved to our lives that I wondered what we had ever done without them. Dirty work, they did it, thoroughly and unfailingly dotting the last "i" and crossing the last "t". Most of all, they never complained, were never unpredictable or erratic.

I was secretly glad they had come out so inferior to their originals. They were almost a cross between a robot and an obedient child. More intelligent than the robot and capable of carrying out complicated tasks, with none of the tantrums or emotional upsets of the child.

While, had I been successful in cloning myself . . . my real, complete self . . . I would have had to deal with an intelligence and a guile equal to my own every time I tried to attain certain goals. I realized that now in retrospect and breathed a sigh of relief at not having obtained the original goal.

****

The sky was overcast so as we descended there was no visible moon.

Good. I set the Military scout ship down in the sands beside the Great Pyramid.

I did not expect any change in Enki's security. It had been non-existent before, I expected it to be non-existent now.

But still, now that we had the services of the clones . . . just in case things might somehow have changed . . . the ones who would be lost or captured with luck would not be us. What Enki's forces might have in that case would be two inexplicable beings which would never be linked to us. After all, as far as Enki knew, we were still and always just radioactive dust on the floor of the Atlantic these 6,000 plus Earth years.

So we sat there and waited for the two clones to bring us back what we were there for.

A copy of the electronic wafer carrying all the communications between Nibiru and Earth.

And after a wait that seemed eternal but was no longer than thirty Earth minutes . . . they did.

They had carried out my complex instructions perfectly. With no emotion, no fear. Obviously there had been no night security watch posted by Enki.

But then why should he post one? As far as he knew he was still the sole ruler of Earth, while we . . . we were memories, if indeed we still had any status at all in his twisted mind.

****

And so the whole story came out as back at our current base I went over all the communications between Nibiru and Earth. Everything was made clear as to what had happened and when.

Yes, the Great Migration had been made.

The multiplicity of dispatches made it all clear, step by step.

The undiminishing supply of gold from Earth had indeed continued to save the planet's atmosphere from thinning out too much for Anunnaki habitation.

But then something else that had no solution happened.

And aged King Anu at last, conservative as he was, and desiring as he did to end his life as he had begun it on the planet Nibiru . . . nevertheless at last saw it was no longer any use.

But it involved an ironic twist.

One of the two problems for Nibiru's continued survival had been the lack of heat at the far reaches of its enormous 3600 Earth year orbit. Like a comet and with a comet's periodicity, it had a tendency to become cold and icy in those far reaches.

What had always saved it from becoming so, were the multiplicity of subterranean volcanic rivers. Boiling lava flows that transmitted some of their roisterous heat to the surface of the planet.

These were always considered, and were, life-preserving features.
Until they became too dominant.

The ambient temperature on Nibiru at some point began to rise. The dispatches showed that over thousands of years this rise in temperature began to present a problem for continued habitability. Due to the gold curtain overhead supplied by the Earth mission, the Anunnaki could indeed breathe freely. But their feet began to be too hot, and at the last almost scorched.

Not only that but the heat was a factor that by its changing nature threatened to get out of control. So much so, that some projections showed that Nibiru could eventually explode from its vast internal pressures.

So the decision had been made. King Anu announced it.

The Anunnaki henceforth would have a new home. The planet his late son Enlil had selected for them, the one with twin suns in the distant constellation of Zeta Reticuli 2. It was , King Anu pointed out, Enlil's heroic legacy to the Anunnaki before his being so tragically lost in space and presumed dead.

Anu at first presumed that Enki would abandon the no longer needed Earth Project and join them on the New Home Planet. The dispatches made that clear.

But that was where Enki's twisted personality obviously took over.

He requested permission to remain where he was. What he was doing, he said, was carrying out an experiment. One that could be important. He would of course be subject to King Anu's desires in this.

And Anu . . . I could only believe that yes he was now entirely senile . . . had given his consent. I have no doubt it was because as far as he knew at that point, Enki was his only surviving son, whose love and devotion he wanted to keep, even though his proposal may have been . . . and surely was . . . against his better judgment.

And so everything was explained. All Enki's treachery condensed into two innocuous words . . . "an experiment" . . . as if that justified it.

I saw clearly it was up to us to put things right. That done, it would be Enlil in the position of the beloved and only son. While Enki would be where he deserved to be. Somewhere in the unbounded regions of oblivion . . .

****

We were back at the entrance to the maze of our predicament, it seemed.

And yet we were not. No, we were a long way from that.

I thought about it.

We were not in such a bad position. We had completely dominated and pacified the two Western Continents. All the inhabitants were under our single command via the network of locally dominating tribes.

Our health . . . there was no question it was returning now in a manner that seemed inexorable. All we had to do was to continue to follow the regimen Doctor Atra had laid out for us.

Yes, it involved a great amount of human slaughter . . .

I was sometimes a little sorry for that.

But . . .

The inevitable question it always came down to was this . . .

How else were we to obtain our indispensable supplies of blood and essence of internal organs? Both were vitally necessary to our own survival.

And so . . .

I did not think overlong about this program ever, because philosophically I knew that certain things were eternally true.

One was that the savage primitive humans would always be at war with one another, anyway.

All I had done was take the momentum of that and channel it to our advantage. Now the slaughter was organized and blended cleverly, I thought, into the command structure we had built to give ourselves absolute rule and military command of what amounted to almost one third of Earth.

Now it seemed to me more and more what we had to do next was clear and obvious. That was to gain control of the other two thirds . . .

****

My plan developing in the light of the new knowledge of the status quo was still rough, but it went something like this . . .

First . . .

We would continue to consolidate our dominion over the two Western Continents.

To do that, due to the excellence of the original concept and its application, it was only necessary now to make periodic visits. Or sporadic ones.

The thing was to keep our visibility, yes. But at the same time it was no longer necessary to stay long in any one place. A single appearance was enough, really, I calculated, now to last five or six generations as far as maintaining our rule. The high priests would pass down the traditions and we would be revered and abjectly worshipped always as the gods of Creation, barring any unforeseen circumstances. And in our absence they would always be breathlessly awaiting our return. Praying for it, anticipating it, talking about it, making it the central point of their existence.

Of course we would always be offered whatever we required or asked for . . .

Human sacrifices . . . tribal virgins . . . food . . . total adoration . . . and gold or silver from those few tribes who had it . . . plus, where it grew, our precious cactus, whose juice and fibers had proved to be such a catalyst for us in restoring our health and our appearance.

So . . .

We had all this . . .

And now perhaps it was time to move on.

I already knew where our next base . . . on the Middle Continent . . . should be, due to my previous reconnaissance flights.

The island off the coast had its advantages, yes . . . but after due consideration those advantages paled before the bright promise that the neck of mountainous land at the top of the Iberian peninsula held out for us . . .

It really had everything we needed.

I wanted to make it a real base, not like those easily attacked ones which were quite sufficient in the Western Continents. After all, being nearer to Enki's forces, it was always possible he might discover us, were we too open in our activities. And that, due to his access to superior technology and military force, might well spell our doom.

The site I picked to avoid all those negative consequences was good . . .

In the mountains, with none or very few human inhabitants. But what I visualized to make it even more secure in case of overflights by Enki's forces was this . . .

I had found a rather spectacular underground cavern, one that led into a vast and high-domed area large enough to contain both our ships and also to furnish sizeable living quarters for us. In addition, there was sufficient space still to construct a kind of rude factory. What I had in mind was to begin producing certain things we might require or that might make our life easier. And still beyond that, there was space for us to store things . . . plus move around freely without being under the observation of anyone.

We would also be safe from any nuclear attack there, if it ever came to that again. That was one episode in history that was going to remain singular if I had anything to say about it . . . and I knew well enough that if and when the time came, the same would not apply to Enki and his forces. Thinking they were the only Anunnaki on the face of Earth, they were totally exposed to a similar such attack as had so devastated us.

Convincing Enlil was now not any problem, though he was still in the throes of lamenting the failure of his own plan to contact his father King Anu directly. Now he lacked all direction, which meant I had to be his rudder.

So I started to arrange things.

Not on the Middle Continent. Not yet.

First, there were things to do here. Not only further consolidation, but work in the laboratory of Doctor Atra. I told him exactly what I wanted. Another twelve clones.

He looked at me as if I were crazy. But then he often did when I proposed something new. I considered it an auspicious beginning . . .

****

First of all, we had a big, important question to answer.

Doctor Atra outlined its parameters for me. The twelve clones we now had . . . were produced from damaged DNA, resulting in the strange beings that they were. Beings never before seen in this or any other world.

The question was now . . .

What kind of clones would our DNA presently produce? Doctor Atra thought they might be very like what we ourselves were. Logically, of course, they had to be. Beings who were almost completely healed of their radiation damage . . .

It was something to think about, so I did for a period of several weeks.

And came at last to a startling conclusion. Startling for me . . . because what I originally intended was to produce copies of ourselves, the twelve Anunnaki who had withstood the worst that the evil Enki could throw at us. Then . . . then we would be doubly strong.

But . . .

My mind went back to my earlier conclusion.

What we would be creating might have an equally negative

potential. Beings who might rebel against their creators . . . danger-ous entities that might have as much lust for power as Enki himself.

An internal danger to our organization and to our goals.

Did I really want a twin brother? Someone as wily and crafty as myself to plot against me? It was the second time I had considered that daunting possibility, and I didn't like it any better the second time around. Besides, a new thought had come to me. If I needed a horrible example of what could happen I only had to look at the case of Enlil and Enki . . . brothers totally opposed to each others' goals and mortal enemies in their souls, no matter how much social convention might make them on occasion declaim the opposite.

So, after much thought, this was my decision.

We would not clone ourselves again.

What we would do instead, was clone our clones.

When I first proposed it, again Doctor Atra shook his head negatively and looked at me with that look that clearly said I was insane . . . but then the look dissolved into something else. I saw the dawn of recognition in his eyes, and saw his headshake then assume a vertical direction.

The thing was almost poetic in its resolution.

Our twelve clones had given us service beyond what any of us had ever expected. They could do anything, never hesitated in ac-cepting any task, never questioned any command . . . and worked tirelessly to carry it out.

They passed like ghosts or spirits among the native populations and so inspired their own brand of awe.

They were weak, physically, yes . . . but in conjunction they were strong . . . and in their best attribute, perhaps, of constant applica-tion to the task . . . whatever task . . . they seemed always to prevail.

They would be perfect for the work I had in mind. The work in the Middle Continent, of constructing the vast underground base in the mountains. We had lasers to do the principal cutting and tractor beams to excavate with and Engineer Bronti to supervise all this ac-cording to the Master Protocols . . . but there was a lot of detailed, dangerous work to be done in the execution of the plan. And the clones would be perfect for this.

Doctor Atra, now that he understood everything about my point of view, agreed heartily. But then he explained something else.

It was something generally true about cloning, something I never knew, though I supposed Enki with his strange attraction towards such things, was long ago cognizant of it.

It was this. Clones, due to some of the microscopic processes involved, tend to be shorter than the originals. We had seen it already in our present clones who were only two thirds our own height.

Now, since we were going to clone clones . . . we could expect that the result would be also something like only two thirds the height of the clone cloned.

I thought about that. Concluded it was all right. Not only all right, but again a potential advantage.

Three foot high beings, ethereal, light in weight . . . could get into spaces and work successfully where more massive beings could not.

Of course I was thinking of my projected new underground base in the mountains.

So I ordered Doctor Atra to go ahead with the plan . . . not to clone ourselves, but instead to clone our clones.

He picked some very special Virgins into which to implant the new twelve clones of our present twelve clones . . . though I don't know it would have made any difference about their quality.

When they came to term and were delivered in the big examining room of the Hospital ship, the offspring were strange looking indeed. But we did not have to worry about their care and early childhood. All that we assigned as a duty to our present twelve clones . . . who we quickly saw obviously enjoyed the multifaceted task. In fact, it was the most emotion I had ever seen them express . . .

****

The time finally came when our new second generation clones were mature enough for us to use them effectively. I say mature, even if because of their height not passing by much the 3 foot mark, it was hard to think of them as full grown, though of course they were. As to what their lifespans might prove to be, we as yet had no inkling. I asked Doctor Atra to run a check on one and give me his estimate.

What he came up with was the following . . . the clones yes had telomeres, little caps that limited their lifespan, much as had the humans. His theory was that the radiation damage we had suffered had somehow done that. However, their prospective lifespans, though laughably short by our own Anunnaki standards, were still much longer than that of humans . . . something like 50,000 Earth years.

So we had no immediate worries along those lines, of their wearing out on us.

I felt the time was ripe to begin our rule over the Middle Continent. Once that was established and we had our permanent base to back us up, with two thirds of Earth under our control, I felt we would be ready to strike at the head of the Great Serpent. At Enki himself . . .

****

The new permanent base.

I had to be the ramrod of it, otherwise it never would have gotten done.

Enlil preferred to lie on his pillows and read fantasies, or watch them projected on the wall of his compartment.

Poor Enlil. Of such royal blood and . . . such an idiot.

The Master Protocols I had brought back at much risk to myself . . . their most important aspects he ignored . . . and instead went immediately and thereafter to the entertainment also included in their vast context. The dancing girls, the orgies . . . the silly romances and the scenes of whatever frivolous activity.

Enlil, as always, was . . . a very difficult person.

Meanwhile I had to contend with rocks and dirt and peaks and valleys and mudslides in my effort to contruct us our great new base, our waystation towards eventual total domination of this planet Earth.

If I expected sympathy from Enlil, I did not receive it.

If I expected help, even less.

Or if I only expected a little comprehension of the importance of the project on his part . . . well, once again I was doomed to disappointment.

But I had not expected it. I knew him all too well from many thousands of Earth years of past experience.

So I forged ahead on my own as best I could with engineer Bronti's help. Together we designed the parameters of what we wanted the great base to be . . . then used our lasers and tractor beams to rough hew it out of the very resistive soil and rock of this rugged range of mountains.

The thing that saved us were the clones. They were like living mechanisms that you wound up and then . . . they never ran down. Unlike mechanisms, too, they had minds of their own . . . intelligence, however inferior to our own, still sufficient to deal with all the difficult tasks we gave to them.

After three months we could see at least the broad outlines of our great base. Could walk inside its vast dimensions and imagine it as it eventually would be . . . with a finished interior, everything lined with stone . . . hangars for our ships, living quarters sufficient for all we Anunnaki and our clones and many more . . . laboratory and factory space . . . electric generators installed and working with power outlets in all convenient places . . . water and heat and some electronic facilities . . . and storage spaces and even private offices . . . everything properly lit and looking like some crude approximation of what might have been a military base back on Nibiru.

I calculated another 6 months of Earth time with a lot of hard work on the part of the clones, was all that was needed to make every part of Bronti's and my design come true.

Meanwhile we had another minor crisis on our hands . . .

****

It really was not a crisis.

We had brought with us in our move to the Middle Continent quite a large supply of both blood and wafers for our maintenance.

Yet it was now on the point of running out.

Food. That was another question. Those supplies ran out even sooner. Our ships' refrigerators could only hold so much. And while our underground facilities eventually might have refrigeration, that was still a long way off.

Of course we always had the option of travelling back to the Western Continents and obtaining new supplies.

I considered that. But on the other hand we had to learn to make our way here in our new environment.

I thought first I might take it upon myself to begin solving these problems on site.

I took the Military scout ship out with a co-pilot and four of our clones aboard and scouted out a tribe of people somewhere to the south of our mountain base.

I set Proteus to project our now standard icon of the magnificent, saintly being, radiant and shining.

It inspired enough awe to bring us several slaughtered sheep as an offering.

But it was done in a very clumsy manner.

I had to tractor aboard what looked to be a possible leader, pacify him, and give instructions as to how the meat was to be cooked and prepared in an attractive manner for us.

With time, that worked out well enough, and we were soon feasting again on freshly slaughtered but now well-cooked meat.

As to human blood and internal organs to be processed in our centrifuge . . . that was a separate problem.

We had to forage for it and . . . as usual it was left to me, Yahweh, to figure out how.

My thinking was that at this point we needed a show of force.

So I stationed myself above the tribe with Proteus displaying the sacred icon.

The people gathered . . . pointed . . . looked up. And yet I saw plainly the effect here for some reason was not as great as in the Western Continents. I needed to add some emphasis to their lagging emotions. Perhaps what they lacked was a sufficient hierarchical organization among themselves. In fact, I was sure that was the problem.

So I tractor beamed one of the crowd up to the ship. I pacified him and told him to be the leader of his people, the chosen one. To let them know their god was angry and for their sins against him, he was now demanding tribute.

Ten virgins, the most comely, must be delivered up after exactly five days at this very spot . . . or destruction would rain down upon them from the wrath of their god.

We returned the terrified man to his tribe, ostentatiously so as to awe the people and bend them to our will.

And then "disappeared" as I turned Blend on, and we went back to our underground base to await results.

****

I had plenty of supervision duties concerning the new underground base to fill those five days. And began to see what had begun as only a concept in my mind was finally becoming reality.

But I was hungry in more than one way.

Yes, we needed the food, the human blood and the wafers. We needed too the intimate feel of women. And these women were different from those of the Western Continents. Perhaps they did not have the same wild, savage appeal of those we had enjoyed for so many thousands of years . . . but yet, they being more culturally advanced, the conquest and the taking of them would bring . . . in my imagination at least . . . more ultimate satisfaction.

I figured that five of the virgins, whose body organs and blood should be in top condition, would be taken into a remote part of the mountains and slaughtered for our use.

Not at first, however.

They would be used along with the other five to slake that other hunger we were beginning to feel, even in our weakening condition.

I anticipated the reaping of the fruits of our evangelistic labors.
But things did not work out exactly as I had planned . . .

****

The appointed day arrived and in the Military scout craft I
hastened to the spot and got all in readiness to receive the bounty
I had requested . . .

The sight that met my eyes was strange and unexpected from the
beginning.

There was no crowd assembled to greet and adore us.

Instead, on a nearby hill, what I saw was a crude wooden cross.
And our ambassador, our chosen representative . . . he was there all
right, but all by himself . . . crucified upside down!

****

Resistance.

Resistance by a native populace in the face of force . . . divine
force.

It was something I never thought we would ever have to deal
with.

Yet here it was.

I had to take affirmative, corrective action . . . immediately.

And so I did.

Yes, they had to feel the wrath of Yahweh . . . so that next time
they would be more compliant to our needs.

First, I aimed a particle beam that turned the cross on the hillside
into a funeral pyre, watched it blaze high.

Now, yes, people came out of their village huts.

Using our augmentation lens I scanned the faces of the women. I
picked out ten of the most attractive, and one at a time, very
ostentatiously, I beamed them aboard.

That night we satisfied one part of our hunger . . .

****

And the next day we satisfied the second part . . .

I took them to an isolated part of the foothills and . . .

****

Beautiful sunsets can not last forever, no . . . nor were they designed to. That is their tragedy.

But for us, the gods, life must last forever. And that, perhaps, is ours . . .

After Doctor Atra and the centrifuge finished their work, we had minimum blood and wafer supply for at least the next month.

****

I moved north in my explorations in the next few days.

To the edge of the continent and across a storm-tossed channel until I found myself over a green and fertile land. I came to a place where sheep and sheepherders were prevalent and where rude collections of huts existed in what might be called villages. This was a territory far out of the sphere of interest or influence to the short-sighted Enki, who seemed only to be concerned with his precious Mesopotamia and the gold operations in Africa.

I needed to pacify the region and prepare to bring it under my rule, and I wondered how best to begin that monumental task. And then the problem resolved itself for me.

Some careless movement of mine inadvertently turned Proteus off. I became conscious of it when I saw the shepherds below staring as if entranced directly up at me as I swooped low and leisurely over them in my survey of the landscape.

Immediately I saw how I could turn this to my purpose . . .

My electronic voice boomed down at them. "I have revealed my Heavenly Chariot to you for a purpose . . . know this, and remember it forever. I am the god of Earth looking down on you even now. And I am not pleased. Not pleased at all . . ."

I let them think about that for a moment. I also saw women and children now coming out of the rude huts and peering upwards at me.

Good.

I went on.

"I have given you all this. This great, good green land for your use. And have you praised me for it? Have you given me any of the increase I have blessed you with? Do you think on me and worship me?"

I could see fright in their faces now. Naked fear.

Better.

"So I am . . . greatly displeased. I could wreak my vengeance on you all now as easily as I breathe. From here in the heavens I could rain my thunder and lightning down on you all now until I pounded you into nothing more than dust."

Now the shepherds were falling to their knees in terror. I saw the women weep and the small children grab at their legs for protection.

Best.

"But your god is a god of mercy. Though his patience is not without limits. No. You have sinned against me greatly, however. That must be atoned for. And so I proclaim that you must do the following. Build me on top of your green earth a replica of what you are looking at now . . . a replica of my Heavenly Chariot. So shall your earthly sights be lifted towards my Glory, a Glory you have been blind to for too many years past. The replica must not be of transitory, perishable wood. No. It must be of stone. The greatest, most massive stones you can find, no matter how far you may need to roam to find them and bring them here. To this very spot."

I was hovering above them now, low in the sky so they could see every detail of my ship. I tilted it towards one side and then the other and I could hear their gasps as they contemplated it.

"This . . . this will be my temple. It must be round in shape even as the roundness of my Heavenly Chariot. And of the same magnitude in size, its height to reach by nature of the stones even as you see now the height of my Chariot. Only then will you gain redemption. Only then will you be relieved of the crushing burden of your great sin against the god of Earth."

And then I left them. Put Proteus on Blend and disappeared from their sight, becoming in an instant a combination of blue sky and clouds that fit perfectly into the rest of the heavenly panorama above them.

I was learning. And I thought I had done well.

The task I had given them would bring them together, and would probably keep them working in a united way towards a common goal for something like a couple of hundred Earth years. My hope was that whenever I found the time to return to them they would be a society completely remolded, putty under my thumb, waiting for whatever orders I might choose to give them.

****

The work went forward on our underground base in the mountains.

When it was at last finished we had quite a creation, given our situation and the crude tools at our disposal. When all was in place I wanted to be the first to give it a runthrough, from the inside out and into the air and back again.

Inside the hangar I climbed aboard the Military scout craft . . .

On the control panel I pressed the newly installed electronic button. The huge but very light hangar door slid upwards leaving me egress.

Outside I hovered for a moment over the grassy plateau, then pressed the switch again and watched the door slide back into place. The clones, with their collection of dyes extracted from nearby vegetation, had done an excellent job. Their painting of the exterior of the great hangar door made it appear, even to me at close distance, almost as part of the steep mountain itself.

I stopped again at a hundred feet up to hover and observe. From that height there was absolutely no way to distinguish where the painting began and the mountainside ended. It was all one mountain as far as the eye could detect.

Good.

I flew around the area for a while, then looked for the site of our base while trying to find any telltale signs that it WAS a base. But there were none. The proof was that I myself at first was lost and did not know which peak was mine, since there were three in rather close proximity, each of which had its grassy plateau.

I had at last to depend on a landmark . . . a gnarled and twisted pine bent practically double on an outcropping of rock . . . to get me back home.

Pressing the button, the great door slid open and I moved lightly and easily inside, then closed the door behind me.

The clean, well-lighted space inside with its high dome, where natural crystal incrustations reflected the light like a million stars, was impressive even for me, its designer. I felt well content with myself.

Why not? We were, I was now sure, completely undetectable from the air should any of Enki's ships chance by. Not that I expected them to. It was becoming more and more clear to me that Enki's interests seemed to lie exclusively in the area of Mesopotamia. There was where he had built his magnificent seven cities for what were, I presumed, his particular set of Earthlings . . . I mean the ones chosen to carry out and participate in his great treason and betrayal of Anunnaki ideals and the unconscionable revelation of our treasured secrets.

More and more it grated across the surface of my mind, the impudence, the disrespect, the sacrilege of Enki . . .

But I reminded myself I must be patient. Must move carefully. Success had only one sure way, while there were a thousand roads to failure.

****

In the Earth years that followed I tried my best to stick to the original plan . . . to gradually conquer and consolidate the Earthlings of the Middle Continent.

The work was different here than it had been in the Western

Continents. The people, perhaps because more cultured, were more resistant to domination, as I had seen in our first incident . . . and also less eager to risk themselves gratuitously in the task of conquering nearby tribes. This presented an obstacle to my easily setting up a system similar to the one that continued to work so well in the lands across the great Atlantic.

I needed to work out a new plan.

First of all, they had to be convinced. Threatened, decimated . . . whatever it took I was ready to supply.

And began immediately.

I gave them the carrot of the great Icon, its robed and bearded figure with its outspread arms a kind of inherent promise of succor and salvation. . . . but I did not spare the stick, either, including public atomization of recalcitrants and rebels.

And so proceeding, over hundreds of Earth years, I at last succeeded in establishing a priestly clan that governed, that made the people obeisant, and who we carefully programmed to carry out our wishes. This priestly clan then, ruled at last all the inhabited lands of the Middle Continent, both north and south of our permanent base.

That included the green and fertile lands north of the channel, the land I had visited so many years previous where vast herds of sheep roamed the landscape. I had commanded them to build me a temple. And while it was not quite that, still it was an impressive ring of giant stones, which to their crude and elemental minds at least, represented the Glory they had seen in the skies of my Heavenly Chariot.

And of course I had not allowed our conquest of the Western Continents to fall into neglect, either. We made frequent visits there and spent our time wherever the impulse guided us to go . . . in any case, whether there or on the Middle Continent, constantly enjoying the benefits of our work . . . not only the blood and essence of internal organs of countless slaughtered Earthlings, but also the attentions of the innumerable virgins we demanded be constantly offered up to us.

I calculated we now controlled two thirds of the world. Our dream was coming true a little at a time. Our hard work and dedication were paying off.

The only thing that stood in our way now of establishing the perfect Earthly kingdom . . . the one that Enki should have but never did establish . . . was the despicable presence of Enki himself.

****

Our gains consolidated, I began now to look towards Enki's Empire . . . with what I admit were covetous eyes.

Why not? I was looking to reclaim domains that rightfully belonged to us, say whatever Enki might and undoubtedly had to Great Anu. His lies might triumph for a time . . . but I felt that, with exquisitely careful planning, and the benefit of surprise, we might make right predominate in the end.

And so I began with little incursions . . . short visits right into the lion's mouth. I had to know in all aspects what the true situation was in the domains of Enki . . . the better so to be able to destroy and conquer it when the time came, when the golden and much anticipated opportunity arose.

Did I mention that we were now restored almost to our original godly status? The regimen Doctor Atra had so wisely put us on so many milleniums in the past had now at last rendered results. I had no fear any longer of mirrors . . . often looked into them, and was never disappointed. I saw myself a god again, a true Anunnaki. At last no worse after almost 8,000 Earth years of disfigurement.

It occurred to me that the legions of humans that had been slaughtered in the cause of restoring our lost health and beauty had not died in vain . . . in a sense they were incorporated in us, who would one day soon be the rulers of this otherwise forsaken planet.

We . . . we twelve valiant Anunnaki would change history forever . . . and soon.

There was only one thing missing in our fight to restore what was rightfully ours by birth and history . . . that was our virility in the

microscopic, undetectable visually but still essential quality . . . the
ability to produce children.

We were, even now, still apparently sterile.

We had done ongoing experiments to see if we could make Earthling women conceive from any one of us. We had marked them electronically, retrieved them with our tractor beams and tested them
repeatedly over centuries of time . . . but no, apparently we were not
yet ready to father children.

It was important to be able to do so. Not just for us, or our own
self-concept. No. By producing children we would produce the superior leaders among the Earthlings, the key people who would by ines-
capable genetic connection, lead us on to ultimate and perpetually
enduring triumph.

****

The night sky was overcast, hiding the moon and stars, when I set the
Military scout craft down just outside one of Enki's precious seven
cities.

I told my co-pilot to return for me the following night at the
same place.

I wanted to spend the whole next day gathering intelligence about
just what was going on in Enki's continuing campaign of treachery.

For the two hours before dawn I surreptitiously walked the streets
and observed everything I could. I shook my head in disbelief. There
was no doubt about it. This was a Level 3 city as described in the
Anunnaki Master Protocols!

Not that I had to refer to the Protocols to know that. Even on
Nibiru, in the remotest regions there had been Level 3 cities still in
existence the last time I left it. Though of course most of our cities
were Levels 5 or 6 or 7, while our capital, where King Anu reigned
was of course a 10.

But, yes, I had personally walked similar streets in Level 3's, and
more than once. While it was planned to eventually bring them all to
level 7, such plans were expensive to implement . . . and besides there

was always a certain rustic charm about a Level 3 in its comparatively primitive quality.

A charm I was all too cognizant of now. Because while this city might have been primitive to an Anunnaki, for an Earthling so primitive himself it was wildly inappropriate . . . too much for his savage spirit to be able to appreciate or even utilize in any intelligent way. And so, very dangerous. Dangerous to stability, dangerous eventually perhaps to Anunnaki rule. Something that Enki should know, but did not. Or more likely, in his arrogant way, merely chose to kick aside.

Pearls before swine would be the briefest yet far from most complete way to express my condemnation of what Enki had done in allowing to be constructed his seven cities. But that Anunnaki expression falls short, hardly gathers up all the hundred ramifications of sacrilege and social destruction he had unleashed in building his seven cities here on Earth.

As the sun came up, so did the city begin to pulse with life . . .

Being dressed as I was in my Anunnaki uniform was not too bad, I saw, as it gained me some instant respect. Not, I was quick to note, to the degree it should have. Earthlings should have been taught to genuflect immediately and cease all locomotion until I had passed a respectable distance from them.

Instead, all I got was a sort of salute from the men and a sort of curtsy from the women, both lamentably imprecise. That, I realized, was due to the decadence of Enki and his mistaken belief in levelling himself with his creation . . . which as an idea was way beyond absurdity.

But my rising indignation at what I saw was combatted by an almost equally strong force of nostalgia.

I could almost believe I was back on Nibiru. Even though the people, as to intellectual capacity, were of course in their potential about as the base of a mountain is to its summit, still, appearance-wise there was not that much difference between me and them . . . especially as I still lacked some small bit from attaining my former complete physical magnificence.

Their clothing . . . after so many milleniums among the almost naked savages of the Western Continents . . . it was stimulating to once again see beings completely dressed. With full-length clothes and sashes around the waist, and headgear and shoes . . .

But I had to be careful.

What if I met another Anunnaki and was recognized? The risk was great and pressing, so I did not delay in looking to effectuate its solution.

A tailor shop was open. I slipped inside and its hanging curtains closed behind me. That was all I needed. Electronically I quickly pacified the owner, and led him into the ample back room.

It was early enough that no other customers were in the shop.

Rummaging around I found clothing that came close to fitting, and put it on over my own. So advanced were these level 3 City inhabitants that I had a mirror made of glass in which to contemplate my transformation.

Not bad..

Then, behind the front counter I found currency and coins . . . so far advanced were they . . . took a handful of both . . . and was ready to continue my spying mission with no further fear of being detected.

Before I exited, I awakened the shop owner. There was no danger. He would have only a memory of having dozed off, and perhaps a pleasant dream. Nothing more.

****

I spent a very pleasant day in the city. Though every bit of its architectural beauty and utility was physical evidence of the traitorous mind of Enki, still, with all my resentment of that, I could not help but be carried away by sentimental memories of my Home Planet . . . perhaps made sharper, more poignant by the fact that Nibiru now was a planet devoid of Anunnaki habitation, now a mere memory itself in our long racial history.

After the crudity of the Western Continents, this city was almost heaven.

Commercial shops there were aplenty . . . doctor's offices and apothecaries . . . marketplaces . . . wheeled vehicles . . . a library . . . a university!

I walked through the university grounds, torn between admiring it and deprecating the degree of treachery of Enki, in having so easily and cavalierly given away so many of our secrets of progress to these ignorant and undeserving Earthlings.

I was curious about the books in the university library, so I entered there.

And found dangerous sedition openly in print and on display to the populace . . . to whatever slave might wander in off the streets with no restriction . . . publications incorporating Anunnaki lore on Agriculture, Medicine, Architecture . . . I could not continue my perusal because it turned my heart sick . . . this gigantic sell-out of our carefully garnered secrets to a savage tribe whose only claim to any kind of ascendancy at all was due to what we gave them . . . and nothing more. To compound my growing rage, I had to meet a troupe of strolling musicians playing, however inadequately, upon Anunnaki instruments . . . lutes and other stringed instruments that they themselves never would have come up with in another million years!

When I left the university grounds I was almost dizzy with emotion . . . negative emotion . . . anger and frustration against the traitor Enki.

I almost reeled down a side street and saw a welcome sight. A great fountain whose waters rose and fell in pleasing cascades. I suddenly became conscious that the day was hot, that I was a stranger in a very strange land . . . and I lusted in that instant for nothing more than the healing touch of those inviting waters.

I did not dream that moments later I would be lusting for substances much more solid. Nor that Anunnaki and Earth history were again about to converge in a strange and unexpected way . . .

****

She was not bad looking, the lady who came to the fountain while I was still cooling myself with the waters I misted towards my face with the fanning motion of my hands.

But as soon as I saw her I sat down on one of the stone benches surrounding the fountain.

I needed to do that.

Needed to recline and rest and concentrate on nothing else but contemplating her.

Something about her. Who can say what it was? I, who have had ten thousand women . . . who have fathered hundreds of children, most of them unknown to me . . . suddenly had to have this woman at this time . . . and with the hope of fathering a child by her.

And then . . .

Then she was leaving, taking my aching heart with her . . .

****

I caught up with her down the particular radiating street she had taken.

What would I say? What could I say? That I was a god, member of a race who had created hers?

But why should I say anything at all? After all, all I needed to do was to electronically pacify her and she would be mine.

But . . . in the ontological sense, would she?

I felt the intense need to approach her not as a superior to a slave, but as an equal . . . a dangerous presumption, I admit, and one perhaps destined to unnecessary failure.

Yet I could no more resist its attraction for me, than I could resist the attraction of the lady herself.

This . . . this was real romance . . . not just naked physical conquest of which I had had my fill . . . so, almost breathless, I pursued it on that basis.

Pursued her . . .

We talked. Do not ask me about what. I had to be careful not to reveal myself too much. So I suppose the conversation was mundane and banal, full of commonplaces and vague observations. But there was a second conversation going on . . . on a completely different plane, a silent one conducted mostly between the rapidly changing expressions on our faces, our eyes and the subtle postures of the body that each of us assumed.

Her features were not that outstanding, I admit. But they had a certain inclination upwards, a certain independent haughty air . . . completely missing in the primitives I had been living with for so many milleniums . . . so much so that in my mind at some point our roles suffered a reversal.

Suddenly I was the slave and she was my Queen. My unobtainable Queen.

But I must . . . whatever risk it entailed . . . obtain my Queen.

That was the message my rebel loins passed to my brain now.

I forgot about spy missions. Lost my perspective on almost everything . . .

I found out that her mother had died some time ago and that she lived here with only her aged father.

I had to have her freely given favors . . . or die. I asked her to step out on her balcony sometime after dusk and when she asked why I told her. . . . why to see the moon together. She squeezed my hand, smiled at me and rolled her dark, almond eyes in a most enchanting way.

****

I saw her aged father meet her at the door of their home . . .

From his extreme decrepitude I saw there might be little physical obstacle between my desire and its fulfillment . . . if I knew anything about Earthlings.

It was strange.

Old age . . . something we Anunnaki hardly know even after a half million years . . . attacks humans it seems to us almost immediately after their adolescent years. In fact, human life is in such a constant state of flux that it is not at all remarkable that it is very difficult for humans to achieve anything of any magnitude. Which is, I should state plainly here, exactly correct and correspondent to their status . . . which is that of a slave race, born for service of a mundane variety and nothing more.

But I was thinking about mundane things myself at this moment. Things like . . .

Where was her bedroom? That was all I had to know in my turbulent remnant of a mind. My hope was it would be on the second story, immediately behind the balcony.

I waited to see if I would see her again.

As dusk fell, I saw her emerge onto her balcony overlooking the narrow street . . . and to me, below , that seemed a silent cry for help . . .

And I . . . I was more than ready to answer that call.

She smiled down on me, the Queen blessing her faithful servant . . . then went inside again.

Tonight, I told myself. We had had Act 1. Let the evening wear on a little, take the edge off itself. When the aged father would surely fall asleep . . . then, perchance she would come out again to look at the full moon. Act 2.

Then . . . then, I would be home. Then I might know paradise. And have full participation in Act 3, the all important climactic act. Such was my fantasy.

****

Sometimes fantasies can come true.

This time when she emerged on the balcony things had progressed. For one thing the moon had doubled in size and hung low above the narrow street as if it had exclusive domain there and nowhere else.

My lady fair looked down on me and threw me something. Some kind of fragrant flower, which in the rays of the moon I deftly caught.

All very nice. Much more than that. To me my fate seemed to hang in the balance of her attitude towards me, though my mind told me clearly it did not. I had come to the city on a mission . . . and yet . . . maybe this was part of it in some way I as yet did not fully comprehend.

But I had a big problem now. Between the desire and its fulfillment. There was the physical space that I had somehow to overcome, between me and my love.

And she turned now even as I thought that, and went inside again.

My heart sank. So I was to be shut out at last. This was only a flirtation, one that cost her nothing and left me dangling on the frayed end of the cord of my own desire. I was a fool . . .

But wait . . .

Maybe not so great a fool after all . . .

If my eyes did not deceive me she was lowering a twisted sheet . . . just the idea it was from her bed made her eager slave's heart double its activity.

The muscular expenditure of energy in my climbing was for me like that of a master musician who tunes his instrument before he begins his concert performance . . .

My lips melded into hers . . . we were welded the one into the other for a long time . . . almost long enough for the moon to decide to desert our street and move on to other conquests . . . but I have no idea whether it did or not.

Did she tractor beam me, or pacify me in some way? It could have been . . .

But somehow we were together in her bed and if I were the victim this time, well . . . there never in history had ever been a more willing one . . .

****

Back home at our mountain base I gave Enlil the benefit of my espionage mission.

I thought I was rather clever in the way I played upon his emotions . . . as a great musician might play upon his instrument . . .

pointing out that in the city, which I had learned was called Ur, there were solid emanations of every aspect of Enki's betrayal of our race.

The university alone was really all I needed to make my point.

I had seen the subjects that they were teaching there. Mathematics. Astronomy. Agriculture. Medicine. Law. The Fine Arts. And all the little technological advances that go with those. The damage was incalculable.

To give away Anunnaki secrets like this . . .

It was sedition, it was outright treason on the face of it . . .

It was to have your servants and slaves instead of being, as they should, ignorant and subservient . . . suddenly drunk on unearned knowledge, arrogant and armed for rebellion . . .

The Anunnaki way of life itself was in imminent danger.

The only possible counterbalance that might yet save Earth was what we represented . . . the old, established, proven ways . . . where rank and privilege and prestige still held sway . . . and hierarchy was not a dirty word, but instead the very staff and bread of life.

Enlil was easily enough convinced. He hated his brother Enki . . . or at least he hated his success, which had been gained at the price of Enlil's own apparent annihilation. For him, revenge was what whetted his thirst for living now, and he eagerly looked forward to the execution of that revenge.

So all was in readiness. And yet . . .

Now, strangely, even though we had succeeded in dominating two thirds of the world, exactly as per my ingenious plan . . . I found myself wanting to delay the day of judgment . . . the day when the great sword of vengeance would drop upon Enki and his cohorts.

Not out of any pity for them.

The pity was rather all for myself.

I had to see my lady love again, and carry out our affair to wherever it might lead . . .

Against all my wishes, and much to my own consternation, love had suddenly taken precedence over vengeance.

Which was all right, I told myself. Vengeance could wait . . . love could not.

****

And then it came. One of the greatest and most gratifying surprises of my life since my life was challenged and forever changed by the terrible atomic blast that destroyed Atlantis.

She was with child!

My lady love of Ur was with child . . .

If it really was from me then it was the first . . . the first since Atlantis. And if it was genuine, then it meant so many things and so much to us . . .

That we were no longer infertile. No longer sterile. That the long rigorous regimen of Doctor Atra was at last bearing fruit. Literal fruit. The fruit of my loins made flesh in the womb of the woman of Ur . . .

I felt again like a god . . . like a true Anunnaki.

And if so, if she really were pregnant by me, then . . . while the child might be a hybrid, thanks to Enki's genetic manipulations he would not be sterile and would be able to reproduce.

Our child inevitably would have to reflect the genetic superiority of his Anunnaki father . . . combined with the Earthly beauty of the mother.

So two goals now solidified themselves into what I considered to be our racial objectives.

One was to be ultra-sure to carefully conserve the Olympian headquarters of Enki when we made our attack against him.

Two was to protect at all costs the baby that was to be born from my lady love in Ur . . .

Meanwhile, I saw no need to reveal to Enlil or any of the other Anunnaki just yet the secret of my renewed virility . . . of my now proven paternity. I might be the first and so far the only one of us so empowered. It gave me a certain advantage, and I have never been one to easily surrender an advantage without good cause. So I kept my silence on this subject, awaiting future events.

****

My lady love of Ur gave birth. The child was a male . . . and I learned she had called his name Abram.

Against my biological impulses, I forced myself to restrain for the present from announcing the birth to the other Anunnaki.

Meanwhile . . .

There were pressures building for me to act . . .

Enlil was eager for the attack against Enki, and it strained my powers a little to keep him convinced we were approaching things just right. Slowly and with extreme caution.

I pointed out that while the time was indeed near, it was not yet.

There was still some consolidation work to be done on the Middle Continent peoples to have everything under such strict control as we had over the Western Continents.

Of course nothing could probably ever match the domination we had established over the Western Continents . . . but then, the tribes there being so essentially primitive after all reduced everything to very simple terms for us.

Meanwhile . . .

Our health now advanced still another degree.

I calculated that probably we were more healthy now than before Atlantis . . . and certain tests of Doctor Atra tended to confirm my estimate.

As for appearance, my mirror, now my best friend, told me the whole story at a glance. I saw a true god reflected there . . . and the memory of the misshapen monster I had once been began gradually to fade from my mind, like the trace memory of a half-forgotten nightmare . . .

The others made similar progress. And you would have thought that at that point we might have given up our regimen of blood and wafers . . .

But no, that would be not to know true Anunnaki attitudes in an affair of this magnitude. There was no use gambling against fate . . . what had worked would continue working as long as we continued the regimen. The regimen was proven not only for its obvious restorative powers, but now it seemed it even offered improvement somewhere beyond even our normal godlike beauty and health.

And on the other hand . . .

If we stopped . . . what?

We did not know. Would we retrogress? Doctor Atra was not sure. So he advised us for the present at least to continue.

Besides, strange as it may seem, over the long milleniums of time we had actually conceived a taste for both things . . . the blood and the wafers.

Why not? Long habit can accustom you to anything . . . plus the results were something we could all see for ourselves.

Even Enlil looked once again the handsome god he formerly had been . . . the only difference was he was a little rounder than before, a little more fully packed, a little overweight.

That, however, was not to be marvelled at. Seeing as how he spent so much of his time in idle pursuits. One of his favorites was throwing darts at a target in his quarters. Of that he organized competitions which, not surprisingly, he always won.

Not that he was any better, or even as good, as his competitors . . . frankly I think even the clones, or maybe even especially the clones because of their patient and methodical approach to the game, could have beaten him . . . but obviously none dared. He was, after all, Enlil, our Commander, and probable heir to the throne of the Anunnaki.

It was not his only idle pastime. Another was juggling . . . all kinds of objects. Even, if he wanted to produce emotion in his audience, wafers and . . . and yes, on a few occasions, even our refrigerated bottles of blood.

Actually, if he dropped one of those latter, at this time of our existence, it was no longer any great matter. We had whole rivers of blood and freightloads of internal organs on a regular basis flowing in now to our underground base, where within our ample facilities they were processed, stored, and cooled by Mother Earth plus a kind of primitive refrigeration system that Bronti had found in the Master Protocols.

We did not need at all that much, true. Yet, there was nothing wrong in having an ample reserve in case of unforeseen emergencies. Besides, such a procedure only added to the efficacy of the disciplinary procedures over the tribes we ruled. I never underestimate the power of death and annihilation, properly administered, as a means of establishing a satisfactory working order with primitives. An order which they themselves need and literally cry out for. So everyone benefitted in every way . . .

What saved Enlil from becoming completely gross in his restored physiognomy were the sex orgies we regularly conducted in the underground base.

We had more space now, more facilities, and could be more inventive and creative. And while all of us might become completely drunk on native liquors, the sober clones, who had no taste for alcohol, were always there to do the mundane chores and keep order. We could depend on them to, at the end of such festivities, either return the girls to their native habitats or slaughter them to increase our stores of blood and wafers. The decision as to which fate awaited them often depended on Enlil, whether he was satisfied or not with the night's activities . . . or even just on his momentary whim.

The nice thing about it was that, in spite of what I considered to be Enlil's lack of judgment, we Anunnaki as a race always benefitted either way he went.

His gesture of thumbs up meant, now that I at least was restored to normal fertility, another possible improvement in the race of Earthlings.

Thumbs down was not negative, because it meant we would increase our store of blood and wafers, which also eventually would mean improvements for the race of Earthlings.

So we were really rather altruistic in what we did.

Though I participated in all these activities with my usual enthusiasm, yet I did not, either. Not entirely.

I was still taken with my lady of Ur, and she was much in my thoughts . . . though as time passed, not so much she herself, as our son. He was already grown at this point into a young man, strong and handsome. I was not only proud of him . . . I saw in his make-up something of our potential future. He had to be a part of that, however I had to arrange things to make it that way.

I visited them both on a somewhat regular basis, though at times Earth years might go by between one visit and another.

But time, of course, took its toll so quickly, as always, in the case of Earthlings. In a ridiculously short period of time, my lady love grew gray and matronly . . . revealing to me a truth I knew or should have known long before . . . how futile at last it was to love one of the Earthlings except strictly on a short range scale or for the purpose of producing children. I resolved never to do it again.

Even though my son, too, was subject to the same incursions of time, I thought to use him yet in something advantageous both for himself and me.

And when his mother died, I knew now that my available time for such utilization was short.

Besides, I found it increasingly difficult any longer to resist the petulant insistence of Enlil . . . that we at last make our mighty strike. Our stroke of final vengeance against the traitor Enki . . .

And so one night I appeared to my son, after first calling him out to the balcony of the house of his late mother where he now lived alone.

The blue-white light of the tractor beam apparently emanated from the starry sky itself, since I had Proteus on Blend. I had set the ship's position under automatic control and could work the tractor beam with my Commander's belt remote.

The effect of this on Abram was of course strong, as I could see. And I wanted to take full advantage of it to get my message across.

"Abram," I told him. "You must leave Ur. You have been chosen for an important mission. Ur and all the other Sumerian cities will be destroyed by Divine Edict. Do this thing for me and for your future."

He was staggered. But still resistant.

"What . . . what are you saying? I can't just leave. I have relatives here. My mother's family. Cousins. I know no other city except Ur."

I told him of his glowing future if he followed my instructions. I told him to bring any family members he wanted with him. In fact, bring them all, all his relatives. But to leave as soon as possible to escape the terrible fate that Ur must inevitably soon suffer.

He was obviously stunned. But at last he assured me he would obey. I kissed his forehead as he knelt before me, then beamed myself back aboard . . .

****

Now . . . now at last . . . it was time to strike.

****

The night sky was overcast, heavy with portents to my observation as to what was soon to take place.

Enlil was aboard the Military scout craft with us. Half-drunk, but present. He wouldn't miss this. How could he? It was what he had lived . . . or at least existed . . . for, now almost these 8,000 years.

That was an eternity for Earthlings, 8,000 Earth years. For us Anunnaki, being quasi-immortal, not much time at all . . . something less than a quarter of a year. Still, perhaps influenced by the Earthly environment, and certainly influenced by our tragic circumstances, to me it seemed something like a very long time now, too.

Did I say Enlil was half-drunk? I was half wrong about that.

He laughed and babbled, babbled and laughed. Drank from his flask, sang, or tried to . . . lolled about and generally made a fool of himself.

He was, in spite of his drunkenness, not about to miss any of this. That was obvious.

But his attitude didn't help. He contributed nothing, except increasing the general anxiety I felt.

There were thirty reasons our raid could go wrong. And only one or two factors working in our favor.

Still, those factors were magna factors.

There was Enki's temperament which I knew all too well. His

tendency to foolishly trust in others . . . I was a good example of that, how he always treated me well when all the time I was a spy in the employ of Enlil . . . that now was all in our favor.

To amplify that weakness . . . how to do that . . . was what I had found out in my own investigations, and what I knew from my past association as Enki's most trusted Aide.

Which was this.

Tomorrow was to be a great celebration. It was in Earthly years the annual celebration of the 2nd Anunnaki Mission on Earth. The one with Enki in charge instead of Enlil, the change that had so injured Enlil's oversensitive psyche. And I knew from past experience what the celebration would be . . . or at least what general lines it would follow.

Everyone would gather at the Space Center on the Sinai peninsula to celebrate the great occasion.

I had taken part in those myself many times. At the gathering on the Eve there would be wine and native beverages and general conviviality . . . encouraged as always by Enki's bent towards bringing everyone towards a common level.

For him that was progress, while for me it was regression towards a potential state of anarchy and chaos. That was something I felt so strongly about I was now risking my own life to eradicate it, before it could spread any further.

Well, that was not my only motive. Hardly. 8,000 Earth years of being a radiation-ravaged monster could not make me feel affectionate in any way towards Enki.

I had as great an impetus towards revenge as Enlil. Greater. Because he was a drunken clown . . . while I was trying to be the cold, calculating instrument of revenge. I had the nuts and bolts of it firmly in my mind, while he . . .

He thought as usual by wishing something you could make it come true.

Well, if you were high enough up in the Anunnaki hierarchy that policy could sometimes seem to be correct.

What he failed to realize ever since the atomic blast, was how radically things had changed. We both wanted to restore the true hierarchy, yes. But he had no grasp as to how to do it, while I . . . well this night would prove whether I had or not.

And if I had, my thought was that alone would prove something else. Who had the inherent right in the future to decide the fate of Earth.

The Great Mission was progressing, except for Enlil's antics, normally enough. There was no way I could not find my target area. I had rehearsed it enough to do it in my sleep.

Sleep was what overcame the distracting antics of Enlil as time slid by us, for which I and my other crew were thankful.

We were myself and the two pilots. That was tailored exactly to my objectives which I had figured out a thousand times before tonight.

I didn't really see how we could go wrong, in spite of my earlier statement about the probabilities. Perhaps the presence of the now sound asleep Enlil made me feel that way. I don't know. Anyway, if I ever thought we were going to fail, I simply wouldn't be on this mission now . . .

****

We broke out into an open patch. The full moon cast down its light and seemed like a kind of temporary anodyne against anxiety. Yet I needed the clouds for the success of the Mission.

I had studied the weather patterns carefully and over an extended period of time. Above all, I knew the prevailing winds at this season of the year. They would be very important to me.

What I expected to see when we arrived at the Sinai in . . . I saw by the time indicator on the dash, about ten minutes . . . was something very close to the following . . .

Six ships parked on the runway outside the Administration building.

There would be the great spaceship, the Mother Ship . . . and five Military scouts. As to their crews and passengers, numbering exactly 205 unless someone had died or arrived from Nibiru since my own departure . . . after their wine drinking and conviviality in the Enki way, they should all be asleep in the personnel quarters next to the Administration building by the time of our arrival, about 3 a.m.

I hoped once again everything would go according to my meticulous plan . . . but knew too well that nothing ever does in spite of considering every possible contingency.

And . . . here we were.

I had Proteus on Blend, so we looked like a field of stars to anyone looking up. But no one was, or should be . . . what would they be guarding against, after all?

Not us. We had been dead some 8,000 Earth years as far as they knew. With no sign of us in all that time. I almost felt sympathy for a moment with Enlil's liberal point of view about not making any personnel have to work the night before a day-long celebration. Almost, but not quite. I knew that I myself, I, Yahweh, would have the normal around the clock watch on duty . . . and would make it a point to check on them personally, ready to punish any slackers. It was the true Anunnaki way, the caution and prudence even in the midst of prosperity that had made us great.

But for right now, I was almost grateful for Enki's mistaken liberalism, his laxness. It could only help assure the success of our own Great Mission. After the conviviality of the anniversary's Eve, all of Enki's personnel would sleep late. On this particular occasion, much later than any one of them could ever possibly imagine . . .

Through the night vision, as we approached our target, I noted one thing wrong immediately.

The great spaceship was there all right. But instead of five scouts, there were only four . . .

What did that mean?

I didn't know. And as a military Commander, I don't like unknowns.

Yes, Enki's personal Flagship was there, easily identifiable. The only one painted his royal gold, the others gray. So he would be there to die on schedule.

Good.

And then I saw it. The fifth scout parked away from the others on the margin of the grounds of the Space Station.

So everything was in order. Everything orchestrated for the symphony of destruction about to rain down from the skies . . .

Extermination was not my only goal. This was our one great opportunity for something else. To steal the great spaceship, the Mother Ship, with all the power and technology it had aboard.

And, for my own personal uses, to steal Enki's personal scout, his magnificently outfitted and equipped Flagship.

Had we more pilots we would steal more, of course. But we did not. Only myself and the two behind me, on each side of the snoring Enlil, the supposed great god Enlil . . .

Given those parameters and only one bomb, with one chance to administer it in the interest of the greatest good, my choices were greatly simplified.

Yes, perhaps . . .

But I never liked maybes.

Anyway, it was time to act.

I banked sharply and swept low over the spaceport looking for any signs of life. Saw none.

I set us down deftly in back of the administration building, in the deepest shadow afforded by the moon now peeping through the surrounding layer of clouds.

Enlil's snoring was a grateful sound, assuring he would at least not interfere with our work, which had to be carried out precisely and precipitately to have any chance at succeeding.

So sleep decadent gods always, was the thought that coursed unbidden through my mind.

There was urgent work to be done. First we went to the spaceship we were going to appropriate.

I saw it there looming gigantically to one side in the lambent moonlight. "The Mother Ship . . ." My whispered words under the moon were full of reverence, as well they might be.

Of course the Mother Ship. It had a plethora of extra command equipment, enough in itself to shift the balance of power and make us nothing less than the new Kings of Earth.

A few strides and we were there, but then I swore softly to myself.

The code to open the ramp door I had. But there was a detail . . . always the unexpected details.

I had forgotten how high it was. The door was three feet beyond my reach.

Two pairs of hands were there to boost me up. These pilots were not like Enlil . . . they knew nothing of privilege and godly prissiness . . . they saw a problem and acted immediately to solve it, without a protesting word. As I pressed the electronic buttons, I resolved to find a way to reward them once I was in charge. If we lived though this Mission . . .

The ramp slid down. Silently and smoothly. It was a sensual pleasure just to see it work, and to anticipate the great reassuring mass of technology inside, which would surely succor us in our just fight for ultimate domination of the Earth.

One pilot was now inside. It was his ball of wax now, and I had every confidence in him.

I looked towards the administration building for signs of life or any light.

None.

I breathed more freely.

Next was Enki's gold personal scout, his Flagship. I used the access code, and my second pilot was quickly inside and seated, giving me the thumbs up signal.

What I had to do next was get out of there. After that, not much. Just blow up the entire complex. With a little Military scout ship ill-adapted for the purpose and with the potentially hampering presence of a snoring god beside me . . .

****

I was five miles up now. Not just in ship's altitude . . . my own adrenalin and heart rate made me feel personally higher than that. In the face of great accomplishment, the mind plays tricks. You suddenly see your future and in that future you may alternately be . . . a giant or a dwarf, with the two opposing images alternating on what seems some kind of rogue electronic control in the brain.

Right at this moment I felt like a giant.

But then . . .

Enlil gasped and snorted, and I feared the worst. His idiot orders given on any whim could quickly doom our Mission. And then . . . thankfully he fell back into his steady snoring.

Because of the unexpected moonlight, I did not need the night vision to see that both the Flagship and the great Mother Ship were no longer on the runway. Of course I knew they weren't, since I had waited for them to clear the spaceport before I myself ascended in the Military scout.

But as I said, in crisis situations, the mind plays tricks . . . or tries to.

Now, looking around, I saw them both not far away from me. At least I saw lights in the sky that corresponded to their dimensions, and that was the reassurance my vagrant mind so badly needed.

I was ready. I was not going to wait any longer for this fulcrum of fate on whose high apex I now rested to degenerate into something that would have no consequence on this planet Earth.

I saw I was near the center of the complex, and entered first the code. Then pulled back the lever that would open the bay that Bronti had fashioned for me that would . . . what? . . . change the future of this alien world, I hoped.

My heart did not stop beating. Just that it suddenly felt like it . . .

I would have to wait a moment that seemed like eternity itself to know the ultimate result of 8,000 Earth years of planning this sweet culmination . . . this bittersweet revenge.

And then it came.

I saw it, entranced . . .

A giant orange ball of cloud and flame that seemed to boil and jump upwards towards me. I banked sharply and accelerated to the maximum, while angling upwards. I had no desire to be caught in my own mousetrap.

I quickly thus left the broiling holocaust behind me.

I found it ironic but not surprising that Enlil . . . the revenge on his brother at last launched after such a long wait . . . did not even wake at my maneuver. His mouth only fell open further, and his snoring increased in volume.

Now I headed the ship towards the region Enki had christened Sumer. The seven cities . . .

I maneuvered then most carefully, to make sure I covered the entire area of their extent.

While I employed a technique well known on Nibiru . . .

When a section of the planet needed rain, this is what you did, what I was doing now.

With compressed air you blew out millions of tiny seeds along with a billion particles of crop dust . . . in this case pre-gathered from the fields of the Iberian Peninsula . . . to saturate the atmosphere.

If the winds held true, Enki's distorted dream of what Earth should be would be dead.

With that vain vision gone, our own would have its slow but solid beginning in place. The first step on the first rung of a new ladder, not stretching into heaven, no . . . but to the exact place where I wanted it to go . . .

I, Yahweh . . . the new god of Earth.

****

Back at our underground mountain base, I felt euphoric . . . when I was finally able to awaken the lethargic Enlil, he at last began to realize with me the significance of what we had accomplished.

We had the great Mother Ship. We had Enki's Flagship. Both safely hidden away in our great underground hangar.

Enki . . . his cohorts . . . all the other Anunnaki on Earth besides ourselves . . . were now vapor, scattered atoms with no focus . . . enjoying the very fate Enki had so maliciously willed for us.

This world . . . Earth . . . this round globe . . . was now ours.

Ours in its entirety. Not one third of it. Not two thirds of it. It was now totally ours . . . ours to make of it what we would.

As to what that would be I had no doubts. It would be everything that Enki's world was not. Honorable. Structured. Functional. Hierarchical. Run for the benefit of the Anunnaki and the Anunnaki race . . . not for the scapegrace primitive Earthlings who without our science and our care would never even have come into existence . . . at least not for millions of years more of evolution, and even then they would have been more ape and less like us.

So we owed them nothing, while on the contrary they owed us everything. Something so simple to understand . . . and yet the late Enki had never quite understood it. His mistaken liberality got in the way . . . that he must be, for some obsessive reason comprehensible only to himself, always the Friend of Humanity.

Well, he had his reward now.

Oh, yes.

The realization seeped through my pores like a balm . . .

Yes.

Enki now . . .

. . . lived in that very self-same realm called Oblivion, the one he had tried so treacherously to send us to, and almost succeeded . . .

Almost, but not quite . . . here we were revived, we twelve, not almost as good as new, but in my opinion, better. Doctor Atra's difficult but effective regimen over so many thousands of years had at last left us in that very desirable state. If I were handsome before . . . and I was . . . I was handsomer now . . . an even more effusive glow around my features as my mirror told me clearly. And I was a father again . . .

In two ways, a father, I thought. To my Earthling child, my Abram . . . but also now the new Father of Earth itself.

In reality its god.

Oh, of course that honor remained to the titular ruler, Enlil. But I knew, and I think that he also, at least at night in his most secret dreams, somehow realized who was the real power behind the throne.

And of course at some point in the future I expected Enlil to be recalled to the New Home Planet in Zeta Reticuli 2 . . . either to accept the crown from the aged hands of his father, King Anu . . . or be offered it by the Anunnaki Grand Council when Anu at long long last passed on.

Of course certain things had to happen first. Anu needed to be informed of the new situation on Earth. Of Enki's treachery and the nature of that treachery . . . and that at last true justice had been established, and the Earth rule returned to its rightful possessor, the great Enlil.

But I cautioned Enlil the time was not quite ripe for that, as yet.

There were things to be done first. We had to assure that none of Enki's forces had survived the blast. That would take time.

We had to secure the planet. I had to insure that the seven cities of what Enki called the region of Sumer, had indeed been demolished by my tactics. For him those cities had been almost sacred, but for me the depth of his treachery had made me see them for what they really were. Blasphemous.

Well, such blasphemy had to be punished. I had accomplished that, I was sure, but still . . . all had to be verified beyond any doubt.

That I would do in the coming days. Once done, I had then to contact my son.

What I had in mind for him was something hugely important. While it was true we now ruled the world, we ruled it in name only. To make that rule actual rather than theoretical I had to make firm plans.

It might very well be that segments of the population formerly ruled by Enki might actually resent our rule. Might put up resistance. Even rebel. Such were the dangerous seeds planted in their minds by Enki's liberal policies, I knew well. And so, instead of recognizing themselves as the slaves and servants they were created to be, they might dare to try to arrogate to themselves the rights that belonged only to Anunnaki. Or so I feared.

The remedy that came to mind one night when sleep evaded me was this . . .

Once we had created an Invincible Army in Atlantis.

Perhaps that was what was needed here. To conquer and keep control of Enki's former domains, and to be ready to go anywhere on the globe to carry out my wishes on a moment's notice.

Of course they would not be totally like the Invincible Army of Atlantis. Nor could they ever be . . . without considerable genetic manipulation, which we were not yet prepared to make. Rather it occurred to me they could be something like the Su of the Western Continents, who had served us so well for so long before the fatal sickness struck them down. Rather like the Su, yes . . . if they could be trained to be so totally merciless and cruel, so unforgiving to anyone designated as an enemy. Of course, they needed an ultimate authority to make those designations . . . in other words, a god.

My mind began to work in that direction. Plans and visions sprang up in my brain. I thought perhaps I had the key to everything in my son, Abram. Through him and his seed I could work. My blood would always be a strong controlling factor . . . and once he recognized me as his god, his people's god . . . I should be able to implement my plan.

They could carry out the glorious work of the remaining conquest that still lay before us. To put Enki's rebellion to the sword among all Earthlings . . . and implement the proper respect due to a god. A very proper task for a Chosen People . . .

After that sleepless night in which all this had come to me, I knew it was good . . . and I got up and went forth with strong appetite to an Anunnaki breakfast in our underground retreat. Followed, of course, by my ration of wafers plus a generous libation of the life-giving blood I had become almost addicted to. Before downing the last of it, I watched with satisfaction the smoke curling upwards from the cold metal container, a testimony to Engineer Bronti's refrigeration units taken from the Protocols. And imagined in its suggestive depths the almost certain fulfillment of my dreams.

****

The New Times, the good times, the times without Enki when Enlil ruled once again supreme . . .

It was no longer just a dream.

Those good times had come. They were here. Rather I had made them eventuate, made them exist and I was very proud of what I had accomplished.

I suggested to Enlil we move very soon into Enki's headquarters on Mount Olympus. While our underground base was secure and nice, it was nothing like the Olympus layout. Besides there really was no need now for security. We twelve were the only Anunnaki left on the face of Earth. And there was no Earthling who could ever challenge us on an individual basis . . . though, yes, we had to look out for any possible rebel elements, any mistaken followers of the late Enki.

When the time came to begin to make the change, I took everyone there in Enki's gold colored personal Flagship. The great Mother Ship for this first visit we left in the underground base. The Flagship was incredible. Comfort to the Nth degree. All the latest in technology, which made our own Military scout and Hospital ship look crude by comparison.

We had aboard we twelve Anunnaki plus twelve of our ghostly little clones, some of them even smaller than the twelve originals, being, as they were, clones of the original clones. We continued to find them extremely useful, and it was my intent to put them to work immediately at Mount Olympus to search and secure everything, and then to carry out their usual cleaning and organizational tasks at which they were incomparable.

And when we got to Enki's headquarters, my mind quickly formulated an analogy. As our two battered ships were to Enki's grand Flagship, so was our underground base to the fantastic layout near the top of Mount Olympus.

I walked around it ecstatic. Yes, I had known it 8,000 Earth years before when I was Enki's chief aide and advisor. So it was hardly new. And yet after so many years of being in hiding, of living in ill health and deprivation, it was like sunburst to find ourselves lords of this celestial manor, this great mansion in the clouds.

Besides the comfort, the scope, the fantastic mountain views, which to people who had been living in exile or underground too long was like something analogous to a release from prison . . . there was one thing so far beyond anything we had known for so long that just the sight of it made my heart beat fast . . .

The laboratory . . . the scientific laboratory . . . even though we might have all the Anunnaki Master Protocols, we had very few instruments with which to implement them . . .

But here, here was everything we might want.

Not only all the Anunnaki technology was concentrated here in one way or another, but more . . . because Enki, much as I detested him for good reason . . . had been in the vanguard of genetic and scientific discovery and invention.

We luxuriated in our new Headquarters for awhile . . . just relaxed and enjoyed ourselves at last. Took advantage of the comforts, baths, the sweeping views punctuated always by low swooping clouds . . . the recorded Anunnaki music . . . the carpets so soft beneath our feet and the elaborate cooking and serving facilities which the clones began to utilize creatively to all our great glee.

Strangely, in this moment of triumph, my thoughts wandered towards Enki, my former master.

He was gone, yes, but still I needed to put him in his place. His mistake was clear to me. He had tried to make a silk purse of a sow's ear. In trying to elevate humanity, he had offended the Anunnaki sense of Destiny. A Destiny based on our superiority and the faithful maintenance of that superiority through class and code as the essential keys to ascendancy in a hard universe.

In so far as he failed to comprehend that, Enki was not a true Anunnaki and thus deserved to die.

I felt no pity for him, nor should any right-thinking Anunnaki once we made the facts clear to their comprehension.

Why should I?

If he had always stood in the way of right administration of an alien planet with an inferior culture which we ourselves had created only for a very specific purpose. And so their role in our society was clear from the start. It was never to surpass anything grander than service and slavery.

For some odd reason, Enki had not understood in this situation something very simple. The key to success lay not in mistakenly and futilely trying to raise an inferior life form to our level, but on the contrary . . . to be assiduous in always keeping them in their place so as properly to get on with the only real business of the Planet, which was to advance the Anunnaki way of life.

****

We had a potential great triumph, one bought with 8,000 Earth years of patience. I was hardly after such pains and planning going to lose all now in some impulsive gamble.

No, on the contrary. I had to be even more careful now in what I did and how I did it, if I wished to attain my ultimate ends. And I knew I must never forget one thing. I was working with backward and recalcitrant people here in the as yet unconquered zone which included all of Mesopotamia and everything surrounding it in a large and as yet undefined radius. Yes, of course, these people were far advanced as compared to the savage people of the Western Continents . . . and for that very reason were apt to be far more dangerous. Which only goes to prove my point that Enki's policies were totally mistaken.

It was true I had struck down his most proud achievement . . . his glorious Sumer.

I could not help gloating about that.

The destruction of the seven cities he so cherished . . . in his ignorance not realizing that each and every one of them was a threat, a potential dagger to the heart of everything he should have revered above all else. The Anunnaki Way of Life. The manner of preserving it was not imitation by an ignorant and inferior race of humans . . . but in keeping such knowledge from them. A truth too simple for him to grasp.

But now I had to see for myself. Had I really done what I thought I had done? Destroyed the entire population of Sumer?

****

I made a radiation check from high above the city of Ur.

As I had hoped, the reading came out . . . lethal.

Good. But I had to know more.

I looked through the augmentation lenses much superior to the ones in our old Military scout ship . . . I was alone on my mission aboard Enki's gold Flagship.

The scene I saw below was very satisfying.

People in the streets, their bodies sprawled in every conceivable direction. Most of them dead, but not all. Some wandered dazedly around . . . aimless . . . bouncing off walls and sometimes retracing their steps in their obvious confusion.

How satisfying! Justice was delayed, but at last now it had come, thanks to my actions.

Some of these people spawned by the treachery of Enki raised their arms to heaven. Some evidently saw me . . . I did not have Proteus Blend on, because there was no need. And some of those who did might have thought I was their golden redemption, their savior . . . because as I increased the power of augmentation I could see the imploring looks on their anguished faces, the question in their rolling eyes. How had Enki their god allowed this terrible thing to happen? And now that it had inexplicably happened . . . was he here now on a mission of mercy . . . to save them?

Well, I would relieve them of that delusion.

I picked an image from the infinite selection on Proteus control. It was from what some might call the demons from Hell. I flicked this one on full force. The image of a demonically gleeful Devil . . .

To send them off in first class fashion towards final extinction.

To let them know I was not Enki. And that Enki himself was powerless to stop me anymore . . . had even preceded them to their own now imminent destination . . .

****

The other cities of Sumer I soon found were suffering in a similar manner.

I congratulated myself again on my perspicacity. My tactic of letting the prevailing winds carry death to the inhabitants of Sumer with their cargo of radiation from our bomb blast. And then, exactly as I had calculated, the rains I had induced had finished the job . . . taking all the incoming fallout from the stratosphere and delivering it gently to the streets and buildings of the seven Sumerian cities.

That, together with the bombing raid that had annihilated Enki and all his Anunnaki cohorts was a master stroke of strategy. Much too great a feat ever to be enclosed within the narrow bounds of the old Anunnaki saying of killing two birds with one stone.

Oh, yes.

It was a twin accomplishment of such magnitude that no popular saying could ever capture its complete magnificence.

I was proud to have been its sole author.

The beauty of it was that we had lost nothing but the dangerous and unrealistically presumptuous population of Sumer, that, had they lived, would have been primed and ready for a revolt against our own prudent rule, so different from Enki's mistaken liberalism.

We still had the seven cities themselves for whatever use I might decide to put them someday. After the 500 Earth years I calculated it would take for them once again to be inhabitable.

On the other hand, if at any time they became bothersome to me . . . if, for example, at some future point they became a refuge for rebel earthlings . . . I would simply bomb them out of existence, now that I had Enki's supply of nuclear bombs as part of my own personal arsenal.

Inside the Flagship of Enki I could hardly contain my exhilaration. I laughed and slapped my knee and laughed and slapped again and again . . .

****

Next, I took a turn over the place of our recent victory.

Our bomb had left its imprint . . . a huge black scar enclosing miles of earth was all that was left of the former Space Base on the Sinai Peninsula.

I was sorry to lose the services of the Base . . . but not at all in losing those who had manned it, which included all the Anunnaki expedition, ironically celebrating the anniversary of Enki's second arrival to Earth.

We had now the most important keys to power. Enki's headquarters on Mount Olympus, the Great Pyramid . . . even in the future the seven cities of Sumer, should we ever need them.

The only thing we did not have was a formal launching or landing place for space travel. But that we could build back with Earthling slave labor when the time came . . . and for the immediate present there was no need.

I headed north, just to finish my general survey of the region, and soon found myself over what on our maps I had called the Great Salt Sea, the one the locals called the Dead Sea.

Beyond its southern edge I came across something strange.

I remembered there had been two cities there, thriving against all odds in the rugged landscape. Where were they? I saw no evidence of them.

I went lower. The ridges of rock running through where the cities had been were twisted and riven, great chunks strewn everywhere, and lots of little pieces, too. Not just rock, either, but rock that had been charred and seared.

So what had happened here?

I hovered above the scene and tried to figure it out. Suddenly the entire sequence came to me. First, the atomic explosion as we blew Enki and his cohorts to smithereens. They must have felt its effects here. Too distant for any direct effect, true. But what if . . . ?

What if the subterranean reverberations had been strong enough to trigger a local Earthquake?

That fit what I was looking at. There were cracks and fissures visible in the rugged area.

But there was obviously something else involved. Some other factors.

I dared to land the Flagship, get out and and look around. There was a strange, acrid odor to the air. I noticed it most strongly near the fissures. Some kind of underground bubbles of gas might have been liberated, broken open by the Earthquake that opened the fissures. All right. What else?

I noticed a plethora of yellow colored, greasy looking little crudely shaped globes scattered around over the entire area. I picked one up. Its odor hit my nostrils hard. Sulfur.

Now I pretty much had the entire picture. The Earthquake from our atomic blast opened the fissures and liberated the methane gas into the atmosphere. Some friction among the rock generated sparks and the whole area became instantaneously a conflagration. The rich deposits of sulfur had ignited, adding to the fiery scene.

And so perished two savage but primitively prosperous cities, the ones their inhabitants called Sodom and Gomorrah.

Interesting. Perhaps I could some way turn their destruction to my advantage.

But what I had to do first and fast, was get out of there. No use risking the effects of some other sudden conflagration, which conceivably could still occur at any moment . . .

****

I moved on to part three of my inspection.

The people of this place I was surveying now would be important to our future. I had plans for them. They could, indeed, be the very scourge of god's vengeance on Earth . . .

Not the people who presently inhabited the area. No, I was not thinking of them. They were . . . eminently expendable. But of those who under my direction would soon come to inhabit it . . .

Canaan. That was what Earthlings called the strategically located land in question. I had directed my son Abram to lead his people to the border of Canaan and there await instructions. Now it was time to begin to give him a few basic ideas of what his role should be, and his tribe their basic indoctrination lecture.

****

As I approached I put Proteus to project the Generic icon that had been so successful for me in the Western and Middle Continents. Its radiant image seemed to successfully inspire awe in the hearts of all who saw it . . . so for purposes of uniformity, and with no reason to abandon a method that had produced so many past successes, I went with it again now.

Canaan was . . . not entirely what I would have wished. Half desert, another fourth too mountainous . . . not the ideal land to settle in. And yet it was, too, a large portion of it green enough with plenty of vineyards in ample evidence.

And even the rugged part was not so bad . . . not if what I wished to produce in the tribe I proposed to adopt as my scourge was hardiness . . . an ability to respond to conditions and obstacles that would make faint the hearts of the majority of Earthlings.

I saw from above I had their attention . . . the attention of my waiting tribe, my potentially Chosen People. Their gazes were riveted on me as I hovered there above their extensive encampment. My son Abram had done well in assembling all his near and most remote familiars to embark on this new enterprise. It was an auspicious beginning.

One that obviously necessitated a formal speech of some kind.

So I gave them one through my words, properly augmented to godlike volume over the Flagship's voice projection system.

Something like this . . .

"You are my Chosen Race. The one I have picked from all others to help me dominate the world. You must swear undying allegiance to me, your omnipotent, omniscient god, and only in that way will you and your children prosper."

I paused for emphasis and to let my point sink in. These were, after all, only savage Earthlings I was addressing, not a group of

Anunnaki . . . and I was not at all certain how much of my very simplified message they would be able to understand.

"How will they prosper, your children? One day they will inhabit all of this magic land . . . it will be solely theirs. The way will be difficult, yes, and the time perhaps longer than your individual lives. But eventually we will triumph. You must be warlike and totally obedient to my orders. Because others now inhabit the land that I have promised you. But they can not stand against the sword of your god once it is raised against them . . . not if you are faithful, not if you believe in me and no other."

Here I augmented the already thunderous volume.

"And for those who do not believe, who do not have faith in me, it were better for them that they were to batter out their brains now against the rocks, rather than suffer the punishment of their august, only Lord."

I paused to let them think about that.

"Those of you who have doubts should ponder the fate of those former great cities to the south. The ones known as Sodom and Gomorrah. Look what happened to them in the storm of the Lord's wrath. Because they were stubborn and wicked and attracted to other gods . . ."

I had them going, I could see. But now I decided to press my psychological impact . . .

"And what about the city of Ur, and all the seven cities of once powerful and prosperous Sumer? They had defied me, and gone against my wishes, and worshipped other gods. Where are those people now? I tell you the only sound to be heard there is the sound of the wind moaning through deserted streets . . . streets where the skeletons of ten thousand dead lie crumbling into dust . . .

"I tell you now that Ur is a forbidden city, a deserted city, a cursed city . . . as are all the seven cities of Sumer. Because they worshipped a foreign god and adopted strange ways that were not my ways.

"But I in my mercy led you safely out of Ur before the seven cities suffered their just punishment."

Most were on their knees by now, lifting their eyes upwards

towards me where I hovered some hundred feet above them. Among them I saw Abram, my son, properly reverent with folded hands.

Good.

I needed to say something about him. "The noble Abram is your leader, the leader I have chosen for you. Obey him in all things, because he carries behind him from this day forward my authority. And to show that new authority now, today, I wish to change his name to one more noble, one more befitting his new role as my chosen leader. From now on, he shall be called no longer Abram, but Abraham. I have spoken."

For a while of intense silence I had only the panorama of bowed heads and prostrate figures to contemplate, which I viewed with considerable satisfaction.

Then one patriarch arose. It almost made me sick to see someone so visibly attacked by the curse of Earthlings, age . . . someone who undoubtedly in his youth had been, while never certainly of an Anunnaki beauty, still, at least presentable and functional. Not like this present simulacrum of a man. I saw his arms tremble, his degenerated lips in the middle of his long white beard quiver uncontrollably even as he spoke.

"Almighty," he said. "We need to know . . . what name should we call you by, you who will rule our destiny?"

That was a good, if unexpected question. No one had ever asked it before. Well, I could have given them a generic name, something like The Awesome One. Not bad. But something made me want to put myself into the equation. Why not?

"Yahweh," I said.

But the patriarch being in his dotage . . . maybe hard of hearing and certainly with quivering lips and quavering voice, repeated something different.

"Oh, Lord . . . I hear you . . . yes, Mighty Jehovah, we will worship you forever."

Jehovah?

You idiot! . . . pronounce it right or I can kill you here and now. Which might not be such a bad idea. Maybe inspire a little instant respect.

But on second thought . . . Enlil was a problem. He might not like it, were he to find out, that I instead of him were being worshipped as a god.

Jehovah . . . Enlil would not identify that name with me.

Besides . . .

It had a certain nobility, a certain grand and godlike exotic ring to it. Something I could go along with.

For a new chapter in my life, in the life of Planet Earth, why not a new, bold name to go with it? The more esoteric and exotic the better.

"Yes, you say well," I told the patriarch in booming tones thrown electronically right in front of his face though I was now 50 feet above him. "And remember, no other gods before me. I am the god of you, my Chosen People, and the only legitimate god of the world. I will always be your god and lead you in magnificent ways. But your worship and your loyalty must be perfect. You must revere me and never question my demands on you. For there will be many. I leave you with that thought and will from time to time return to guide you. My plans for you are both great and grand and beyond your present comprehension. But the time to carry them out is not yet. Meanwhile, go about your daily lives as before . . . except in all things follow the dictates of Abraham. I have spoken."

And following a long pause, I added as an afterthought . . .

"I, Jehovah."

****

And later I thought to myself . . . what was that all about? I didn't need to say that. After all there were no other opposing gods left on Earth. Enki and all his crew had been obliterated in the nuclear blast at Sinai.

Hadn't they?

****

We had a decision to make back at our new command quarters on Mount Olympus.

The question was not new. I had made my negative decision about it long ago. Just that now, with us in sole power on Mount Olympus, the situation was different.

Enlil said he wanted us to discuss it as a group.

With the extensive technology available in Enki's laboratory, Doctor Atra announced we could now easily clone ourselves. It would be possible to populate Earth with hundreds, or even thousands of our clones. Not like our twenty-four faithful little ghosts who had served and continued to serve us so well . . . not at all. No, authentic copies of all us twelve in our present robust state of health were now available if we so wished, in whatever numbers desired.

The question was . . . did we want that? Had it been up to me, there would have been no discussion. But I had to humor Enlil this time because he became so insistent about it.

There was some desultory discussion among the group. Two or three thought yes, it would be a good idea to strengthen our Anunnaki forces which were now after all only us twelve. Most, using good sense, refrained from making any statement one way or another. They wisely knew that all decisions had to be made by Enlil . . . and perhaps knew also that I would be the deciding factor in any decision made by him.

The upshot of that was we three held a private meeting in Enlil's quarters . . . Enlil, Doctor Atra and myself.

Obviously there were various factors to be considered here. First was Anunnaki law and custom. On Nibiru, cloning of Anunnaki was forbidden by law, and for good reason. It tended to contribute to confusion and disorder . . . even chaos . . . and so was against the very Anunnaki spirit.

We would ordinarily not consider it at all except for our special situation. So few in numbers and . . . we were all still sterile.

Well, not quite all. I had my son Abraham, born some 50 years previous, to prove that I myself had regained my virility.

But only Doctor Atra was the very recent recipient of that

information, and I had convinced him not to reveal that fact as yet to anyone, for my own private reasons. As to why I was the first and so far the only one, Doctor Atra had his theories. When the atomic blast came, perhaps I was a bit more sheltered than the others . . . or my natural recuperative powers were stronger.

But clones . . . were they the answer to our problem of being so few in number?

Enlil seemed to have no definite opinion, and looked to me to speak to the issue.

I did. "Anunnaki law forbids it. We had to do it only under extreme circumstances . . . to combat the treachery of Enki. But that is now past. Doctor Atra assures me that we will soon, along with our restored health and vitality, also attain our ability to produce children in the natural way. If we wish to have more clones at our service, we can always do that. Clone our already existing clones. That would not really be against Anunnaki law because they in no way resemble us . . . they are just pale wraiths of our radiation damaged selves, and so present no problems. No problems of mistaken identity or shared authority. They are servants and slaves, very like the Earthlings are."

Enlil approved everything I said. There would be no cloning, even though we had the capability. Except possibly of our existing clones as necessity might arise.

I think that in his heart Enlil felt the same as I did in rejecting the idea of a clone. Much as he might not trust others, he would trust even less a copy of himself. The capacity for deviousness and capricious change of heart in his copy was simply too great to be comtemplated with any tranquillity, even by him.

I could see in his bored expression that he was, as usual eager to return to his juggling or his darts, or to nap anticipating that evening's schedule for a group session of free sex with a groggy and prepacified group of maidens . . .

So I left quietly and did not push my victory. It WAS a victory because after all how would it look to my Chosen People . . . to have two or three or more Jehovahs?

No other gods? True, not even myself if it was not me, but only my simulacrum.

****

Everything was going my way.

Gradually, true.

But on the other hand . . .

The short Earth years flew by.

We still had a long way to go to totally dominate Earth and safely subjugate all populations.

The most troublesome areas were Mesopotamia and its immediate surroundings. That was due to the Enki influence which would not die. There were people and peoples still infected with the absurd idea of rights and privileges. That was what I was concerned with stamping out.

But everything indicated it might take a long time.

Then there was the continent known as Africa. It was a mess. Egypt worshipped a god who had been the son of Enki . . . Marduk . . . that the Egyptians themselves had come to call Ra. That subversion had to be taken care of. After all, they had no way to know that Marduk/Ra had been obliterated in our nuclear attack on the Sinai Space Station. But I let it go for the time being, thinking that all I needed to do eventually was to make a name change . . . from Ra to Jehovah.

A lot of Africa was untamed, primitive . . . almost as primitive as the Western Continents.

As time went by I began to think more and more of precious metals. Formerly gold had been only a means to saving the atmosphere of Nibiru. Now I began to look at it in a different light. It was a metal that Earthlings valued highly. A status symbol and sign of prestige, of royal authority. As such, I wanted to assure I had always the largest supply as a leverage for my divinity and the control of my subjects.

I contemplated two things. Re-opening the gold mining operations of Africa . . . and taking advantage of what the native population had already done in that respect in the southern entity of the Western Continents.

Also I thought this.

My Chosen People . . . eventually I might put them in charge of administering and keeping order in the world. Under my own august authority, of course. They could be, perhaps, both troops and canny administrators.

But of course that could only come after centuries of seasoning and training. Not so easily would I yet surrender even a part of the administration of the planet to anyone besides myself.

Yet I did think it better eventually to have things run that way. The thing was for we gods to always appear as just that . . . gods. It would not do to mix too closely into the day-to-day running of things . . . too much familiarity with us might eventually breed a kind of contempt.

I thought of Enlil . . . how could anyone respect him much less revere him if they knew him and his weaknesses as intimately as I did?

Distance . . . a show of authority and magnificence . . . power . . . all those things were necessary to keep that definite divisorial line always in place. That absolutely essential demarcation between Divinity and the savage, barbarian inferior races of Earth.

As I said, I had a lot of work to do.

****

Absolute unquestioning loyalty under any circumstance. Thoughtless, automatic . . . it had to be that way if my Chosen People were to be the Whip of God. The arm of Jehovah.

There were necessarily going to be a number of tests which they had to pass. Otherwise I would drop them and select some other tribe.

The first one I thought of was this . . .

****

"Abraham . . . Abraham . . . do you hear me? This is Jehovah, your only god . . ."

I was in the gold Flagship of Enki, now my own personal Flagship, hovering at dawn some 200 feet in the air above Abraham's village.

Long ago, when he was still a child in Sumer, I had impressed into his right ear lobe a tiny gold microwafer which was a radio receptor.

I gave him now his instructions. His test.

"Abraham . . . the time has come to prove your loyalty to your god, Jehovah . . . I need a sacrifice . . . this time not just a lamb . . . the sacrifice must be of your son. Of your beloved son, Isaac. You must arise now . . . this is urgent . . . go to the altar, take Isaac with you. Tell him you are going to sacrifice a lamb. But once you are at the altar, I want you to sacrifice him instead."

Now I watched Abraham carefully, with the ship set on Proteus Blend so it would not be visible to him or his son Isaac or anyone else.

I observed him in the early dawn follow my instructions and walk with his son the quarter mile to the raised stone altar.

So far, so good. Abraham seemed my true child, always obedient to higher authority, as it must be.

Then they were there.

What would happen next?

If the results were not good, I would drop Abraham's tribe as the Chosen People and look elsewhere for my leadership . . .

****

The large knife glistened in the early sunlight.

I saw it clearly, poised in the air above Isaac's body tied to the altar.

There was no question of sincerity here. Abraham, tears running down his aged cheeks, was set to do the one thing he could never do. Kill his son.

That was enough for me.

"Abraham . . . put down your knife! You have passed my loyalty test. Untie your son. He is your link to the future. A glorious future. He is a hero, as are you."

My amplified, augmented divine voice boomed down at him this time from the skies.

I saw him follow my command, then embrace his son . . . and at last collapse into the sand.

"Abraham," I told him. "Jehovah is and must be exigent. Be content. You have passed an important test. You have done well."

****

Abraham had done well, true. But then, after all, Abraham was my own son. It was only natural that he should obey his father, even though he had no inkling I was indeed his natural father. But my blood beat in his veins . . . I had no doubt but what some of my own DNA in his nervous system made it like finely attuned antennae to receive even my unspoken messages.

That I had a son was still a secret to everyone at Anunnaki headquarters except for Doctor Atra, and I wanted to keep it that way. I had a unique advantage, being the only one so far to be able to procreate the great Anunnaki heritage.

In spite of Abraham's now well-demonstrated quality of blind loyalty and unquestioned obedience, even to the point of almost murdering his son Isaac whom he loved so much . . . I was not satisfied with the progress of the rest of the tribe.

But I determined to continue my experiments and tests until such time as I would be satisfied. And until I was, there was no way I would allow the tribe to assume the post of the Whip of Jehovah, no matter how desperately I desired to begin to utilize that whip.

There were, after all, rebellions to be put down. Not so much in the Western Continents that had never been infected with Enki's virus of rebellion and dreams of equality. But in the Middle Continent, yes.

While I was able to meet these crises with a show of Divine Force, still, to have a stable administration I would have much preferred to use my whip and myself stay out of the picture . . . again to keep the separation I wanted, so essential to running a taut planet . . . a regulated planet where everyone knew his place and feared to the depths of his being ever trying to jump up out of it.

And Abraham, ironically, now that he had proved his undoubted loyalty, I realized one day was getting old and feeble.

To work with Earthlings with their incredibly brief lifespans . . . well, while it has its advantages as I have said before, preventing them from thinking too much of long range plans which might be dangerous . . . it is always a shock to realize still once again how delicate and fragile Earthlings are. How their desperate lives pass like a race towards the finish line of death . . . so quickly before your eyes.

I could have with genetic tampering with Doctor Atra's help expanded Abraham's lifespan.

But on the other hand I couldn't, either.

That would have been against our code and our ultimate goals and would set a dangerous precedent. No, we could give little rewards here and there to humans but never anything genetic . . . that would be to fall into the sin of Enki. That was something I would not do. Not I, Jehovah, the god of Earth.

But I was sorry to see Abraham go. I mourned him. He was after all part Anunnaki and my son . . . and had given me faithful service. If all the tribe were like him, my dream of having my Invincible Army would be at least half complete.

But I knew they weren't. I had to find something that would toughen them up, somehow make them equal to the grand task they had to carry out in my name.

****

For a long time nothing occurred to me.

I had the administration of Earth to think about and deal with constantly.

The gold production at last was prospering and we all started using gold ornaments in our dress and in decorative touches at the Mount Olympus headquarters.

Enlil especially went crazy for the shiny metal, in what I thought to be a quite ridiculous way. He had an enormous gold belt around his middle . . . since that middle seemed to be ever expanding due to his completely sybaritic and irresponsible life style, the belt had to expand over time too . . . and soon came to be more girdle than belt . . . though as a girdle, even the fine spun molecular fibers of gold proved inferior to the ever-increasing magnitude of their task.

He really disgusted me, Enlil, and I came to ask myself how long I would have to put up with his inanities and ineptitudes. How long I would have to pretend he ruled Earth when I knew and everybody knew . . .

But let that go.

I used the precious metal now to negotiate sometimes with tribes and as an incentive to them to reinforce the absolute hierarchical imperative of the planet . . . and in that I thought I was really quite ingenious.

It cost me nothing.

The gold itself, after all, was produced by natural processes inside Earth. The mining was done by my slaves, closely regulated by overseers I myself appointed for their particular cruelty and attitude of unbending strictness. That was necessary since above all the slaves must be kept in line. Their working together otherwise gave them a dangerous sense of unity of purpose, something I wanted to discourage in everyone except in my Chosen People.

Most of my overseers were from that Chosen People. After their tours of duty I permitted them to bring back to the tribe a certain quantity of gold. I did that purposely. Eventually I wanted them to control a certain amount thus of the world's wealth. To be able to lend to other tribes and never be in debt themselves. To dominate, in other words, monetarily. Which was an attractive adjunct to eventually being able to dominate other tribes militarily.

In such managerial chores the time passed quickly. And one day I suddenly realized what at first seemed an incredible fact . . .

Isaac, the late Abraham's son, the one who had almost been sacrificed to me, himself was now grown senile. I realized I had to pick his successor from his twin sons, that to pick the right one was important to my cause.

Jacob and Esau . . . they were quite a pair. Almost total opposites.

At first I thought in Esau. He was virile, of sun-burnished, reddish hair, an abundant thatch on his head as well as a mat of it on his chest and spread all over his muscular body. He was an outdoors man, a hunter . . . strong and closely allied to nature and the land. Those were not bad qualities.

But on second thought . . .

His twin brother Jacob . . . darker in all respects, mentally as well as physically . . . not so open in his aspect or his speech . . .

His wiliness impressed me. It could be exactly the quality I needed upon which to build my army, my Whip of God.

I began to watch them both. From above and afar, in the Flagship.

One day, using the technology available in my Flagship, I witnessed the following scene.

Esau, tired from his day-long hunt, came home where Jacob was busily cooking up a rich-smelling stew.

Esau in his open way asked for some of the stew.

Jacob said, "The stew I can give you. Give you right now, as hot and meaty and nourishing as it is . . . the best I've ever made. In an instant you can be sitting there in comfort eating it to your heart's content. As many servings as you might want." He paused. "But . . ."

"But what?" demanded the famished Esau.

"But I need something in return."

"Say it, it's yours. After all, you're my brother. Anyway, I have no strength with which to resist. I'm dying of hunger."

"Just sign this document and then swear to what I tell you."

Esau waved his right arm as if brushing away a fly. "I'll sign or swear anything, brother, as long as it's you who presents it to me. But serve that stew up."

Jacob put the quill pen and sheep parchment in front of Esau, who made his mark.

"Now swear."

"Swear what?"

"Your birthright you assign to me."

"What? . . . Jacob, this is ridiculous. If you think my birthright can be taken away by this . . ."

Jacob shrugged and grinned. "Then swear."

Esau did. "Now give me the stew."

A smile of great contentment overcame Esau's red-bearded face as he luxuriated in the smell and substance of the delicious stew, and seemed to lose himself in its steaming contents . . .

****

Abraham was gone. Isaac was gone.

Swept into the dustbins of Earth time.

But now . . . now at least I had Jacob.

Jacob the wily. Jacob the clever. Jacob who knew what he wanted and how to get it.

I had something rare and valuable here and I knew it.

I knew it doubly when I later heard that the blind and dying Isaac had been deceived by Jacob into giving his final blessing and inheritance not to the older brother, Esau, but to Jacob.

This . . . this was my man . . . my building block to the future.

****

I was to watch Jacob cheat and deceive his way into constantly escalating prosperity many times. At last I determined to let him know he had won my heart . . . and that it was his DNA I wanted to instill in future generations of my Chosen People as part of my very personally directed breeding program.

In fact, he had so won my heart I had to let him know on a more personal level.

And in a way, too, it would be his final test . . .

****

From the Flagship I was watching Jacob's massive party in their travel.

It was night, and for some reason Jacob had arisen, and decided to send across the Jabbok River both his wives and his two concubines along with his eleven sons. That left Jacob alone in the camp and I . . . I saw my opportunity.

I beamed down from the Flagship.

To beam down when I am the sole occupant of the Flagship is something very easily done, once I have set the very sophisticated ship's control on hold.

Just that to insure my own return, I also factor in inside the tractor beam a kind of spiral staircase, which has a temporary ultra-light physical reality. In case the electronic system should fail . . . an extremely remote possibility . . . I could physically walk right up it to the access door of the Flagship.

This time I used Proteus to shield both the Flagship and the tractor beam from Jacob's eyes. For what I had in mind I wanted to approach him from out of the night in an anonymous fashion, as if I were just some pilgrim Earthling.

Touching ground, I walked the short distance to Jacob's camp.

I entered from out of the night and into the circle of light generated by his flickering campfire with only the briefest of greetings. Then, without further preamble I challenged the startled Jacob to a wrestling match on the spot.

For one thing I wanted to see if he was physically strong enough to be my leader. One thing was wiles, another was muscles . . .

Besides, I wanted to see how he might meet an unexpected crisis.

He did not shrink from the challenge.

We met in a solid mutual bodylock and for hours neither of us could get the advantage.

I was agreeably surprised to say the least.

But I could not let any Earthling beat me, not even Jacob.

So there, even as we continued to twist and turn and strain amidst mutual grunts and groans and the campfire at last flickered its last, leaving us still struggling under the light of the stars . . .

It occurred to me what I had to do.

I used a technique that had to make me win, based on my knowledge of a weakness in human physiology. I chopped my right hand at his hip, my crisp blow immediately knocking it out of its socket.

That should have been enough.

But it wasn't.

He still hung on.

"I will not let you go until you bless me."

That told me two things. He knew I was something more than human, which showed his mental acuity. And . . . he had a grit and dogged determination like few others.

I was well pleased. I pretended not to know his name, asked it.

"Jacob."

"No, it is not. Not any longer. From now on it will be Israel . . . because you have proved yourself fit to be a worthy opponent of both men and god. I bless you here in the name of Jehovah."

I touched his forehead.

Then I used my belt Proteus to allow both the tractor beam and the lighted ship to become visible.

As he watched in awe, I stepped into the nearby bluish-white tractor beam. I could have tractored myself aboard, of course. Instead, I chose to make a leisurely climb around the twisting ultra-light spiral stairway. It must have seemed to him something like a filmy, blue-white stairway into heaven, an impression that certainly would do no harm to my cause.

I saw him drop to his knees and several times touch his forehead to the ground, then raise both his arms to heaven.

I turned and gave him a last sweeping and measured wave before entering the Flagship.

I was well content with my little charade.

I had now beyond any doubt confirmed that I had found the foundation rock of my house. The house that would assure world order and that would continue to endure for many Earth centuries into the future.

****

Jacob was perfect, but still the rest of his tribe left me discontent. They had nothing of his cunning, of his physical and moral strength, his solidity of purpose.

At last it occurred to me. An evolutionary package that would insure that those who survived were the best and strongest of the lot. If I do say so myself, it was a stroke of genius, my sudden inspiration.

To perpetuate the strong and make them ever stronger . . . how simple. All I needed was an environment to effectuate that, and it was near at hand.

As for the weak . . . they would inevitably perish along the way, which was exactly how I wanted it.

I remembered the Dinosaurs of my revered ancestor's great experiment . . . he had come out of that with the greatest fighting machines ever produced . . . it was not his fault that the Intergalactic Federation had decided that what he was doing was wrong. The weakness was on their part, not his.

And as to the Intergalactic Federation . . . with so much territory to cover the likelihood of their ever investigating my own activities on outpost Earth . . . were so negligible as to approach the vanishing point.

My idea was so delightful to me that I took its contemplation slowly . . . like eating some delicate confection you do not wish ever to be completely consumed.

Though my mind had leaped ahead to the end plan, I reviewed my idea as if it had not, looking carefully now at every individual step . . . as if I did not know where it would lead to.

Let's see . . .

Egypt was a territory I had not yet addressed. As to how to conquer it and bring it directly under my rule.

Its history was too intertwined with Enki's son, Marduk, who the Egyptians called Ra, to give me any comfort.

So as a still unconquered and innately rebel territory Egypt was a challenge. But perhaps I could turn that challenge to my advantage somehow . . .

What if I transferred that challenge to my Chosen People?

Just as I had wrestled Jacob to test his mettle, what if I put the whole tribe into a kind of wrestling match . . . to strengthen them . . . to make the strong stronger and the weak disappear? A kind of manipulated evolution which appealed to me both for my present and my long range purposes.

And then circumstance came to my aid. I saw a way to solve two problems at one time . . .

****

What happened was a strange tale indeed, the details of which I will not go into here.

It had to do with one of Jacob's sons, Joseph. He had been sold into slavery by his jealous brothers and ended up in Egypt. However, such was his ability he quickly rose from his slavery to be the main advisor to the Egyptian Pharaoh. Blood will tell, after all, and I saw again the wisdom of my choice in picking Jacob to build my Chosen Race around.

But there was more to it than that. In reality, much as I was the real ruler of Earth in its entirety rather than Enlil, so it was with Joseph and the Pharaoh. The real ruler in all but name was Joseph himself.

I lost no time in appearing to Joseph in my generic saintly image as generated by Proteus.

"I am the god of your father Jacob, " I told him. "And the god of his father Isaac. And the god of Isaac's father Abraham. Before Abraham was, I am. I am the god of all Earth."

Joseph was quickly won over with all that, and had he not been I would have done whatever it took to win him.

I told him about Egypt and my concerns about it. How it had strayed from Jehovah, their true god, to continue to worship certain false gods.

"Ra?" he said, angling his handsome face sideways at me.

"Ra."

He told me how he had been troubled himself by having to pay public allegiance to the Egyptian god when in his childhood his father

Jacob had brought him up to revere Jehovah. "Did you . . . did you really wrestle with him? Was that really you?"

"It was. I am your god and you are my Chosen People. It was a test for your father and later I gave him a revelation, too. I tested him more than once, just as I did Abraham. Are you ready to hear my plan now, and what you must do to carry it out?"

I described everything for him in great detail.

How Ra was an evil influence of Satanic origin. How he was the spawn of the Devil . . . and how, though the Devil had been destroyed by the wrath of Jehovah, and though the Devil's spawn, Ra himself, had also been destroyed in the same fiery wrath . . . unfortunately, his image remained. Remained and was still dominant in Egypt. I was eventually going to change that, I promised him, and establish myself, the true god here . . . but first the heathen idols of Ra that were so widespread in Egypt must be destroyed. His image must be eradicated and then I could establish the new image of the only true god, Jehovah.

Concomitant with that, I told him, I wanted to bring my Chosen People here, to Egypt. They would help me in my fight against Ra, infiltrating their loyalty to me, first of all . . . and secondly, they would be preparing themselves, in ways that might be beyond his understanding, but that eventually would make them soldiers of Jehovah. And that if they performed well, these soldiers of god would be led into a land of milk and honey, an Earthly paradise over which they would rule alone for thousands of years, their descendants as numerous as the stars in the sky, their enemies powerless against them . . .

****

And so I appeared next to Jacob and told him to settle in Egypt, he and all his tribe. And that while things might not seem to go so smoothly at first and possibly not smoothly at all at any time during his lifetime . . . that still, I could assure him that by this in many ways traumatic experience, the Chosen People would be forged into a new mold and model . . . one that would endure in the place of honor for many thousands of years.

At first Jacob resisted my ideas. After all, I had told him and his people previously that Canaan would be theirs and he could not understand why they must now go instead to Egypt.

I finally convinced him by telling him mine was not a promise broken, but only a promise delayed. A promise whose fulfillment, once it came, would then be ten times more glorious than I had painted it before. That Canaan and the Israelite rule over it would be greatly strengthened by the hiatus in Egypt, where the Israelites would eventually, after much travail, elevate themsselves to become the very Scourge of god, able to conquer Canaan and its peoples and to ever more be its only rulers . . . that itself only a step to their eventual rule over all Earth as god's stewards and administrators.

Jacob obeyed his god, as I knew he would.

****

As long as Joseph lived and ruled over Egypt things went well in my Egypt pacification plan.

All the images of the devil god Ra were smashed to smithereens, much to my satisfaction. Though there were loyalists, still, to his memory under the rule of Enki . . . he was after all, Enki's son, and therefore a favorite of many . . . still, I knew I had one thing irrevocably always on my side. That was the incredibly brief Earthling lifespan, automatically cancelling out direct memory and therefore any serious continuity of attitude or action.

I myself appeared in my generic saintly form generated by Proteus several times in different places, announcing myself as Jehovah, the god of Earth. First of all, of course, around the area of the Great Pyramid, and then over a period of years near various tribal centers.

So my campaign was going well and I had no doubt that over time it would succeed totally.

But then Joseph died . . .

****

And it was time to initiate part 2 of my plan.

There were still unbelievers in Egypt. Those who chose Ra over Jehovah even though his images had by now all been long ago destroyed. Perhaps they lusted for his empty promises of equality with the gods and his other seditious nonsense inherited from the nefarious Enki himself.

The new Pharaoh was what might have looked to ordinary eyes to be a problem . . . a professed advocate of Ra. He reacted negatively against the growing presence of Jacob's descendants. They were multiplying fast . . . much faster than the Egyptians themselves. He saw them as a threat and said so.

Then made a move that startled everyone by its suddenness. Jacob's tribes . . . there were now twelve of them . . . were declared enemies of Egypt and ordered to depart immediately.

When they did not, his official decree came quickly down. They were to be no longer residents, but slaves. Slaves of the Pharaoh and subject to his exclusive will or whim.

I saw all this and laughed.

Laughed, because, had this Pharaoh's attitude not existed I would have had to order it.

This was what I wanted . . . it fit my plans exactly.

To be more precise . . .

His actions forumulated part 2 of my plan. Without my having to do anything . . .

Which was to expose my Chosen Ones to a breeding experiment, almost exactly the one of my own conception. As I said earlier, one not so far removed either from that of my grandfather who regulated the dinosaurs on Earth.

My own experiment was different in its details, of course. It would not be genetic manipulation I would be instituting . . . and thus would be quite different from either the dinosaurs or the experiments on Atlantis that eventually produced the Perfect Warrior.

What it would constitute would be a kind of forced and greatly accelerated artificial evolution.

I had already calculated it this way. The Chosen People as they stood did not live up to my expectations. Not in hardihood and vigor, though they stood better in craft, and in grasping imagination. I wanted first of all however, physical specimens that would be able to crush any opposition. And I had not attained that yet.

But maybe after several generations of hard enslavement I would.

How many generations? I didn't know. Whatever it took, was my basic attitude.

Meanwhile, if the Pharaoh tried in his picayune way to re-establish Ra I would let him do it.

When I later at my choosing asserted my power against a non-existent opponent whose ashes were even now blowing with any vagrant breeze somewhere across the Sinai desert . . . the impact would be such that there would no longer exist in Egypt even one single believer in the devil Ra . . .

While all would quickly convert to the powerful deity that was myself . . .

I, Jehovah.

****

Meanwhile, I had many more problems than that of Egypt and my Chosen People, my potential Whip of God.

The principal one was Enlil.

While he was dormant, playing with his darts and doing his ridiculous juggling and romancing Earth women he was no problem.

It was when he emerged from that role that I became concerned. Because he could ruin everything. Turn all my grandiose plans into dust with a word . . . or even just a gesture of disgust.

I saw the deep injustice of that, and could no longer take it.

I decided to act before I myself was acted upon.

His whims were getting more and more unpredictable and . . . and with time he might even have done the unthinkable. Replaced me.

And with Enlil in real command rather than just apparently so . . .

what would happen to Earth? I shuddered at the thought. I could picture it metaphorically rudderless in the great primordial seas of space with only its irresponsible Royal psychopath at the helm . . . the planet itself thus doomed to become inevitably a hapless victim just begging to be conquered . . . by some outside invader, by upstart Earthlings, by a chain of foreseeable and preventable circumstance, if not merely by the always certain progress of ever encroaching Chaos itself.

I could not let that happen. Enlil without me to control and guide him would be, terrible as the thought was, worse than Enki . . . worse because under his pusilanimous lack of leadership there was no way his rule could last even at the outside more than a hundred Earth years.

So . . .

I had no choice. No recourse. I had to take corrective action and soon.

Having the crisis upon me, I did not hesitate. Courage has never been a quality lacking in me.

In the Western Continents we had found our salvation in the contents of a certain cactus. It had greatly accelerated our return to health.

But Doctor Atra had made a study and found other uses of a different growth of cacti.

Which contained a deadly, undetectable poison.

A fact he confided only to me. I had held it in reserve all these centuries of Earth time.

It was something now that, judiciously applied, might effectively act as an anodyne to remove the pain of Enlil's ineffective leadership forever . . .

****

It was an evening, not an unusual one at all, when the Mount Olympus headquarters was alight with music and activity.

The twenty girls from . . . I believe what I had christened and we had come to call the Iberian Peninsula, were all prepacified and thus free of any inhibitions they might have had.

They were all sinuous and swaying, lips open, and inviting . . . and things were proceeding normally. Certain exquisite preliminaries were taking place, tantalizing everyone involved . . . one girl put on her own erotic show, doing certain things to herself before us all that in its detail entered into territory previously unknown even to us . . .

The big erotic culmination was about to begin.

And that was when my opportunity arose.

Enlil himself, already tipsy, asked me to serve him another drink of his favorite Greek liquor. That libation was so thick and potent that it could mask any other aroma . . . even of a liquid extracted from a cactus.

So I went into the next room and poured him another drink of the potent Greek libation. But first I put into his glass enough of the distilled cactus liquid to kill an elephant.

Came back and with an appropriately subservient flourish and a hypocritical smile put it before him.

His fate at that bold moment . . . was sealed.

And so mine. Ruler of Earth not only in fact, but soon also to be in name.

I thought of the dispatches I must eventually then send to the new Anunnaki Home Planet there in Zeta Reticuli 2 . . .

How Enlil had died heroically in responding to the traitorous attack of Enki . . . fighting to preserve Anunnaki values.

How I had been forced to take over, against my will, to avoid the chaos of insurrection.

I was savoring that as I stood there contemplating the now wild scene.

Bodies were combining in unpredictable ways as if activated by forces no one understood. Immediate necessity had to be fulfilled, and that was all that mattered to anyone in the almost palpable heat of the moment.

Enlil was caught up in it. He left his drink where I had set it and dedicated his entire energy to the voluptuous young maiden now insinuating herself upon his supine form.

Well, I told myself, I could wait.

But then I couldn't.

Could not because . . .

Liamo swept by. He was one of us twelve, of course. Not anyone so essential . . . just a hospital administrator. He must have thought the drink was his. Anyway, he swept it up, and I watched horrified as he downed its contents at a gulp.

****

Doctor Atra's official medical verdict was vital to me, and he did not disappoint me . . . knowing as he did what I had tried to do.

Liamo had died, he said sadly, from a case of over-excitement. The sexual stimulation had just been too much, an anomaly . . . just one of those strange things that happen once in a million years.

Everyone seemed to be satisfied with that. Everyone . . . being the eight surviving Anunnaki besides myself, Doctor Atra and Enlil . . . was not important, of course, but Enlil was . . . he accepted it also without question, even felt superior I surmised from later conversations, because he himself though extremely excited had not succumbed to any such attack. So, in his strange mind, the medical decision flattered him.

I volunteered to dispose in an honorable way of the body.

A burial at sea.

Enlil nodded, impressed by my sincerity and sagacity.

They all in fact thought me quite noble, and applauded my suggestion. Of course, how could they not, once Enlil had given his stamp of approval . . .

****

Late the next afternoon, just at sunset over the broad Atlantic I released the hatch of the Military scout and watched the body of the late Liamo plunge downwards towards the blue waters.

It could have been Enlil, I thought with some bitterness . . . visualizing the exalted position that would have left me in.

But on the other hand there was the chilling thought . . . what if my murder attempt had been detected? I myself would then be the inert and lifeless thing I had released to find its way to ultimate destruction . . . prey to gravity and watery impact and then to the myriad denizens of the distant and forbidding deep.

I shuddered, and swung the Military scout back towards Mount Olympus . . .

****

Jacob's twelve tribes, what everyone now began to call the Israelites because of the new name I had bestowed upon him as the father of a new nation . . . were either faring very badly or very well in Egypt over a long period of time.

Whether they were doing well or badly depended entirely on the point of view.

At first glance it seemed they hardly could do worse, and as if their god Jehovah had deserted them.

They were poor, they had few possessions anymore of their own, almost everything taken over by Pharaoh's men. They had no lives of their own any longer, their whole agenda again controlled by the wishes of the Pharaoh. They were put to work dawn to dusk at the most laborious, backbreaking tasks. They toiled endlessly under the hot Egyptian sun fashioning bricks from clay and straw and baking them in enormous kilns that added to the already killing heat. Many of the weaker Israelites simply could not stand this regimen, sickened and died. Only the strongest and hardiest, the most healthy, were able to endure.

Which was exactly the way I wanted it. So . . . from my perspective things were going well. Quite well.

After almost three hundred Earth years of this I was one day observing them from on high doing this same backbreaking work under a broiling sun . . .

The difference, I thought. The palpable difference. Almost night and day.

Where early on a lot of frail and sickly people had been in evidence, that was not true now.

I observed them closely with magnification.

The women had a simple, straightforward, active dark beauty, their bodies slender and lithe where their ancestors had tended to be soft and puffy and overweight. The men when they moved showed rippling muscles and had an obvious strength which gave them dominance even over the enormous and tiring tasks they had to do . . . so that they went about those daunting tasks cheerily, with few complaints, and even with slaps on the back among themselves and grins and flourishes.

My plan was a success, I saw. These . . . these could truly become the warriors of god, Jehovah's Whip on Earth . . .

There was one more step to take.

I said genetics would play no part in this, my shaping of my warriors, but now it occurred to me that I still needed one fantastic exemplar of what the ideal warrior should be.

And genetics could play its part in that . . .

There was one particular lady in the group of Israelites working so devotedly below me who caught my attention.

The lithest of them, and tall, with long abundant dark hair that fell across her shoulders and well-developed chest . . . and eyes that seemed like a pair of dark, mysterious wells.

That night I tractored her up to the Flagship, pacified her and kissed her. All around her eyes I circled my lips like troops, and kept up the campaign until I saw she was hypnotized by me and ready to be taken like a city. I told her she was about to be granted a great honor . . . to be ravished by a god.

I saw the excitement grow until at last it spilled over out the great wells of her eyes . . .

****

Shortly after our child was born, I again brought her and the boy aboard the Flagship.

"His name shall be called Joshua," I told her, patting the boy's dark locks as I spoke. "He shall be the Israelite's greatest warrior. You will see it. They will bless his name. He will win many victories for Israel, their songs shall praise him."

She was ecstatic, but then her expression darkened.

"What's wrong?"

"My Lord . . . you are Joshua's father. But . . . shall I see you again? I don't know even what to call you. Are you . . . are you our god . . . are you the great Jehovah?"

Well, I was, of course. But I was not about to tell her that, not after I had had time to think about it . . .

It would not be prudent to let it be noised about that Jehovah was having children with his Chosen People. It led, it seemed to me, to a certain lack of respect. The line between Divinity and Humanity must always be a sharp, well-defined one, even with a Chosen People. I was not about to fall into the nefarious Enki's mistaken ideas . . .

So I extemporized and prevaricated with her . . .

"I am not permitted to tell you my name. Nor are you permitted to tell anyone your child's father is divine. But I tell you this . . . no, I am not the great Jehovah who no one can approach in his singular magnificence. No. But I am . . . close to his throne. And that is all I can say. You are indeed honored among women to have been specially picked to mother my child."

She seemed well content with that. At first. But then . . .

Her beautiful clear brow knitted up.

"My Lord . . . there is a problem. I have a child and the elders look upon me strangely because I have no husband. I have no standing with the tribe . . . I am perilously close to being outcast. They could even decide to stone me . . ."

Her wide eyes opened even wider with terror.

I had the remedy for that and gave it to her in a wooden box inlaid with precious jewels.

"The box alone would be enough to accomplish the purpose. But look inside."

She did . . . and the gold bar, late of the Southern continent of the Western Continents, sparkled in the light inside the Flagship.

Her eyes formulated other questions, so I answered them for her before she could speak them.

"Now you have a dowry, given to you by someone close to the throne of god. It will buy you a husband, anyone you want. You do not have to take the first who comes calling because there will be many. You can pick the handsomest or the richest, or perhaps find some pleasing combination of the two."

Of course I was right and she was quickly married and elevated to important social status among her tribe.

And I looked forward eagerly to the development of Joshua, who I hoped to make my Model Warrior.

****

A few Earth years later, something incredible happened.

We were having dinner, just seven of us Anunnaki . . . the other four being at our underground base in Iberia . . . in the main dining room of our Mount Olympus Headquarters.

Outside, the setting sun made marvellous effects of light and shadow upon the several peaks in our sight. It gave a celestial atmosphere to everything, and tended by its magnificence to yes, make us feel like the gods of Earth we now were.

The mood was jovial and toasts were being drunk. To Enlil, of course . . . to myself, to Doctor Atra . . . to the aged King Anu . . . to our Home Planet Nibiru, now a lifeless derelict which, because of its unstable volcanic core might even one day explode . . .

We talked about that and our engineer Bronti even gave a little talk about Nibiru's possibilities of survival. He didn't seem to think they were very good. The internal heat at last, he thought, would prove too much for the planet's integrity, and would eventually end up blowing it apart.

At the end of his speech we toasted the planet where all of us had been born and grew up.

Then of course we had to toast the new Home Planet of the Anunnaki in the Constellation Zeta Reticuli 2.

We knew from the dispatches received in the Great Pyramid on a periodic basis that things were going well there. Just as our dispatches to them indicated the same on Earth . . . I had decided not yet to say anything about the death of Enki and his cohorts . . . but that time would come, and perhaps soon. I in fact looked forward to it, because as soon as Anu knew that Enlil lived and that he had lost his other son Enki, he would want Enlil to come home, probably to assume the rule over all the Anunnaki on the new Home Planet.

Which I knew would leave me in charge of Planet Earth. I already was, of course, in everything except name. Still, I wanted the name, too. Jehovah, the one and only god of Earth.

That in fact I came to realize, is what I wanted more than anything.

I was glad now in retrospect my plan to murder Enlil had gone awry. It would have been a mistake, I realized. Better to let him go back to the Home Planet . . . we would both be safely happy then. He to rule there, I to rule here.

Those were my thoughts when . . .

There was a strange sound coming from somewhere outside.

****

I was the first out on the grounds.

The sun had set, it was dark now.

My belt flash in my hand pierced that darkness.

I received a terrible shock.

Caught in the rays was a clearly defined face. A face from what I thought was the dead past. A face I knew all too well . . .

The others, perhaps loggy from their drinks, were still inside.

My mind reeled. It simply could not be. Impossible . . .

But I knew what I was seeing. Even if it was just a glimpse before, with an agility he had always been famous for, he ducked and pivoted away from the light and blended somehow into darkness. I slashed the blade of my light desperately like a sword against the gloom, but could not discover him again.

Marduk! Marduk, the son of Enki! Who the Egyptians called their god Ra . . .

He should have been killed in the nuclear blast of the Sinai Space Station. Everyone . . . all of Enki's forces should have been there for the special celebration.

That, I thought about later. What I thought about now, was . . . get him! Before he gets me.

But he did. Get me. With a laser blast that knocked me down. Down and out.

I descended into my own personal blackness deeper than the night's . . . uttering his cursed name.

When the others revived me, I told them who I had seen.

They had found no one.

But I . . . I looked around and saw clear evidence that someone had tried to board the great Mother Ship. The correct code had already been entered to open up its sliding panel . . . that was obvious because it gaped open now. No one inside, everything secure, but . . .

It was clear to me we had avoided total disaster by a matter of seconds.

It changed everything.

****

Security.

That was the new watchword. Now that we knew Marduk and possibly others had survived our atomic attack.

I went over everything in my mind.

All of Enki's ships were accounted for. The Mother Ship and the

Flagship we had. The others were destroyed in the blast. No question about it. So . . .

How could Marduk have survived?

At last I came up with a theory. Marduk . . . and perhaps others . . . maybe had been on duty inside the Great Pyramid. Not as a regular security watch, because my own nocturnal visits there while Enki lived proved there hadn't been any.

But maybe . . .

Maybe someone had been stationed there just that particular night. Purpose? To send and receive messages about the celebration to the New Home Planet. That would explain how he had escaped destruction. If true, he would have been left there at the Great Pyramid . . . perhaps the plan having been to be picked up the following day.

But no. While it could be, it was against normal procedure. Enki wanted everyone there for the annual celebration . . . that I well knew from personal experience.

There were other possible explanations.

Marduk could have been that night of our sweet revenge at Enki's headquarters on Mount Olympus . . . for whatever reason . . .

Perhaps he was taken ill shortly before the celebration and had been left there to recuperate.

Yes, that could be. It fit his profile. He was such a spoiled brat, always looking to be pampered beyond reason and thinking special treatment was always his due, never wanting to expose himself to any hardship. And then of course Enki his father had as always been to blame in the cultivating of such an attitude. Never one to be demanding of anyone, much less his beloved son.

I could almost see that happening in my mind's eye now.

The terrible thing was that, however it had happened, it was a fact. No question of that. I had seen his terrible, unmistakable face so reminiscent of the monster Enki.

The thing was now . . . what was I to do about it?

As I already said, security, thanks to me, was now the number one new policy of our rule.

Constant watches all around, everywhere. The Great Pyramid, our underground base in Iberia, Mount Olympus . . . everywhere.

To keep those watches we needed more manpower. I immediately authorized Doctor Atra to clone our clones again. This time to produce another hundred of them which we could employ as needed to keep constant vigil everywhere without thereby draining our own vital energies.

But that, I realized, was only defense. What I really needed to do was go on the offense.

Find Marduk.

Find Marduk and eradicate him and his followers as soon as possible . . .

****

Using my Flagship I made a thorough air search of Egypt.

And there was nothing . . . nothing from the air that I could see that indicated any presence of Marduk.

But in the very course of my surveillance I came across an interesting scene . . .

****

It was not unusual to see the Israelite slaves being beaten by their brutal Egyptian overseers. Not at all. It was, in fact, routine . . . and I had no objection to it. It was part of the refining process that was working out so successfully in producing a hale and hearty race that could eventually be of great service to me, a race free of weaklings and cowards.

However on this occasion . . .

Something truly unusual, unprecedented, was taking place.

A young man standing nearby the beating scene stepped forward aggressively. He was well-dressed and obviously not a slave himself.

But it was what he did next that caught my rapt attention.

He looked around first, to see if any Egyptian besides the overseer might be nearby. None were. Then he grabbed the long wooden club of the overseer in his own widespread two hands. With that leveraged grip he flipped the Egyptian sideways onto the sands.

But the Egyptian was up quickly, now flashing a drawn knife. They circled each other.

When the Egyptian made his move forward to stab, the athletic young man sidestepped and brought his right knee hard into the stomach of the attacker.

When the stunned overseer dropped his knife in the sand, the young man grabbed it and, without hesitation, buried it to the hilt into the overseer's heart.

I had to move on. But before I did I imprinted something into the still trembling right arm of the young man. He wasn't even conscious of it. Why should he be? It didn't hurt. It was just a tiny microcircuit to transmit a locating signal, nothing more. It would leave on his arm a little subcutaneous bump not even noticeable. All done from above by laser beam equipment with the help of the augmentation lenses. He didn't notice me because I had Proteus on Blend, so I was just a patch of sky above him should he even have looked up, which he did not.

Later I could find out who he was and always locate him electronically when I needed to do so. Joshua was almost grown now and in my plans he was to be the model for me of the ideal Israelite soldier, of course . . . but it would not hurt to have as an ally someone else in reserve . . . someone like this very interesting young man I had just been watching.

****

It was time to move on now out of the land of Egypt and into the surrounding territories in my relentless search for Marduk, the son of Enki.

That he must be exterminated, and the sooner the better, there was no question. He posed a tremendous potential danger. My entire empire could be at risk now because of him.

I wondered how he had been able to mount the attempted theft of our Mother Ship on Mount Olympus. To do so he had to over-come tremendous difficulties. First of all, it was obvious he had no ship of his own. Those had all been positively identified and then destroyed in our nuclear attack. Of that I was sure. So, what did that mean?

It meant that Marduk was somehow managing to survive on Earth with neither a space ship nor military scout to help him.

I didn't like that, because of what it meant.

What it meant was he had the support of some deviant Earth-lings. They were hiding him, supplying him . . . probably even wor-shipping him as their god. The Egyptian god, Ra.

Well, if so, they would soon feel the wrath of Jehovah, the only true god of Earth. Ra was nothing in comparison to the great Jeho-vah. That was the truth whose inevitable brunt he would soon feel.

I had to find his headquarters. My sweep of Egypt seemed to indicate it was not in that territory . . . so the question was . . . where?

Wherever it was I would find it and destroy it. It was only a question of time . . .

****

It was over the land of Canaan, the land I had promised to Jacob and his descendants, that it happened . . .

It was dusk and outside a certain village I happened to be watch-ing an episode that had no apparent importance in itself. Three ap-parently tipsy men sharing the contents of some kind of flask.

That in itself did not interest me. What did was what I saw through augmentation . . . something that was carved on the head of each one's staff.

How brazen!

Incredible effrontery . . . not to mention sacrilege to the god of Earth himself.

I could not take it. I tractored them up to my Flagship and ques-tioned them at length. Yes, it was true. They had seen Marduk. They called him the great god Ra . . . he had promised them peace and prosperity if they followed him, which they had been convinced to do.

I told them they had fallen in league with the Devil. Just before I jettisoned them from five miles up, watching their bodies with the absurdly waving arms tumble all the way to at last impact the hot sands below . . .

Thus perish always all enemies of Jehovah . . .

I told myself that, and it gave me some measure of satisfaction.

I kept their three staffs as first, a reminder of how I had to rededicate myself now to wipe out this threat . . . and second as graven proof to show Enlil. Because the carved head of each staff contained the unmistakable and hateful image of Marduk, the son of the traitorous Enki.

I told myself it was now time. Time to activate the Whip of God.

The vengeance of Jehovah would now echo across the land. Yea, even across the sacred and promised land of Canaan.

****

His name, I found out, was Moses. The young man who had killed the Egyptian overseer. He had an interesting past, I learned. He was an Israelite, yes. But adopted by an Egyptian princess and raised as a noble before the episode I had witnessed had forced him to flee Egypt.

When I looked for him I found him tending flocks for his father-in-law not far away from the place I had now established as my base for the coming campaign against Marduk and all those who supported him.

That base was atop what I myself had long ago while posing as Enki's devoted Aide christened Mount Sinai. It was convenient in many ways . . . geographically, strategically, logistically.

Of course it was nothing like the base on Mount Olympus. This one was rustic in the extreme . . . but then I did not anticipate this particular mission would take me long. While it did last, I wanted Sinai to be recognized by my Chosen People as well as their opponents as the Mountain of God. I was prepared to launch psychological as well as military warfare.

Of course, first, I had to liberate the Israelites from their slavery in Egypt . . . the 400 Earth years of which had, I felt with considerable satisfaction, apparently produced the results I had been trying to obtain.

But . . . the preparation began here, outside Egypt.

I needed to convince Moses. Enlist him in the campaign early. I had plans for him, hoped to use him in many ways. But first I had to get his attention . . .

I tried a simple technical ruse.

I used Proteus to project an image of fire upon a bush close to him.

Saw him observe it open mouthed.

I called his name with electronic amplification. "Moses, Moses!"

"Here I am," he said shakily, looking around and seeing no one.

I decided to give him the whole routine. "Do not come any closer. Take off your sandals for you are standing on Holy Ground. I . . ." and here I increased both volume and timbre of my electronically projected voice . . . "I am the God of your ancestors . . . the God of Abraham, the God of Isaac and the God of Jacob."

I went on. "You can be sure I have seen the misery of my people in Egypt. I have heard their cries for deliverance from their harsh slave drivers. Yes, I am aware of their suffering. So I have come to rescue them from the Egyptians and lead them out of Egypt into their own good and spacious land. It is a land flowing with milk and honey . . . the land where the Canaanites, Hittites, Amorites, Perizzites, Hivites and Jebusites live.

"And . . ."

I paused for effect.

"And you have been chosen to lead my people, the Israelites, out of their bondage in Egypt."

****

In the days that followed, Moses, in spite of all he had seen and heard, was still not ready to accept my word about anything. I saw that.

"God," he whimpered. "God . . . I am not ready for this. Not ready. Give it to my brother Aaron who is quick with his tongue, not like me, a rude and simple man."

I had to convince him. He who I had seen was so resilient in the thick of battle . . . and yet here so evidently confused and diffident when great plans were unexpectedly laid upon his shoulders.

I tried a new tack.

"Don't call me that."

"What?"

"God."

"But you are. Aren't you?"

"Of course I AM . . . before you were, I AM . . . that's not the point."

"But, God . . ."

"There you go again."

"What, then . . . what should I call you?"

I tried to give him suggestions. It was important.

"Well, you could begin with Your Lordship. Our Heavenly Father is all right. I like Mighty Jehovah, All Powerful Monarch of Earth and Sky . . . but, be creative, use your own powers of imagination and expression."

"Yes, your Heavenly Lordship."

He was starting to get the idea, dimly. I had to educate him. He was after all who I proposed to be the leader of my people, the one who would bring them out of Egypt.

"You see, the word 'god', though accurate, is too brief to properly express Majesty. Three letters . . . ? Three letters are just right to set down what is an ass or a dog . . . but hardly begins to imply infinite majesty. Do you get my drift?"

"I understand, Your Majesty, Ruler of the Clouds and the Vaulted Sky."

"Now you're getting it. The lyric at least and some of the music. Which brings up another subject. I want you to keep a history of everything we accomplish together. All the mighty deeds and enemies vanquished, miracles done, lands won."

"But Mighty Jehovah, I have told you I am slow of tongue . . . and of pen, too. I hardly see how I could ever . . ."

I grew impatient. "All right, then. All right. Have Aaron do it . . . someone. But it must be done. We do not want our marvellous deeds to go unrecorded. There must be chronicles of some sort. Do you understand?"

"Yes, Your Heavenly Conqueror."

"And that's not all. You could encourage the writing of supplemental literature."

"Supplemental literature? Your Universal Lordship, this ignorant shepherd remains in the dark as to your august meaning. What . . . ?"

I saw I needed to help him out.

"Poems. Poems of praise and awe about the grandeur of their god. Lyrical, ecstatic poems to the Majesty of the Great Jehovah who led them out of bondage . . ."

"But, Your Heavenly Lordship, that hasn't happened yet."

"It will. The Mighty Jehovah who makes Israel's enemies to cringe with fear in the night, at the mere thought of his mighty power, of . . . well, I want your people to do the writing, not me."

"I shall work on it, Heavenly Father."

"See that you do. And not just poems, but songs. And hymns. Hymns to the Mighty Arm of the Powerful Jehovah, Terror of the Skies . . . and so forth."

I gave him some other examples of what his artists might create.

"And keep it all in a book of some kind. Along with a record of achievements . . . all the things the Great Jehovah has led his Chosen People to accomplish, etcetera, etcetera . . . set down in an official way in an ornate style."

I realized the foregoing sounded a little on the grotesque side and even comical in a way, though we Anunnaki are not known for having any kind of sense of humor. But those are the lengths I had to go to with the Israelites, who, for all their progress, were still at best a backward and benighted people in any galactic sense, although on

Earth they were still my favorites. My objective in recording it is just to show how difficult was my task.

Being a god to a backward, ignorant tribe is not an easy matter. The Jews have just enough intelligence and initiative to make it ten times as difficult as being, for example, the god of the Mah-Yahs.

Unlike the savage Western Continent tribes, the Israelites have no idea of the psychology of a god . . . or protocol or procedures or even any common sense about it.

They definitely can not see the forest for the trees, and have difficulty seeing beyond their own noses. The future . . . is something they measure in earthly days or weeks or months . . . which in the deep vats of sidereal time is very close to being nothing at all, mere ephemera with no more weight than a fly's wings.

And that is just to begin to state the problem.

They may know which side their bread is buttered on, yes. But they have no idea of the provenance of that bread or what its greater significance in the scheme of things might be. They are short-sighted, mundane and matter-of-fact to the point of absurdity. With no vision of grandeur and greatness . . . without my first having to draw everything out for them.

Indeed, I was fast learning that everything had to be spelled out for them first, then put in dramatic form for it to penetrate that hard shell of worldliness that surrounds their Semitic heads like a protective helmet.

But, well . . . that was the Mission I had given myself when I decided to make them into my fierce warriors who would one day help enforce my rule on Earth. And at times I wondered if I had not made a big mistake . . . trying to make a silk purse out of a sow's ear, as we say on Nibiru . . . or said . . . still saying I'm sure on the new Home Planet of Zeta Reticuli 2.

Perhaps I should say more exactly that to try to fashion the Unconquerable, Invincible Perfect Warrior from a race more content to be sharp-trading merchants and sheepherders is a daunting task.

Is it any wonder they set my godly teeth on edge and sometimes make the lightning of my temper flash?

Maybe I was a fool ever to have sold Enlil such an idea in the first place . . . though to tell the truth it all dated back to his own original concept in Atlantis to create the Invincible Army. There of course we had had applied genetics on our side, and no Jewish initiative or capriciousness to work against.

****

Moses still, in spite of everything I had said to him and taught him, had all kinds of protests. I could see he was shocked beyond all measure at the prospect of himself having the heavy responsibility of leading the Israelites out of Egypt.

I did my best to reassure him. I, Jehovah, would use my supernatural powers to strike at the very heart of Egypt.

But he persisted. "Look, the Israelites will not believe me. They won't do what I tell them. They'll just say, 'The Lord never appeared to you. That's just your story.'"

"What do you have in your hand?"

"A shepherd's staff."

"Throw it down on the ground."

He did so. I used Proteus to project an image of a writhing snake upon it.

The terrified Moses turned and ran.

I called him back. "Take hold of the bottom end of the staff."

Trembling, he did, and I turned off Proteus so he again held just a shepherd's staff in his hands.

"Now, put your hand inside your robe."

When he took it out, I projected a leprous image upon the hand.

Again he trembled in fear.

"Now put it back."

When he drew his hand out again, I turned off Proteus and so he saw his hand once more as normal.

He fell to his knees and touched his forehead to the ground. "Great Jehovah, I am yours to command. Whatever I can do, I will do in your name, as your most humble servant."

That was more like it, I thought. Nevertheless this becoming air of humility was of surprisingly short duration.

Moses in fact soon began to vocalize other objections, but gradually I overcame them all. Now I had the two leaders of my campaign against Ra in place . . . my ideal Warrior and Leader who was also my son, Joshua . . . and Moses, who I was beginning to see could be useful in many ways.

Joshua had become tall and stalwart . . . well muscled, long arms and legs . . . strong jaw and a countenance of serious mien.

As with Abraham and Moses, I had made sure Joshua could receive my most intimate communications.

In their case it was an implant in an ear lobe. With Joshua it was the gift of a special permanent ear ring never to be removed,

inside of which there was a molecular transceiver.

It served several purposes. When I wanted I could speak to him directly, without others hearing unless I wanted them to . . . in which case I would just turn up the volume. Also I could listen in to his conversations with others and keep a close line on what their attitudes were.

Then, too, in the depths of night, when the sound of his steady breathing told me he was asleep . . . I could give him soft, whispered reinforcement. For example, he was told he must always strive to be a great fierce warrior to help fulfill his people's destiny . . . and that always, always, he was to be fiercely and blindly loyal to Jehovah and his teachings and instructions.

I saw things progressing in a very favorable light.

Soon the Whip of Jehovah would be ready to fall upon Ra and all who dared to follow him.

I had planned well my work. Now I would execute my plan . . .

****

I told Enlil of my plan and easily obtained his approval. As long as the darts and juggling were available to distract him, and the endless

string of girls especially recruited according to his changing specifications . . . I don't think anything really mattered to him.

By now the new clones I had ordered were grown to usable size.
They all came from the first generation of clones, and so were equal
in size to the second generation . . . about 3 feet tall. I stationed them
strategically in our enclaves around the globe to best meet our security requirements. Since there was no obvious immediate threat from
Marduk, most of the Anunnaki group in their attitudes fell once again
into what I would classify as a kind of tranquil oblivion. But not I. I
was, after all, Jehovah.

And I wanted to keep things that way.

That evening I drank instead of one, two frosty metal containers
of blood smoking in my hands . . . and dutifully swallowed twice my
normal ration of wafers, too.

****

The exodus of the Israelites from Egypt had to be a grand production . . . and I took pains to make it so.

After all, the idea of Jehovah, the single god of Earth had been
challenged by Ra, and I had to reinforce it here in great theatrical
ways . . . ways which would be devastating to any rebel or potential
challenger.

Moses was my intermediary in all this.

He would predict and prognosticate and perform miracles . . .
quote me, Jehovah, and in my name issue any needed ultimatums.

And yes, I engineered all kinds of "miracles" to make the Pharaoh
release the Israelites.

Mostly what I did was take advantage of my advance knowledge
of what was already happening in the realm of nature. A drought was
encroaching upon Egypt and so I announced through Moses that I
was the cause of various effects of the drought's progress, what I chose
to call . . . with good dramatic instincts I believe . . . plagues. Gnats
and flies and locusts and frogs from the evaporating Nile . . . the
ensuing proliferation of a certain algae that tended to turn the waters

of the Nile and all its tributaries red, which I claimed to be blood wrought by my own furious and miraculous hand . . .

The ravages of the host of infections that inevitably followed these noxious effects of the drought I also took credit for, having Moses announce them as a further product of my continuing wrath against Egypt.

And so I began to appear very great in the eyes of the Egyptians.

Especially as Ra, their great god and defender made no appearance to try to counteract my supposed actions. Actually I was hoping all along that he would. It would have greatly simplified my task in the pacification of Egypt. I would then simply blast him to oblivion is some very public way, and so in one blow capture the total loyalty of all Egypt.

But Marduk was too canny to be drawn into such a trap.

Still, my own credit as a god in Egypt because of all the "plagues" was grown very great.

So much so the Pharaoh himself at last feared for his life and sovereignty.

"Get out!" He told Moses finally one day, with a mixture of desperation and fury. "Go and take your people and all your belongings with you. Just get out!"

And so the Great Exodus began . . .

****

I set Proteus in a special way, so as deliberately to create the greatest spectacle in the sky I could. That was for the benefit of both the Israelites and the Egyptians. For those latter who still stubbornly persisted in their mistaken allegiance to Ra, it would teach them a lesson they would never forget . . .

I guided the departing column of Israelites on their way out of Egypt with the image of a gigantic thundercloud during daylight hours. Then as dusk passed and night approached I put Proteus to project an equally huge fire in the sky.

I thought that would be appropriate to get my campaign to eradicate Marduk and his image from Earth well under way.

But then . . . the Pharaoh thought better of his desperation to be rid of the Israelites. He suddenly saw them as an asset, saw his source of slave labor drifting away and didn't know how he would get his buildings and irrigation projects built without them.

He sent an army after them.

Poor fools! So slow in the learning process. They obviously still did not fully comprehend whose might they were up against.

****

They soon found out.

The fleeing Israelites came to a great natural obstacle in their flight.

The Red Sea.

Did either the Israelites or their pursuers think I was not ready to deal with that? I, Jehovah . . . ?

Well, if so, they soon saw they were wrong.

I opened a path through the Red Sea for the Israelites. Used the tractor beams to keep back the sea on either side and infra red on the sea bed itself so that almost dry land beckoned to them as their road to freedom.

They followed that road to the other side.

And then . . .

The foolish Egyptians led by some particularly prime fool as military Commander . . . chose to follow.

I waited until the majority of their forces were caught within the environs of the Red Sea. Then withdrew my tractor beams and let the massive standing wall of water on either side fall now directly over them, knocking them every which way, swept by fatal chaotic forces entirely beyond their control . . . towards swift and suffocating death.

It made me laugh.

For them to fall so predictably into my trap. I expected more intelligent opposition.

****

My next major strategical move was to gather all my newly liberated Chosen People around the base of Mount Sinai.

Again, I was prepared to give the maximum of theatrical effects. It had to be that way for the success of the Ra project.

If they were to be the Whip of God they had to believe entirely in the power and magnificence of that god.

I would make them do so . . .

****

It was Moses, of course, who I had allowed with no further interference of my own to lead his people on the long march to the base of Mount Sinai. I wanted to give him all the delegated authority I could to make his position strong.

And now . . .

Now I studied the expression on his face, on his people's faces as, agonized with fatigue and trauma, they all stared up towards the top of the mountain.

Moses, I could see was nervous . . . apprehensive. After all he had led his people across a desert wilderness to this rendezvous.

For what? That was the question that must have reverberated within his seething mind.

Yes, they had seen my awesome power against the Egyptians at the Red Sea, but still this had to be a crucial moment for him. Nothing less than a crisis if . . . if after the harrowing journey there was no god to meet them at the end of it.

And apparently, from what they could see at this moment, there wasn't.

I had the Flagship's Proteus on Blend, so to the Israelites or anyone else outside I was just part of the background of mountain and sky . . . even though I was really already landed and securely ensconced on a wide plateau near the summit of Mount Sinai.

I couldn't blame the Israelites for being a little skeptical at this point. They must have wondered why, if I was so powerful, I had apparently previously abandoned them for over four hundred years to the doubtful mercies of the Egyptian Pharaohs and their hard-driving overseers.

Having lived so long like slaves, it must have been difficult to hear the words of Moses telling them they were God's Chosen People.

Of course they never would have understood that all that hardship had produced a race superior in all physical aspects to the one that had first entered into captivity. Now they were stronger than their captors. No question about that. Stronger perhaps than any other race on Earth.

But I had to make a show of power. Several shows if I wanted to regain their confidence.

Moses, following my instructions, began to climb. I studied through my electronic amplification, the anxious expression on his face.

When he was halfway up the mountain I spoke to him.

"Moses!" I called out in my best and deepest tones, well amplified by electronic means.

He stopped immediately and I saw his expression change. The emotion that came through to me was relief. At least he would not now be ridiculed as some visionary fool, or the dupe of some power that no one else understood. All the Israelites had now heard my booming voice address him directly.

I carried through the pretense that I was talking to him, and him alone. But most of what I said and the way I said it was designed to strike awe and fear and at the same time confidence into the faltering hearts of the Israelites as I saw them at this moment.

"Give these instructions to the descendants of Israel . . . You have seen what I did to the Egyptians. You know how I brought you to myself and carried you across great danger on eagle's wings. Now if you will obey me and keep my covenant, you will be my own special treasure from among all the nations of Earth . . . for all Earth belongs to me. And you will be to me a kingdom of priests, my holy nation.

"Moses . . . give this message to the Israelites . . ."

Of course there was no necessity to repeat the message to them. They had heard everything. Their faces told the story.

They were mine.

****

I talked to Moses on the mountaintop and reassured him he was doing well, something he seemed to need to hear rather too desperately I thought.

After that, he said his brother Aaron had things he wanted to ask me about. I told him on his way down the mountain to send his brother up.

Later, Aaron, rather breathless from the climb, approached me on my mountaintop and spoke to me from outside my Flagship. Which to him, or anyone, was something very like a cloud, thanks to Proteus.

He had been put in charge by Moses of compiling the Book about Jehovah's great and mighty deeds. He let me know he wanted to make that sacred Book into something even more, embracing a complete history of the Jewish people.

I told him I found his project good.

"But . . . but your Heavenly Majesty, there are some things I need to set down in compiling this monumental history."

He seemed to hesitate and his voice almost failed him.

"Yes?"

"Well . . . I need to know . . . who created humankind?"

I saw his hand tremble as he held some kind of crude stylus over a sheepskin, prepared to write my answer.

"Who?" I started my rhetorical question on low volume. Then raised it . . ."Who?", raising the volume still more. And finally full volume, watching its force literally knock Aaron backwards . . ."WHO DO YOU THINK?"

I left it at that, secure that I had gotten my meaning across to Aaron, who picked himself up now, looked nervously over his shoulder and then turned and scurried quickly down the mountainside.

You see, there was no use complicating things. They couldn't handle that. It was better in all respects for them to consider me as God of the Universe. God of everything. Better for them, better for me, better for my mission of eradicating Ra and his followers, and securing the planet for the true Anunnaki way of life.

****

I was hovering high above Mount Sinai now as I watched the Israelites come marching in and gradually disperse themselves around its base.

I had asked them to come here again after three days, all purified and washed and clean and ready to receive my messages.

It was time for the display . . .

I used Proteus at full power to project an image of thunder and lightning above the summit of Mount Sinai. Then I changed the image to one of flame as I descended once again to my established landing plateau.

Once there I blasted the mountain full of sonar energy for a brief moment so that it actually shook.

I sent two soft laser beams of celestial light to fall briefly over the faces of Joshua and Moses, which caused a gasp of awe from the assembled Israelites.

I then altered my electronic voice projection controls so that I spoke with a timbre based on the actual sound of thunder.

Showmanship like this was exactly what had always been missing in the lamentable reign of Enki over Earth, and I was now out to implement it. It had worked extremely well in the Western Continents, and there was no reason to suppose it would not work equally well with more advanced races, even my evolved race of Chosen People.

"Moses!" I commanded, watching the people now all fall down to their knees, their faces turned away from my mighty power.

This I found very fulfilling to me. Deep within me something spoke to let me know this was my destiny. What I had always wanted. And what I was seeing now, the awe and abject worship, was what I hoped to see eventually in every settlement of Earth, my adopted

planet . . . where Jehovah and Jehovah alone would be recognized as
its rightful ruler . . .

While I had their attention and while Moses was for the second
time making the difficult climb up to meet me, I read the Israelites a
few simple rules, which came from the very first level of the Anunnaki
Protocols. There were ten of them and for convenience and
showmanship I had already inscribed them by laser onto two stone
tablets.

Among those rules I slipped in something of extreme importance
to me in the campaign I had planned against the wily Marduk.

That was the prohibition against idols of any kind. Actually I
had nothing against them making idols of me . . . or rather of the
generic saintly image I had projected now over all the reaches of Earth
as mine. That would have been rather flattering.

The problem was that with the general low quality of artistic
workmanship I would not have come out well in many instances.

Not only that, but in my mission to find and exterminate the
nefarious Marduk, this would introduce an unnecessary complica-
tion. As it was, all I had to look for now were idols or reproductions of
any kind of Marduk\Ra. I would smash them and the people who carried them with an equal and altruistically distributed relentless zeal.

After all . . .

I, Jehovah, had no time to microscopically inspect each image to
see if it might be mine or his. Better it was to simply exterminate all
idols and people who made them . . . and so I would all the quicker
defeat Ra and restore the planet to its former healthy and unified
state.

My decree here from Mount Sinai against idols would facilitate
that plan greatly.

A vagrant thought entered my mind. The Sphinx. It had been
built under Enlil's rule and so carried his facial features. Someday I
would like to change that. I could do it with lasers, gradually working
it until what were Enlil's features were finally metamorphosed into
mine. But that . . . brought problems with it, at least for now . . . so I
put it off for a possible future resolution.

I gave the Israelites through Moses certain ceremonies to follow and a list of anniversaries to celebrate. All that would be important to maintain my reign as their one and only god.

I also gave them basic agricultural instructions, elementary things all taken from level 1 of Annunnaki protocols.

Poor Moses obviously could not physically handle all this . . . the two stone tablets and the parchment scrolls . . . so I assigned four of my small clones to help him down the mountainside with this important cargo.

And while they made their way downwards, I took advantage of the opportunity to once again address the Israelites with my voice of thunder . . .

I kept repeating in different ways my one basic and most important message.

"Never pray to or swear by any other gods. Do not even dare to mention their names."

Ra or Marduk unmentioned, I thought to myself, was Ra or Marduk without existence.

Then I warmed to my main message.

"I will lead you into the Promised Land. The Land of Milk and Honey, promised to your ancestors." Here I got a little carried away by my own eloquence, a little grandiose. "I will fix your boundaries from the Red Sea to the Mediterranean Sea, and from the southern deserts to the Euphrates River."

That I knew had to sound good to them. The assurance that all that land would be theirs.

Now it was time to hit them with what I wanted, what my real objective was . . .

"I will help you defeat the people now living in the land, and you will drive them and their false god out ahead of you."

It was subtle, it was good, it was adroitly applied at the very last.

And now they knew they would have to spearhead my drive to annihilate the greatest threat to Earth since Enki himself. His son, Marduk, who the sinful Egyptians had once worshipped as the sun god Ra.

I sighed, relaxed and looked at the panorama below me, where my Chosen People stood in awe, ready to carry out whatever mission I might choose to give them.

It had been a good day's work.

****

I was fairly sure Marduk must be hiding somewhere in the Land of Canaan. The evidence showed it . . . there was no other reason for his likeness to have been discovered among Canaanites at a good distance from Egypt.

One of the greatest dangers about Marduk was that he might revive on Earth again the cult of Enki. Among those who would make a hero of Enki, the alleged friend of humanity . . . who did not realize that in becoming the friend of Earthlings he had in the process sold out his own people, the Anunnaki.

But there were other dangers, too. As it was, at least until Marduk revealed himself, I had been the only Anunnaki on Earth capable of bearing children. This was very important, giving me a unique advantage over Enlil and the others of our group, none of whom to date had been able to exit their sterile state.

It had now been some six hundred Earth years since my masterfully planned atomic strike against the forces of evil had taken place, that saw Enki and his cohorts reduced to radioactive dust.

How many Earthling children might Marduk have produced in all that time? With an unlimited supply of Earth women at his disposal . . .

It boggled my mind to think about it. True, he was stranded in a backward society with none of the Anunnaki technology at his disposal. We used to have a saying on Nibiru . . . that in the Kingdom of the Blind, the one-eyed man would meet a quick death unless he were also a master of technology. But perhaps . . . perhaps superior intelligence and knowledge and a great dose of cunning . . . which I knew Marduk had . . . could overcome all other obstacles.

And I suddenly remembered something.

Atop Mount Olympus we Anunnaki had heard stories of a certain hero who had arisen among the Greek people. That had been no concern of mine as long as he did not upset the scheme of government I had established among the Greeks . . . which he did not. His reputed exploits were mostly merely local displays of unusual strength and agility, nothing more.

But still . . .

Before I started what could be an all-consuming campaign to ravage and devastate the Land of Canaan . . . perhaps I should make sure first that I was not looking for Marduk in the wrong place . . .

****

I left the Israelites in their camp at the base of Mount Sinai with Moses' brother Aaron in charge until my return.

Moses I took with me on my exploratory journey back to where the Greeks were the dominant population.

I thought it might be an experience that would make him eternally loyal to Jehovah, seeing in the Flagship the absolute power at my command. Also, I let him see me as I am, not as the projected generic saintlike image he was familiar with.

I didn't think that too much of a risk. After all, with my present glowing health and vigor I WAS a god as compared to any Earthling. Unless . . . unless this Greek hero, this Hercules, turned out to be something really special. But that I doubted.

Inside my Flagship, our journey now well under way, I allowed Moses to ask any question that might occur to him.

But for him that was an opportunity missed. He seemed to be absolutely struck dumb with awe and fear of what was happening to him. I hoped time and experience might cure that.

But no . . .

He was dazed, thunderstruck. It was simply too much for him. His jaw worked wordlessly, his eyes rolled. I saw that at last . . . and escorted him back inside the Flagship to my own elegant quarters where I indicated to him he could have a nice nap and that afterwards we would talk . . . about the campaign I wanted in Canaan and other matters of his leadership over the Israelites.

Meanwhile I could explore the area of the Greeks until I came across this supposed hero, this Hercules . . .

****

Eventually I had to land and ask people. Myself in the Proteus-belt-produced guise of just another Greek Earthling, of course.

At last I found Hercules and we talked.

Not long, because the first sight of him had told me everything. Certainly not the primitive lion's skin he wore nor the equally primitive club he carried. That could have been any Earthling savage. But then, up close . . .

Those facial features . . . a certain way he had of pursing the mouth and squinting his eyes. It was almost like seeing the hated Marduk himself again.

So it was true. Marduk was producing children among the Earthlings. At least there was no denying this one was his.

I asked him about his father and he said the rumor was that it was Zeus, a local god. The great god Zeus, from whom he derived his superior physical strength and courage.

Zeus the Greeks might call him, yes. I didn't know if that was deliberate misdirection on his part, the attempt by use of an alias with native populations to lull my suspicions . . . or merely some quirk of language similar to the one that made me Jehovah. It didn't matter. It didn't matter because I was obviously in the presence of an undeniable son of Marduk/Ra.

I asked Hercules when he had last seen his father. It turned out not since he was a mere child. That was encouraging. That tended to make me believe that Marduk was not here, that I was on the right track in Canaan.

I made a mental note that this Hercules could be dangerous to my cause. He had too much influence with the Greek populace, for one thing. But the factor that outweighed everything, that made me determine to get rid of him when the time came, was this . . . he was at one remove undeniably the spawn of Enki, a product of the seed of the Devil himself.

I could never ally myself with that.

But when I got back to my Flagship, I received a major shock . . .

****

Moses.

Where was he?

At first I could find him nowhere, and I got more and more desperate.

Had he somehow managed to leave the electronically sealed ship? Impossible.

When I finally found him, it was not a relief. Not at all.

Somehow he had maneuvered his way into the power room. The hatches are normally sealed off, but evidently some electronic safety switch had malfunctioned.

I pulled him out, put him once again atop my own bed. But was I too late? It appeared so. He was senseless and barely breathing.

****

I put the Flagship on hover over Mount Sinai and now devoted once again my full attention on the condition of Moses.

He was now conscious, though obviously still disoriented.

I knew certain things. There was no way he could have avoided a massive dose of radiation, sleeping as he did right next to the power source of the Flagship. There were shields, of course, but he had penetrated beyond them in his distracted state.

What the effects of all that would be I did not know. It would not be the same as an atomic explosion, no . . . but then again . . . what would it be?

It was night over Mount Sinai. In the quiet blackness near the base, I opened a hatch and gently led Moses out to the edge of the Israeli camp.

Under the circumstances, I thought it the best thing to do . . .

****

It was time to start the campaign.

I had to know about my leader, Moses. Would he be able to lead the Whip of God?

I made a decision. He must at the very least be permitted to be put to the test.

And so . . .

I let him run things entirely.

And . . . it was a disaster.

All the Israelites had to do was attack the unsuspecting Amorites, who occupied the first lands we must conquer . . . of our all-encompassing march to possess every inch of Canaan without permitting any other living soul to survive within its boundaries. It was the only way to stamp out Marduk and the influence of Enki.

According to all my calculations, it should have been an easy victory.

But the weak link in the chain of my strategic moves, was Moses himself.

He vacillated, equivocated, contradicted his own orders . . . showed cowardice in the face of resistance . . . and that infected his troops, who retreated when they should have advanced.

It was ignominious and impermissible.

I, Jehovah, could not be humiliated this way.

I had to act. Decisively and now.

****

We lost hundreds of men in the debacle with the Amorites.

The next day after the battle I called Moses up to my command position on the high plateau of Mount Sinai.

Not ostentatiously this time.

Instead I made the words of my request oscillate almost subliminally in the receptor adorning his right ear lobe.

He came to me, up the side of the mountain.

Like a beaten dog.

I was astounded by his appearance and his aspect.

There were patches of white in his beard and in his hair. His lips quivered when he talked.

He was turning into an old man right before my eyes.

I knew it was not psychological, these effects. They were physiological, caused by the radiation damage he had suffered from the power source of the Flagship.

The question was . . . how was I going to handle it?

****

For the moment, to avoid further defeat and humiliation I had to appoint a new Military Commander. Moses was out, Joshua was in. And I had full confidence in Joshua, my secret son.

I appeared surreptitiously at night, outside his tent, not this time as a burning bush as with Moses, but as a cool, phosphorescent spot of moving light. And when I spoke to him, it was in a low, controlled voice.

He followed me up the mountainside under the ghostly moonlight and we did not exchange a word until I asked him to sit down in my command quarters inside the Flagship.

I gave him a refreshing drink and a platter containing several disk-like white confections.

He ate and drank a little, and then I turned off my belt Proteus so that he no longer saw me as just glowing phosphorescent light . . .

"You are the first Earthling to see Jehovah as he really is," I announced gravely. That was not strictly true. Certainly his mother had. But she was no longer living. And . . . Moses had . . . but then Moses had deteriorated so rapidly soon afterwards that I felt sure he now hardly remembered the encounter.

"And you are . . . very handsome," Joshua said in an admiring tone.

"In saying that you compliment yourself, " I replied. "Because . . . but let that go for now . . . I called you here to discuss your very important mission. For you will be the new Military Commander of all the Israelite forces."

"Moses?"

"Moses is aging prematurely. He is no longer himself. He will still be a leader of his people . . . an inspiration and a patriarch . . . just no longer a military Commander. You saw the debacle against the Amorites . . . we can have no more of that. Even Jehovah can not guarantee victory if his Military Commander disobeys him and leads the people into unhallowed ways . . ."

I explained to him the general idea behind the Canaan campaign. Which was basically one of scorched Earth and extermination. Only in that way could I guarantee to the Israelites and their descendants the land I had promised their forefathers. I told him of the suspected presence of the infidel Marduk, another name for the former Egyptian god Ra, and how he must be found and put to death. How all his idols wherever found must be smashed. How even the children . . . especially the children since Ra might be their father . . . must be exterminated along with every other living thing.

I told him all this, which I saw was difficult for him to understand, the need for such wholesale slaughter.

I reassured him. Talked of the promise of the future, and how that future could only be obtained by following to the letter all my instructions, and how glorious would be the results at last for him and all his people.

I told him my way was the only way, and it was all for the ultimate good of the Nation of Israel, which would be richly blessed . . . and all their descendants more numerous than the stars in the heavens or the grains of sand in the desert.

But before we went into battle again, this time to be certain conquerors, I told him there were two things I wanted to do to strengthen the will of the people . . .

"One has to do with the white confections you have obviously enjoyed here. These are of divine origin, designed to give special strength, and I want them to be consumed by our people before our next battle. To further strengthen their will, I want them to travel in the desert for four days. A forced march. Then they will appreciate the gentle swells and apple orchards of Canaan and its green fields, and build a true lust to possess them. You, Joshua, will lead them. It will be your first command."

"And the second thing, My Lord? What is that?"

"We need a symbol. Something to concentrate in a small area all that your people represent. It needs to be built, and not in just any way. In fact, here are the plans . . ."

I unrolled them and we talked for half an hour about the requirements. How it must be constructed of Acacia wood, with gold overlays everywhere as detailed on my plans . . . with everything to the exact dimensions specified.

For Joshua, of course, I emphasized how sacred the Ark of the Covenant would be and what an important religious symbol it was.

For myself, I thought how convenient it would be for me . . .

I would have my listening devices inside the Ark . . . so I would always know if the priests were happy or discontent, being loyal to me or mentioning other gods.

And . . .

The Ark being a natural electrical condenser I could use my remote controls to blast anyone I thought might be dangerous or disloyal . . . without having to assume any direct blame.

****

Other things in governing my Earth occupied my attention for the next month.

But when I finally returned to Mount Sinai and learned the Ark of the Covenant was completed, and as I saw, completely according to my exact specifications, I was so pleased I ordered a big celebration . . .

I even invited seventy of the Israelite leaders to climb up the mountainside, with Moses leading them and Joshua hard behind him.

There on my command plateau, we had an outdoor dinner together, these Israelite leaders and their god. My Flagship's Proteus was set to make it appear a cloud, while I myself appeared as my generic saintly image.

The meal itself was a little awkward, and being spontaneous not well planned out.

I had to slip the food inside the surrounding aura of the image to my mouth, yes. . . . but apparently no one noticed anything odd about that. The meal itself was catered by six of my clones. Between my image and their ghostly, silent presence the Israelite leaders were obviously awed.

After we ate together, I talked to them.

Very seriously.

About the Ark, how sacred it was, how it would lead them to many victories. And that if anyone touched it or tried to open it without my authorization, how they would be instantly killed. How the Ark itself would automatically know if anyone were disloyal or had evil thoughts in his mind. In that case Jehovah's vengeance would be swift and fatal . . . lightning would strike the offender dead.

On that same note I continued about how in our coming campaign to secure Canaan for Israel and Israel's descendants for all time to come it was necessary to be merciless to all enemies.

"The Lord your God will soon destroy the nations whose land he is giving you, and you will displace them and settle in their villages and towns and cities and homes."

I paused for effect, and then went on.

"As for all the habitations of the nations the Lord your God is giving you as a special possession . . . and I mean all of them, no matter how humble or how wealthy and ornate . . . you must destroy every living thing in them. So will these evil ones be prevented from teaching you their detestable customs in the worship of their exotic gods, which would cause you to sin deeply against the Lord your God."

I paused and looked around at each one of them, to see if my little lesson had sunk in. Apparently it had, I saw to my satisfaction. They were nodding and looking sideways at each other, clutching each others' robes in a kind of mutual silent symphony of support.

All right. That done, something of a lighter nature occurred to me. Something that needed immediate correction.

It came about because of my night excursion to pick up Joshua. Certain things had come to my attention then so that now I had to give them this short lecture, too, about basic hygiene.

I began it without preamble other than to say I was not pleased with my nocturnal visit because of this deficiency encountered. And then I went right to the remedy.

"Mark off an area outside the camp for a latrine. Each of you must have a spade as part of your equipment. Whenever you relieve yourself, you must dig a hole with the spade and cover the excrement. The camp must be holy, for the Lord your God moves around in your camp to protect you and to defeat your enemies. He must not see any shameful thing among you, or he might turn away from you."

I then turned to higher matters.

I talked much about Moses, and extolled his leadership, his historical role in bringing his people out of Egypt. Now, I said, he could gracefully retire and be a venerable patriarch as he deserved to be, having given already almost a hundred years of service since he himself was a youth in Egypt.

That was a lie, of course . . .

Moses was only forty Earth years old. But I had to justify what had happened to him some way.

I could not take responsibility for it, because I was supposed to be all-powerful. Since the Israelites had not known him in his youth, he being raised by the Egyptian nobility and thus outside the ranks of the enslaved Israelites, I was taking little risk.

Anyway, who was going to deny the Great Jehovah, or challenge his holy word?

I told them of the four day forced march we would perform

together, and how it would further prepare them for the series of battles coming up in the process of conquering Canaan.

Finally I formally appointed Joshua as the new Military Commander.

And we drank a toast together, and they all bowed down before me, each outdoing the other in their fluent and fantastic protestations of loyalty to the death to their holy god.

****

The four day march through the wilderness . . .

It was harrowing for all concerned.

I was above in my Flagship watching everything closely.

I had a second goal for leading them through the wilderness besides hardening their spirit and purpose.

In the back of my mind I suspected Marduk might be hidden here. Where he thought I would never look for him. Well, if he thought that, he thought wrong.

Here I was.

Wily he might be, yes . . . but no wilier than I. I, Jehovah, who after all had been clever enough to serve the nefarious Enki, and even make him love and respect me, all the while spying for Enlil without ever raising the ghost of a suspicion in Enki's naive mind.

That . . . that was to be the essence of wily.

I was easily equal to the task before me. I would root out Marduk, the supposed god Ra . . . wherever his lair might prove to be.

Serpents might have holes, yes, but the rain would seek them out. In this case I was the rain, not beneficial but mortal rain . . .

a rain of deadly laser rays that would reduce the great god Ra to undistinguished dust . . .

Just let him show his ugly head.

I would quickly . . . oh, so quickly . . . make Hercules an orphan.

We did not find any evidence of him the first day. All right. At least now I knew for sure where he was not. And where he was, would surely eventuate under my relentless pursuit.

On the morning of the second day of the forced march the people cried out for food. They had brought animals to slaughter, yes, for the evening meal. But for the morning . . . there was nothing.

So I gave them something. Something divine from above. The food of the gods . . .

Quartered wafers. Thousands of them. I scattered them everywhere around, then announced in my most godly voice that it was theirs to eat.

They did so, began gathering the sections of wafers up in baskets and assuaging their morning hunger with them.

Good.

They were the same wafers that had done so much to restore us few Anunnaki. The ones I had served to Joshua in our meeting. I had decided to use them with the Israelites now for good reason.

It would make them stronger, more aggressive . . . more ready for battle . . . why not, if each wafer represented the concentrated life essence of more than one being.

And we had such a surplus of them in both our headquarters . . . the one on Mount Olympus as well as the underground facilities on the Iberian peninsula . . . their storage occupying rooms we needed for other purposes . . . so their use here meant to me a gain two ways.

And I saw them . . . the Israelites . . . improve in strength and purpose each day.

So that when we returned to Mount Sinai after the fourth day I was well content.

They were swelled with success and anticipation. Ready for battle.

We had not caught Marduk this time, true. But we surely would in the imminent campaign against the inhabitants of Canaan.

Even the Amorites would not stop us now.

****

This time we cut through the Amorites like a hot knife through butter.

In only two days.

We celebrated their complete annihilation with dancing and drinking that went on far into the night.

I watched from above, well content, and had something to drink myself.

****

Moses was dying.

It was obvious to me. He was now a doddering ancient physiologically, due to the radiation he had absorbed in the accident.

I was sorry about it. I gave him a great number of wafers to eat, but he had no appetite for them, his weak arms letting them fall to the ground before they reached the trembling lips of his mouth.

At last I came to him one day and personally took him and his brother Aaron up to Mount Nebo, just across from the City of Jericho, which was our next Military Objective.

From there he had a good view of Canaan, the Promised Land.

I told him I was sorry he would not live to see his people occupy it, though that was coming very soon.

I don't know if he heard or understood me. He was in his dotage now, mumbling incomprehensibly and rehearsing who knows what personal dramas in his wandering mind.

But at least, while fighting for breath in his brother's arms, he had a last look at what he had labored for.

They found his lifeless body in his tent the next day . . .

We gave him a grand funeral. On the positive side, psychologically it was just what my troops needed before going into battle. It roused them to combat intensity. Somehow they came to blame the death of their great patriarch on the enemy forces.

It is possible I gave them that impression in my own eulogy delivered over his grave from an apparently empty sky . . .

****

It was time to cross the Jordan River.

Once across we would go up against the walled city of Jericho, that seemed at first glance . . . and at second glance even more . . . an insurmountable obstacle.

So I helped Joshua prepare his way there. But first he took the time to formally dedicate the coming victory to the memory of great Moses.

Then, as per my instructions, he made the party carrying the Ark of the Covenant cross the river first.

As they did so, I activated a tractor beam from above.

I stopped the water upstream so the Israelites, as in the crossing of the Red Sea, could safely pass to the opposite side.

I thought it made an impressive beginning.

But the sixteen foot high stone walls of Jericho still seemed impregnable.

****

I needed to give the Israelites courage for what lay ahead.

I landed my mighty Flagship on the side of the Jordan River nearest Jericho. And there, while all the people watched in awe, I called Joshua forth.

In my most imperial amplified voice, loud enough for all the Israelites to hear, I gave Joshua his orders . . .

"I, Jehovah, who am the god of all Earth, have given you, the Israelites, god's Chosen People, this city of Jericho. I have given you its king, and all its mighty warriors. Now listen well to this, for you must obey exactly my commands . . .

"It will take seven days to demolish the walls of Jericho. Seven days. Joshua, your entire army is to march around the city once a day for the first six days. Seven priests . . . not six, not eight . . . seven priests will walk ahead of the Ark of the Covenant, each priest carrying a ram's horn.

"Then . . . then, Joshua . . . on the seventh day you are to march around the city SEVEN times, with the priests blowing the horns. Now the priests are to give together one mighty, long blast on the horns . . . this must be at a signal and with all their might, all their power . . . then, Joshua, you signal your people to give a mighty, coordinated shout together."

I paused and lowered my voice.

"When all this is done, exactly as I have spoken . . . if it is done well and with spirit . . . then the high walls of great Jericho, that impregnable fortress, will collapse, and our forces . . . all our forces . . . can charge straight into the city."

A wild, spontaneous cheer went up at this, and I saw I had spoken well to what they could understand.

****

The week went by slowly. I could feel the momentum accumulate day by day. Apparently the inhabitants of Jericho had seen my Flagship and were too terrified to come out. They must have been watching everything in fear and wonderment.

Of course a lot of this was pure theater. Drama enacted as much for the the inhabitants of Jericho as for the Israelites and Joshua.

I could have knocked the walls of Jericho down the first minute of the first day, or even vaporized them along with the city itself.

But . . .

That would not have fulfilled my purpose.

Not at all.

I wanted the Israelites themselves to feel powerful, invincible. If they were eventually to become my right hand, the veritable Whip of God, they must feel that way. Besides, I could not myself easily search and ravish every inch of ground in search of Marduk and his allies . . . but my Israelite army could . . .

****

On the morning of the seventh day, just before dawn, I assembled them and gave them their final instructions.

"Understand this, when Jehovah's might has been shown, and Jericho's walls fall, and you enter into the great city that your god has given you. . . . Understand that everything made of silver or gold is sacred to the Lord and may not be destroyed, but must be brought unto me, Jehovah. Also, if you find any idols of heathen gods . . . any idols at all . . . they must be brought to me for my inspection so I can deal with this blasphemy personally. But understand this, too . . . and hear me well . . . everything else in the city IS to be destroyed. Destroyed totally, as an offering to the Lord. Then the city itself is to be put to the torch."

"If you . . . if any one of you . . . takes something for his own use, I tell you that you yourself will bring trouble on all Israel, and you will be destroyed, too.

"Now listen carefully to this. You are to leave nothing living in the city. Nothing. No one. Kill all the men and women. Young, old . . . the sick. Kill them all. Kill the dogs, the sheep, the cattle, all the animals . . . all of them."

I saw the expression on some faces . . . an expression that I didn't like. Something very like horror or remorse.

So I raised the volume and repeated everything I had said. That seemed to sink in and bring the recalcitrants around . . .

It was now dawn.

Time to move.

Seven times I watched the Israelites march around the great walls of the city.

The seventh time on Joshua's signals it all took place at once. The priests with all their might blasted away on the ram's horns. The people raised a mighty shout.

And as both those events took place simultaneously, the sixteen foot high stone walls of Jericho began to tremble. Then to shake.

The shaking built to a crescendo and then . . .

The great walls came crashing down.

Pandemonium ensued. There were shouts of terror from inside Jericho.

Shouts of jubilation and triumph from the attacking Israelites.

Then just the wild screams and groans and whimpers from the dying people and animals as the Whip of God was applied to Jericho, and the triumphant Israelites swept in and onward to a great and crushing victory.

It was a moment I savored and treasured.

They were performing well, my Chosen People, at last. My training programs, survival of the fittest . . . everything at last in that moment was seen as working out.

If Marduk or any of his allies, or any children conceived by him were present in Jericho . . . all would be exterminated. If they were not here, but in our next city or town or village to conquer, well . . . they would meet the same fate.

The Israelites did not need to know, nor would I ever reveal to any of them, even Joshua . . . that I had triggered the collapse of the walls of Jericho.

Yes, I had used the volume of their rams' horns and their shouts.

But that in itself would not have broken the wall's stone foundation.

It had to be multiplied a hundred times.

Which I did. I captured it on a special receptor, multiplied it . . . and by infusing meticulously syncopated pulsed reverberation demolished a single layer of stones all around the entire perimeter of the base.

That was the true scientific basis of the Fall of Jericho.

But the Israelites would never know that. Their confidence soared, and they were well on the way to becoming something not too distant from the concept behind my forever lost Invincible Army of Atlantis . . . the veritable Whip of God.

Which was exactly what I wanted.

****

I had to get back to headquarters atop Mount Olympus, because there were always a dozen things pending in administering my Planet . . . things that needed my personal attention, things I could certainly not trust the slothful Enlil to take care of. Then too, I had a couple of storage holds on the Flagship filled with gold and silver from the conquest of Jericho that I needed to unload.

I had to get back to Mount Olympus, yes. But on the other hand, I did not want to lose the momentum of the marvelous Israelite victory at Jericho, either. A momentum hard won, and that might prove difficult to regain should we lose it.

I decided I had more to gain by staying than going back. For one thing, if this campaign were successful in finding and eradicating Marduk and all his followers, I could then move forward one giant step in the administration of the planet.

That is, with the last of the rebel Anunnaki on Earth gone, it would then be time to begin to adjust our relations with the Home Planet. Time to tell our story to King Anu . . .

How Enki had tried to destroy us and assume sole power with his unprovoked surprise attack . . . and then had tried to cover his cowardly action with a completely false version of events transmitted to the Home Planet.

How he had never suspected that some of us might survive, and live to finally, after 8,000 Earth years, begin to set things right. Gradually, over a series of transmissions, I planned to tell of our heroic struggle to once again assert Anunnaki values onto a recalcitrant Earth population, led astray by the false and treasonous promises of Enki, against all accepted standards.

But I could not do that while Marduk, the so-called great Egyptian god Ra, still lived. He not only continued the treason begun by Enki, but would cause trouble by his lying contradiction of what had really happened in the great drama taking place on Earth.

So I stayed at Jericho, and immediately immersed my energies in helping Joshua plan our next battle.

Joshua now stepped forward the way I always thought he would. I knew he had the potential, had in his blood the craft and cunning of Jacob as well as my own, plus my physical health and beauty and massive strength.

Of strategic cunning, his plan was an epitome. I was proud of him.

The city of Ai was the next objective of the campaign. Alone with him in the Flagship, I watched his engaging smile flash at me several times while he outlined his plan.

I liked it. It was clever and had elements of deception in it which I could hardly have improved upon myself.

At night he would first set in place a secret ambush in back of the city, hidden from the inhabitants' sight by a hill . . . behind which was a valley where his men would lie in wait.

Then in the ensuing day he would form up his main troops and move towards the front gate of the city.

If, as expected, the soldiers of Ai would move out that front gate to fight and protect their city, Joshua would initiate part two of his strategy.

This was the part I liked best.

Joshua would make it seem as if the Israelites were terrified of the men of Ai, and under his leadership they would turn and begin to retreat.

Ah, yes . . .

And then . . .

Then, as the Ai followed them in hot pursuit . . . at a certain point in the action when all the Ai men had exited the city, then the waiting ambush would be sprung.

The warriors waiting behind the city would spring into lethal action.

Yes. Those hidden Israelites would then fall like a fury upon the wide open abandoned city and sack and burn it . . . demolish it . . . killing all the women and children left inside, as well as any animals.

That was good in itself, but then according to the plan, it got better.

When the Israelites fleeing from in front of the city would see the smoke rising from that city behind their pursuers, they themselves would turn in their full force upon those pursuing soldiers of Ai.

If the Ai retreated they would be caught by the Israelites now streaming forth from the front gates of the city to catch them in a trap . . . a trap from which there would be no escape.

If they did not retreat, the superior force of Israel, led by Joshua, and no longer feigning their theatrical cowardice, would quickly cut them down, every man. That, at least, is what I hoped.

I approved the plan and slapped Joshua on his muscular back. I let him know he had done well, that I was pleased. He spontaneously gave me an embrace, which I just as spontaneously accepted.

He was, after all was said and done, blood . . .

****

From my Flagship invisible to those below because I had Proteus on Blend, I dropped low over the city of Ai to watch the battle in every state of its exciting progress.

I could see the secondary Israeli ambush force in waiting in their hidden valley. Watched Joshua and his main force approach the city. Saw the gates open and the men of Ai pour out to do battle. Heard their screams of exultation when the Israelis soon turned and ran, and saw them follow hard after.

The force in ambush then fell upon the rear of the defenseless city. I saw the women and children being cut down in the streets with a merciless efficiency I was proud of having engendered. Nothing stopped those invading Israelites. Not cries and supplications, nor women with babes in arms . . . they let nothing stand in their way, following my orders blindly.

I was proud of them.

They were close, very close to becoming the true Whip of God.

When it was over only the King of Ai was left standing.

But not for long. As I watched, I saw Joshua hang him high and then leave his body to twist in the wind, suspended from the city's scorched front gates . . .

****

Next we went against the Southern Cities. I was basically leaving everything to Joshua now, as long as he was successful, which he continued to be. I assumed a role of just an observer as long as I was not needed.

First Joshua went against the city of Makkedah. When he finished, every inhabitant was dead, including the King.

And who knew? Perhaps Ra himself had been hiding in the city, ready to work his treachery from there. If so, he now had entered the realm of oblivion, where he and Enki and all their followers so richly belonged . . .

****

Next was Libnah.

That city was also quickly doomed by Joshua's fierce and perspicacious actions.

There were no survivors.

Things were going well. Exceedingly well.

****

After that victory over Libnah, I landed before the Israelite forces, with great ostentation, and stepped out of my gold Flagship . . . which Proteus made appear to be a cloud come down to earth . . . to give a little speech.

I resisted the temptation to be prolix. Reminded them only of a few key things . . .

How I had promised this land of Canaan to their ancestors, Abraham and Isaac and Jacob and Joseph and Moses . . . how it would prove to be a land of Milk and Honey for them . . . but also how they had to earn it . . . to show by their actions how they deserved it by carrying out Jehovah's orders . . . whose righteous wrath was set against the present inhabitants of this sweet land . . . because they were usurpers and sinners . . . because they had worshipped false gods and made idols of those gods . . .

Here I held up some idols with the face of Ra himself, that Joshua had brought me from the ruins of Libnah . . . showing clearly how deeply the treason of Enki and his son Marduk, the supposed Egyptian god Ra, had penetrated.

With a dramatic gesture I smashed the idols to smithereens before the Israelite multitude watching me in my saintly generic manifestation.

They cheered wildly, the waves of their adulation sweeping at me with a palpable force, causing a deep emotion inside me. At last I knew I was god of this tribe, that down to the last atom of their being they trusted me, adored me, worshipped me . . . and would follow me into Hell itself.

They were . . . at last . . . the Whip of God.

They would be my righteous right hand to punish rebels and evildoers in the New Kingdom I was creating on Earth. Free of Enki and his influence, where I would always be the sole and unchallenged ruler and god.

****

The campaign accelerated and gained even more momentum after my inspirational speech.

The city of Lachish was next. It fell on the second day, the entire population slaughtered.

Eglon was conquered in a single day.

Then Hebron, with all its surrounding towns.

Next, Debir.

In all cases not a single person was left alive.

Soon the whole region was in our sole control. The hill country, the Negev, the western foothills and the mountain slopes.

And to confirm my judgment in planning the campaign . . . in every city were found idols of Ra . . . idols which I took great pleasure in smashing in front of my Israelite troops.

****

It was time to circle back and move on against the Northern kings.

They rallied desperately, trying to unite against our oncoming force.

But we were unstoppable. The Israelites knew now they were

doing the sacred work of the Lord . . . and this knowledge drove them to truly heroic deeds.

All the cities of the North were razed, their kings and every inhabitant put to the sword, their idols of Ra brought to me to be duly smashed to smithereens before the enchanted eyes of all the assembled Israelites.

In all, thirty one kings and their cities were destroyed.

****

There was more to be done. Not all of Canaan had been conquered, but most of it had been.

I had the instinctive feeling that in all these mass exterminations we had surely done to death both Marduk and any other possible Anunnaki survivors of our nuclear raid, plus certainly any and all followers. With great satisfaction, I was certain their noxious, nefarious influence had been finally erased from the face of Earth.

Which left me free now to begin the corrective communications with the Home Planet. That was what was uppermost in my mind as I guided my Flagship back towards Mount Olympus.

I put the controls of the Flagship on automatic while catching up with the setting down of this continuing history . . .

****

As I am just finishing writing this down, in this very moment I look out and see something incredibly strange up ahead.

What is it?

Either a trick of the atmosphere, a mirage . . . or . . .

I can't believe this, what my own eyes are trying now to tell me . . . it seems to have every appearance of a huge Mother Ship, and yet it can't be ours, nor anything like

PART 2
THE TRIAL OF JEHOVAH

On station in orbit around the planet called Earth, the special task force of the Intergalactic Federation aboard the huge Mother Ship met in the ample conference room to discuss their present mission.

There was no disagreement about the basics of that mission.

Which was simply to try to bring some semblance of justice to outlying planets judged to be victims of Cultural Abuse according to the tenets of Intergalactic Law.

In this particular present case only the specifics had yet to be worked out as a preliminary to trial.

Observations had clearly shown there was more than ample reason to believe atrocities had been committed on the remote planet Earth. Atrocities principally engineered by the Anunnaki known as Yahweh, recently representing himself to be a god, or even God Himself, with the allegedly divine name of Jehovah.

The culprit was in custody and had been assigned an Advocate, who had now advised he was ready with his defense.

And so the trial itself could commence. At the end of the meeting the President with the vote of the Council in favor, so ordered . . .

****

The Federation Counsel drew himself up to his full seven feet, not an unusual height at all for his own Home Planet, but rare here among the assembled Federation members representing many different galaxies. He looked them over now with a steady gaze before beginning . . .

"The Federation will show that atrocities . . . indeed a whole string of atrocities . . . have shamelessly been committed against the backwards people of the outlying Planet called Earth. Said atrocities are crimes in themselves . . . horrible crimes . . . and are against all Intergalactic Law and policy. We ask that the six members on our Jury panel, who are not members of the Federation, and who were chosen by lot at the beginning of our Mission . . . that these six members listen closely to what we will present, and at the end of that we believe the evidence will show that they must convict the accused, Yahweh, or Jehovah."

The look on the Federation Counsel's handsome, but rather feline face, was one of serene confidence as he finished crisply and took his seat. Which caused one of the Jury members to turn and whisper to the member just beside her . . ."He looks like the cat that just swallowed the canary."

The Defendant's Counsel then rose. He had a face rather like the craggy side of a mountain, and ponderous mannerisms to go along with that look.

"These reports of atrocities, if true, certainly would merit the punishment the learned Federation Counsel seems so eager for. But are they true? What proof is there that they ever happened? We know of none . . . and lacking that proof, the Federation's case falls helpless to the ground. And in that instance, your choice as a jury is crystal clear . . . you must find the Defendant guiltless and return him to the important position he holds on Earth."

The Chief Jurist then rose from his place on the massive bench raised several feet above the floor of the large compartment. He walked down now to the six jurors observing him intently as he approached . . .

The Chief Jurist then talked intimately with the jurors, telling them this was a landmark case, asking them if they were comfortable and if there was anything they needed that he might supply them with. He then touched each on the shoulder once, bowed and returned to his place.

"The Federation may present its case."

The Federation Counsel as he rose seemed lost in deep thought. He pursed his lips, pensively stroked the flaring catlike whiskers framing his chin . . .

"There is good reason to believe the Defendant was the author of the nuclear assassination of all the forces of the Anunnaki Enki . . . known on this planet, to the Intergalactic Federation, and in places across the Galaxy as the Friend of Humanity."

The Defense Counsel rose in an agitated manner. "Objection! The Defendant is not accused of any such crime! Such a crime has not even been established."

The Chief Jurist leaned forward high above them. "Sustained."
The Federation Counsel quickly replied . . .

"Strike that remark, strike it. I shouldn't have made it. After all a nuclear attack usually leaves no corpus delecti."

There was uproar in the courtroom, from the jury and the forty-odd off duty members of the ship's crew who made up the spectators . . .

****

The Federation Counsel's expression was contrite. With an audible clicking of his heels, he made a kind of semi-demi-bow towards the Jury.

"I am deeply sorry for my earlier transgression. Let me only talk from here forward of the specific crimes the Defendant is charged with in this tribunal. War against innocent people. Genocide. Intentional extermination of tribes and races whose territory he was illegally invading."

"Objection. There is no proof of that!"

The Federation Counsel now looked with feline contempt at the Defense Counsel. "No proof? Your honor, we ask permission to show the visual record made of the attack on Jericho."

There was another uproar among the spectators in the court.

****

At the end of the showing of the videodisk on the big screen, there was a hushed silence in the courtroom.

The faces of the spectators and the jury seemed to show revulsion, some at the point of becoming physically ill.

All eyes seemed to rest on the Defendant, Yahweh, who shifted nervously in his chair.

The Defense Counsel rose. "Your Honor, I can clear this up . . . this wrong impression. But I need to call the Defendant himself to the witness stand. Now."

"That is perfectly in line with our policy and procedure," the

Chief Jurist pronounced in measured tones. "Do so."

When Yahweh had seated himself in the witness chair, the Defense Counsel after pacing back and forth with his hamlike hands clasped behind his back, began.

His tone was soothing, reassuring.

"This attack on Jericho we have just seen . . . taken by a Federation cameraperson SURREPTITIOUSLY from long range . . . the Jury needs to know. Where were you when it was going on? Because we did not see you anywhere on the videodisk."

"That's right. I was in my Flagship, above the battle scene."

"So you were . . . just an observer, is that not correct?"

"Correct."

"You did nothing to influence the outcome of the battle?"

"Nothing."

"So you were in accordance with general policies and procedures of the Intergalactic Federation, were you not?"

"I believe so."

"Nothing more."

Federation Counsel rose. "I wish to cross-examine."

"Policy permits you to. Proceed," responded the Chief Jurist.

"The mere presence of your Flagship. Was that not enough in itself to influence the outcome of the battle?"

"Yes. It could have been . . . but . . ."

"But what?" The curt question had a sarcastic tinge to it.

"I had the ship's Proteus control on Blend. Which made me invisible to any outside observer."

There was a kind of gasp from the audience of jurors and spectators, and the feline face of the Federation Counsel momentarily suffered a visible falling, which included the tips of his extended catlike whiskers. "Nothing more, your Honor," he announced brusquely and sat down.

****

Defense Counsel then reexamined the Defendant.

"So . . . as learned Federation Counsel has so helpfully just indicated to us . . . is it not true you could have won the battle at any moment in time simply by revealing your Flagship's presence . . . which would have struck supernatural terror into the hearts of the people of Jericho?"

"Yes."

"And yet you deliberately refrained from using that weapon of terror. Is that not right?"

"That is right."

There was another gasp in the courtroom. The six jurors stirred, looked at each other.

"Nothing further, your Honor." The Defense Counsel quickly seated himself.

The Federation Counsel rose and began to raise his right hand. Then he seemed to change his mind, turned and again sat down. He appeared flustered. His whiskers seemed to fall still lower.

****

Next the Federation Counsel called its first witness.

A woman who gave her name only as Ruth.

"And you are a survivor of the massacre? A citizen of Jericho?"

"Objection. Massacre? It was a battle. A battle between Earthlings, who are known for their barbaric savagery throughout the galaxies."

The Chief Jurist sustained the objection.

"Are you the only survivor of the . . . battle?" asked the Federation Counsel.

"As far as I know, yes. Is . . . is this a dream?" Her disoriented, frightened eyes roamed uncertainly around the courtroom.

"It will seem so for you later," Federation Counsel assured her. "In the interests of Justice, we had to bring you here. But this trial is real, and we need your testimony. Tell us now how you survived the . . . battle. What did you see and hear?"

"I heard screams and shouts of the dying. Pleadings for mercy by friends and relatives, who were cut down in the middle of those pleadings. I ran to the roof, to a little alcove there. Then I must have fainted. When I awoke at last it was night. There was nothing but a strange deathlike silence in the city of Jericho . . . what had been the city of Jericho. I slipped away just before what still remained was put to the torch . . . and Jericho, my home, was just a flame against the darkness."

"Tell us. What offense had your people of Jericho committed against the Israelites to bring down such savage fury against you?"

"None, my Lord, that I know of."

"Tell me, did you ever hear the name of Jehovah in all this nightmare?"

"Yes. I heard it shouted often by the invading Israeli troops."

The Federation Counsel nodded wisely. "Thank you. No more questions." He turned towards the Defense Counsel. "Your witness."

"Thank you. Honored Witness, you asked a question earlier yourself. We all heard it . . . is this a dream?"

"Yes. I do not understand all this . . . what it is."

"So is it possible that your testimony here was just a dream, or part of a dream? That it had no more daylight substance than that?"

Near pandemonium broke out among the spectators now in the court.

The Chief Jurist rapped ineffectively with his gavel, then summarily suspended proceedings until the following day.

****

The following Earth day, the trial resumed.

According to accepted Federation procedure, the Federation was permitted, as it would have been at any time, to call the Defendant to the witness stand. Which it did now.

"Yahweh . . . is that your correct Anunnaki name?"

"Yes."

"But what about Jehovah. What is that?"

"It is another name I sometimes use. Earthlings . . . some of them . . . have difficulty pronouncing Yahweh and it comes out Jehovah."

"Is that your name when you are posing as a god?"

"Objection!" The Defense Counsel had leaped to his feet and thrown his right arm into the air.

"Sustained. Federation Counsel will be cautious in his questioning."

"Yes, your Honor. Well, Yahweh . . . let's be honest here. The idea for this attack on Jericho was all yours, was it not?"

"No."

"Oh? Had you not, posing as a Divine Entity, promised this land, this land known as Canaan, to the Israelites?"

"No."

"In spite of the fact that they had no title to it. No right, legal or moral or otherwise in any way?"

"No. I promised them nothing."

"Well, tell us . . . tell us all here today, once and for all . . . are you Divine?"

"No."

"I see . . . I see. But whether you are Divine or not, is it not true you ordered extermination of all the people in Jericho?"

"No."

"Your Honor. We call our next witness."

The Chief Jurist announced, "Bring Joshua to the stand."

****

A hush fell over the courtroom.

Joshua, when brought in, supported by two attendants, was obviously in a state of confusion even greater than that previously seen in the Earthling Ruth.

His eyes rolled, his mouth opened and his tongue lolled.

Then those eyes perceived and locked on Yahweh.

He snapped out of his disoriented state, and shook himself free from his supporters.

"My Lord . . . my Lord!"

Joshua went to Yahweh, knelt at his feet. "What is this, Heavenly One? Is this a dream? What is all this?"

The Federation Counsel turned towards the Jury. "You have heard," he said, arms crossed, his full height of seven feet in the moment very evident, his white whiskers bristling.

The attendants now guided Joshua to the witness chair.

Federation Counsel approached. "Your name is Joshua?"

"Yes."

"Military Commander of the Israelite forces?"

"Yes."

"Who destroyed Jericho?"

"Yes."

"And you do recognize the being seated there?" He pointed towards the Defendant.

"Yes."

"Who is he?"

"He is . . . the mighty Jehovah."

"What status does he have with you, the Israelites?"

"Status? . . . he is our god. . . . the God of Israel . . . we are his Chosen People."

"I see. I see. Well, Joshua, before you went into the battle against Jericho, did you have a conference with this being . . . with this Jehovah?"

"Yes."

"And, tell me . . . did he not order you to exterminate everyone in the city? The city of Jericho?"

"Yes."

"And you accepted that?"

There was an objection from the Defense Counsel. "Your Honor, Joshua is not on trial here."

The objection was sustained.

"Tell us why you accepted such an order."

"Why? We never asked ourselves why. He was . . . he is our god. The Great Jehovah. We had no choice. We had to carry out his will."

"Oh. What would happen if you did not?"

"We would be destroyed. We would be victims of the wrath of God."

"So Jehovah told you he was god of all Earth?"

"Yes. He is." Joshua here looked at Yahweh, and fell forward to his knees. The court attendants lifted him up and once again positioned him in the witness chair.

"I want to question you now about the instructions given you before the attack on Jericho. Did Jehovah . . . the being seated there across from you . . ." Federation Counsel indicated Yahweh and paused dramatically . . ."Did he tell you to be merciless to the enemy?"

"Yes."

"To kill every living thing?"

"Yes."

"Kill all the men of Jericho?"

"Yes."

"The women?"

"Yes."

"The elderly and the infirm?"

"Yes."

"The children? The little children?"

"Yes. They might be the spawn of the Devil."

"The Devil? Who might that be?"

"Marduk, the great god Ra of the Egyptians. Zeus to the Greeks."

"Were even suckling babes to be killed?"

"Yes. Any one of them could be Ra's spawn."

"All of them?"

"Yes."

"No exceptions?"

"None."

"Even the dogs and cats were to be killed?" The Federation Counsel cast a significant glance in the direction of the audience of off-duty crew members, some of whom shared his own slightly feline facial features.

"Yes."

"And what was the object of all this slaughter . . . this all-out war. This extermination."

"The object? Why the object was to carry out the will of Jehovah, our god."

"And what was that will specifically?"

"To conquer Canaan."

"Why did you feel you had to conquer Canaan?"

Joshua's handsome face assumed almost a beatific expression and he now spoke softly, reverently. "Because Canaan was the Promised Land. It was to be our land, a Land of Milk and Honey. Ours to have and to hold forever."

"The Promised Land? Promised by who?"

"By our great god Jehovah."

"But Joshua . . . Captain Joshua . . . surely you knew the land of Canaan was almost completely occupied by other tribes. Didn't you?"

"Yes."

"And they had done nothing against the Israelites?"

"No. Except occupy our land."

"But it was their land first. You see that, don't you?"

"No. How could it be their land if Jehovah had promised it to the Israelites? Since the days of Abraham our god had promised it to us. Through the days of Isaac and Jacob and Moses he had promised it . . . and it was up to me to bring that promise about, with Jehovah's instruction and help."

"But didn't you feel bad about having to destroy all the native populations? Kill all the women and children?"

"No. Because it was our god's will. They . . . the people of Jericho . . . were all guilty of great, unpardonable sin. They were worshipping other gods, false gods . . . and Jehovah would never permit that. They had to be destroyed."

The Federation Counsel sighed deeply, silently performed a slow pace back and forth in front of the jury.

At last, as if words failed him, he sighed again, shrugged his shoulders, opened his long arms wide, then let them drop to his side.

Then he looked at the Judge.

"Nothing else, Your Honor."

But as he said those words, something electrifying happened.

Joshua suddenly pitched forward from the witness chair towards Yahweh, falling to his knees.

"My Lord Jehovah . . . I understand nothing of what is going on here. I would gladly have my own body rendered from head to toe rather than offend you by any deed or word of my mouth. Tell me now . . . what should I do? Say but the word and I will slay them all . . ."

Joshua reached to draw a sword that was not there . . . just before being led away . . .

There was uproar in the courtroom.

****

It was the next day aboard the Galactic Federation Mother Ship.

The time in the trial for closing arguments.

Though in Federation procedure no time was too late to produce either new evidence or new argument, since the ultimate objective always was to effectuate the emergence of the truth in any case.

And the Defense Counsel now seemed inspired.

Perhaps he had seen he had no case in the evidence produced up until this time.

Now he came forth with a new theory entirely.

"Your Honor . . . members of the Jury . . . spectators . . . listen to me, please." His craggy face seemed composed, focused as never before in the trial since the opening statement.

His intensity drew the audience in to him, they seeming to sense the great importance he was placing on his next few words . . .

"You must find the Defendant not guilty. You must, because . . . he was not at any time acting for himself, or acting on his own initiative."

This caused a stir in the courtroom, a stir which Defense Counsel took advantage of to lend more emphasis to what he said next . . .

"All the Defendant did was FOLLOW ORDERS of a higher Commander. Orders he could not disobey. Nor was it in his nature as an Anunnaki to disobey those orders. Which you will hear now from his own lips. I call the Defendant again to the witness stand . . ."

The Chief Jurist had to ask the spectators for quiet before proceeding.

Then the Defense Counsel asked his questions of Yahweh.

"Was any of this plan to conquer Jericho done on your own initiative?"

"No."

"On whose orders was it done?"

"On the orders of Enlil, my superior."

"You had no input on his decisions?"

"None. For Anunnaki the decision of a superior is law. You have no choice but to execute it."

"Thank you. The Defense rests . . ." There was an expression of deep satisfaction on the Defense Counsel's craggy countenance.

"And the Federation?" The Chief Jurist looked inquiringly at the Federation Counsel.

"No, your Honor. The Federation can not rest . . . not after what we have heard here from the Defense today. Not until the Jury has heard this, which we believe will conclude the case in all respects and leave no doubt in their own or anyone's minds . . . It is absolutely incontrovertible evidence . . ."

He paused.

"Incontrovertible and decisive because . . . because it was written by the Defendant himself."

There was an audible collective gasp across the courtroom.

As it died, the Federation Counsel with his long arms now made a dramatic gesture, pointing towards one darkened extremity of the courtroom floor.

His tone was commanding, vibrant with what seemed to be indignation.

"Bring in the manuscript now! The manuscript from which I intend to read everything pertinent to close out this case."

An attendant did so.

The Federation Counsel now made a point of standing stock still and again drawing himself up to his full seven foot height.

As the leather-bound manuscript was delivered into his hands, he made a big production of accepting it, then turning to the Jury and showing them the title on the cover.

The title, emblazoned boldly in large gold letters. The title which consisted of only two words . . .

I, JEHOVAH.

But the Federation Counsel did not stop there. He had a dramatic moment and he was not going to let its full potential escape him.

"And if the jury is not convinced after I read sections from this document . . . then I intend to call still another key witness. The Earthling called Aaron, brother to the Earthling called Moses, who will read to us from another document written in his own hand. Which is a record of his tribe and which will confirm everything admitted in I, JEHOVAH. A document titled THE HOLY SCRIPTURE. And then . . . then the Federation will rest its case."

The confident smile on the feline face of the Federation Counsel was proportionate to his outsize height . . .

****

EPILOG

The tall, stalwart figure felt the acrid atmosphere almost seem to singe his lungs and tear at his tender nostrils as he watched the Federation Mother Ship leave its orbit and head for outer space.

Well, all right. What could he do? It was accept this uncertain fate, to be cast adrift and be totally alone on this obscure out-of-the-way planet . . . or be put to death. Maybe the "or" really didn't matter, because maybe either section of the Federation's sentence came at last to the same thing, the same bleak end.

But then again, maybe not.

He was who he was, after all. Even without weapons, or technology or advantage of any kind over the primitive and savage population the Federation Judge had so sternly warned him about.

Night was coming on . . . and who knew how long it was.

Who knew what savage animals might live lurking in the rapidly encroaching shadows . . . waiting to tear him apart and eat him.

He climbed a large tree, keeping a wary eye out and his ears open. After a while he made a bed of the thick branches and quickly felt himself, half dead from anxiety and fatigue, against his will, dozing off . . .

****

The next day . . . he assumed it was the next day . . . and who knew how many hours later . . . he awoke to once again face his uncertain future.

His mind reeled at recent events that had overwhelmed him. He who had seemed at the very pinnacle of his ambition, being the sole god of Earth in actual practice if not quite yet in title.

He wondered if Enlil would ever find anyone to take his place as god of the Israelites. He doubted it. Doubted that any of the remaining Anunnaki on Earth could carry out the Mission he, Yahweh, had assigned himself for the general good of all.

He thought about the Israelites and the beliefs he had carefully nurtured in them over the generations. What would they come to think eventually now of their great god Jehovah? How would they explain to themselves his sudden disappearance?

CALEB LEVI

Will they expect my return at any moment?

Am I still their god, the god of the Jews?

Or will they have lost faith in me? Have I already been abandoned by them?

But those . . . those were all now just idle speculations. Speculations of someone who was very likely to die quite soon at the hands of the barbarous inhabitants of this backward, hostile planet.

A wave of bitterness swept over him, threatened to overcome him.

The Federation almost certainly felt poetic justice, or at least ironical enjoyment at his carefully engineered plight. Of that he was sure. He laughed a kind of acid and half-choked laugh at the thought.

He was not half an hour out of the tree when his first crisis . . . which he knew too well could be also his last . . . confronted him.

There they were, a group of naked savages, come for him . . . all aggression and teeth and ready to have him for their breakfast.

The situation sparked a sudden thought.

Well, maybe they should be educated on how to cook. On the uses of fire, of which they were undoubtedly ignorant. As to that, he could soon find out.

He pulled from a pocket a pair of flintlike stones he had picked up earlier and struck a spark from them now in front of their riveted eyes.

They contracted backward from him like an amoeba.

There were gasps, and groans of fear.

Good.

He would continue while he lived with his little theater.

He knelt before them, struck the flint stones together now next to a little pile of dried leaves he had previously prepared for his own private use.

The sparks caught . . .

The flames leapt up . . .

And his erstwhile attackers jumped a concomitant distance backwards.

Better.

He leaped up and shouted some nonsense syllables at them now in a sing-song tone.

Then . . .

He broke off a branch and lit it from the flames leaping up from the pile of dry leaves.

At this . . .

Some of the attackers ran away, terrified, grunting loudly.

Others fell to their knees, their crude wooden spears dropping heedlessly from their hands . . .

Those remaining stared at him with what looked like awe and fear . . . and something like abject adoration.

Best.

So . . . maybe this planet could use a god. Was indeed ripe for the presence of a god.

And maybe . . .

He looked once more at the fawning, terror-stricken savages.

Maybe now they had one.

—THE END—